THE BETTY NEELS COLLECTION

Betty Neels's novels are loved by millions
of readers around the world, and this
very special *2-in-1 collection* offers
a unique opportunity to relive the magic
of some of her most popular stories.

We are proud to present these classic romances
by the woman who could weave an
irresistible tale of love like no other.

So sit back in your comfiest chair
with your favorite cup of tea and
enjoy these best of Betty Neels stories!

D1627022

BETTY NEELS

Romance readers around the world were sad to note the passing of Betty Neels in June 2001. Her career spanned thirty years, and she continued to write into her ninetieth year. To her millions of fans, Betty epitomized the romance writer, and yet she began writing almost by accident. She had retired from nursing, but her inquiring mind still sought stimulation. Her new career was born when she heard a lady in her local library bemoaning the lack of good romance novels. Betty's first book, *Sister Peters in Amsterdam,* was published in 1969, and she eventually completed 134 books. Her novels offer a reassuring warmth that was very much a part of her own personality, and her spirit and genuine talent live on in all her stories.

BETTY NEELS

The Right Kind of Girl
and
Nanny by Chance

Recycling programs
for this product may
not exist in your area.

ISBN-13: 978-0-373-60660-3

THE RIGHT KIND OF GIRL AND NANNY BY CHANCE

Copyright © 2014 by Harlequin Books S.A.

The publisher acknowledges the copyright holder
of the individual works as follows:

THE RIGHT KIND OF GIRL
Copyright © 1995 by Betty Neels

NANNY BY CHANCE
Copyright © 1998 by Betty Neels

Printed in U.S.A.

CONTENTS

THE RIGHT KIND OF GIRL

CHAPTER ONE

MRS SMITH-DARCY had woken in a bad temper. She reclined, her abundant proportions supported by a number of pillows, in her bed, not bothering to reply to the quiet 'good morning' uttered by the girl who had entered the room; she was not a lady to waste courtesy on those she considered beneath her. Her late husband had left her rich, having made a fortune in pickled onions, and since she had an excellent opinion of herself she found no need to bother with the feelings of anyone whom she considered inferior. And, of course, a paid companion came into that category.

The paid companion crossed the wide expanse of carpet and stood beside the bed, notebook in hand. She looked out of place in the over-furnished, frilly room; a girl of medium height, with pale brown hair smoothed into a French pleat, she had unremarkable features, but her eyes were large, thickly lashed and of a pleasing hazel. She was dressed in a pleated skirt and a white blouse, with a grey cardigan to match the skirt—sober clothes which failed to conceal her pretty figure and elegant legs.

Mrs Smith-Darcy didn't bother to look at her. 'You can go to the bank and cash a cheque—the servants want their wages. Do call in at the butcher's and tell him that I'm not satisfied with the meat he's sending up to the house. When you get back—and don't be all day over a couple of errands—you can make an appointment with my hairdresser and get the invitations written for my luncheon party. The list's on my desk.'

She added pettishly, 'Well, get on with it, then; there's plenty of work waiting for you when you get back.'

The girl went out of the room without a word, closed the door quietly behind her and went downstairs to the kitchen where Cook had a cup of coffee waiting for her.

'Got your orders, Miss Trent? In a mood, is she?'

'I dare say it's this weather, Cook. I have to go to the shops. Is there anything I can bring back for you?'

'Well, now, love, if you could pop into Mr Coffin's and ask him to send up a couple of pounds of sausages with the meat? They'll do us a treat for our dinner.'

Emma Trent, battling on her bike against an icy February wind straight from Dartmoor and driving rain, reflected that there could be worse jobs, only just at that moment she couldn't think of any. It wasn't just the weather—she had lived in Buckfastleigh all her life and found nothing unusual in that; after all, it was only a mile or so from the heart of the moor with its severe winters.

Bad weather she could dismiss easily enough, but Mrs Smith-Darcy was another matter; a selfish lazy woman, uncaring of anyone's feelings but her own, she was Emma's daily trial, but her wages put the butter on the bread of Emma's mother's small pension so she had to be borne. Jobs weren't all that easy to find in a small rural town, and if she went to Plymouth or even Ashburton it would mean living away from home, whereas now they managed very well, although there was never much money over.

Her errands done, and with the sausages crammed into a pocket, since Mr Coffin had said that he wasn't sure if he could deliver the meat before the afternoon, she cycled back to the large house on the other side of the town where her employer lived, parked her bike by the side-door and went into the kitchen. There she handed over the sausages, hung her sopping raincoat to dry and went along to the little cubby-hole where she spent most of her days—making out cheques for the tradesmen, making appointments, writing notes and keeping the household books. When she wasn't doing that, she arranged the flowers, and answered the door if Alice, the housemaid, was busy or having her day off.

'Never a dull moment,' said Emma to her reflection as she tidied her hair and dried the rain from her face. The buzzer Mrs Smith-Darcy used whenever she demanded Emma's presence was clamouring to be answered, and she picked up her notebook and pencil and went unhurriedly upstairs.

Mrs Smith-Darcy had heaved herself out of bed and was sitting before the dressing-table mirror, doing her face. She didn't look up from the task of applying mascara. 'I have been buzzing you for several minutes,' she observed crossly. 'Where have you been? Really, a great, strong girl like you should have done those few errands in twenty minutes…'

Emma said mildly, 'I'm not a great, strong girl, Mrs Smith-Darcy, and cycling into the wind isn't the quickest way of travelling. Besides, I got wet—'

'Don't make childish excuses. Really, Miss Trent, I sometimes wonder if you are up to this job. Heaven knows, it's easy enough.'

Emma knew better than to answer that. Instead she asked, 'You wanted me to do something for you, Mrs Smith-Darcy?'

'Tell Cook I want my coffee in half an hour. I shall be out to lunch, and while I'm gone you can fetch Frou-Frou from the vet. I shall need Vickery with the car so I suppose you had better get a taxi— it wouldn't do for Frou-Frou to get wet. You can pay and I'll settle with you later.'

'I haven't brought any money with me.' Emma crossed her fingers behind her back as she spoke, for it was a fib, but on several occasions she had been told to pay for something and that she would be reimbursed later—something which had never happened.

Mrs Smith-Darcy frowned. 'Really, what an incompetent girl you are.' She opened her handbag and found a five-pound note. 'Take this—and I'll expect the correct change.'

'I'll get the driver to write the fare down and sign it,' said Emma quietly, and something in her voice made Mrs Smith-Darcy look at her.

'There's no need for that.'

'It will set your mind at rest,' said Emma sweetly. 'I'll get those invitations written; I can post them on my way home.'

Mrs Smith-Darcy, who liked to have the last word, was for once unable to think of anything to say as Emma left the room.

It was well after five o'clock when Emma got on to her bike and took herself off home—a small, neat house near the abbey where she and her mother had lived since her father had died several years earlier.

He had died suddenly and unexpectedly, and it hadn't been until after his death that Mrs Trent had been told that he had mortgaged the house in order to raise the money to help his younger brother, who had been in financial difficulties, under the impression that he would be repaid within a reasonable time. There hadn't been enough money to pay off the mortgage, so she had sold the house and bought a small terraced house, and, since her brother-in-law had gone abroad without leaving an address, she and Emma now managed on her small pension and Emma's salary. That she herself was underpaid Emma was well aware, but on the other hand her job allowed her to keep an eye on her mother's peptic ulcer...

There was an alley behind the row of houses. She wheeled her bike along its length and into their small back garden, put it in the tumbledown shed outside the kitchen door and went into the house.

The kitchen was small, but its walls were distempered in a cheerful pale yellow and there was room for a small table and two chairs against one wall. She took off her outdoor things, carried them through to the narrow little hall and went into the sitting-room. That was small, too, but it was comfortably furnished, although a bit shabby, and there was a cheerful fire burning in the small grate.

Mrs Trent looked up from her sewing. 'Hello, love. Have you had a tiring day? And so wet and cold too. Supper is in the oven but you'd like a cup of tea first...'

'I'll get it.' Emma dropped a kiss on her mother's cheek and went to make the tea and presently carried it back.

'Something smells heavenly,' she observed. 'What have you been cooking?'

'Casserole and dumplings. Did you get a proper lunch?'

Emma assured her that she had, with fleeting regret for most of the sausages she hadn't been given time to eat; Mrs Smith-Darcy had the nasty habit of demanding that some task must be done at once, never mind how inconvenient. She reflected with pleasure that her employer was going away for several days, and although she had been given a list of things to do which would take at least twice that period it would be like having a holiday.

She spent the next day packing Mrs Smith-Darcy's expensive cases with the clothes necessary to make an impression during her stay at Torquay's finest hotel—a stay which, she pointed out to Emma, was vital to her health. This remark reminded her to order the central heating to be turned down while she was absent. 'And I expect an accurate statement of the household expenses.'

Life, after Mrs Smith-Darcy had been driven away by Vickery, the chauffeur, was all of a sudden pleasant.

It was delightful to arrive each morning and get on with her work without having to waste half an hour listening to her employer's querulous voice raised in criticism about something or other, just as it was delightful to go home each evening at five o'clock exactly.

Over and above this, Cook, unhampered by her employer's strictures, allowed her creative skills to run free so that they ate food which was never normally allowed—rich steak and kidney pudding with a drop of stout in the gravy, roasted potatoes—crisply brown, toad-in-the-hole, braised celery, cauliflower smothered in a creamy sauce and all followed by steamed puddings, sticky with treacle or bathed in custard.

Emma, eating her dinners in the kitchen with Cook and Alice, the housemaid, savoured every morsel, dutifully entered the bills in her household ledger and didn't query any of them; she would have to listen to a diatribe about the wicked extravagance of her staff from Mrs Smith-Darcy but it would be worth it, and Cook had given her a cake to take home, declaring that she had made two when one would have done.

On the last day of Mrs Smith-Darcy's absence from home Emma arrived in good time. There were still one or two tasks to do before that lady returned— the flowers to arrange, the last of the post to sort out and have ready for her inspection, a list of the invitations accepted for the luncheon party...

She almost fell off her bike as she shot through the gates into the short drive to the house. The car was before the door and Vickery was taking the cases out of the boot. He cast his eyes up as she jumped off her bike.

'Took bad,' he said. 'During the night. 'Ad the doctor to see 'er—gave her an injection and told 'er it were a bug going round—gastric something or other. Alice is putting 'er to bed, miss. You'd better go up sharp, like.'

'Oh, Vickery, you must have had to get up very early—it's only just nine o'clock.'

'That I did, miss.' He smiled at her. 'I'll see to yer bike.'

'Thank you, Vickery. I'm sure Cook will have breakfast for you.'

She took off her outdoor things and went upstairs. Mrs Smith-Darcy's door was closed but she could hear her voice raised in annoyance. She couldn't be very ill if she could shout like that, thought Emma, opening the door.

'There you are—never where you're wanted, as usual. I'm ill—very ill. That stupid doctor who came to the hotel told me it was some kind of virus. I don't believe him. I'm obviously suffering from some grave internal disorder. Go and phone Dr Treble and tell him to come at once.'

'He'll be taking surgery,' Emma pointed out reasonably. 'I'll ask him to come as soon as he's finished.' She studied Mrs Smith-Darcy's face. 'Are you in great pain? Did the doctor at Torquay advise you to go to a hospital for emergency treatment?'

'Of course not. If I need anything done I shall go into a private hospital. I am in great pain—agony...' She didn't quite meet Emma's level gaze. 'Do as I tell you; I must be attended to at once.'

She was in bed now, having her pillows arranged just so by the timid Alice. Emma didn't think that she looked in pain; certainly her rather high colour was normal, and if she had been in the agony she described then she wouldn't have been fussing about her pillows and which bed-jacket she would wear. She went downstairs and dialled the surgery.

The receptionist answered. 'Emma—how are

you? Your mother's all right? She looked well when
I saw her a few days ago.'

'Mother's fine, thanks, Mrs Butts. Mrs Smith-
Darcy came back this morning from a few days at
Torquay. She wasn't well during the night and the
hotel called a doctor who told her it was a bug and
that she had better go home—he gave her something—I don't know what. She says she is in great
pain and wants Dr Treble to come and see her immediately.'

'The surgery isn't finished—it'll be another half
an hour or so, unless she'd like to be brought here
in her car.' Mrs Butts chuckled. 'And that's unlikely,
isn't it?' She paused. 'Is she really ill, Emma?'

'Her colour is normal; she's very cross…'

'When isn't she very cross? I'll ask Doctor to visit
when surgery is over, but, I warn you, if there's anything really urgent he'll have to see to it first.'

Emma went back to Mrs Smith-Darcy and found
her sitting up in bed renewing her make-up. 'You're
feeling better? Would you like coffee or tea? Or
something to eat?'

'Don't be ridiculous, Miss Trent; can you not see
how I'm suffering? Is the doctor on his way?'

'He'll come when surgery is finished—about half
an hour, Mrs Butts said.'

'Mrs Butts? Do you mean to tell me that you
didn't speak to Dr Treble?'

'No, he was busy with a patient.'

'I am a patient,' said Mrs Smith-Darcy in a furious voice.

Emma, as mild as milk and unmoved, said, 'Yes,
Mrs Smith-Darcy. I'll be back in a minute; I'm going
to open the post while I've the chance.'

There must be easier ways of earning a living, she
reflected, going down to the kitchen to ask Cook to
make lemonade.

She bore the refreshment upstairs presently, and
took it down again as her employer didn't find it
sweet enough. When she went back with it she was
kept busy closing curtains because the dim light from
the February morning was hurting the invalid's eyes,
then fetching another blanket to put over her feet, and
changing the bed-jacket she had on, which wasn't
the right colour...

'Now go and fetch my letters,' said Mrs Smith-
Darcy.

Perhaps, thought Emma, nipping smartly downstairs once more, Dr Treble would prescribe something which would soothe the lady and cause her
to doze off for long periods. Certainly at the moment Mrs Smith-Darcy had no intention of doing
any such thing.

Emma, proffering her post, got the full force of
her displeasure.

'Bills,' said Mrs Smith-Darcy. 'Nothing but
bills!' And went on that doubtless, while her back
was turned, those whom she employed had eaten
her out of house and home, and as for an indigent

nephew who had had the effrontery to ask her for a
small loan... 'Anyone would think that I was made
of money,' she said angrily—which was, in fact, not
far wrong.

The richer you are, the meaner you get, reflected
Emma, retrieving envelopes and bills scattered over
the bed and on the floor.

She was on her knees with her back to the door
when it was opened and Alice said, 'The doctor,
ma'am,' and something in her voice made Emma turn
around. It wasn't Dr Treble but a complete stranger
who, from her lowly position, looked enormous.

Indeed, he was a big man; not only very tall but
built to match his height, he was also possessed of a
handsome face with a high-bridged nose and a firm
mouth. Pepper and salt hair, she had time to notice,
and on the wrong side of thirty. She was aware of
his barely concealed look of amusement as she got
to her feet.

'Get up, girl,' said Mrs Smith-Darcy and then
added, 'I sent for Dr Treble.' She took a second look
at him and altered her tone. 'I don't know you, do I?'

He crossed the room to the bed. 'Dr Wyatt. I have
taken over from Dr Treble for a short period. What
can I do for you, Mrs Smith-Darcy? I received a message that it was urgent.'

'Oh, Doctor, I have had a shocking experience—'
She broke off for a moment. 'Miss Trent, get the doctor a chair.'

But before Emma could move he had picked up

a spindly affair and sat on it, seemingly unaware of the alarming creaks; at the same time he had glanced at her again with the ghost of a smile. Nice, thought Emma, making herself as inconspicuous as possible. I hope that he will see through her. At least she won't be able to bully him like she does Dr Treble.

Her hopes were justified. Mrs Smith-Darcy, prepared to discuss her symptoms at some length, found herself answering his questions with no chance of embellishment, although she did her best.

'You dined last evening?' he wanted to know. 'What exactly did you eat and drink?'

'The hotel is noted for its excellent food,' she gushed. 'It's expensive, of course, but one has to pay for the best, does one not?' She waited for him to make some comment and then, when he didn't, added pettishly, 'Well, a drink before I dined, of course, and some of the delightful canapés they serve. I have a small appetite but I managed a little caviare. Then, let me see, a morsel of sole with a mushroom sauce—cooked in cream, of course—and then a simply delicious pheasant with an excellent selection of vegetables.'

'And?' asked Dr Wyatt, his voice as bland as his face.

'Oh, dessert—meringue with a chocolate sauce laced with curaçao—a small portion, I might add.' She laughed. 'A delicious meal—'

'And the reason for your gastric upset. There is nothing seriously wrong, Mrs Smith-Darcy, and it

can be easily cured by taking some tablets which
you can obtain from the chemist and then keeping
to a much plainer diet in future. I'm sure that your
daughter—'

'My paid companion,' snapped Mrs Smith-Darcy.
'I am a lonely widow, Doctor, and able to get about
very little.'

'I suggest that you take regular exercise each
day—a brisk walk, perhaps.'

Mrs Smith-Darcy shuddered. 'I feel that you don't
understand my delicate constitution, Doctor; I hope
that I shan't need to call you again.'

'I think it unlikely; I can assure you that there is
nothing wrong with you, Mrs Smith-Darcy. You will
feel better if you get up and dress.'

He bade her goodbye with cool courtesy. 'I will
give your companion some instructions and write a
prescription for some tablets.'

Emma opened the door for him, but he took the
handle from her and ushered her through before closing it gently behind him.

'Is there somewhere we might go?'

'Yes—yes, of course.' She led the way downstairs
and into her office.

He looked around him. 'This is where you work
at being a companion?'

'Yes. Well, I do the accounts and bills and write
the letters here. Most of the time I'm with Mrs Smith-
Darcy.'

'But you don't live here?' He had a pleasant, deep

voice, quite quiet and soothing, and she answered his questions readily because he sounded so casual.

'No, I live in Buckfastleigh with my mother.'

'A pleasant little town. I prefer the other end, though, nearer the abbey.'

'Oh, so do I; that's where we are…' She stopped there; he wouldn't want to know anything about her—they were strangers, not likely to see each other again. 'Is there anything special I should learn about Mrs Smith-Darcy?'

'No, she is perfectly healthy although very overweight. Next time she overeats try to persuade her to take one of these tablets instead of calling the doctor.' He was writing out a prescription and paused to look at her. 'You're wasted here, you know.'

She blushed. 'I've not had any training—at least, only shorthand and typing and a little bookkeeping—and there aren't many jobs here.'

'You don't wish to leave home?'

'No. I can't do that. Is Dr Treble ill?'

'Yes, he's in hospital. He has had a heart attack and most likely will retire.'

She gave him a thoughtful look. 'I'm very sorry. You don't want me to tell Mrs Smith-Darcy?'

'No. In a little while the practice will be taken over by another doctor.'

'You?'

He smiled. 'No, no. I'm merely filling in until things have been settled.'

He gave her the prescription and closed his bag.

The hand he offered was large and very firm and she wanted to keep her hand in his. He was, she reflected, a very nice man—dependable; he would make a splendid friend. It was such an absurd idea that she smiled and he decided that her smile was enchanting.

She went to the door with him and saw the steel-grey Rolls-Royce parked in the drive. 'Is that yours?' she asked.

'Yes.' He sounded amused and she begged his pardon and went pink again and stood, rather prim, in the open door until he got in and drove away.

She turned, and went in and up to the bedroom to find Mrs Smith-Darcy decidedly peevish. 'Really, I don't know what is coming to the medical profession,' she began, the moment Emma opened the door. 'Nothing wrong with me, indeed; I never heard such nonsense. I'm thoroughly upset. Go down and get my coffee and some of those wine biscuits.'

'I have a prescription for you, Mrs Smith-Darcy,' said Emma. 'I'll fetch it while you're getting dressed, shall I?'

'I have no intention of dressing. You can go to the chemist while I'm having my coffee—and don't hang around. There's plenty for you to do here.'

When she got back Mrs Smith-Darcy asked, 'What has happened to Dr Treble? I hope that that man is replacing him for a very short time; I have no wish to see him again.'

To which remark Emma prudently made no answer. Presently she went off to the kitchen to tell Cook that her mistress fancied asparagus soup made with single cream and a touch of parsley, and two lamb cutlets with creamed potatoes and braised celery in a cheese sauce. So much for the new doctor's advice, reflected Emma, ordered down to the cellar to fetch a bottle of Bollinger to tempt the invalid's appetite.

That evening, sitting at supper with her mother, Emma told her of the new doctor. 'He was nice. I expect if you were really ill he would take the greatest care of you.'

'Elderly?' asked Mrs Trent artlessly.

'Something between thirty and thirty-five, I suppose. Pepper and salt hair…'

A not very satisfactory answer from her mother's point of view.

February, tired of being winter, became spring for a couple of days, and Emma, speeding to and fro from Mrs Smith-Darcy's house, had her head full of plans—a day out with her mother on the following Sunday. She could rent a car from Dobbs's garage and drive her mother to Widecombe in the Moor and then on to Bovey Tracey; they could have lunch there and then go on back home through Ilsington— no main roads, just a quiet jaunt around the country they both loved.

She had been saving for a tweed coat and skirt, but she told herself that since she seldom went anywhere, other than a rare visit to Exeter or Plymouth, they could wait until autumn. She and her mother both needed a day out…

The weather was kind; Sunday was bright and clear, even if cold. Emma got up early, fed Queenie, their elderly cat, took tea to her mother and got the breakfast and, while Mrs Trent cleared it away, went along to the garage and fetched the car.

Mr Dobbs had known her father and was always willing to rent her a car, letting her have it at a reduced price since it was usually the smallest and shabbiest in his garage, though in good order, as he was always prompt to tell her. Today she was to have an elderly Fiat, bright red and with all the basic comforts, but, she was assured, running well. Emma, casting her eye over it, had a momentary vision of a sleek Rolls Royce…

They set off in the still, early morning and, since they had the day before them, Emma drove to Ashburton and presently took the narrow moor road to Widecombe, where they stopped for coffee before driving on to Bovey Tracey. It was too early for lunch, so they drove on then to Lustleigh, an ancient village deep in the moorland, the hills around it dotted with granite boulders. But although the houses and cottages were built of granite there was nothing forbidding about them—they were charming even on a chilly winter's day, the thatched roofs gleaming with the last of the previous night's frost, smoke eddying gently from their chimney-pots.

Scattered around the village were several substantial houses, tucked cosily between the hills. They were all old—as old as the village—and several of them were prosperous farms while others stood in sheltered grounds.

'I wouldn't mind living here,' said Emma as they passed one particularly handsome house, standing well back from the narrow road, the hills at its back, sheltered by carefully planted trees. 'Shall we go as far as Lustleigh Cleave and take a look at the river?'

After that it was time to find somewhere for lunch. Most of the cafés and restaurants in the little town were closed, since the tourist season was still several months away, but they found a pub where they were served roast beef with all the trimmings and home-made mince tarts to follow.

Watching her mother's pleasure at the simple, well-cooked meal, Emma promised herself that they would do a similar trip before the winter ended, while the villages were quiet and the roads almost empty.

It was still fine weather but the afternoon was already fading, and she had promised to return the car by seven o'clock at the latest. They decided to drive straight home and have tea when they got in, and since it was still a clear afternoon they decided to take a minor road through Ilsington. Emma had turned off the main road on to the small country lane when her mother slumped in her seat without uttering a sound. Emma stopped the car and turned to look at her unconscious parent.

She said, 'Mother—Mother, whatever is the matter…?' And then she pulled herself together—bleating her name wasn't going to help. She undid her safety-belt, took her mother's pulse and called her name again, but Mrs Trent lolled in her seat, her eyes closed. At least Emma could feel her pulse, and her breathing seemed normal.

Emma looked around her. The lane was narrow; she would never be able to turn the car and there was little point in driving on as Ilsington was a small village—too small for a doctor. She pulled a rug from the back seat and wrapped it round her mother and was full of thankful relief when Mrs Trent opened her eyes, but the relief was short-lived. Mrs Trent gave a groan. 'Emma, it's such a pain, I don't think I can bear it…'

There was only one thing to do—to reverse the car back down the lane, return to the main road and race back to Bovey Tracey.

'It's all right, Mother,' said Emma. 'It's not far to Bovey… There's the cottage hospital there; they'll help you.'

She began to reverse, going painfully slowly since the lane curved between high hedges, and it was a good thing she did, for the oncoming car behind her braked smoothly inches from her boot. She got out so fast that she almost tumbled over; here was help! She had no eyes for the other car but rushed to poke her worried face through the window that its driver had just opened.

'It's you!' she exclaimed. 'Oh, you can help. Only, please come quickly.' Dr. Wyatt didn't utter a word but he was beside her before she could draw another breath. 'Mother—it's Mother; she's collapsed and she's in terrible pain. I couldn't turn the car and this lane goes to Ilsington, and it's on the moor miles from anywhere...'

He put a large, steadying hand on her arm. 'Shall I take a look?'

Mrs Trent was a nasty pasty colour and her hand, when he took it, felt cold and clammy. Emma, half-in, half-out of the car on her side, said, 'Mother's got an ulcer—a peptic ulcer; she takes alkaline medicine and small meals and extra milk.'

He was bending over Mrs Trent. 'Will you undo her coat and anything else in the way? I must take a quick look. I'll fetch my bag.'

He straightened up presently. 'Your mother needs to be treated without delay. I'll put her into my car and drive to Exeter. You follow as soon as you can.'

'Yes.' She cast him a bewildered look.

'Problems?' he asked.

'I rented the car from Dobbs's garage; it has to be back by seven o'clock.'

'I'm going to give your mother an injection to take away the pain. Go to my car; there's a phone between the front seats. Phone this Dobbs, tell him what has happened and say that you'll bring the car back as soon as possible.' He turned his back on Mrs Trent, looming over Emma so that she had to crane her neck to see his face. 'I am sure that your mother has a perforated ulcer, which means surgery as soon as possible.'

She stared up at him, pale with shock, unable to think of anything to say. She nodded once and ran back to his car, and by the time she had made her call she had seen him lift her mother gently and carry her to the car. They made her comfortable on the back seat and Emma was thankful to see that her mother appeared to be dozing. 'She'll be all right? You'll hurry, won't you? I'll drive on until I can turn and then I'll come to the hospital—which one?'

'The Royal Devon and Exeter—you know where it is?' He got into his car and began to reverse down the lane. If the circumstances hadn't been so dire, she would have stayed to admire the way he did it— with the same ease as if he were going forwards.

She got into her car, then, and drove on for a mile or more before she came to a rough track leading on to the moor, where she reversed and drove back the way she had come. She was shaking now, in a panic that her mother was in danger of her life and she wouldn't reach the hospital in time, but she forced herself to drive carefully. Once she reached the main road and turned on to the carriageway, it was only thirteen miles to Exeter...

She forced herself to park the car neatly in the hospital forecourt and walk, not run, in through the casualty entrance. There, thank heaven, they knew who she was and why she had come. Sister, a cosy body with a soft Devon voice, came to meet her.

'Miss Trent? Your mother in is Theatre; the professor is operating at the moment. You come and sit down in the waiting-room and a nurse will bring you a cup of tea—you look as though you could do with it. Your mother is in very good hands, and as soon as she is back in her bed you shall go and see her. In a few minutes I should like some details, but you have your tea first.'

Emma nodded; if she had spoken she would have burst into tears; her small world seemed to be tumbling around her ears. She drank her tea, holding the cup in both hands since she was still shaking, and presently, when Sister came back, she gave her the details she needed in a wooden little voice. 'Will it be much longer?' she asked.

Sister glanced at the clock. 'Not long now. I'm sure you'll be told the moment the operation is finished. Will you go back to Buckfastleigh this evening?'

'Could I stay here? I could sit here, couldn't I? I wouldn't get in anyone's way.'

'If you are to stay we'll do better than that, my dear. Do you want to telephone anyone?'

Emma shook her head. 'There's only Mother and me.' She tried to smile and gave a great sniff. 'So sorry, it's all happened so suddenly.'

'You have a nice cry if you want to. I must go and

see what's happening. There's been a street-fight and we'll be busy...'

Emma sat still and didn't cry—when she saw her mother she must look cheerful—so that when somebody came at last she turned a rigidly controlled face to hear the news.

Dr Wyatt was crossing the room to her. 'Your mother is going to be all right, Emma.' And then he held her in his arms as she burst into tears.

CHAPTER TWO

EMMA DIDN'T CRY for long but hiccuped, sniffed, sobbed a bit and drew away from him to blow her nose on the handkerchief he offered her.

'You're sure? Was it a big operation? Were you in the theatre?'

'Well, yes. It was quite a major operation but successful, I'm glad to say. You may see your mother; she will be semi-conscious but she'll know that you are there. She's in Intensive Care just for tonight. Tomorrow she will go to a ward—' He broke off as Sister joined them.

'They're wanting you on Male Surgical, sir—urgently.'

He nodded at Emma and went away.

'Mother's going to get well,' said Emma. She heaved a great sigh. 'What would I have done if Dr Wyatt hadn't been driving down the lane when Mother was taken ill? He works here as well as taking over the practice at home?'

Sister looked surprised and then smiled. 'Indeed

he works here; he's our Senior Consultant Surgeon, although he's supposed to be taking a sabbatical, but I hear he's helping out Dr Treble for a week or two.'

'So he's a surgeon, not a GP?'

Sister smiled again. 'Sir Paul Wyatt is a professor of surgery, and much in demand for consultations, lecture-tours and seminars. You were indeed fortunate that he happened to be there when you needed help so urgently.'

'Would Mother have died, Sister?'

'Yes, love.'

'He saved her life...' She would, reflected Emma, do anything—anything at all—to repay him. Sooner or later there would be a chance. Perhaps not for years, but she wouldn't forget.

She was taken to see her mother then, who was lying in a tangle of tubes, surrounded by monitoring screens but blessedly awake. Emma bent to kiss her white face, her own face almost as white. 'Darling, everything's fine; you're going to be all right. I'll be here and come and see you in the morning after you've had a good sleep.'

Her mother frowned. 'Queenie,' she muttered.

'I'll phone Mr Dobbs and ask him to put some food outside the cat-flap.'

'Yes, do that, Emma.' Mrs Trent closed her eyes.

Emma turned at the touch on her arm. 'You're going to stay for the night?' A pretty, young nurse smiled at her. 'There's a rest-room on the ground floor; we'll call you if there's any need but I think your mother will sleep until the morning. You can see her before you go home then.'

Emma nodded. 'Is there a phone?'

'Yes, just by the rest-room, and there's a canteen down the corridor where you can get tea and sandwiches.'

'You're very kind.' Emma took a last look at her mother and went to the rest-room. There was no one else there and there were comfortable chairs and a table with magazines on it. As she hesitated at the door the sister from Casualty joined her.

'There's a washroom just across the passage. Try and sleep a little, won't you?'

When she had hurried away Emma picked up the phone. Mr Dobbs was sympathetic and very helpful—of course he'd see to Queenie, and Emma wasn't to worry about the car. 'Come back when you feel you can, love,' he told her. 'And you'd better keep the car for a day or two so's you can see your ma as often as possible.'

Mrs Smith-Darcy was an entirely different kettle of fish. 'My luncheon party,' she exclaimed. 'You will have to come back tomorrow morning and see to it; I am not strong enough to cope with it—you know how delicate I am. It is most inconsiderate of you…'

'My mother,' said Emma, between her teeth, 'in case you didn't hear what I have told you, is dangerously ill. I shall stay here with her as long as necessary. And you are not in the least delicate, Mrs Smith-Darcy, only spoilt and lazy and very selfish!'

She hung up, her ear shattered by Mrs Smith-Darcy's furious bellow. Well, she had burnt her boats, cooked her goose and would probably be had up for libel—or was it slander? She didn't care. She had given voice to sentiments she had choked back for more than a year and she didn't care.

She felt better after her outburst, even though she was now out of work. She drank some tea and ate sandwiches from the canteen, resisted a wish to go in search of someone and ask about her mother, washed her face and combed her hair, plaited it and settled in the easiest of the chairs. Underneath her calm front panic and fright bubbled away.

Her mother might have a relapse; she had looked so dreadfully ill. She would need to be looked after for weeks, which was something Emma would do with loving care, but they would be horribly short of money. There was no one around, so she was able to shed a few tears; she was lonely and scared and tired. She mumbled her prayers and fell asleep before she had finished them.

Sir Paul Wyatt, coming to check his patient's condition at two o'clock in the morning and satisfied with it, took himself down to the rest-room. If Emma was awake he would be able to reassure her…

She was curled up in the chair, her knees drawn up under her chin, the half of her face he could see tear-stained, her thick rope of hair hanging over one shoulder. She looked very young and entirely without glamour, and he knew that when she woke in the morning she would have a job uncoiling herself from the tight ball into which she had wound herself.

He went and fetched a blanket from Casualty and laid it carefully over her; she was going to be stiff in the morning—there was no need for her to be cold as well. He put his hand lightly on her hair, touched by the sight of her, and then smiled and frowned at the sentimental gesture and went away again.

Emma woke early, roused by a burst of activity in Casualty, and just as Sir Paul Wyatt had foreseen, discovered that she was stiff and cramped. She got up awkwardly, folding the blanket neatly, and wondered who had been kind during the night. Then she went to wash her face and comb her hair.

Even with powder and lipstick she still looked a mess—not that it mattered, since there was no one to see her. She rubbed her cheeks to get some colour into them and practised a smile in the looking-glass so that her mother would see how cheerful and unworried she was. She would have to drive back to Buckfastleigh after she had visited her and somehow she would come each day to see her, although at the moment she wasn't sure how. Of one thing she was sure—Mrs Smith-Darcy would have dismissed her out-of-hand, so she would have her days free.

She drank tea and polished off some toast in the canteen, then went to find someone who would tell her when she might see her mother. She didn't have

far to go—coming towards her along the passage
was Sir Paul Wyatt, immaculate in clerical grey and
spotless linen, freshly shaved, his shoes brilliantly
polished. She wished him a good morning and, without waiting for him to answer, asked, 'Mother—is
she all right? May I see her?'

'She had a good night, and of course you may
see her.'

He stood looking at her, and the relief at his words
was somewhat mitigated by knowing that her scruffy
appearance seemed even more scruffy in contrast
to his elegance. She rushed into speech to cover her
awkwardness. 'They have been very kind to me
here...'

He nodded with faint impatience—of course, he
was a busy man and hadn't any time to waste. 'I'll
go to Mother now,' she told him. 'I'm truly grateful to you for saving Mother. She's going to be quite
well again, isn't she?'

'Yes, but you must allow time for her to regain
her strength. I'll take you up to the ward on my way.'

She went with him silently, through corridors and
then in a lift and finally through swing-doors where
he beckoned a nurse, spoke briefly, then turned on
his heel with a quick nod, leaving her to follow the
nurse into the ward beyond.

Her mother wasn't in the ward but in a small room
beyond, sitting up in bed. She looked pale and tired
but she was smiling, and Emma had to fight her
strong wish to burst into tears at the sight of her. She

smiled instead. 'Mother, dear, you look so much better. How do you feel? And how nice that you're in a room by yourself...'

She bent and kissed her parent. 'I've just seen Sir Paul Wyatt and he says everything is most satisfactory.' She pulled up a chair and sat by the bed, taking her mother's hand in hers. 'What a coincidence that he should be here. Sister told me that he's a professor of surgery.'

Her mother smiled. 'Yes, love, and I'm fine. I really am. You're to go home now and not worry.'

'Yes, Mother. I'll phone this evening and I'll be back tomorrow. Do you want me to bring anything? I'll pack nighties and slippers and so on and bring them with me.'

Her mother closed her eyes. 'Yes, you know what to bring...'

Emma bent to kiss her again. 'I'm going now; you're tired. Have a nap, darling.'

It was still early; patients were being washed and tended before the breakfast trolley arrived. Emma was too early for the ward sister but the night staff nurse assured her that she would be told if anything unforeseen occurred. 'But your mother is most satisfactory, Miss Trent. The professor's been to see her already; he came in the night too. He's away for most of the day but his registrar is a splendid man. Ring this evening, if you like. You'll be coming tomorrow?'

Emma nodded. 'Can I come any time?'

'Afternoon or evening is best.'

Emma went down to the car and drove herself back to Buckfastleigh. As she went she planned her day. She would have to go and see Mrs Smith-Darcy and explain that she wouldn't be able to work for her any more. That lady was going to be angry and she supposed that she would have to apologise... She was owed a week's wages too, and she would need it.

Perhaps Mr Dobbs would let her hire the car each day just for the drive to and from the hospital; it would cost more than bus fares but it would be much quicker. She would have to go to the bank too; there wasn't much money there but she was prepared to spend the lot if necessary. It was too early to think about anything but the immediate future.

She took the car back to the garage and was warmed by Mr Dobbs's sympathy and his assurance that if she needed it urgently she had only to say so. 'And no hurry to pay the bill,' he promised her.

She went home then, and fed an anxious Queenie before making coffee. She was hungry, but it was past nine o'clock by now and Mrs Smith-Darcy would have to be faced before anything else. She had a shower, changed into her usual blouse, skirt and cardigan, did her face, brushed her hair into its usual smoothness and got on to her bike.

Alice opened the door to her. 'Oh, miss, whatever's happened? The mistress is in a fine state. Cook says come and have a cup of tea before you go up to her room; you'll need all your strength.'

'How kind of Cook,' said Emma. 'I think I'd rather have it afterwards, if I may.' She ran upstairs and tapped on Mrs Smith-Darcy's door and went in.

Mrs Smith-Darcy wasted no time in expressing her opinion of Emma; she repeated it several times before she ran out of breath, which enabled Emma to say, 'I'm sorry if I was rude to you on the phone, Mrs Smith-Darcy, but you didn't seem to understand that my mother was seriously ill—still is. I shall have to go to the hospital each day until she is well enough to come home, when I shall have to look after her until she is quite recovered—and that will take a considerable time.'

'My luncheon party,' gabbled Mrs Smith-Darcy. 'You wicked girl, leaving me like this. I'm incapable...'

Emma's efforts to behave well melted away. 'Yes, you are incapable,' she agreed. 'You're incapable of sympathy or human kindness. I suggest that you get up, Mrs Smith-Darcy, and see to your luncheon party yourself. I apologised to you just now—that was a mistake. You're everything I said and a lot more beside.'

She went out of the room and closed the door gently behind her. Then she opened it again. 'Will you be good enough to send my wages to my home?' She closed the door again on Mrs Smith-Darcy's enraged gasp.

She was shaking so much that her teeth rattled against the mug of tea Cook offered her.

'Now, don't you mind what she says,' said Cook. 'Nasty old lady she is, too. You go on home and have a good sleep, for you're fair worn out. I've put up a pasty and one or two snacks, like; you take them home and if you've no time to cook you just slip round here to the back door—there's always a morsel of something in the fridge.'

The dear soul's kindness was enough to make Emma weep; she sniffed instead, gave Cook a hug and then got on her bike and cycled home, where she did exactly what that lady had told her to do—undressed like lightning and got into bed. She was asleep within minutes.

She woke suddenly to the sound of the door-knocker being thumped.

'Mother,' said Emma, and scrambled out of bed, her heart thumping as loudly as the knocker. Not bothering with slippers, she tugged her dressing-gown on as she flew downstairs. It was already dusk; she had slept for hours—too long—she should have phoned the hospital. She turned the key in the lock and flung the door open.

Professor Sir Paul Wyatt was on the doorstep. He took the door from her and came in and shut it behind him. 'It is most unwise to open your door without putting up the chain or making sure that you know who it is.'

She eyed him through a tangle of hair. 'How can I know if I don't look first, and there isn't a chain?' Her half-awake brain remembered then.

'Mother—what's happened? Why are you here?' She caught at his sleeve. 'She's worse...'

His firm hand covered hers. 'Your mother is doing splendidly; she's an excellent patient. I'm sorry, I should have realised... You were asleep.'

She curled her cold toes on the hall carpet and nodded. 'I didn't mean to sleep for so long; it's getting dark.' She looked up at him. 'Why are you here, then?'

'I'm on my way home, but it has occurred to me that I shall be taking morning surgery here for the next week or two. I'll drive you up to Exeter after my morning visits and bring you back in time for evening surgery here.'

'Oh, would you? Would you really do that? How very kind of you, but won't it be putting you out? Sister said that you were taking a sabbatical, and that means you're on holiday, doesn't it?'

'Hardly a holiday, and I'm free to go in and out as I wish.'

'But you live in Exeter?'

'No, but not far from it; I shall not be in the least inconvenienced.'

She looked at him uncertainly, for he sounded casual and a little annoyed, but before she could speak he went on briskly, 'You'd better go and put some clothes on. Have you food in the house?'

'Yes, thank you. Cook gave me a pasty.' She was suddenly hungry at the thought of it. 'It was kind of you to come. I expect you want to go home—your days are long…'

He smiled. 'I'll make a pot of tea while you dress, and while we are drinking it I can explain exactly what I've done for your mother.'

She flew upstairs and flung on her clothes, washed her face and tied back her hair. Never mind how she looked—he wouldn't notice and he must be wanting to go home, wherever that was.

She perceived that he was a handy man in the kitchen—the tea was made, Queenie had been fed, and he had found a tin of biscuits.

'No milk, I'm afraid,' he said, not looking up from pouring the tea into two mugs. And then, very much to her surprise he asked, 'Have you sufficient money?'

'Yes—yes, thank you, and Mrs Smith-Darcy owes me a week's wages.' Probably in the circumstances she wouldn't get them, but he didn't need to know that.

He nodded, handed her a mug and said, 'Now, as to your mother…'

He explained simply in dry-as-dust words which were neither threatening nor casual. 'Your mother will stay in hospital for a week—ten days, perhaps— then I propose to send her to a convalescent home— there is a good one at Moretonhampstead, not too far from here—just for a few weeks. When she returns home she should be more or less able to resume her normal way of living, although she will have to keep to some kind of a diet. Time enough for that, however. Will you stay here alone?' He glanced at her. 'Perhaps you have family or a friend who would come…?'

'No family—at least, father had some cousins somewhere in London but they don't—that is, since he died we haven't heard from them. I've friends all over Buckfastleigh, though. If I asked one of them I know they'd come and stay but there's no need. I'm not nervous; besides, I'll try and find some temporary work until Mother comes home.'

'Mrs Smith-Darcy has given you the sack?'

'I'm sure of it. I was very rude to her this morning.' Anxious not to invite his pity, she added, 'There's always part-time work here—the abbey shop or the otter sanctuary.' True enough during the season—some months away!

He put down his mug. 'Good. I'll call for you some time after twelve o'clock tomorrow morning.' His goodbye was brief.

Left alone, she put the pasty to warm in the oven, washed the mugs and laid out a tray. The house was cold—there had never been enough money for central heating, and it was too late to make a fire in the sitting-room. She ate her supper, had a shower and went to bed, reassured by her visitor's calm manner and his certainty that her mother was going to be all right. He was nice, she thought sleepily, and not a bit pompous. She slept on the thought.

* * *

It was raining hard when she woke and there was a vicious wind driving off the moor. She had breakfast and hurried round to Dobbs's garage to use his phone. Her mother had had a good night, she was told, and was looking forward to seeing her later—reassuring news, which sent her back to give the good news to Queenie and then do the housework while she planned all the things she would do before her mother came home.

She had a sandwich and a cup of coffee well before twelve o'clock, anxious not to keep the professor waiting, so that when he arrived a few minutes before that hour she was in her coat, the house secure, Queenie settled in her basket and the bag she had packed for her mother ready in the hall.

He wished her a friendly good morning, remarked upon the bad weather and swept her into the car and drove away without wasting a moment. Conversation, she soon discovered, wasn't going to flourish in the face of his monosyllabic replies to her attempts to make small talk. She decided that he was tired or mulling over his patients and contented herself with watching the bleak landscape around them.

At the hospital he said, 'Will half-past four suit you? Be at the main entrance, will you?' He added kindly, 'I'm sure you'll be pleased with your mother's progress.' He got out of the car and opened her door, waited while she went in and then, contrary to her surmise, drove out of the forecourt and out of the city. Emma, unaware of this, expecting him to be about his own business in the hospital, made her way to her mother's room and forgot him at once.

Her mother was indeed better—pale still, and hung around with various tubes, but her hair had been nicely brushed and when Emma had helped her into her pink bed-jacket she looked very nearly her old self.

'It's a miracle, isn't it?' said Emma, gently embracing her parent. 'I mean, it's only forty-eight or so hours and here you are sitting up in bed.'

Mrs Trent, nicely sedated still, agreed drowsily. 'You brought my knitting? Thank you, dear. Is Queenie all right? And how are you managing to come? It can't be easy—don't come every day; it's such a long way...'

'Professor Wyatt is standing in for Dr Treble, so he brings me here after morning surgery and takes me back in time for his evening surgery.'

'That's nice.' Mrs Trent gave Emma's hand a little squeeze. 'So I'll see you each day; I'm so glad.' She closed her eyes and dropped off and Emma sat holding her hand, making plans.

A job—that was the most important thing to consider; a job she would be able to give up when her mother returned home. She might not be trained for anything much but she could type well enough and she could do simple accounts and housekeep adequately enough; there was sure to be something...

Her mother woke presently and she talked cheerfully about everyday things, not mentioning Mrs Smith-Darcy and, indeed, she didn't intend to do so unless her mother asked.

A nurse came and Emma, watching her skilful handling of tubes and the saline drip, so wished that she could be cool and calm and efficient and—an added bonus—pretty. Probably she worked for the professor—saw him every day, was able to understand him when he gave his orders in strange surgical terms, and received his thanks. He seemed to Emma to be a man of effortless good manners.

Her mother dozed again and didn't rouse as the tea-trolley was wheeled in, which was a good thing since a cup of tea was out of the question, but Emma was given one, with two Petit Beurre biscuits, and since her hurried lunch seemed a long time ago she was grateful.

Her mother was soon awake again, content to lie quietly, not talking much and finally with an eye on the clock, Emma kissed her goodbye. 'I'll be here tomorrow,' she promised, and went down to the main entrance.

She had just reached it when the Rolls came soundlessly to a halt beside her. The professor got out and opened her door, got back in and drove away with nothing more than a murmured greeting, but presently he said, 'Your mother looks better, does she not?'

'Oh, yes. She slept for most of the afternoon but she looks much better than I expected.'

'Of course, she's being sedated, and will be for the next forty-eight hours. After that she will be free of pain and taking an interest in life again. She's had a tiring time...'

It was still raining—a cold rain driven by an icy wind—and the moor looked bleak and forbidding in the early dusk. Emma, who had lived close to it all her life, was untroubled by that; she wondered if the professor felt the same. He had said that he lived near Exeter. She wondered exactly where; perhaps, after a few days of going to and fro, he would be more forthcoming. Certainly he was a very silent man.

The thought struck her that he might find her boring, but on the following day, when she ventured a few remarks of a commonplace nature, he had little to say in reply, although he sounded friendly enough. She decided that silence, unless he began a conversation, was the best policy, so that by the end of a week she was no nearer knowing anything about him than when they had first met. She liked him—she liked him very much—but she had the good sense to know that they inhabited different worlds. He had no wish to get to know her—merely to offer a helping hand, just as he would have done with anyone else in similar circumstances.

Her mother was making good progress and Emma scanned the local paper over the weekend, and checked the advertisements outside the news agents in the hope of finding a job.

Mrs Smith-Darcy had, surprisingly, sent Alice

with her wages, and Emma had made a pot of coffee and listened to Alice's outpourings on life with that lady. 'Mad as fire, she was,' Alice had said, with relish. 'You should 'ave 'eard 'er, Miss Trent. And that lunch party—that was a lark and no mistake—'er whingeing away about servants and such like. I didn't 'ear no kind words about you and your poor ma, though. Mean old cat.' She had grinned. 'Can't get another companion for love nor money, either.'

She had drunk most of the coffee and eaten all the biscuits Emma had and then got up to go. 'Almost forgot,' she'd said, suddenly awkward, 'me and Cook thought your ma might like a few chocs now she's better. And there's one of Cook's steak and kidney pies—just wants a warm-up—do for your dinner.'

'How lucky I am to have two such good friends,' Emma had said and meant it.

Going to the hospital on Monday, sitting quietly beside Sir Paul, she noticed him glance down at her lap where the box of chocolates sat.

'I hope that those are not for your mother?'

'Well, yes and no. Cook and Alice—from Mrs Smith-Darcy's house, you know—gave them to me to give her. I don't expect that she can have them, but she'll like to see them and she can give them to her nurses.'

He nodded. 'I examined your mother yesterday evening. I intend to have her transferred to Moretonhampstead within the next day or so. She will remain there for two weeks at least, three if possible, so that when she returns home she will be quite fit.'

'That is good news. Thank you for arranging it,' said Emma gratefully, and wondered how she was going to visit her mother. With a car it would have been easy enough.

She would have to find out how the buses ran—probably along the highway to Exeter and then down the turn-off to Moretonhampstead halfway along it—but the buses might not connect. She had saved as much money as she could and she had her last week's wages; perhaps she could get the car from Mr Dobbs again and visit her mother once a week; it was thirty miles or so, an hour's drive...

She explained this to her mother and was relieved to see that the prospect of going to a convalescent home and starting on a normal life once more had put her in such good spirits that she made no demur when Emma suggested that she might come only once a week to see her.

'It's only for a few weeks, Emma, and I'm sure I shall have plenty to keep me occupied. I've been so well cared for here, and everyone has been so kind. Everything's all right at home? Queenie is well?'

'She's splendid and everything is fine. I'll bring you some more clothes, shall I?' She made a list and observed, 'I'll bring them tomorrow, for the professor didn't say when you were going—when there's a vacancy I expect—he just said a day or two.'

When she got up to go her mother walked part of

the way with her, anxious to show how strong she had become. By the lifts they said goodbye, though, 'I'm a slow walker,' said Mrs Trent. 'It won't do to keep him waiting.'

For once, Emma was glad of Sir Paul's silence, for she had a lot to think about. They were almost at Buckfastleigh when he told her that her mother would be transferred on the day after tomorrow.

'So tomorrow will be the last day I go to the hospital?'

'Yes. Talk to Sister when you see her tomorrow; she will give you all the particulars and the phone number. Your mother will go by ambulance. The matron there is a very kind woman, there are plenty of staff and two resident doctors so your mother will be well cared for.'

'I'm sure of that. She's looking foward to going; she feels she's really getting well.'

'It has been a worrying time for you—' his voice was kind '—but I think she will make a complete recovery.'

Indoors she put the pie in the oven, fed an impatient Queenie and sat down to add up the money in her purse—enough to rent a car from Mr Dobbs on the following weekend and not much over. She ate her supper, packed a case with the clothes her mother would need and went to put the dustbin out before she went to bed.

The local paper had been pushed through the letter-box. She took it back to the kitchen and turned to the page where the few advertisements were and there, staring her in the face, was a chance of a job. It stated:

Wanted urgently—a sensible woman to help immediately for two or three weeks while present staff are ill. Someone able to cope with a small baby as well as normal household chores and able to cook.

Emma, reading it, thought that the woman wouldn't only have to be sensible, she would need to be a bundle of energy as well, but it was only for two or three weeks and it might be exactly what she was looking for. The phone number was a local one too.

Emma went to bed convinced that miracles did happen and slept soundly.

In the morning she waited with impatience until half-past eight before going round to use Mr Dobbs's phone. The voice which answered her was a woman's, shrill and agitated.

'Thank heaven—I'm at my wits' end and there's no one here. The baby's been crying all night…'

'If you would give me your address. I live in Buckfastleigh.'

'So do I. Picket House—go past the otter sanctuary and it's at the end of the road down a turning on the left. You've got a car?'

'No, a bike. I'll come straight away, shall I?'

She listened to a jumble of incoherent thanks and, after phoning the surgery to cancel her lift with Sir Paul, hurried back to the house. Queenie, having breakfasted, was preparing to take a nap. Emma left food for her, got into her coat, tied a scarf over her head and fetched her bike. At least it wasn't raining as she pedalled briskly from one end of the little town to the other.

Picket House was a rambling old place, beautifully maintained, lying back from the lane, surrounded by a large garden. Emma skidded to the front door and halted, and before she had got off her bike it was opened.

'Come in, come in, do.' The girl wasn't much older than Emma but there the resemblance ended, for she was extremely pretty, with fair, curly hair, big blue eyes and a dainty little nose. She pulled Emma inside and then burst into tears. 'I've had a dreadful night, you have no idea. Cook's ill with flu and so is Elsie, and the nurse who's supposed to come sent a message to say that her mother's ill.'

'There's no one who could come—your mother or a sister?'

'They're in Scotland.' She dismissed them with a wave of the hand. 'And Mike, my husband, he's in America and won't be back for weeks.' She wiped her eyes and smiled a little. 'You will come and help me?'

'Yes—yes, of course. You'll want references…?'

'Yes, yes—but later will do for that. I want a bath

and I've not had breakfast. To tell the truth, I'm not much of a cook.'

'The baby?' asked Emma, taking off her coat and scarf and hanging them on the elaborate hat-stand in the hall. 'A boy or a girl?'

'Oh, a boy.'

'Has he had a feed?'

'I gave him one during the night but I'm not sure if I mixed it properly; he was sick afterwards.'

'You don't feed him yourself?'

The pretty face was screwed up in horror. 'No, no, I couldn't possibly—I'm far too sensitive. Could you move in until the nurse can come?'

'I can't live here, but I'll come early in the morning and stay until the baby's last feed, if that would do?'

'I'll be alone during the night...'

'If the baby's had a good feed he should sleep for the night and I'll leave a feed ready for you to warm up.'

'Will you cook and tidy up a bit? I'm hopeless at housework.'

It seemed to Emma that now would be the time to learn about it, but she didn't say so. 'I don't know your name,' she said.

'Hervey—Doreen Hervey.'

'Emma Trent. Should we take a look at the baby before I get your breakfast?'

'Oh, yes, I suppose so. He's very small, just a month old. You're not a nurse, are you?'

'No, but I took a course in baby care and house-wifery when I left school.'

They were going upstairs. 'Would you come for a hundred pounds a week?'

'Yes.' It would be two or three weeks and she could save every penny of it.

They had reached the wide landing, and from somewhere along a passage leading to the back of the house there was a small, wailing noise.

The nursery was perfection—pastel walls, a thick carpet underfoot, pretty curtains drawn back from spotless white net, the right furniture and gloriously warm. The cot was a splendid affair and Mrs Her-vey went to lean over it. 'There he is,' she said un-necessarily.

He was a very small baby, with dark hair, screwed up eyes and a wide open mouth. The wails had turned to screams and he was waving miniature fists in a fury of infant rage.

'The lamb,' said Emma. 'He's wet; I'll change him. When did he have his feed? Can you remember the time?'

'I can't possibly remember; I was so tired. I suppose it was about two o'clock.'

'Is his feed in the kitchen?'

'Yes, on the table. I suppose he's hungry?'

Emma suppressed a desire to shake Mrs Hervey. 'Go and have your bath while I change him and feed him. Perhaps you could start breakfast—boil an egg and make toast?'

Mrs Hervey went thankfully away and Emma took the sopping infant from his sopping cot. While she was at it he could be bathed; everything she could possibly need was there…

With the baby tucked under one arm, swathed in his shawl, she went downstairs presently. The tin of baby-milk was on the table in the kind of kitchen every woman dreamt of. She boiled a kettle, mixed a feed and sat down to wait while it cooled. The baby glared at her from under his shawl. Since he looked as if he would cry again at any minute she talked gently to him.

She had fed him, winded him and cuddled him close as he dropped off and there was still no sign of his mother, but presently she came, her make-up immaculate, looking quite lovely.

'Oh, good, he's gone to sleep. I'm so hungry.' She smiled widely, looking like an angel. 'I'm so glad you've come, Emma—may I call you Emma?'

'Please do,' said Emma. She had her reservations about feeling glad as she bore the baby back to his cot.

CHAPTER THREE

By THE END of the day Emma realised that she would have her hands full for the next week or two. Mrs Hervey, no doubt a charming and good-natured woman, hadn't the least idea how to be a mother.

Over lunch she had confided to Emma that she had never had to do anything for herself—she had been pampered in succession by a devoted nanny, a doting mother and father, and then an adoring husband with money enough to keep her in the style to which she had been accustomed. 'Everyone's ill,' she had wailed. 'My old nanny ought to be here looking after me while Mike's away, but she's had to go and look after my sister's children—they've got measles. And the mother of this wretched nanny who was supposed to come. Just imagine, Emma, I came home from the nursing home and Cook and Elsie got ill the very next day!'

'You were in the nursing home for several weeks? Were you ill after the baby was born?'

'No, no. Mike arranged that so I could have plenty

of time to recover before I had to plunge into normal life again.'

Emma had forborne from telling her that most women plunged back into normal life with no more help than a willing husband. She'd said cautiously, 'While I'm here I'll show you how to look after the baby and how to mix the feeds, so that when Nanny has her days off you'll know what to do.'

'Will you? How sensible you are.'

'Hasn't the baby got a name?'

'We hadn't decided on that when Mike had to go away. We called him "Baby"—I suppose he'll be Bartholemew, after Mike's father, you know. He's very rich.'

It seemed a pity, Emma had reflected, to saddle the baby with such a name for the sake of future money-bags. 'May I call him Bart?' she'd asked.

'Why not?' Mrs Hervey had cast an anxious glance at Emma. 'You're quite happy here? It's a long day...'

As indeed it was.

After the first day, ending well after nine o'clock in the evening, Emma saw that she would have to alter things a bit. A little rearranging was all that was required. Bart needed a six o'clock feed, so she agreed to make it up the evening before for his mother to warm up.

'I'll come in at eight o'clock and get your breakfast, and while you are having it I'll bath Bart and make up his feed for ten o'clock. When he's had his two o'clock feed I'll leave him with you—he'll sleep for several hours and you will be able to rest if you want to.

'I'd like to go home for an hour or two, to do the shopping and so on, but I'll be back in plenty of time to see to his evening feed and get your supper. I'll stay until nine o'clock, so that you can get ready for bed before I go, then all you need to do is feed him at ten o'clock. I'll make up an extra feed in case he wakes at two o'clock.'

Mrs Hervey looked at her with her big blue eyes. 'You're an angel. Of course you must go home—and you will stay until nine o'clock?'

'Yes, of course.'

'You'll have lunch and supper with me, won't you?'

'Thank you, that would be nice. How about shopping? It wouldn't hurt Bart to be taken for an airing in his pram.'

'I'd be scared—all the traffic, and it's so far to the shops. I've always phoned for anything I want.'

'In that case, I'll take him for half an hour in the mornings when the weather's not too bad.'

'Will you? I say, I've just had such a good idea. Couldn't you take him with you in the afternoons?'

Emma had been expecting that. 'Well, no. You see, it's quite a long way and I go on my bike—I haven't anywhere to put the pram. Besides, you are his mum; he wants to be with you.'

'Oh, does he? You see, I'm not sure what to do when he cries...'

'Pick him up and see if he's wet. If he is, change him, and give him a cuddle.'

'It sounds so easy.'

'And it will be very nice if you know how to go on, so that when the nanny comes you can tell her how you want things done.'

Mrs Hervey, much struck with this idea, agreed.

It took a day or two to establish some sort of routine. Mrs Hervey was singularly helpless, not only with her son but about the running of a household; she had always had time to spend on herself and this time was now curtailed. But although she was so helpless, and not very quick to grasp anything, she had a placid nature and was very willing to learn.

The pair of them got on well and Bart, now that his small wants were dealt with promptly, was a contented baby.

Emma phoned her mother during the week and was relieved to hear that she had settled down nicely, and when Emma explained that she had a job, just for a week or two, and might not be able to go and see her, she told her comfortably that she was quite happy and that Emma wasn't to worry.

It was on Saturday that Sir Paul Wyatt, on his way home from a conference in Bristol, decided to visit Mrs Trent. He had seen nothing of Emma in Buckfastleigh, and on the one occasion when he had given way to a wish to visit her the house had been locked up and there had been no sign of her. Staying with friends, probably, he'd decided, and didn't go again.

Mrs Trent was delighted to see him. She was making good progress and seemed happy enough. Indeed, he wondered if she might not be able to return home very shortly. Only her enthusiastic description of Emma's new job made him pause, for, if he sent her home, Emma would have to give it up, at least for a few weeks, and he suspected that the Trent household needed the money.

'Emma has a local job?' he asked kindly.

'Yes. She is able to cycle there every day. It's with a Mrs Hervey; she lives at the other end of Buckfastleigh—a very nice house, Emma says. There is a very new baby and Mrs Hervey's cook and maid are both ill and the nanny she has engaged was unable to come, so Emma's helping out until she turns up and the other two are back.'

'Mrs Hervey is a young woman, presumably?'

'Oh, yes. Her husband is away—in America I believe. Mrs Hervey seems quite lost without him.'

He agreed, that might be so.

'I'm keeping you, Professor,' she went on. 'I'm sure you want to go home to your own family. It was very kind of you to come and see me. I told Emma not to come here; from what she said I rather think that she has very little time to herself and I shall soon be home.'

'Indeed you will, Mrs Trent.'

They shook hands and she added, 'You won't be seeing her, I suppose?'

'If I do I will give her your love,' he assured her.

Fifteen minutes later he stopped the car outside his front door in the heart of Lustleigh village. The house was close to the church, and was a rambling thatched cottage, its roof at various levels, its windows small and diamond-paned. The door was arched and solid and its walls in summer and autumn were a mass of colour from the climbing plants clinging to its irregularities.

He let himself in, to be met in the narrow hall by two dogs—a Jack Russell with an impudent face and a sober golden Labrador. He bent to caress them as a door at the end of the hall was opened and his housekeeper came trotting towards him. She was short and stout with a round, pink-cheeked face, small blue eyes and a smiling mouth.

'There you are, then,' she observed, 'and high time too, if I might say so. There's as nice a dinner waiting for you as you'd find anywhere in the land.'

'Give me ten minutes, Mrs Parfitt, and I'll do it justice.'

'Had a busy day, I reckon. Time you took a bit of a holiday; though it's not my place to say so, dear knows you've earned it.' She gave an indignant snort. 'Supposed to be free of all that operating and hospital work, aren't you, for six months? And look at you, sir, working your fingers off to help out old Dr Treble, going to conferences...'

Sir Paul had taken off his coat, picked up his bag

and opened a door. 'I'm rather enjoying it,' he observed mildly, and went into his study.

There was a pile of letters on his desk and the light on the answer-phone was blinking; he ignored them both and sat down at his desk and, lifting the phone's receiver, dialled a number and waited patiently for it to be answered.

Emma had soon discovered that it was impossible to get annoyed or impatient with Mrs Hervey. She had become resigned to the mess she found each morning when she arrived for work—the table in the kitchen left littered with unwashed crockery used by Mrs Hervey for the snack she fancied before she went to bed, the remnants of that snack left to solidify in the frying-pan or saucepan. But at least she had grasped the instructions for Bart's feeds, even though she made no attempt to clean anything once it had been used. She was, however, getting much better at handling her small son, and although she was prone to weep at the slightest set-back she was invariably good-natured.

Towards the end of the week Emma had suggested that it might be a good idea to take Bart to the baby clinic, or find out if there was a health visitor who would check Bart's progress.

'Absolutely not,' Mrs Hervey had said airily. 'They talked about it while I was in the nursing home but of course I said there was no need with a trained nanny already booked.'

'But the nanny isn't here,' Emma had pointed out.

'Well, you are, and she'll come soon—she said she would.' Mrs Hervey had given her a sunny smile and begged her not to fuss but to come and inspect various baby garments which had just arrived from Harrods.

By the end of the week Emma was tired; her few hours each afternoon were just sufficient for her to look after her house, do the necessary shopping, see to Queenie and do the washing and ironing, and by the time she got home in the evening she was too tired to do more than eat a sandwich and drink a pot of tea before tumbling into bed. She was well aware that she was working for far too many hours, but she told herself it was only for a few weeks and, with the first hundred pounds swelling the woefully meagre sum in their bank account, she went doggedly on.

All the same, on Saturday evening, as nine o'clock approached, she heaved a sigh of relief. Sunday would be a day like any weekday, but perhaps by the end of another week someone—the cook or the housemaid—would be back and then her day's work would be lighter. She had been tempted once or twice to suggest that Mrs Hervey might find someone to come in each day and do some housework, but this had been dismissed with a puzzled, 'But you are managing beautifully, Emma; you're doing all the things I asked for in the advert.'

Emma had said no more—what was the use? She only hoped that Mrs Hervey would never fall on hard times; her cushioned life had hardly prepared her for that.

She was about to put on her coat when Mrs Hervey's agitated voice made her pause. She took off her coat again and went back upstairs to find her bending over Bart's cot. 'He's red in the face,' she cried. 'Look at him; he's going to have a fit, I know it!'

'He needs changing,' said Emma.

'Oh, I'm so glad you're still here.' Mrs Hervey gave her a warm smile and went to answer the phone.

She came back a few moments later. 'A visitor,' she said happily. 'He's on his way. I'll go and get the drinks ready.'

Emma, still coping with Bart's urgent needs, heard the doorbell presently, and voices. Mrs Hervey was laughing a lot; it must be someone she knew very well and was glad to see. She had, so far, refused all invitations from her friends and hadn't invited any of them to come to the house. 'I promised Mike that I'd stay quietly at home and look after Baby,' she had explained to Emma. 'As soon as Nanny is here and settled in then I shall make up for it.' Her eyes had sparkled at the thought.

Bart, now that she had made him comfortable once more, was already half-asleep; Emma was tucking him up when the door was opened and Mrs Hervey came in and, with her, Sir Paul Wyatt.

Emma's heart gave a delighted leap at the sight of him while at the same time she felt a deep annoyance; she looked a fright—even at her best she was nothing to look at, but now, at the end of the day, she wasn't worth a glance. What was he doing here anyway? She gave him a distant look and waited to see who would speak first.

It was Mrs Hervey, bubbling over with pleasure. 'Emma, this is Sir Paul Wyatt; he's a professor or something. He's Mike's oldest friend and he's come to see Bart. He didn't know that I was home—I did say that I would go to Scotland until Mike came home. Just fancy, he's turned into a GP, just for a bit while Dr Treble is away.' She turned a puzzled gaze to him. 'I thought you were a surgeon?'

'I am. This is by way of a change. Emma and I have already met; I operated upon her mother not so long ago.' He smiled at her across the room. 'Good evening, Emma. You are staying here?'

'No, I'm just going home.'

'Rather late, isn't it?'

'Oh, well, that's my fault,' said Mrs Hervey cheerfully. 'Bart went all red and was roaring his head off and Emma hadn't quite gone so she came back. I thought he was ill.'

He lifted an enquiring eyebrow as Emma said in a no-nonsense voice, 'He needed changing.'

He laughed. 'Oh, Doreen, when will you grow up? The sooner Mike gets back the better!' He had gone to lean over the cot and was looking at the sleeping infant. 'The image of his father. He looks healthy enough.' He touched the small cheek with a gentle finger. 'Why do you not have a nanny, and where are the servants?'

Mrs Hervey tugged at his sleeve. 'Come downstairs and have a drink and I'll tell you.'

Emma, longing to go, saw that Bart was already asleep.

'How do you get back?' he enquired of Emma.

'I bike—it's only a short way.' She added, in a convincingly brisk tone, 'I enjoy the exercise.'

He held the door open and she followed Mrs Hervey downstairs, got into her coat once again and heard him telling Mrs Hervey that he could spare ten minutes and no more. She wished them goodnight and then let herself out of the house and pedalled furiously home.

It was already half-past nine and, although she was hungry, she was too tired to do more than put on the kettle for tea. She fed a disgruntled Queenie and poked her head into the fridge and eyed its sparse contents, trying to decide whether a boiled egg and yesterday's loaf would be preferable to a quick bath and a cup of tea in bed.

A brisk tattoo on the door-knocker caused her to withdraw her head smartly and listen. The tattoo was repeated and she went to the door then, suddenly afraid that it was bad news of her mother. She put up the new chain and opened the door a few inches, her view quite blocked by the professor's bulk.

He said testily, 'Yes, it is I, Emma.'

'What do you want?' The door was still on the

chain but she looked up into his face, half-hidden in the dark night. 'Mother?' she asked in a sudden panic.

'Your mother is well; I have seen her recently. Now, open the door, there's a good girl.'

She was too tired to argue. She opened it and he crowded into the narrow hall, his arms full.

'Fish and chips,' said Emma, suddenly famished.

'A quick and nourishing meal, but it must be eaten immediately.'

She led the way into the kitchen, took down plates from the small dresser and then paused. 'Oh, you won't want to eat fish and chips…'

'And why not? I have had no dinner this evening and I am extremely hungry.' He was portioning out the food on to the two plates while she laid the cloth and fetched knives and forks.

'I was making tea,' she told him.

'Splendid. You do not mind if I join you?'

Since he was already sitting at the table there seemed no point in objecting, and anyway, she didn't want to!

They sat opposite each other at the small table with Queenie, aroused by the delightful smell, at their feet, and for a few minutes neither of them spoke. Only when the first few mouthfuls had been eaten did Sir Paul ask, 'How long have you been with Doreen Hervey?'

Emma, gobbling chips, told him.

'And what free time do you have? It seems to me that your day is excessively long.'

'I come home each afternoon just for an hour or two...'

'To shop and wash and clean and make your bed? You are too pale, Emma; you need fresh air and a few idle hours.'

'Well, I'll get them in a week or two; the nanny said it would be only a few weeks, and Mrs Hervey told me today that the housemaid is coming back in just over a week.'

'Of course you need the money.'

He said it in such a matter-of-fact way that she said at once, 'Yes, I do, I won't be able to work for a bit when Mother comes home.' She selected a chip and bit into it. She had small very white teeth, and when she smiled and wasn't tired she looked almost pretty.

It was surprising, he reflected, what fish and chips and a pot of tea did for one. He couldn't remember when he had last had such a meal and he was glad to see that Emma's rather pale cheeks had taken on a tinge of colour.

He got up from the table, took their plates to the sink and poured the water from the kettle into the bowl.

'You can't wash up,' said Emma.

'I can and I shall. You may dry the dishes if you wish.'

'Well, really...' muttered Emma and then laughed. 'You're not a bit like a professor of surgery.'

'I am relieved to hear it. I don't spend all day and every day bending over the operating table, you know. I have a social side to my life.'

She felt a pang of regret that she would never know what that was.

As soon as the last knife and fork had been put away he wished her a pleasant good evening and went away. She felt deflated when he had gone. 'Only because,' she explained to Queenie, for lack of any other listener, 'I don't get many people—well, many men.'

Half an hour later Sir Paul let himself into his house, to be greeted as he always was by his dogs and his housekeeper.

'Dear knows, you're a busy man, sir, but it's long past the hour any self-respecting man should be working. You'll be wanting your dinner.'

'I've dined, thank you, Mrs Parfitt. I would have phoned but there was no phone.'

'Dined? With Dr Treble?' She sniffed. 'His housekeeper is a careless one in the kitchen—I doubt you enjoyed your food.'

'Fish and chips, and I enjoyed every mouthful.'

'Not out of newspaper?' Mrs Parfitt's round face was puckered in horror.

'No, no. On a plate in the company of a young lady.'

Mrs Parfitt twinkled at him. 'Ah, I'm glad to hear it, sir. Was she pretty?'

'No.' He smiled at her. 'Don't allow your thoughts to get sentimental, Mrs Parfitt—she needed a meal.'

'Helping another of your lame dogs over the stile, were you? There's a pile of post in your study; I'll bring you a tray of coffee and some of my little biscuits.'

'Excellent. They should dispel any lingering taste of my supper.'

Mrs Parfitt was right; there were a great many letters to open and read and the answering machine to deal with. He was occupied until the early hours of the morning, when he took the dogs for a brisk walk, and saw them to their baskets and finally took himself off to bed. He hadn't thought of Emma once.

'Fancy you knowing Paul,' said Mrs Hervey, when Emma arrived in the morning. 'He's a stunner; if Mike hadn't turned up I could have fallen for him. Not that he gave me any encouragement.' She sighed. 'You see, he'll pick a suitable wife when he decides he wants one and not a minute sooner. I don't believe he's ever been in love—oh, he's dozens of girlfriends, of course, but it'll take someone special to touch his heart.'

Emma nodded. It would have to be someone like Mrs Hervey, pretty as a picture, amusing and helpless; men, Emma supposed, would like that. She thought with regret that she had never had the opportunity to be helpless. And she would never, she decided, taking a quick look in the unnecessary looking-glass in the nursery, be pretty.

That her eyes were large and thickly lashed and

her hair, confined tidily in a French pleat, was long and silky, and that her mouth, though too wide, was gentle and her complexion as clear and unblemished as a baby's quite escaped her attention.

Sir Paul Wyatt, fulfilling his role of general practitioner in the middle of the following week, allowed his thoughts to dwell on just those pleasing aspects of Emma's person, only relinquishing them when the next patients came into the surgery.

Surgery finished, he went on his rounds; the inhabitants of Buckfastleigh were, on the whole, a healthy bunch and his visits were few. He drove himself home, ate his lunch, took the dogs for a walk and then got into the Rolls and drove back to Buckfastleigh again.

Emma was at home; her elderly bike was propped against the house wall and the windows were open. He knocked on the door, wondering why he had come.

She answered the door at once, an apron tied round her slender middle, her hair, loosed from its severe plait, tied back with a ribbon.

She stared up at him mutely, and he stared back with a placid face.

'Not Mother?' she said finally, and he shook his head.

'Is Mrs Hervey all right? Bart was asleep when I left.'

He nodded and she asked sharply, 'So why have you come?' She frowned. 'Do you want something?'

He smiled then. 'I am not certain about that... May I come in?'

'Sorry,' said Emma. 'Please do—I was surprised to see you...' She added unnecessarily, 'I was just doing a few chores.'

'When do you have to go back?' He was in the hall, taking up most of the space.

'Just after four o'clock to get Mrs Hervey's tea.'

He glanced at his watch. 'May we have tea here first? I'll go and get something—crumpets—while you do the dusting.'

Emma was surprised, although she agreed readily. Perhaps he had missed his lunch; perhaps surgery was earlier than usual that afternoon. She stood in the doorway and watched him drive away, and then rushed around with the duster and the carpet-sweeper before setting out the tea things. Tea would have to be in the kitchen; there was no fire laid in the sitting-room.

She fed Queenie, filled the kettle and went upstairs to do her face and pin her hair. Studying her reflection, she thought how dull she looked in her tweed skirt, blouse and—that essentially British garment—a cardigan.

She was back downstairs with minutes to spare before he returned.

It wasn't just crumpets he had brought with him— there were scones and doughnuts, a tub of butter and a pot of strawberry jam. He arranged them on a dish while she put the crumpets under the grill and boiled the kettle, all the while carrying on an undemanding conversation about nothing much so that Emma, who had felt suddenly awkward, was soothed into a pleasant feeling of ease.

They had finished the crumpets and were starting on the scones when he asked casually, 'What do you intend doing when you leave Doreen Hervey, Emma?'

'Do? Well, I'll stay at home for a bit, until Mother is quite herself again, and then I'll look for another job.'

He passed her the butter and the jam. 'You might train for something?'

'I can type and do shorthand, though I'm not very good at either, and people always need mother's helps.' She decided that it was time to change the conversation. 'I expect Mother will be on some kind of a diet?'

'Yes—small meals taken frequently, cut out vinegar and pickles and so on.' He sounded impatient. 'She will be given a leaflet when she comes home. The physicians have taken over now.' He frowned. 'Is it easy to get a job here?'

Her red herring hadn't been of much use. 'I think so. My kind of a job anyway.'

'You're wasted—bullied by selfish women and changing babies' nappies.'

'I like babies.' She added tartly, 'It's kind of you to bother, but there is no need—'

'How old are you, Emma?'

'Almost twenty-six.'

He smiled. 'Twenty-five, going on fifteen! I'm forty—do you find that old?'

'Old? Of course not. You're not yet in your prime. And you don't feel like forty, do you?'

'Upon occasion I feel ninety, but at the moment at least I feel thirty at the most!' He smiled at her and she thought what a very nice smile he had—warm and somehow reassuring. 'Have another doughnut?'

She accepted it with the forthright manner of a polite child. She was not, he reflected, in the least coy or self-conscious. He didn't search too deeply into his reasons for worrying about her future, although he admitted to the worry. It was probably because she was so willing to accept what life had to offer her.

He went presently, with a casual goodbye and no mention of seeing her again. Not that she had expected that. She cycled back to Mrs Hervey and Bart, reflecting that she was becoming quite fond of him.

It was the beginning of the third week, with another hundred pounds swelling their bank balance, when Mrs Hervey told her that the new nanny would be with them by the end of the week, and Cook and the housemaid would return in three days' time.

'And about time too,' said Mrs Hervey rather pettishly. 'I mean, three weeks just to get over flu…'

Emma held her tongue and Mrs Hervey went on, 'You'll stay until the end of the week, won't you,

Emma? As soon as Cook and that girl are here I shall have a chance to go to the hairdresser. I'm desperate to get to Exeter—I need some clothes and a facial too. You'll only have Bart to look after, and Nanny comes on Friday evening. I dare say she'll want to ask your advice about Bart before you go.'

'I think,' said Emma carefully, 'that she may prefer not to do that. She's professional, you see, and I'm just a temporary help. I'm sure you will be able to tell her everything that she would want to know.'

'Will I? Write it all down for me, Emma, won't you? I never can remember Bart's feeds and what he ought to weigh.'

Certainly, once the cook and housemaid returned, life was much easier for Emma. She devoted the whole of her day to Bart, taking him for long rides in his pram, sitting with him on her lap, cuddling him and singing half-forgotten nursery rhymes while he stared up at her with his blue eyes. Cuddling was something that his mother wasn't very good at. She loved him, Emma was sure of that, but she was awkward with him. Perhaps the new nanny would be able to show Mrs Hervey how to cuddle her small son.

It was on her last day, handing over to a decidedly frosty Nanny, that she heard Sir Paul's voice in the drawing-room. She listened with half an ear to the superior young woman who was to have charge of Bart telling her of all the things she should have done, and wondered if she would see him. It seemed that she wouldn't, for presently Mrs Hervey joined them, remarking that Sir Paul had just called to see if everything was normal again.

'I asked him if he would like to see Bart but he said he hadn't the time. He was on his way to Plymouth.' She turned to the nanny. 'You've had a talk with Emma? Wasn't it fortunate that she was able to come and help me?' She made a comic little face. 'I'm not much good with babies.'

'I'm accustomed to take sole charge, Mrs Hervey; you need have no further worries about Bart. Tomorrow, perhaps, we might have a little talk and I will explain my duties to you.'

It should surely be the other way round, thought Emma. But Mrs Hervey didn't seem to mind.

'Oh, of course. I'm happy to leave everything to you. You're ready to go, Emma? Say goodbye to Bart; he's got very fond of you...'

A remark which annoyed Nanny, for she said quite sharply that the baby was sleeping and shouldn't be disturbed. So Emma had to content herself with looking at him lying in his cot, profoundly asleep, looking like a very small cherub.

She would miss him.

She bade Nanny a quiet goodbye and went downstairs with Mrs Hervey and got on her bike, warmed by that lady's thanks and the cheque in her pocket. Three hundred pounds would keep them going for quite some time, used sparingly with her mother's pension.

When she got home, she took her bike round to

the shed, went indoors and made some supper for Queenie, and boiled an egg for herself. She felt sad that the job was finished, but a good deal of the sadness was because she hadn't seen the professor again.

There was a letter from her mother in the morning, telling her that she would be brought home by ambulance in two days' time. How nice, she wrote, that Emma's job was finished just in time for her return. Emma wondered how she had known that, and then forgot about it as she made plans for the next two days.

It was pleasant to get up the next morning and know that she had the day to herself. It was Sunday, of course, so she wouldn't be able to do any shopping, but there was plenty to do in the house—the bed to make up, wood and coal to be brought in, the whole place to be dusted and aired. And, when that was done, she sat down and made a shopping list.

Bearing in mind what Sir Paul had said about diet, she wrote down what she hoped would be suitable and added flowers and one or two magazines, Earl Grey tea instead of the economical brand they usually drank, extra milk and eggs—the list went on and on, but for once she didn't care. Her mother was coming home and that was a cause for extravagance.

She had the whole of Monday morning in which to shop, and with money in her purse she enjoyed herself, refusing to think about the future, reminding herself that it would soon be the tourist season again and there were always jobs to be found. It didn't matter what she did so long as she could be at home.

Her mother arrived during the afternoon, delighted to be at home again, protesting that she felt marvellous, admiring the flowers and the tea-tray on a small table by the lighted fire in the sitting-room. Emma gave the ambulance driver tea and biscuits, received an envelope with instructions as to her mother's diet and went back to her mother.

Mrs Trent certainly looked well; she drank her weak tea and ate the madeira cake Emma had baked and settled back in her chair. 'Now, tell me all the news, Emma. What was this job like? Were you happy? A nice change looking after a baby?'

Emma recounted her days, making light of the long hours. 'It was a very nice job,' she declared, 'and I earned three hundred pounds, so I can stay at home for as long as you want me to.'

They talked for the rest of that afternoon and evening, with Queenie sitting on Mrs Trent's lap and finally trailing upstairs with her to curl up on her bed.

Emma, taking her some warm milk and making sure that she was comfortable before she went to bed herself, felt a surge of relief at the sight of her mother once more in her own bed. The future was going to be fine, she told herself as she kissed her mother goodnight.

CHAPTER FOUR

EMMA AND HER MOTHER settled down into a quiet routine: gentle pottering around the house, short walks in the afternoon, pleasant evenings round the fire at the end of the day. For economy's sake, Emma shared her mother's small, bland meals, and found herself thinking longingly of the fish and chips Sir Paul had brought to the house.

There was no sign of him, of course, and it wasn't likely that she would see him again; the new doctor had come to take over from Dr Treble and the professor had doubtless taken up his normal life again. She speculated a bit about that, imagining him stalking the wards with a bunch of underlings who hung on to any words of wisdom he might choose to utter and watched with awe while he performed some complicated operation. And his private life? Her imagination ran riot over that—married to some beautiful young woman—she would have to be beautiful, he wouldn't look at anyone less—perhaps with children—handsome little boys and pretty little girls.

If he wasn't married he would certainly have any number of women-friends and get asked out a great deal—dinner parties and banquets and evenings at the theatre and visits to London.

A waste of time, she told herself time and again—she would forget all about him. But that wasn't easy, because her mother talked about him a great deal although, when pumped by Emma, she was unable to tell her anything about his private life.

Mrs Trent had been home for a week when he came to see her. Emma had seen the Rolls draw up from her mother's bedroom window and had hurried down to open the door, forgetting her unmade-up face and her hair bunched up anyhow on top of her head. It was only as she opened the door that she remembered her appearance, so that she met his faintly amused look with a frown and her feelings so plain on her face that he said to her at once, 'I do apologise for coming unexpectly, but I had half an hour to spare and I wanted to see how your mother was getting on.'

'Hello,' said Emma gruffly, finding her voice and her manners. 'Please come in; she will be glad to see you.'

She led the way into the little sitting-room. 'I was going to make Mother's morning drink and have some coffee. Would you like a cup?' She gave him a brief glance. 'Shall I take your coat?'

'Coffee would be delightful.' He took off his overcoat and flung it over a chair and went to take Mrs

Trent's hand, which gave Emma the chance to escape. She galloped up to her room, powdered her nose, pinned up her hair and tore downstairs again to make the coffee and carry it in presently, looking her usual neat self.

Sir Paul, chatting with her mother, looked at her from under his lids and hid a smile, steering the conversation with effortless ease towards trivial matters. It was only when they had finished their coffee that he asked Mrs Trent a few casual questions. He seemed satisfied with her answers and presently took his leave.

As he shook hands with the older woman she asked, 'Are you still working here as a GP? Has the new doctor arrived?'

'Several days ago; he will be calling on you very shortly, I have no doubt.'

'So we shan't see you again? I owe you so much, Sir Paul.'

'It is a great satisfaction to me to see you on your feet again, Mrs Trent. Don't rush things, will you? You're in very capable hands.' He glanced at Emma, who had her gaze fixed on his waistcoat and didn't meet his eye.

When he had driven away Mrs Trent said, 'I'm sorry we shan't see him again. I felt quite safe with him...'

'I expect the new doctor is just as kind as Dr Treble. I'm sure he'll come and see you in a day or two, Mother.'

Which he did—a pleasant, youngish man who asked the same questions that Sir Paul had asked, assured Emma that her mother was making excellent progress and suggested that she might go to the surgery in a month's time for a check-up.

'No need really,' he said cheerfully. 'But I should like to keep an eye on you for a little while.' As Emma saw him to the door he observed, 'I'm sure you're looking after your mother very well; it's fortunate that you are living here with her.' It was a remark which stopped her just in time from asking him when he thought it would be suitable for her to look for a job again.

The days slid past, each one like the previous; Mrs Trent was content to knit and read and go for short walks, and Emma felt a faint prick of unease. Surely by now her mother should be feeling more energetic? She was youngish still—nowadays most people in their fifties were barely middle-aged and still active—but her mother seemed listless, and disinclined to exert herself.

The days lengthened and winter began to give way reluctantly to spring, but Mrs Trent had no inclination to go out and about. Emma got Mr Dobbs to drive them to the surgery, when a month was up, after reminding her mother that it was time she saw the doctor again.

She had already spoken to him on Mr Dobbs's phone, voicing her vague worries and feeling rather silly since there was nothing definite to tell him, but he was kindness itself as he examined Mrs Trent.

He said finally, 'You're doing very well, Mrs Trent—well enough to resume normal life once more. I'll see about some surgical stockings for you—you do have a couple of varicose veins. Recent, are they?'

'Oh, yes, but they don't bother me really. I'm not on my feet all that much.' Mrs Trent laughed. 'I'm getting rather lazy...'

'Well, don't get too lazy; a little more exercise will do you good, I think. The operation was entirely successful and there is no reason why you shouldn't resume your normal way of life.' He gave her an encouraging smile. 'Come and see me in a month's time and do wear those stockings—I'll see you get them.'

'A nice young man,' declared Mrs Trent as they were driven home by Mr Dobbs and Emma agreed, although she had the feeling that he had thought her over-fussy about her mother. Still, he had said that her mother was quite well again, excepting for those veins...

It was several days later, as she was getting their tea, that she heard her mother call out and then the sound of her falling. She flew to the sitting-room and found her mother lying on the floor, and she knew before she picked up her hand that there would be no pulse.

'Mother,' said Emma, and even though it was use-

less she put a cushion under her head before she tore
out of the house to Mr Dobbs and the phone.

An embolism, the doctor said, a pulmonary embolism, sudden and fatal. Emma said, in a voice
which didn't sound like hers, 'Varicose veins—it
was a blood clot.' She saw his surprised look. 'I've
done my First Aid.' She raised anguished eyes to his.
'Couldn't you have known?'

He shook his head. 'No, there were no symptoms
and varicose veins are commonplace; one always
bears in mind that a clot might get dislodged, but
there is usually some warning.'

'She wouldn't have known?'

'No, I'm certain of that.'

There was no one to turn to, no family or very
close friends, although the neighbours were kind—
cooking her meals she couldn't eat, offering to help.
They had liked her mother and they liked her and she
was grateful, thanking them in a quiet voice without
expression, grief a stone in her chest.

They came to the funeral too, those same neigh-
bors, and the doctor, Cook and Alice from Mrs
Smith-Darcy's house, taking no notice of that lady's
orders to remain away. Mrs Hervey was there too,
and kind Mr Dobbs. The only person Emma wanted
to see was absent—Sir Paul Wyatt wasn't there, and
she supposed that he had no reason to be there anyway. That he must know she was certain, for the doctor had told her that he had written to him...

There was no money, of course, and no will. She

remembered her mother telling her laughingly that when she was sixty she would make one, but in any case there was almost nothing to leave—the house and the furniture and a few trinkets.

Emma, during the next few empty days, pondered her future. She would sell the house if she could find a small flat in Plymouth, and train properly as a shorthand typist and then find a permanent job. She had no real wish to go to Plymouth but if she went to Exeter, a city she knew and loved, she might meet Sir Paul—something, she told herself, she didn't wish to do. Indeed, she didn't want to see him again.

A new life, she decided, and the sooner the better. Thirty wasn't all that far off, and by then she was determined to have built herself a secure future. 'At least I've got Queenie,' she observed to the empty sitting-room as she polished and dusted, quite un-necessarily because the house was clean, but it filled the days. She longed to pack her things and settle her future at once, but there were all the problems of unexpected death to unravel first, so she crammed her days with hard work and cried herself to sleep each night, hugging Queenie for comfort, keeping her sorrow to herself.

People were very kind—calling to see how she was, offering companionship, suggesting small out-ings—and to all of them she showed a cheerful face and gave the assurance that she was getting along splendidly and making plans for the future, and they went away, relieved that she was coping so well.

'Of course, Emma has always been such a sensible girl,' they told each other, deceived by her calm manner.

Ten days after the funeral, her small affairs not yet settled, she was in the kitchen, making herself an early morning cup of tea and wondering how much longer she would have to wait before she could put the house up for sale. She would keep most of the furniture, she mused, sitting down at the kitchen table, only to be interrupted by a bang on the doorknocker. It must be the postman, earlier than usual, but perhaps there would be something interesting in the post. The unbidden thought that there might be a letter from Sir Paul passed through her mind as she opened the door.

It wasn't a letter from him but he himself in person, looming in the doorway and, before she could speak, inside the house, squashed up against her in the narrow little hall.

At the sight of him she burst into tears, burying her face in the tweed of his jacket without stopping to think what she was doing, only aware of the comfort of his arms around her.

He said gently, 'My poor girl. I didn't know— I've been in America and only got back yesterday evening. I was told what had happened by your doctor. He wrote—but by the time I had read his letter it was too late to come to you. I am so very sorry.'

'There wasn't anyone,' said Emma, between great

heaving sobs. 'Everyone was so kind...' It was a muddled remark, which he rightly guessed referred to his absence. He let her cry her fill and presently, when the sobs became snivels, he offered a large white linen handkerchief.

'I'm here now,' he said cheerfully, 'and we'll have breakfast while you tell me what happened.' He gave her an avuncular pat on the back and she drew away from him, feeling ashamed of her outburst but at the same time aware that the hard stone of her grief had softened to a gentle sorrow.

'I'm famished,' said Sir Paul in a matter-of-fact voice which made the day normal again. 'I'll lay the table while you cook.'

'I must look a fright. I'll go and do something to my face...'

He studied her with an impersonal look which she found reassuring. Not a fright, he reflected, but the face far too pale, the lovely eyes with shadows beneath them and the clear skin blotched and pinkened with her tears. 'It looks all right to me,' he told her and knew that, despite the tearstains, she was feeling better.

'As long as you don't mind,' she said rather shyly, and got out the frying-pan. 'Will fried eggs and fried bread do?' she asked. 'I'm afraid there isn't any bacon...'

'Splendidly. Where do you keep the marmalade?'

They sat down eventually, facing each other across the kitchen table and Emma, who had had no appetite for days, discovered that she was hungry. It wasn't until they had topped off the eggs with toast and marmalade that Sir Paul allowed the conversation to become serious.

'What are your plans?' he wanted to know, when he had listened without interruption to her account of her mother's death.

'I'll have to sell this house. I thought I'd find a small flat in Plymouth and take a course in office management and then get a proper job. I've enough furniture and I'll have Queenie.'

'Is there no money other than the proceeds from the house?'

'Well, no, there isn't. Mother's pension won't be paid any more of course.' She added hastily, anxious to let him see that she was able to manage very well, 'I can put the house up for sale just as soon as I'm allowed to. There are still some papers and things. They said they'd let me know.'

'And is that what you would like to do, Emma?'

'Yes, of course.' She caught his eye and added honestly, 'I don't know what else to do.'

He smiled at her across the table. 'Will you marry me, Emma?'

Her mouth dropped open. 'Marry you? You're joking!'

'Er—no, I have never considered marriage a joke.'

'Why do you want to marry me? You don't know anything about me—and I'm plain and not a bit interesting. Besides, you don't—don't love me.'

'I know enough about you to believe that you would make me an admirable wife and, to be truthful, I have never considered you plain. As for loving you, I am perhaps old-fashioned enough to consider that mutual liking and compatibility and the willingness to make a good marriage are excellent foundations for happiness. Since the circumstances are unusual we will marry as soon as possible and get to know each other at our leisure.'

'But your family and your friends…?' She saw his lifted eyebrows and went on awkwardly, 'What I mean is, I don't think I'm used to your kind of life.' She waved a hand round the little kitchen. 'I don't expect it's like this.'

He said evenly, 'I live in a thatched cottage at Lustleigh and I have an elderly housekeeper and two dogs. My mother and father live in the Cotswolds and I have two sisters, both married. I'm a consultant at the Exeter hospitals and I frequently go to London, where I am a consultant at various hospitals. I go abroad fairly frequently, to lecture and operate, but at present I have taken a sabbatical, although I still fulfil one or two appointments.'

'Aren't you too busy to have a wife? I mean—' she frowned, trying to find the right words '—you lead such a busy life.'

'When I come home in the evenings it will be pleasant to find you there, waiting to listen to my grumbles if things haven't gone right with my day, and at the weekends I will have a companion.'

'You don't—that is, you won't mind me not loving you?'

'I think,' he said gently, 'that we might leave love out of it, don't you?' He smiled a tender smile, which warmed her down to the soles of her feet. 'We like each other, don't we? And that's important.'

'You might fall in love with someone...'

She wasn't looking at him, otherwise she would have seen his slow smile.

'So might you—a calculated risk which we must both take.' He smiled again, completely at ease. 'I'll wash up and tidy things away while you go and pack a bag.'

'A bag? What for?'

'You're coming back with me. And while Mrs Parfitt fattens you up and the moor's fresh air brings colour into your cheeks you can decide what you want to do.' When she opened her mouth to speak he raised a hand. 'No, don't argue, Emma. I've no intention of leaving you alone here. Later you can tell me what still has to be settled about the house and furniture and I'll deal with the solicitor. Are the bills paid?'

He was quite matter-of-fact about it and she found herself telling him that there were still a few outstanding. 'But everyone said they'd wait until the house was sold.'

He nodded. 'Leave it to me, if you will. Now, run along and get some things packed. Has Queenie got a basket?'

'Yes, it's beside the dresser.'

She went meekly upstairs, and only as she was packing did she reflect that he was behaving in a high-handed fashion, getting his own way without any effort. That, she reminded herself, was because she was too tired and unhappy to resist him. She was thankful to leave everything to him, but once she had pulled herself together she would convince him that marrying him was quite out of the question.

And, since he didn't say another word about it as he drove back to Lustleigh, she told herself that he might have made the suggestion on the spur of the moment and was even now regretting it.

It was a bright morning and cold, but spring was definitely upon them. Lustleigh was a pretty village and a pale sun shone on its cottages. It shone on Sir Paul's home too and Emma, getting out of the car, fell in love with the house at first glance.

'Oh, how delightful. It's all nooks and crannies, isn't it?'

He had a hand under her elbow, urging her to the door. 'It has been in the family for a long time, and each generation has added a room or a chimney-pot or another window just as the fancy took it.' He opened the door and Mrs Parfitt came bustling down the curving staircase at the back of the hall.

'God bless my soul, so you're back, sir.'

She cast him a reproachful look and he said quickly, 'I got back late last night and went straight to the hospital and, since it was already after midnight and I wanted to go to Buckfastleigh as early as possible, I didn't come home. They put me up there.' He still had his hand on Emma's arm. 'Mrs Parfitt, I've brought a guest who will stay with us for a little while. Miss Trent's mother died recently and she needs a break. Emma, this is my housekeeper, Mrs Parfitt.'

Emma shook hands, conscious of sharp, elderly eyes looking her over.

'I hope I won't give you too much extra work…'

Mrs Parfitt had approved of what she saw. All in good time, she promised herself, she would discover the whys and wherefores. 'A pleasure to have someone in the house, miss, for Sir Paul is mostly away from home or shut in that study of his—he might just as well be in the middle of the Sahara for all I see of him!'

She chuckled cosily. 'I'll bring coffee into the sitting-room, shall I, sir? And get a room ready for Miss Trent?'

Sir Paul took Emma's coat and opened a door, urging her ahead of him. The room was long and low, with small windows overlooking the narrow street and glass doors opening on to the garden at the far end. He went past her to open them and let in the dogs, who danced around, delighted to see him.

'Come and meet Kate and Willy,' he invited, and Emma crossed the room and offered a balled fist.

'Won't they mind Queenie?' she wanted to know.

'Not in the least, and Mrs Parfitt will be delighted;

her cat died some time ago and she is always talking of getting a kitten—Queenie is much more suitable. I'll get her, and they can get used to each other while we have our coffee.'

While he was gone she looked around the room. Its walls were irregular and there were small windows on each side of the inglenook, and a set of heavy oak beams supporting the ceiling. The walls were white but there was no lack of colour in the room—the fine old carpet almost covered the wood floor, its russets and faded blues toning with the velvet curtains. There were bookshelves crammed with books, several easy-chairs, and a vast sofa drawn up to the fire and charming pie-crust tables holding reading lamps—a delightful lived-in room.

She pictured it in mid-winter, when the wind whistled from the moor and snow fell; with the curtains drawn and a fire roaring up the chimney one would feel safe and secure and content. For the first time since her mother's death she felt a small spark of happiness.

Sir Paul, coming in with Queenie under his arm, disturbed her thoughts and saw them reflected in her face. He said casually, 'You like this room? Let us see if Queenie approves of it… No, don't worry about the dogs—they'll not touch her.'

Mrs Parfitt came in to bring the coffee then, and they sat drinking it, watching the dogs, obedient to their master, sitting comfortably while Queenie edged round them and finally, to Emma's surprise, sat down and washed herself.

'The garden is walled—she won't be able to get out; she'll be quite at home in a few days. I've taken your bag upstairs; I expect you would like to unpack before lunch. This afternoon we'll walk round the village so that you can find your way about. I'll take the dogs for a run and see you at lunch.'

Emma, soothed by the room and content to have someone to tell her how to order her day, nodded. It was like being in a dream after the loneliness of the last week or two. It wouldn't last, of course, for she had no intention of marrying Sir Paul. But for the moment she was happy to go on dreaming.

She was led away presently, up the charming little staircase and on to a landing with passages leading from it in all directions.

'A bit of a jumble,' said Mrs Parfitt cheerfully, 'but you'll soon find your way around. I've put you in a nice quiet room overlooking the garden. Down this passage and up these two steps. The door's a bit narrow...'

Which it was—solid oak like the rest of the doors in the cottage and opening into a room with a large circle of windows taking up all of one wall. There was a balcony beyond them with a wrought-iron balustrade and a sloping roof. 'For your little cat,' explained Mrs Parfitt. 'I dare say you like to have her with you at night? I always had my Jenkin—such a comfort he was!'

'How thoughtful of you, Mrs Parfitt. I hope you'll like Queenie; she's really very good.'

'Bless you, miss, I like any cat.' She trotted over to another door by the bed. 'The bathroom's here and mind the step down, and if there's anything you need you just say so. You'll want to hang up your things now. Lunch is at one o'clock, but come downstairs when you're ready and sit by the fire.'

When she had gone Emma looked around her; the room had uneven walls so that the bay window took up the longest of them. There was a small fireplace in the centre of one short wall and the bedhead was against the wall facing the window. That was irregular too, and the fourth wall had a deep-set alcove into which the dressing-table fitted. She ran a finger along its surface, delighting in the golden brown of the wood.

It was a cosy room, despite the awkwardness of its shape, and delightfully furnished in muted pinks and blues. She unpacked her things and laid them away in the tallboy, and hung her dress in the cupboard concealed in one of the walls. She had brought very little with her—her sensible skirt and blouses, her cardigan and this one dress. She tidied away her undies, hung up her dressing-gown and sat down before the dressing-table.

Her reflection wasn't reassuring and that was partly her fault, for she hadn't bothered much with her appearance during the two weeks since her mother had died—something she would have to remedy. She did her face and brushed her hair and pinned it into its neat French pleat and went downstairs, peering along the various passages as she went.

It was indeed a delightful house, and although Sir Paul had called it a cottage it was a good deal larger than that. There was no sign of him when she reached the hall but Mrs Parfitt popped her head round a door.

'He won't be long, miss. Come into the kitchen if you've a mind. Your little cat's here, as good as gold, sitting in the warm. Taken to us like a duck to water, she has.'

Indeed, Queenie looked as though she had lived there all her life, stretched out before the Aga.

'You don't mind her being here? In your kitchen?'

'Bless you, miss, whatever harm could she do? Just wait while I give the soup a stir and I'll show you the rest of it...'

She opened a door and led the way down a short passage. 'This bit of the house Sir Paul's grandfather added; you can't see it from the lane. There's a pantry—' she opened another door '—and a wash-house opposite and all mod cons—Sir Paul saw to that. And over here there's what was the stillroom; I use it for bottled fruit and jam and pickles. I make those myself. Then there's this cubby-hole where the shoes are cleaned and the dogs' leads and such like are kept. If ever you should want a good thick coat there's plenty hanging there—boots too.'

She opened the door at the end of the passage.

'The back garden, miss; leastways, the side of it with a gate into the path which leads back to the lane.' She gave a chuckle. 'Higgledy-piggledy, as you might say, but you'll soon find your way around.'

As she spoke the gate opened and Sir Paul and the dogs came through.

'Ready for lunch?' he wanted to know, and swept Emma back with him to the sitting-room. 'A glass of sherry? It will give you an appetite.'

It loosened her tongue too, so that over Mrs Parfitt's delicious lunch she found herself answering his carefully casual questions and even, from time to time, letting slip some of her doubts and fears about the future, until she remembered with a shock that he had offered her a future and here she was talking as though he had said nothing.

He made no comment, but began to talk about the village and the people living in it. It was obvious to her that he was attached to his home, although according to Mrs Parfitt he was away a good deal.

He took her round the house after lunch. There was a small sitting-room at the front of the cottage, with his study behind it. A dining-room was reached through a short passage and, up several steps to one side of the hall, there was a dear little room most comfortably furnished and with rows of bookshelves, filled to overflowing. Emma could imagine sitting there by the fire, reading her fill.

There was a writing-desk under the small window, with blotter, writing-paper and envelopes neatly arranged upon it, and the telephone to one side. One could sit there and write letters in comfort and peace, she thought. Only there was no one for her to write to. Well, there was Mr Dobbs, although he was always so busy he probably wouldn't have time to read a letter, and she hardly thought that Mrs Hervey would be interested. Cook and Alice, of course, but they would prefer postcards…

Sir Paul had been watching her. 'You like this room?'

She nodded. 'I like the whole cottage; it's like home.'

'It is home, Emma.'

She had no answer to that.

She was given no time to brood. During the next few days he walked her over the moor, taking the dogs, bundling her into one of the elderly coats by the back door, marching her along, mile after mile, not talking much, and when they got home Mrs Parfitt had delicious meals waiting for them, so that between the good food and hours in the open air she was blissfully tired at the end of each day, only too willing to accept Sir Paul's suggestion that she should go early to bed—to fall asleep the moment her head touched the pillow.

On Sunday he took her to church. St John's dated from the thirteenth century, old and beautiful, and a mere stone's throw from the cottage. Wearing the dress under her winter coat, and her only hat—a

plain felt which did nothing for her—Emma sat beside him in a pew in the front of the church, and
watched him read the lesson, surprised that he put
on a pair of glasses to do so, but enthralled by his
deep, unhurried voice. Afterwards she stood in the
church porch while he introduced her to the rec-
tor and his wife, and several people who stopped to
speak to him.

They were friendly, and if they were curious they
were far too well-mannered to show it. They all gave
them invitations to come for a drink or to dine, promising to phone and arrange dates, chorusing that they
must get to know Emma while she was in Lustleigh.

'We are always glad to see a new face,' declared a
talkative middle-aged woman. 'And as for you, Paul,
we see you so seldom that you simply must come.'

He replied suitably but, Emma noted, made no
promises. That made sense too; their curiosity would
be even greater if she were to return home and never
be seen again there. Sir Paul would deal with that
without fuss, just as he did everything else. She remained quiet, smiling a little and making vague remarks when she had to.

After Sunday lunch, sitting by the fire, the Sunday papers strewn around, the dogs at Sir Paul's feet
and Queenie on her lap, Emma said suddenly, 'You
have a great many friends...'

He looked at her over his glasses and then took
them off. 'Well, I have lived here for a number of
years, and my parents before me, and their parents

before them. We aren't exactly cut off from the world but we are a close-knit community.' He added casually, 'I believe you will fit in and settle down very well here.'

His gaze was steady and thoughtful, and after a moment she said, 'I don't understand why you want me to marry you.'

'I have given you my reasons. They are sound and sensible. I am not a young man, to make decisions lightly, Emma.'

'No, I'm sure of that. But it isn't just because you're sorry for me?'

'No, certainly not. That would hardly be a good foundation for a happy marriage.'

He smiled at her and she found herself smiling too. 'We might quarrel…'

'I should be very surprised if we didn't from time to time—which wouldn't matter in the least since we are both sensible enough to make it up afterwards. We are bound to agree to differ about a number of things—life would be dull if we didn't.'

Early the following week he drove her to Buck-fastleigh. 'You're having coffee with Doreen Hervey,' he told her. 'Unless you want to come with me to the solicitor and house agent. Will you stay with her until I fetch you?'

'Should I go with you?'

'Not unless you wish to. From what you have told me, everything is settled and you can sell your house. The solicitor has already been in contact with the house agent, hasn't he? It's just a question of tying up the ends. Would you like to go there and see if there's anything you want to keep? There's plenty of room at the cottage.'

'You're talking as though we are going to be married.'

For a moment he covered her clasped hands with one of his. He said quietly, 'Say yes, Emma, and trust me.'

She turned her head to gaze at his calm face. He was not looking at her, but watching the road ahead. Of course she trusted him; he was the nicest person she had ever met, and the kindest.

'I do trust you,' she told him earnestly, 'and I'll marry you and be a good wife.'

He gave her a quick glance—so quick that she hadn't time to puzzle over the look on his face. She dismissed it, suddenly filled quite joyously with quiet content.

CHAPTER FIVE

EMMA AND PAUL had a lot to talk about as he drove back later that day. Everything, he assured her, was arranged; it was now only a question of selling the house.

He had settled the few debts, paid the outstanding bills and returned to Doreen Hervey's house, where he found Emma in the nursery, hanging over Bart's cot, heedless of Nanny's disapproval.

Mrs Hervey, sitting meekly in the chair Nanny had offered, had been amused. 'Wait till you've got one of your own,' she had said.

Emma had turned her face away, her cheeks warm, and listened thankfully to his easy, 'One would imagine that you were worn to a thread looking after Bart, Doreen. When will Mike be home?'

He had taken her to her house then, and helped her decide which small keepsakes she wished to have—a few pieces of silver, some precious china, her mother's little Victorian work table, her father's silver tankard, photos in old silver frames.

Standing in the small sitting-room, she had asked diffidently, 'Would you mind if Mr Dobbs and Cook and Alice came and chose something? They were very kind to me and to Mother...'

'Of course. We'll take the car and fetch them now.'

'Mrs Smith-Darcy will never let them come.'

'Leave it to me. You stay here and collect the things you want while I bring them here.'

She didn't know what he had said but they were all there within twenty minutes, and she had left them to choose what they wanted.

'If I could have some of Mrs Trent's clothes?' Alice had whispered. Alice was the eldest of numerous children, whose wages went straight into the family purse. She had gone away delighted, with Cook clutching several pictures she had fancied. As for Mr Dobbs, he had had an eye on the clock in the kitchen for a long time, he had told her.

Sir Paul had taken them all back and mentioned casually on his return that he had arranged to send everything but the furniture to a charity shop. Emma had been dreading packing up her mother's clothes and the contents of the linen cupboard. She had thanked him with gratitude.

He had popped her back into the car then, taken her to Buckland in the Moor and given her lunch at the country hotel there. She had been conscious that her first sharp grief had given way to a gentle sorrow and she had been able to laugh and talk and feel again. She had tried to thank him then. 'I told you that I would never be able to repay you for all you did for Mother, and now I'm doubly in your debt.'

He had smiled his kind smile. 'Shall we cry quits? After all, I'm getting a wife, am I not? And I fancy the debt should be mine.'

That evening, as they sat round the fire, with the dogs and Queenie sprawling at their feet, he suggested that they might go to Exeter on the following day. 'You have plenty of money now,' he reminded her, and when she told him that she had only a few pounds he said, 'You forget your house. Supposing I settle any bills for the present and you pay me when it is sold?'

'I already owe you money for the solicitor and all these debts...'

'You can easily repay those also, but all in good time. I'm sure that the house will sell well enough.'

'Thank you so much, then; I do need some clothes.'

'I have yet to meet a woman who didn't. At the same time we might decide on a date for our wedding. There is no point in waiting, is there? Will you think about it and let me know what you would like to do?'

When she didn't reply he went on quietly, 'Supposing we go along and see the vicar? He can read the banns; that will give you three weeks to decide on a date. It will also give you a breathing-space to think things over.'

'You mean if I should want to back out?'

'Precisely.' He was smiling at her.

'I'll not do that,' said Emma.

She was uncertain what to buy and sat up in bed that night making a list. Good clothes, of course, suitable for the wife of a consultant surgeon and at the same time wearable each day in the country. 'Tweeds,' she wrote. 'Suit and a top-coat'—even though spring was well settled in it could be cold on the moor.

One or two pretty dresses, she thought, and undies, shoes—and perhaps she could find a hat which actually did something for her. She would need boots and slippers—and should she look for something to wear in the evenings? Did those people she'd met at the church give parties or rather grand dinners?

She asked Paul at breakfast. He was a great help.

'The dinner parties are usually formal—black tie and so on, short frocks for the ladies. I suppose because we tend to make our own amusements, celebrating birthdays and so on. But more often, as far as I remember, the ladies wear pretty dresses. You'll need a warm wrap of some kind, though, for the evening. It'll stay chilly here for some time yet.' He looked across at her list. 'Don't forget a warm dressing-gown and slippers.'

'I need rather a lot…'

'You have plenty of money coming to you.'

'How much should I spend?'

He named a sum which left her open-mouthed. 'But that's hundreds and hundreds!'

Poker-faced, he observed that good clothes lasted a long time and were more economical in the long run.

'You really don't mind lending me the money?'

'No. I'll come with you and write the cheques. If you outrun the constable, I'll warn you.'

Thus reassured, Emma plunged into her day's shopping. She would have gone to one of the department stores but Paul took her instead to several small, elegant and very expensive boutiques. Even with a pause for coffee, by lunchtime she had acquired a tweed suit, a cashmere top-coat—its price still made her feel a little faint—more skirts, blouses and sweaters, a windproof jacket to go with them, and two fine wool dresses.

When she would have chosen shades which she considered long-wearing he had suggested something more colourful—plaids, a dress in garnet-red, another in turquoise and various shades of blue, silk blouses in old rose, blue and green, and a dress for the dinner parties—a tawny crêpe, deceptively simple.

He took her to lunch then. Watching her crossing through her list, he observed, 'A good waterproof, don't you think? Then I'll collect the parcels and go to the car and leave you to buy the rest. Will an hour be enough?'

'Yes, oh, yes.' She paused, wondering how she should tell him that she had barely enough money to buy stockings, let alone undies and a dressing-gown.

'You'll need some money.' He was casual about it, handing her a roll of notes. 'If it isn't enough we can come again tomorrow.'

They bought the raincoat, and a hat to go with it, before he left her at a department store. 'Don't worry about the time; I'll wait,' he told her, and waited until she was inside.

Before she bought anything she would have to count the notes he had given her. There was no one else in the Ladies, and she took the roll out of her handbag. The total shocked her—she could have lived on it for months. At the same time it presented the opportunity for her to spend lavishly.

Which she did. Might as well be hung for a sheep as for a lamb, she reflected, choosing silk and lace undies, a quilted dressing-gown, and matching up stockings with shoes and the soft leather boots she had bought. Even so, there was still money in her purse. Laden with her purchases, she left the shop and found Paul waiting for her.

He took her packages from her. 'Everything you need for the time being?' he asked.

'For years,' she corrected him. 'I've had a lovely day, Paul; you have no idea. There's a lot of money left over…'

'Keep it. I'm sure you'll need it.' He glanced sideways at her. 'Before we marry,' he added.

It was at breakfast the next morning that he told her that he would be away for a few days. 'I have an appointment in Edinburgh which I must keep,' he told her. 'If you want to go to Exeter for more shopping ask Truscott at the garage to drive you there and bring you back here. I'll have a word with him before I go.'

'Thank you.' She was very conscious of disappointment but all she said was, 'May I take the dogs out?'

'Of course. I usually walk them to Lustleigh Cleave in the early morning. If it's clear weather you'll enjoy a good walk on the moor.'

'I can christen the new tweeds,' said Emma soberly. He wouldn't be there to see them; she had been looking forward to astonishing him with the difference in her appearance when she was well-dressed. That would have to wait now. 'You're leaving today?'

'In an hour or so. Mrs Parfitt will look after you, Emma, but feel free to do whatever you like; this house will be your home as well as mine.'

He had gone by mid-morning, and when she had had coffee with Mrs Parfitt she went to her room with Queenie and tried on her new clothes.

They certainly made a difference; their colours changed her ordinary features to near prettiness and their cut showed off her neat figure. It was a pity that Paul wasn't there to see the chrysalis changing into a butterfly. She had to make do with Queenie.

She had to admit that by teatime, even though she had filled the rest of the day by taking the dogs for a long walk, she was missing him, which was, of course, exactly what he had intended.

Mrs Parfitt, when Emma asked her the next day, had no idea when he would be back. 'Sir Paul goes off for days at a time,' she explained to Emma. 'He goes to other hospitals, and abroad too. Does a lot of work in London, so I've been told. Got friends there too. I dare say he'll be back in a day or two. Why not put on one of your new skirts and that jacket and go down to the shop for me and fetch up a few groceries?'

So Emma went shopping, exchanging good mornings rather shyly with the various people she met. They were friendly, wanting to know if she liked the village and did she get on with the dogs? She guessed that there were other questions hovering on their tongues but they were too considerate to ask them.

Going back with her shopping, she reflected that, since she had promised to marry Paul, it might be a good thing to do so as soon as possible. He had told her to decide on a date. As soon after the banns had been read as could be arranged—which thought reminded her that she would certainly need something special to wear on her wedding-day.

Very soon, she promised herself, she would get the morning bus to Exeter and go to the boutique Paul had taken her to. She had plenty of money still—her own money too... Well, almost her own, she admitted, once the house was sold and she had paid him back what she owed him.

The time passed pleasantly, her head filled with the delightful problem of what she would wear next, and even the steady rain which began to fall as she walked on the moor with the dogs did nothing to dampen her spirits.

She got up early and took them out for a walk before her breakfast the next day and then, with Mrs Parfitt's anxious tut-tutting because she wouldn't get the taxi from the garage ringing in her ears, she got on the bus.

It was a slow journey to the city, since the bus stopped whenever passengers wished to get on or off, but she hardly noticed, and when it arrived at last she nipped smartly away, intent on her search for the perfect wedding-outfit.

Of course, she had had her dreams of tulle veils and elaborate wedding-dresses, but theirs wasn't going to be that sort of wedding. She should have something suitable but pretty, and, since she had an economical mind, something which could be worn again.

The sales lady in the boutique remembered her and nodded her head in satisfaction at the vast improvement in Emma's appearance now that she was wearing the tweed suit. The little hat she had persuaded her to buy had been just right... She smiled encouragingly. 'If I may say so, madam, that tweed is exactly the right colour for you. How can I help you?'

'I want something to wear at my wedding,' said Emma, and went delightfully pink.

The sales lady concealed a sentimental heart under her severely corseted black satin. She beamed a genuine smile. 'A quiet wedding? In church?'

Emma nodded. 'I thought a dress and jacket and a hat…'

'Exactly right, madam, and I have just the thing, if you will take a seat.'

Emma sat and a young girl came with the first of a selection of outfits. Very pretty, but blue would look cold in the church. And the next one? Pink, and with rather too many buttons and braid for her taste—it was too frivolous. The third one was the one—winter white in a fine soft woollen material, it had a short jacket and a plain white sheath of a dress.

'I'll try that one,' said Emma.

It fitted, but she had known that it would. Now that she was wearing it she knew that it was exactly what she had wanted.

The sales lady circled her knowingly. 'Elegant and feminine. Madam has a very pretty figure.'

'I must find a hat…'

'No problem. These outfits for special occasions I always team up with several hats so that the outfit is complete.' She waved a hand at the girl, who opened drawers and tenderly lifted out a selection and offered them one by one.

Emma, studying her reflection, gave a sigh. 'I'm so plain,' she said in a resigned voice, and removed a confection of silk flowers and ribbon from her head.

The sales lady was good at her job. 'If I may say

so, madam, you have fine eyes and a splendid complexion. Perhaps something... Ah, I have it.'

It looked nothing in her hand—white velvet with a pale blue cord twisted round it—but on Emma's head it became at once stylish, its small soft brim framing her face.

'Oh, yes,' said Emma, and then rather anxiously, 'I hope I have enough money with me.'

The older woman waved an airy hand. 'Please do not worry about that, madam. Any money outstanding you can send to me when you return home.'

Emma took off the hat and, while it and the outfit were being packed up, counted the money in her purse. There was more than enough when she was presented with the bill. She paid, feeling guilty at spending such a great deal of money. On the other hand she wanted to look her very best on her wedding-day. They would be happy, she promised herself, and stifled the sadness she felt that her mother wouldn't see her wed.

There were still one or two small items that she needed. She had coffee and then bought them, and by that time she was hungry. She had soup and a roll in a small café tucked away behind the high street and then, since the bus didn't leave for another hour or so, wandered round the shops, admiring the contents of their windows, thinking with astonishment that, if she wanted, she could buy anything she desired, within reason. She would have plenty of money of her own when the house was sold; she would get Paul to invest it in something safe and use the interest. She need never ask him for a penny, she thought, and fell to wondering where he was and what he was doing.

Sir Paul, already on his way back from Edinburgh, had turned off the main road to pay a visit to his mother and father, and, as he always did, gave a smile of content as he took the Rolls between the gateposts and along the short drive which led to their home—an old manor-house built of Cotswold stone, mellow with age and surrounded by a large, rambling garden which even at the bleakest time of year looked charming.

One day it would be his, but not for many years yet he hoped, catching sight of his father pottering in one of the flowerbeds. He drew up before the door, got out and went to meet him and together they walked to the house, going in through the garden door. 'My dirty boots, Paul; your mother will turn on me if I go in through the front door.'

They both laughed. His mother, to the best of his knowledge, had never turned on anyone in her life. She came to meet them now. Of middle height, rather stout and with a sweet face framed by grey hair stylishly dressed, she looked delighted to see him.

'Paul—' she lifted her face for his kiss '—how lovely to see you. Are you back at work again? Going somewhere or coming back?'

'Coming back. I can't stay, my dear, I need to get home—but may I come next weekend and bring the girl I'm going to marry to meet you both?'

'Marry? Paul—is it anyone we know?'

'No, I think not. She has lived at Buckfastleigh all her life except for her time at boarding-school. Her mother died recently. I hope—I think you will like her.'

'Pretty?' asked his mother.

'No—at least, she has a face you can talk to— peaceful—and she listens. Her eyes are lovely and she is also sensible and matter-of-fact.'

He didn't look like a man in love, reflected his mother. On the other hand, he was of an age to lose his heart for the rest of his life and beyond; she only hoped that she was the right girl. He had from time to time over the years brought girls to his parents' home and she hadn't liked any of them. They had all been as pretty as pictures, but he hadn't been in love with any of them.

'This is wonderful news, Paul, and we will make her very welcome. Come for lunch on Saturday. Can you stay until Monday morning?'

'I've a teaching round in the afternoon. If we leave soon after breakfast I can take Emma home first.'

'Emma—that's a pretty and old-fashioned name.' He smiled. 'She's rather an old-fashioned girl.'

Watching him drive away presently, his mother said, 'Do you suppose it will be all right, Peter?'

'My dear, Paul is forty years old. He hasn't married sooner because he hadn't found the right girl. Now he has.'

* * *

Emma got off the bus in the village, walked the short distance to Paul's house, went along the alley and in through the side-door. Mrs Parfitt would be preparing dinner and she didn't want to disturb her. She went through to the hall and opened the drawing-room door, her parcels clamped under one arm.

Sir Paul was sitting by the fire, with the dogs resting their chins on his feet and Queenie on the arm of his chair. Emma gave a squeak of delight, dropped her parcels and hurried across the room.

'Paul! Oh, how lovely; you're home. Don't get up...'

He was already on his feet, his eyes very bright, scanning her happy face. He said lightly, 'Emma, you've been shopping again.' And she pulled up short beside him, conscious that she had been quite prepared to fling herself into his arms. The thought took her breath so that her voice didn't sound quite like hers.

'Well, yes, my wedding-dress.' She added earnestly, 'I couldn't buy it the other day because you mustn't see it until we're in the church.'

'A pleasure I look forward to.' He picked up the box and parcels she had dropped. 'You'd like a cup of tea? I'll tell Mrs Parfitt while you take off your things.'

When she came down the tea-tray was on a little table by the fire—tea in its silver teapot, muffins in their silver dish, tiny cakes.

She was pouring their second cups when he said quietly, 'Next Saturday we are going to my parents' home in the Cotswolds—just for the weekend.'

She almost dropped the pot. 'Oh, well, yes, of course. I—I hope they'll like me.' She put down the teapot carefully. 'I think that perhaps I'm not quite the kind of girl they would expect you to marry, if you see what I mean.'

'On the contrary. You will find that they will welcome you as their daughter.' He spoke kindly but she could sense that it would be of no use arguing about it.

She said merely, 'That's good. I'll look forward to meeting them.'

'If you've finished your tea shall we go along to the vicarage and discuss dates with the vicar? If you're not too tired we can walk.'

The vicarage was on the other side of the church. I suppose I shall walk to my wedding, thought Emma as Paul rang the bell.

The vicar was a man of Paul's age. 'I'll read the first banns this Sunday, tomorrow, which means that you can marry any day after the third Sunday. You've a date in mind?'

They both looked at Emma, who said sensibly, 'Well, it will have to fit in with Paul's work, won't it?' She smiled at him. 'I know I'm supposed to choose, but I think you had better...'

'Will the Tuesday of the following week suit you? I believe I'm more or less free for a few days after that.' He glanced at Emma, who looked back serenely.

'In the morning?' she asked.

'Whenever you like; since I chose the day you must choose the time.'

She realised that she had no idea if there would be anyone else there, and her face betrayed the thought so plainly that Sir Paul said quickly, 'There will be a number of guests at the reception.'

He was rewarded by the look of relief on her face. 'Eleven o'clock,' she said.

The vicar's wife came in then, with a tray of coffee, and they sat for a while and talked and presently walked back to the cottage.

'You said there would be guests,' observed Emma, in a voice which held a hint of coolness.

'It quite slipped my mind,' he told her placidly. 'I'm sorry, Emma. We'll make a list this evening, shall we?' He smiled at her and she forgot about being cool. 'Mrs Parfitt will be in her element.'

The list was more lengthy than she had expected—his parents, his sisters and their husbands, a number of his colleagues from Exeter, friends from London, friends in and around the village, Doreen Hervey and her husband. 'And we must ask Mr Dobbs—I take it there is a Mrs Dobbs?'

'Yes, I think they'd like to come. Shall I write to them?'

'I'll get some cards printed—no time to have them engraved—and I'll phone everyone and tell them the cards will arrive later.' He glanced at his watch. 'I can reach several friends after dinner this evening.'

They told Mrs Parfitt the wedding-date when she came to wish them goodnight. 'The village will turn out to a man,' she told them happily. 'Been wanting to see you wed for a long time, sir. Your ma and pa will be coming, no doubt.'

'Indeed they are, Mrs Parfitt, and we hope you will be our guest too.'

'Well, now—that's a treat I'll enjoy. I'll need a new hat.'

'Then you must go to Exeter and get one. I'll drive you in whenever you wish to go.'

Emma saw very little of Paul until the weekend; he had consulting rooms in Exeter and saw his private patients there, and, in the evenings, although they discussed the wedding from time to time he made no mention of their future. All the guests were coming, he told her, and would she mind very much if he went to Exeter on the day after their wedding? He had promised to read a paper at a seminar; he had hoped to postpone it but it hadn't been possible.

'Well, of course you must go,' said Emma. 'May I come with you? I shan't understand a word but I'd very much like to be there.'

He had agreed very readily, but she wasn't sure if he was pleased about it or not.

They left early on Saturday morning and Emma sat silently beside him, hoping that she had brought the right clothes with her and that his parents would like her. She was then comforted by his quiet, 'Don't worry, Emma, everything will be all right.' And as though Willy and Kate had understood him, they had uttered gentle grumbling barks, and Willy had got down off the back seat and licked the back of her neck.

It was a day when spring had the upper hand and winter had withdrawn to the more remote stretches of the moor, and once they had bypassed Exeter and were racing up the motorway the country showed a great deal of green in the hedges. The car was blissfully warm and smelled of good leather, Paul's aftershave and the faint whiff of dog and, soothed by it, Emma decided in her sensible way that there was no point in worrying about something she knew very little about. So when Paul began a rambling conversation about nothing much she joined in quite cheerfully.

Just past Taunton he stopped for coffee and then turned off the motorway to drive across country—Midsomer Norton, Bath and then onwards towards Cirencester—to turn off presently into a country road which led them deep into the Cotswolds.

'Oh, this is nice,' said Emma. 'I like the houses—all that lovely pale yellow stone. Where are we exactly?'

'Cirencester is to the north-east, Tetbury is away to the right of us—the next village is where we are going.'

When he stopped the car in front of his parents' home, she sat for a moment, peering at it. 'It's beautiful,' she said softly. 'Do you love it very much?'

He said gravely, 'Yes, I do, and I hope that you will love it too. Come inside…' He took her by the elbow and went towards the opening door.

His mother stood there, smiling a welcome. She offered a cheek for his kiss and turned to Emma. 'Emma—such a pretty name—welcome, my dear.' She shook hands and then kissed Emma's cheek and tucked her arm in hers. 'Come and meet my husband.' She paused a moment to look up at her son. 'Paul, you described Emma exactly.'

He smiled but didn't speak, and when they entered the drawing-room and his father came to meet them he shook hands and then drew Emma towards him. 'Father, this is Emma—my father, Emma.'

Mr Wyatt wore his years lightly, and it was obvious where his son had got his good looks. She put out a hand and he took it and then kissed her. 'Welcome, my dear. We are delighted to have you here with us.'

After that everything was perfect. Going to bed that night in the charming bedroom, Emma reflected that she had had no need to worry—Paul's mother and father had been kindness itself, and Paul had taken her round the house and the large garden while Willy and Kate and his father's elderly spaniel trotted to and fro, dashing off following imaginary rabbits and then coming back to trot at their heels.

It had been an hour she didn't think she would

forget; they hadn't talked much but somehow there hadn't been the need for that. All the same, when they had gone back into the house for tea, she'd had the strange feeling that she knew Paul better than she had done.

In the evening, after dinner, they had sat talking about the wedding and who would be coming to it and Mrs Wyatt had admired her dress—one of the pretty ones Paul had persuaded her to have. 'You will make a charming bride,' she had told Emma. 'Paul is a lucky man.'

Emma, curling up in the comfortable bed, promised herself that she would make sure that he was. Not loving him didn't seem to matter, somehow, and she supposed that he felt the same about her. They were friends and they liked each other; everything would be all right, and on this cheerful thought she went to sleep.

They all went to church the next morning, and Emma got stared at. Somehow the news had got around that Sir Paul had got himself engaged at last and everyone wanted to see the bride-to-be. Wedged between father and son, Emma did her best not to notice the interested stares, hoping that they wouldn't be disappointed that she wasn't a girl whose good looks would match her bridegroom's. She peeped up at Paul's face and found him looking at her and took heart at his kind smile, knowing that he understood how she felt.

They left early on Monday morning, and his

mother kissed her and gave her a little hug. 'My
dear, we are so happy for you both. You are exactly
right for Paul and we wish you every happiness. We
shan't see you before your wedding-day—it's something we both look forward to. You'll meet the rest
of the family then—they will love you, too.'

Emma got into the car feeling a pleasant glow of
content; she had been accepted by Paul's family—
something which mattered to her.

They were home by lunchtime but he went back
to Exeter directly after, saying that he might be late
back and that she wasn't to wait up for him. He didn't
say why he was going and she didn't ask, although
she longed to. Instead she offered to take the dogs
for their walk in the late afternoon.

'Yes, do that. But not after teatime, Emma. I'll
give them a good run when I get home.'

He patted her shoulder in what she considered to
be a highly unsatisfactory manner and got back into
the Rolls and drove away. The day, which had begun
so pleasantly, had turned sour, and although she told
herself that she had no reason to complain, she felt
ill done by. She sat still when he had gone, looking
at her ringless hand. Had he forgotten that it was the
custom to give one's intended bride a ring? Or perhaps he thought that the unusual circumstances of
their marriage didn't merit one.

Moping about and feeling sorry for herself would
do no good, she told herself, and, leaving Queenie
by the fire, she took Willy and Kate for a long walk.

She was late getting back to the cottage and Mrs Parfitt said severely, 'Another ten minutes and I'd have been getting worried about you, miss. Sir Paul said most particular that you weren't to go out after teatime. And quite right too!'

It was a remark which cheered her up a little, and tea round the fire, with the lamps lighted against the gloomy day, restored her usual good spirits. She spent a careful half-hour writing her bread-and-butter letter to Mrs Wyatt, then stamped it and left it on the hall table. The postman would take it in the morning.

She lingered over dinner, helped Mrs Parfitt clear the table and, since there was no sign of Paul, went to bed with a book. She read for a long time, one ear cocked for the sound of his footfall, but by midnight she was half-asleep. She put the book down, telling herself that this was no way to behave—there would probably be years of similar evenings, and if she lay in bed worrying about him she would grow old before her time. Queenie, glad at last that the bedside lamp was out, crept up beside her and she fell asleep.

When she went down to breakfast the next morning, Paul was already at the table. His good morning was cheerful and friendly. 'You slept well?' he wanted to know.

'Like a top, whatever that means! What a nice morning it is...'

'Yes, indeed—a pity I have to go back to Exeter this morning. Unfinished business, I'm afraid.'

'Would you like me to take the dogs out?' She buttered toast, not looking at him.

'I'll take them before I go; I'm sure you have a lot to do here.'

What, in heaven's name? Mrs Parfitt got upset if she offered to help in the house, the garden was beautifully kept by the part-time gardener, but there was a chance that she could go to the village shop for Mrs Parfitt...

'Oh, yes, I've lots to do,' she told him serenely.

'You won't mind if I leave you?' And at her cheerful, 'Of course not,' he got up.

On his way to the door, though, he paused and came back to the table. 'I must beg your forgiveness, Emma.' He took a small box from a pocket. 'I have been carrying this round since we left yesterday and forgot all about it.'

He took a ring out of the box and held it in the palm of his hand—sapphires and diamonds in an old-fashioned setting. 'It has been kept in the safe in father's study, waiting for the next bride in the family. It is very old and is handed down from one generation to the next.' He picked up her hand and slipped the ring on her finger.

'It fits,' said Emma.

'As I knew it would.' He bent and kissed her, a quick kiss which took her by surprise. 'That augers well for our future.'

Emma said, 'Thank you, Paul,' and, while she was still trying to think of something else to add to that, he patted her shoulder and was gone.

CHAPTER SIX

EMMA DIDN'T SEE much of Paul during that week; he took her with him to Exeter one day, so that she might do some last-minute shopping, and once or twice he was home early so that they could walk the dogs together. On the Saturday he drove down to Buckfastleigh.

They had been invited by the Herveys to have drinks and at the same time they called at the house agent's. There were enquiries, they were told; it was certain that the house would sell, especially now that the warmer weather was coming.

'You don't mind waiting for the money?' asked Emma worriedly as they got back into the car.

'No, Emma, there's no hurry for that.' He turned to smile at her. 'There's time for us to get an armful of flowers and visit your mother's grave.'

She hadn't liked to ask but that was exactly what she wanted to do. He bought the flowers she chose—roses and carnations—and they took them to the quiet churchyard. Emma's sadness was mitigated by the feel of Paul's great arm round her shoulder and his unspoken sympathy.

The Herveys were delighted to see them and Emma was borne upstairs to see Bart, asleep in his cot. Emma was relieved to see that Nanny had been replaced by an older woman with a pleasant face and a ready smile.

'He's grown,' said Emma. 'He's perfect...'

'He's rather a duck,' said his mother fondly, 'and Nanny's splendid with him—and I'm getting better, aren't I, Nanny?'

On the way downstairs she took Emma's arm. 'Mike took one look at that other nanny and gave her notice,' she confided. 'Didn't fancy her at all—a regular sargeant major, he said she was. This one's an old dear, and she's taught me a lot—you know, how to hold Bart properly and what to do when he yells. I'm not afraid of him any more.'

She was quite serious; Emma murmured sympathetically, reflecting that it was fortunate that the Herveys could afford a nanny.

They had their drinks then, talking about the wedding and the baby and listening to Mike's amusing account of his trip to America. Then the two men went upstairs to see Bart and Mrs Hervey described in great detail what she intended to wear at the wedding.

Listening to her, Emma thought it likely that she would outshine the bride. Not that she minded— she liked Doreen Hervey; she might be helpless and unable to do much for herself but she was kind and friendly and light-hearted, and she went into raptures over Emma's ring.

'It's a family heirloom, isn't it? You deserve it, Emma, for you're such a nice girl, and Paul's the nicest man I know—excepting Mike, of course. He's frightfully rich, of course, and awfully important—but you'd never know, would you? Never says a word about himself—never told anyone why he was knighted... I don't suppose you would tell me? I'll not breathe a word...'

'Well, no,' said Emma. 'He wants to keep it a private matter.'

So private, she thought, that he had never mentioned it to her. She would ask him...

Which she did as they were driving back to Lustleigh, and was thwarted by his placid, 'Oh, you know how it is—names out of a hat and I happened to be lucky.' Even though he sounded placid there was something in his voice which prevented her from asking any more questions. Perhaps, she thought wistfully, when they had been married for a long time and had got to know each other really well he would tell her.

They went to church in the morning and heard their last banns read, and after the service an endless stream of people stopped to wish them well. They all wanted to know the date of the wedding.

'It will be very quiet—just family and a few close friends,' said Paul and, when pressed, told them the

day on which they were to marry, knowing that if
he didn't tell them they would find a reason to call
at the cottage and ask Mrs Parfitt.

If Emma had hoped to see more of Paul during the
next week she was disapointed; even at the weekend
he was called away urgently to operate on a road casualty so that her wedding-day loomed without her
having had the chance to get to know him better.
Indeed, suspicion that he was avoiding her lurked at
the back of her head and became so urgent that on
the evening before her wedding, left to her own de-
vices while he worked in his study, she put down the
book she was reading, thumped on the door and then
entered the study before she could change her mind.

He got up as she went in. 'Emma—what's wrong?
You look as though…' He paused and asked mildly,
'Something has upset you?'

'Yes—no, I'm not sure.' She gave him a worried
look. 'Why don't I see you more often? You're always
going somewhere, and even when you're at home
you keep out of my way. Don't you want to marry
me? It's quite all right if you've changed your mind;
it isn't as if… I wouldn't like you to get married to
the wrong person and be unhappy.'

He came round the desk and took her hands in
his. 'Emma, my dear girl, what can I say to reassure
you? Only that I want to marry you and that you are
the right person. If you haven't seen much of me it is
because I've had a good deal of work, and I'm afraid

that is something you will have to learn to live with.'
He smiled down at her, a tender smile which set her
heart thumping. 'And I haven't changed my mind,
nor will that ever happen.'

'I've been silly,' said Emma. 'I'm sorry—and I've
interrupted your work.'

He turned her round and put an arm round her
shoulders. 'We will sit down and go over the arrangements for tomorrow.' He was propelling her gently
out of the study and back into the drawing-room.
'Are you feeling nervous? No need—you know almost everyone who'll be there. The car will fetch you
tomorrow morning; I know it's only a few yards to
the church but I can't have my bride walking there...'

'The car? But what about you?'

'I'm spending the night at Eastrey Barton—the
family are already there. It is considered very bad
luck, so I'm told, for the bride and groom to spend
the night before their wedding under the same roof.
Mrs Parfitt will look after you and I'll phone you in
the morning.'

'Oh, I thought we'd just have breakfast together
as usual and then walk to church.'

'I have neglected you shamefully, Emma—the
truth is...'

'You forgot that you were getting married!' she
finished for him, unaware that that hadn't been what
he had been going to say.

She spoke matter-of-factly and Sir Paul gave a
soundless sigh. Patience, he reminded himself—she

wasn't ready to hear his reason for avoiding her company, and, when he was with her, treating her with a casual friendliness.

Dressed for her wedding, Emma took a final look at herself in the pier glass, and even to her critical eye she considered that she didn't look too bad. Not beautiful—brides were supposed to look beautiful—not even pretty, but the outfit suited her and the little hat framed her rather anxious face with its soft velvet brim.

She went downstairs to where Dr Treble, who was to give her away, waited, and was much heartened by his surprised admiration. He and Mrs Parfitt, who was on the point of leaving for the church, chorused their approval in no uncertain terms, so that she got into the car feeling more confident.

Her confidence faltered a little as they started down the aisle and she clutched the small bouquet of pink roses which Paul had given her in a nervous hand; she hadn't expected the church to be full of people—the entire village appeared to be in the pews, nodding and smiling at her as she passed them. When she reached the front pews Paul's mother looked round and smiled and nodded too, but Emma scarcely noticed her; her eyes were on Paul's broad back—if only he would turn round and look at her...

He did, smiling a little, and her heart gave a great jump against her ribs so that she caught her breath. Her thoughts were wild; it was a bit late in the day to fall in love with him, wasn't it? And not at all a good idea either, for now everything was going to be a bit complicated.

She stood beside him and the vicar began to speak the opening words of the service. She did her best to listen but odd thoughts kept popping in and out of her head. She had loved him for quite a while, she thought, only she hadn't known it, and if she had would she have married him?

The solemn words the vicar was speaking cut across her reflections at last and she listened then. Never mind the future. She would make her vows and keep to them; she would be a good wife, and if Paul didn't need her love, only her companionship, then she would do her best to be the kind of person he wanted. When the moment came, she spoke her 'I will' in a clear, steady little voice that everyone could hear, and then took comfort from Paul's deep voice, as assured and certain as hers had been.

They exchanged rings then and went to sign the register, and presently were walking down the aisle and out into the bright morning, but before they could get into the Rolls they were surrounded by guests with cameras poised and had to pass through a barrage of confetti and good wishes.

Paul had been holding her hand, and as they reached the car at last gave it an encouraging squeeze. 'So much for our quiet wedding,' he said. 'I'm enjoying it, aren't you?'

'Oh, yes,' said Emma. 'It's the most wonderful

day of my life.' She spoke with such fervour that he looked down at her, but the little hat shaded her face from his as she got into the car.

The rest of the day was like a dream; the cottage was full of people laughing and talking and drinking champagne and eating canapés. Paul had Emma by the hand, and as various friends greeted him he introduced her.

His sisters had been the first to join them after his mother and father—handsome young women who kissed her warmly and listened smilingly as their husbands flattered her gently and congratulated Paul—and after them there were people she realised she would meet again—colleagues from the hospital, several from London, old friends with their wives and of course the Herveys and Mr Dobbs and his wife.

Mr Dobbs had given her a smacking kiss. 'Wait till I tell 'em all about this,' he said. 'I'll make sure that Mrs Smith-Darcy gets the lot. I've taken some photos too.' He transferred his beaming smile to Sir Paul. 'You are a lucky man, and no mistake,' he told him.

Since they weren't going anywhere, the guests lingered, renewing acquaintances, plying Emma and Paul with invitations, and then at last taking their leave. The cake had been cut, the last toast drunk and Emma longed to take off her new shoes. The moment the last guest had gone, she did so. 'You don't mind, do you? Just for a few minutes—they're new...'

'And very pretty. You look charming, Emma, and I do like that hat.' He took her arm as they went indoors to where his mother and father and sisters were waiting. 'We're going out to dinner—just the family—but we can sit around for a while and talk.'

'I'll get Mrs Parfitt to make a pot of tea…'

'A splendid idea, although I suspect she's already got the kettle on.'

As indeed she had, and presently she bustled in with the tea-tray and a plate of cucumber sandwiches. 'After all that cake and bits and pieces,' she explained. 'Not but it wasn't a rare fine party.' Her eyes fell on the dogs, basking in the late afternoon sunshine. 'Queenie's in the kitchen having her tea.'

'And what about you, Mrs Parfitt?' asked Emma. 'You've worked so hard; you must have your tea too…'

'That I shall, ma'am—wetted it not five minutes ago with a nice boiled egg and a bit of toast.'

Emma, in bed that night, thought back over her wedding-day. It had ended on a light-hearted note at Eastrey Barton, where they had all dined splendidly with a great deal of talk and laughter, and she had been happy because Paul had given her a wedding-present—a double row of pearls which she had immediately worn.

When they had returned to the cottage he had kissed her goodnight—a quick, friendly kiss—almost a peck—she thought wistfully, but at least it was a kiss. It had been difficult not to kiss him back, but she hadn't. She would keep to her resolve of being a good companion, however hard it was, and perhaps in time he would come to love her. At least, she told herself stoutly, she had several advantages—she was his wife and she loved him.

The next day he took her to Exeter with him as he had promised, and she sat in the lecture hall and listened to him addressing a large and attentive audience. She understood very little of the lecture—that it was about bones went without saying, and some of it must have been amusing for the audience laughed quite often. When he had sat down they clapped for a long time before someone on the platform got up and made a speech about him in glowing terms.

Emma, sitting at the back of the hall, beamed with pride and Sir Paul, who had seen her the moment he started his lecture, smiled—his dear little Emma…

They had tea with a number of his colleagues—several foreign surgeons and members of the hospital board—and Emma—being Emma—had little to say for herself but listened to the opinions of various learned gentlemen who were quick to observe to Sir Paul that his wife was a charming young lady and a splendid listener. 'Such beautiful eyes,' sighed an Italian surgeon, over in England to exchange ideas with his colleagues. 'I hope we shall meet again.'

Driving back to Lustleigh presently, Paul repeated this. 'How fortunate that I'm not a jealous husband,' he said lightly. 'You were a great success, Emma.'

'Oh, was I? I didn't understand half of what they were talking about but they were all very nice to me.' She turned to look at him. 'Perhaps it was because I'm your wife and they were being polite.'

'No, no. They all fell for you...' He was laughing and that hurt.

'I expect it was my new clothes,' said Emma.

'You enjoyed the lecture?' he asked her.

'Very much, although I didn't understand very much of it. Do you lecture a great deal?'

'From time to time. Sometimes I'm invited to other countries—you shall come with me.'

'Oh, may I? Don't you have a secretary with you?'

'Yes, if it's a long tour, but for the present I shall be in England.'

'Not always at Exeter?'

'No—but I'm usually only away for a day or two—not long.'

At dinner that evening he asked her if she would like to drive to Torquay in the morning. 'It's pleasant at this time of year—not too many people yet, and the dogs love the beach.'

She peeped at him over her glass. He looked tired and preoccupied—a carefree day by the sea would be pleasant. 'I'd love it,' she told him.

They left soon after breakfast, and since it was a clear day, Emma wore a skirt with a cashmere sweater and a velvet beret perched over one eye. 'Very fetching,' said Sir Paul. 'You are sure you'll be warm enough?'

He drove to the A38 and took the fork over Haldon to the coast and, as he had said, Torquay was not too crowded.

'Coffee first or walk the dogs?' he asked her.

'The dogs,' said Emma, conscious of two anxious, whiskery faces turned towards her. So they parked the car and took them down on to the beach and walked arm-in-arm for a mile or more, stopping every now and again to throw sticks for the dogs and look out to sea.

'It looks very cold,' said Emma, and then added, 'I expect you can swim...'

'Yes.' They were standing at the water's edge and he flung an arm around her shoulders. 'You don't?'

'Well, I tried—at school, you know—and once or twice when I went on holiday with Mother and Father. I think I'm a coward.'

His arm tightened. 'Nonsense. You haven't had the chance to learn, that's all. I'll teach you. I've a small yacht which I keep at Salcombe; we'll go there when I'm free.'

'I've never been on a yacht.'

'I shall very much enjoy having you for my crew,' he told her.

He took her to the Imperial Hotel for lunch—lobster bisque and *boeuf en croute*, rounded off by a chocolate soufflé, and washed down by a claret handled by the wine waiter as though it were a precious baby rather than a bottle.

Emma, who knew almost nothing about wines,

took a sip, then another. 'It's perfect—I've never tasted anything as heavenly.'

Sir Paul thought it unlikely that she had, but he expressed the view that it was considered a good wine and that he was glad that she enjoyed it.

The day was fine. They walked again after lunch, on the beach once more but this time in the opposite direction, with the dogs rushing about, barking at the water, begging for sticks to be thrown. Presently they turned back and got into the car and began to drive back to Lustleigh, stopping on the way at a tea-room in one of the villages. It was old-fashioned—a front room in a thatched cottage—but they had a splendid tea of muffins, oozing butter, and a large pot of strong tea, while the dogs sat under the table, gobbling the bits of muffin Emma handed them.

'You'll spoil them,' observed Sir Paul.

She said at once, 'Oh, I'm sorry, I shouldn't have done it.'

He frowned, annoyed with himself for sounding as though he was criticising her. She saw the frown and guessed quite wrongly that he was vexed with her so that she became ill at ease.

The day had been heavenly—just being with him had been wonderful—but now, in her efforts to behave as the kind of wife he had wished for, she drew back from the friendly rapport they had had, still making small talk, but keeping him at arm's length while willingly answering him when he spoke.

He, however, was practised in the art of putting

patients at their ease, and by the time they reached home she was her usual, friendly self and they dined together in the easy companionship that he was so careful to maintain.

That, she was to discover, was to be the last of their days together for some time, for he left directly after breakfast each morning and was rarely home before seven or eight o'clock in the evening. She hid her disappointment and showed a bright face when he got back—ready to listen about his day, even though she understood very little of what he had been doing. She was also careful not to chat at breakfast while he was glancing through his post. True, they had been out to dine on several evenings, but she saw little of him then, though it was pleasant to meet the people he counted his friends.

She filled her days with walking the dogs, working doggedly at a piece of tapestry she had begun with so much enthusiasm, not realising the amount of work and tiny stitches it required before it was finished. She was happy because she loved Paul, but she found herself counting the hours until he came home each evening.

They had been married for several weeks when he told her at breakfast that someone would deliver a Mini that morning. 'For you, Emma, so you can go wherever you want. I'll be home early today and you can take me for a drive in it.'

She smiled widely at him across the table. 'Paul,

thank you—how perfectly splendid.' She added, 'I'll
be very careful...'

He smiled. 'Keep to the roads around here until
you're quite used to it. I'll be home before five
o'clock so be ready for me.'

He dropped a kiss on her head as he went away.

The Mini, a nice shade of blue, arrived at lunch-
time, and she got into it at once and drove to Bovey
Tracey and back and then waited impatiently for
Paul to come home. When he did she drove him to
Moretonhampstead, very conscious of him sitting
squashed up beside her.

'It's a bit small for you,' she said, driving carefully
past the sheep wandering across the road.

'Indeed, but just right for you, I hope, Emma.'

'Yes, oh, yes. It's a wonderful present.'

Back home, as they sat at dinner he asked her,
'Do you find the days long, Emma?'

'Well, yes, a bit. You see, I've had to work all day
for quite a time and I'm not really used to having so
much leisure.'

'Would you like a little job? Voluntary, of course.
There is a nursery at Moretonhampstead. It takes
unwanted babies and toddlers—most of them are
orphaned or abandoned. Not ill, but neglected and
very underfed. Diana Pearson, who is in charge, is
an old friend of mine and she tells me that she needs
more help urgently. Would you like to go there once
or twice a week and give a hand? No nursing, just
common sense and a liking for infants.'

He wanted her to say yes, she was sure—perhaps that was why he had given her the car. She didn't hesitate. 'Yes, I'd love to help,' she told him.

'Good. We'll go there on Monday; I'm not operating until the afternoon. Would you ask Mrs Parfitt to have lunch ready for us at one o'clock? I'll bring you back and have lunch here.' He added, 'One or two days a week and not more than four hours at a time, Emma. It has to be interesting, not tiring and demanding, and never at the weekends.'

The nursery was on the outskirts of the town—a long, low building, with cheerfully coloured walls and a large playroom and several nurseries. Sir Paul walked in as though he knew the place well and went straight to a door with 'Office' written on it.

The young woman who got up as he went in was tall and dark with almost black eyes in a lovely face. She was elegantly dressed and she smiled at him in a way which gave Emma food for thought. Her greeting was casual enough and when Paul introduced her she shook hands with a pleasant murmur and another smile—quite different from the first one, though.

It was obvious that she knew all about Emma, for she said pleasantly, 'We'd love to have you here; we're desperate for help. Paul said two days in a week and not more than four hours at a time.' She put a hand on his arm and smiled at Emma, who smiled back, knowing that she was disliked just as she disliked the speaker. 'Come and look around—there are a lot of small babies at the moment. The travellers bring them in for a week or two's feeding up—the little ones get cold and quickly ill; it's not really an ideal life for babies, although the children seem happy enough.'

They went round the place together, and Emma said she would come each Tuesday and Thursday in the mornings. 'Is nine o'clock too early?'

'We take over from the night staff at eight o'clock, but that'll be too early for you.' Diana stole a look at Paul. 'Won't it, Paul?' She smiled as she spoke, and Emma repressed a desire to slap her. If it hadn't been for Paul's obvious wish that she should have something to occupy her days she would have said there and then that she had changed her mind.

On the way back to the cottage Paul said carefully, 'You'll like Diana—she is a marvellous organiser. She has no need to work and it surprises me that she hasn't married—she's quite lovely, isn't she?'

'She's beautiful,' said Emma. 'Have you been friends for a long time?'

'Two or three years, I suppose. We met at a friend's house and found that we had a good deal in common.'

Emma kept her voice pleasant. 'Instant rapport—that's what it's called, isn't it? You meet someone and feel as though you've known them all your life…' She added before he could reply, 'I'm sure I shall enjoy giving a hand—thank you for thinking of it, Paul.'

'I wondered if you were becoming bored with life—I'm not at home much, am I?'

She said cheerfully, 'Well, I didn't expect you to be—doctors never are, are they?'

That evening he asked her if she would like to spend a weekend with his parents. 'Next weekend I'm free. We could drive up on Saturday afternoon and come back on the Sunday evening.'

'I'd like that.'

But first there was the nursery. She drove there in the Mini and within ten minutes, wrapped in a plastic pinny, she was bathing a very small baby in a room where five other babies were awaiting her attention.

Diana Pearson, elegant and beautiful, sitting behind her desk, had greeted her pleasantly but without warmth. 'Hello, Emma—so you have turned up. So many volunteer ladies change their minds at the last minute. Will you go to the end nursery and start bathings? Someone will be along to give you a hand presently.'

Emma had waited for more information but Diana had smiled vaguely and bent her head over the papers before her. At least she'd been credited with enough good sense to find her own way around, reflected Emma, and anyway she'd met another girl on the way to the nursery, who'd shown her where to find a pinny before hurrying off in the opposite direction.

Emma, not easily flurried, had found the pinny, assembled all that she needed to deal with the babies and picked up the first one...

She had just picked up the second baby, a small, wizened creature, bawling his head off, tiny fists balled in rage, eyes screwed up tightly, when she was joined by a middle-aged woman with a sour expression.

'New, are you?' she wanted to know as she tied her pinny. 'What's yer name?'

Not a local woman, thought Emma, and said pleasantly, 'Emma—Emma Wyatt, and yes, I'm new. I hope you'll tell me when I do something wrong.'

'You bet I will. 'Ere, you that Professor Wyatt's wife?'

'Yes, I am.'

'Well, don't expect me ter call yer 'yer ladyship', 'cos I'm not going to.'

'I'd like it if you'd call me Emma.'

The woman looked surprised. 'OK, I'm Maisie.' She picked up the third baby and began to take off its gown with surprisingly gentle hands. 'He's the worst of the bunch you've got there,' she observed. 'Proper little imp, 'e is—always shouting 'is 'ead off.'

Emma looked down at the scrap on her lap; he had stopped crying and was glaring at her from bright blue eyes. 'He's rather sweet…'

Maisie gave a cackle of laughter. 'Your first day, isn't it? Wait till you've been 'ere a couple of months—that's if you last as long as that.'

'Why do you say that?'

'You'll find out for yerself—Madam there, sitting in her office, doing nothin'—that is, until someone comes along. Pulls the wool nicely over their eyes, that she does. That 'usband of yours—she's 'ad her sights on 'im this last year or more. 'Ad her nose put out of joint and no mistake.' She was pinning a nappy with an expertise Emma envied. 'Better watch out, you 'ad.'

The baby, freshly bathed and gowned, looked up at Emma with interest; she picked him up and tucked his small head under her chin and cuddled him.

''Ere, there ain't no time for cuddling—leastways not in the mornings—there's the feeds to do next.'

So Emma put him back in his cot and set to work on the fourth baby, a placid girl who blew bubbles and waved her small arms at her. Maisie had finished before her; she was already feeding the first baby by the time Emma had tidied everything away and fetched her three bottles from the little pantry.

When the infants had been fed and lay sleeping it off, she and Maisie had to tidy the nursery, put everything ready for the afternoon and then go and have their coffee. They sat together in the small room set aside for them and Emma listened to Maisie's numerous tips about the work.

'Have you been here long?' she asked.

'Upwards of two years. It's a job, see. Me old man scarpered off and the kids are at school all day— keeps me mind off things.'

She blew on her coffee and took a gulp. 'You going ter stick it out? It's not everyone's cup of tea.'

'Well, I like babies,' said Emma, 'and my husband's away almost all day. He told me that Miss Pearson was short-handed and asked if I'd like to help out, so I'll stay for as long as I'm needed. I only come twice a week.'

Maisie eyed her thoughtfully over her mug. 'Persuaded 'im, she did? Men—blind as bats! Never mind the "lady this" and "lady that"—you're a nice young woman, so keep those eyes of yours peeled.'

'Thank you for your advice. Shall I see you on Thursday?'

'Yep. Me, I come every morning—oftener if it gets really busy. Some of the babies will be going back to their mums tomorrow—bin waiting for an 'ouse or flat or whatever, yer see.'

'I hope the same babies will be here when I come on Thursday.'

'Well, Charlie—that's the little 'owler—e'll be with us for a while yet. 'Is mum's in prison for a couple of months—won't 'ave 'im near 'er.'

'Why ever not?'

'Dunno; bit flighty, I dare say.' She put down her mug. 'We gotta bag the wash before we go.'

Diana came out of the office as Emma took off her pinny. 'Going? See you on Thursday and many thanks. Oh, would you ask Paul to call in some time? I need his advice about one of the toddlers—a congenital dislocation of the hip—I think the splint needs adjusting.'

'I'll tell him,' said Emma. 'I'm sure he'll come when he has the time.'

Diana laughed. 'He usually comes whenever I ask him to, whether he's busy or not—we're old friends.'

Emma dredged up a smile. 'That's nice—I'll see you on Thursday.'

She drove back home, ate the lunch Mrs Parfitt had ready for her and then took the dogs for a long walk. She had a great deal to think about.

'It's a good thing I'm married to him,' she told Willy, who was loitering beside her. 'I mean, it's an advantage, if you see what I mean—and I love him. The point is, does he love her? That's something I have to find out. But if he does why did he marry me?' She stopped and Kate came lumbering back to see why. 'If it was out of pity...?' She sounded so fierce that Willy gave a whimper.

Paul was home for tea, which surprised her. 'How nice,' she said, and beamed at him. 'Have you had a busy day?'

'I've beds at the children's hospital and an out-patients clinic at Honiton; I seem to have spent a lot of my time driving from here to there.' He bit into one of Mrs Parfitt's scones. 'Tell me, did you enjoy your morning?'

'Very much. I bathed three babies and fed them. There was someone else there in the nursery—a nice woman who was very friendly and helpful. Oh, and Diana says could you go and see the baby with the dislocated hip? She thinks the splint needs changing.'

'It'll have to be tomorrow evening. I've a list in

the morning and a ward-round in the afternoon and a couple of private patients to see after that.'

'Where do you see them?'

'I've rooms in Southernhay. I'll phone Diana presently and tell her when I'll be free.'

'I'll ask Mrs Parfitt to make dinner a bit later, shall I?'

'Yes, do that if you will. Did you take the dogs out?'

'Yes, it was lovely on the moor. After all it is summer.'

'That doesn't mean to say we shan't get some shockingly bad weather.' He got up. 'I've some phoning to do, then I'll take the dogs for ten minutes.' He smiled at her. 'You must tell me more about the nursery when I get back.'

The following evening he phoned at teatime to say that he would be home later than he had expected and that she wasn't to wait dinner for him. 'I'll get something here,' he told her.

She gave him a cheerful answer and spent the rest of the evening imagining him and Diana dining together at some quiet restaurant. She knew it was silly to do so but she seemed unable to think of anything else.

Perhaps it wasn't so silly either, she told herself, lying in bed later, waiting for the sound of the car and dropping off to sleep at last without having heard it.

He was already at the table when she went down

to breakfast. He wished her good morning. 'You don't mind if I get on? I've a busy day ahead.'

'Did you have a busy time last night?' She kept her voice casually interested.

'Yes. I trust I didn't disturb you when I got back?'

'Will you go and see the baby today? Do you want me to give Diana a message?'

He gave her a thoughtful look. 'No need. I saw her yesterday.'

'Oh, good,' said Emma, bashing her boiled egg, wishing it was Diana.

CHAPTER SEVEN

DIANA'S GREETING WHEN Emma reached the nursery was friendly. It was as though she was trying to erase her rather cool manner towards her; she asked if she was quite happy with the babies, if she would like to alter her hours and expressed the hope that she wasn't too tired at the end of her morning's work. Emma took all this with a pinch of salt, not convinced by all this charm that Diana was going to like her—and, anyway, she didn't like Diana.

It was refreshing, after all that sweetness, to listen to Maisie's down-to-earth talk, which covered everything under the sun—the royal family, the government, the price of fish and chips and the goings-on of the young couple who had rented rooms beneath hers—and all the while she talked she attended to the babies, raising her voice above their small cries.

They had finished the bathing and were feeding them when she said, 'Your old man was 'ere yesterday—late too.'

Emma was feeding Charlie, who was content for

once, sucking at his bottle as though it would be torn from him at any moment. 'Yes, I know,' she said quietly.

Maisie turned her head to look at her. 'You're a quiet one, but I bet me last penny you'll get the better of 'er.'

'Yes, I believe I shall,' said Emma, and smiled down at Charlie's small face. He wasn't a pretty baby—he was too pale and thin for that. It was to be hoped that when his mother claimed him once more—if she ever did—he'd look more like a baby and not a cross old man. She kissed the top of his head and gave him a quick cuddle and then put him over her shoulder so that he could bring up his wind.

It was after they had had dinner together that evening that Paul told her that he was going to Boston in two days' time.

Emma said, 'Boston? You mean Boston, USA?'

'Yes, and then on to New York, Philadelphia and Chicago. I shall be away for ten days, perhaps a little longer.' He said, carefully casual, 'I expect the trip would be a bit boring for you.'

She was quick to decide that he didn't want her with him. 'Yes, I think it might be,' she said. 'Will you be lecturing?'

She looked to see if he was disappointed but his face gave nothing away. 'If you need help of any sort, phone John Taggart, my solicitor; he'll sort things out for you. I've opened an account for you at my bank—I have also arranged for a joint account but I'd like you to have your own money. The house agent phoned to say that he has a possible buyer for your house; send everything to John—he'll deal with it.'

'The dogs will miss you,' said Emma. She would miss him too, but she wasn't going to tell him that. 'There's a card from the Frobishers—they've asked us to dinner. I'll write and explain, shall I?'

'Yes, do that. Suggest we take up their invitation when I get back.'

It was all very business-like and she did her best to match her manner to his. 'Shall I write to your mother and tell her that we shan't be coming for the weekend?'

'I phoned her last night. They are very sorry not to be seeing us.'

'I could drive myself...'

'I'd prefer you not to, Emma.'

The cottage seemed very quiet when he had gone. Emma couldn't bear to be in it and took the dogs for a long walk on the moor; they walked for miles and the austere vastness of it made his absence bearable. 'It's only for just over a week,' she told the dogs. 'But how shall I bear to be away from him for so long?'

A problem solved for her by Diana, who, when Emma went on Tuesday as usual, asked her if she could manage to help out for a third morning.

'We're so short of staff, I don't know which way to turn. I'm so glad that Paul didn't want you to go with him.' She laughed gently. 'Wives can be a bit of an encumbrance sometimes. It was so wise of him to marry someone like you, Emma.'

Emma asked why.

'Well, you're not demanding, are you? You're content to sit at home and wait for him to come back—just what he needed...'

Emma said, 'Yes, I think it is. He leads a busy life.'

Diana laughed again. 'Yes, but he always has time for his friends. He and I have such a lot in common.'

'I expect you have,' said Emma sweetly, 'but not marriage.' Her smile was as sweet as her voice. 'I'll get started on the babies,' she said.

Maisie, already at work with her three, looked up as she went into the nursery. ''Ello, Emma, what's riled you? 'As her 'igh and mightiness been tearing yer off a strip?'

'No—just a slight difference of opinion. I'm going to do an extra morning, Maisie; I hope you'll be here too.'

'Come every day, don't I, love? I'll be here. So'll Charlie there, from wot I 'eard. 'Is mum don't really want 'im, poor little beggar.'

'What will happen to him?' Emma was lifting him from his cot; he was bawling as usual.

'Foster-mum if they can find one, or an orphanage...'

'He's so small...'

'Plenty more like 'im,' said Maisie. 'Maybe there'll be someone who don't mind a bad-tempered kid.'

'Well, I'd be bad-tempered if I were he,' said Emma, smiling down at the cross little face on her lap. 'Who's a lovely boy, then?' she said.

She thought of Paul constantly, and when he phoned from Boston that night she went around in a cloud of content which was, however, quickly dispelled when she went into the nursery the next day.

'Heard from Paul?' asked Diana, with a friendly concern Emma didn't trust.

'Well, yes. He phoned yesterday evening...'

'He always does.' Diana smiled at Emma—a small secret smile, suggesting that words weren't necessary.

She had no right to be jealous, reflected Emma, bathing a belligerent Charlie, for she had no hold on Paul's feelings, had she? He had wanted a companion and the kind of wife to suit his lifestyle. He had never promised love...

That afternoon when she took the dogs on to the moor she saw the clouds piling up over the tors and felt the iciness of the wind. Bad weather was on the way, and even though it was summer the moor could be bleak and cold. She turned for home and was thankful for the bright fire in the drawing-room and the delicious tea Mrs Parfitt had ready for her.

Diana came out of her office as she arrived at the nursery on Thursday. 'Emma, I'm so glad to see you. You know the moor well, don't you? There's a party of travellers camping somewhere near Fernworthy Reservoir—one of them phoned me. We've one of their toddlers here already and he says there are several children sick—not ill enough for the doctor—colds, he thinks, and perhaps flu. He asked me to send someone with blankets, baby food and cough medicine. I wonder if you would go? It's not far but a bit out of the way. Perhaps you can get them to come off the moor until the weather gets warmer again.'

'Yes, of course I'll go. I'll phone Mrs Parfitt, though, so that she can take the dogs out if I'm not back.'

Mrs Parfitt didn't fancy the idea at all. 'Sir Paul would never allow it,' she demurred. 'You going off on your own like that.'

'I'll be gone for an hour or two,' said Emma. 'It's not far away, you know…'

Mrs Parfitt snorted. 'Maybe not, madam, but it's so isolated it could be the North Pole.'

It wasn't quite the North Pole but it was certainly isolated. Emma had a job finding the camp, tucked away from the narrow road which led to nowhere but the reservoir. When she found it eventually it took quite a time to unload the blankets and baby food and hand them over.

There were half a dozen broken-down buses and vans drawn up in a semicircle and their owners clamoured for her attention as she was led from one to another ramshackle vehicle. In one of them she found a sick baby—too ill to cry. 'She's ill,' she told the young woman who was with her. 'She needs medical attention—will you bring her to the nursery? I'll take you now…'

The girl needed a lot of persuading. ''Tis only a cold,' she told Emma. 'There's half a dozen kids as bad. Come in and look if you don't believe me.'

She was right. There were more than half a dozen, though—some of them small babies. Emma, although no nurse, could recognise the signs of whooping cough when she saw it. It would need several ambulances to take them to the nursery. 'Look,' she said to one of the older women, 'I haven't room to take them all, but I'll go back now and send an ambulance for them.'

They gathered round her, all talking at once, but at last she got back into the Mini, with the baby and its mother in the back, and began her journey back to Moretonhampstead. As Diana had said, it wasn't far, but the road was narrow and winding and little used and there were no houses or farms in sight. She was glad when the reached the nursery and she could hand the baby and mother over to Diana.

It was Maisie who led them away while Emma explained to Diana that there were more babies and toddlers needing help. 'An ambulance?' she suggested. 'They are really quite ill and it's so cold for them.'

Diana frowned. 'Wait here. I'll see if I can get help. Go and have a cup of coffee; you must need one.'

When Emma returned Diana shook her head.

'Would you believe it, there's nothing to be had until tomorrow morning—it's not urgent you see…'

'But they need more baby food and someone to clean them up—nappies and warm clothes.'

Diana appeared to think. 'Look, I wouldn't ask it of everyone but you're so sensible, Emma. If I get more stuff packed up would you take it back? Why not go back to Lustleigh and pack an overnight bag just in case you feel you can't leave them? I'll get a doctor to them as soon as I can and you can go straight home once he's got organised.'

'You're sure there's no one available?'

'Quite sure. There's a flap on with a major road accident—whooping cough just doesn't count.'

Emma was only half listening, which was a pity for then she might have queried that, but she was worried about the babies wheezing and gasping, so far from the care they needed. She said, 'All right, I'll go. I wish Paul were here…'

'Oh, my dear, so do I. He's such a tower of strength— we have been so close.' Diana's voice was soft and sad. 'We still are and I know you won't mind; it isn't as if you love each other.' She turned away and dabbed at a dry eye. 'You see, his work is all-important to him; he cannot afford to be distracted by the all-embracing love I—' She choked and took a long breath. 'Of course, he has explained all that to you—he told me how understanding you were.'

Emma said, 'I'd better be on my way,' and left without another word.

She went over the conversation word for word as she drove back to the cottage, and although she hated Diana she had to admit that it was all probably true. Paul didn't love her; he liked her enough to marry her, though, knowing that she would provide the calm background his arduous work demanded, whereas Diana's flamboyant nature would have distracted him.

It was well into the afternoon by now, and the sky was threatening rain. She hurried into the cottage, explained to Mrs Parfitt that she might not get back that night and ran upstairs to push essentials into a shoulder-bag. Mrs Parfitt came after her. 'You didn't ought to go,' she said worriedly. 'Whatever will Sir Paul say when he hears?'

'Well, he doesn't need to know. I'm only going to the reservoir, and don't worry, Mrs Parfitt, there'll be a doctor there tomorrow and I'll come home.' She turned to look at the faithful creature. 'Think of those babies—they really need some help.'

'Sir Paul wouldn't let you go, ma'am, but since you won't listen to me at least you'll have a bowl of soup and a nice strong cup of tea.'

Emma, who hadn't had her lunch, agreed, wolfed down the soup and some of Mrs Parfitt's home-made bread, drank several cups of tea and got back into the car. It was raining now and the wind had got up. She waved goodbye to Mrs Parfitt and Willy and Kate and drove back to the nursery.

It was amazing how much could be packed into

the Mini; it was amazing too how helpful Diana was. 'Don't worry,' she told Emma. 'Someone will be with you just as soon as possible.'

She waved goodbye as Emma drove away, then went into the office and picked up the phone. 'There's no hurry to send anyone out to that camp on the moor. I've sent everything they need and the girl who is taking the stuff is sensible and capable. I'll let you know more in the morning!'

Emma was still a mile or so from the reservoir when she saw the first wisps of mist creeping towards her, and five minutes later she was in the thick of it. It was eddying to and fro so that for a moment she could see ahead and then the next was completely enshrouded.

She had been caught in the moorland mists before now; to a stranger they were frightening but she had learnt to take them in her stride. All the same, she was relieved when she saw the rough track leading to the camp and bumped her way along it until the first of the buses loomed out of the mist. The mist had brought Stygian gloom with it and she was glad to see the lights shining from the open doorways. As she got out several of the campers came to surround her.

They were friendly—happy in the way they lived, making nothing of its drawbacks—but now they were anxious about the babies and Emma, taken to see them, was anxious too. No expert, she could still see that they were as ill as the one she had taken to the nursery. She handed out the blankets, baby food and bags of nappies, drank the mug of strong tea she was offered and prepared to return.

The mist had thickened by now and it was almost dark—to find her way wouldn't be easy or particularly safe; she would have to stay where she was until the morning and, since there were hours to get through, she could curl up in the back of the Mini for the night. She helped with the babies, looking at their small white faces and listening to their harsh breathing and hoping that, despite the awful weather, an ambulance or at least a doctor would come to their aid.

No one came, however, so she shared supper with one of the families and, after a last worried look at the babies, wrapped herself in a blanket and curled up on the Mini's back seat. It was a tight fit and she was cold, and the thin wails of the babies prevented her from sleeping, and when she at last lightly dozed off she was awakened almost immediately by one of the men with a mug of tea.

The mist had lifted. She scrambled up, tidied herself as best she could and got back into the car. If she drove round the reservoir and took the lane on the other side she would reach a hamlet, isolated but surely with a telephone. She explained what she was going to do and set off into the cold, bleak morning.

It was beginning to rain and there was a strong wind blowing; summer, for the moment, was absent. The lane was rutted and thick with mud and there

was no question of hurrying. She saw with relief
a couple of houses ahead of her and then a good-
sized farm.

There was a phone. The farmer, already up, took
her into the farmhouse when she explained, and
shook his head. 'They'm foolish folk,' he observed.
'Only just there, I reckon. Leastways they weren't
there when I was checking the sheep a few days ago.'
He was a kindly man. 'Reckon you'd enjoy a cuppa?'

'Oh, I'd love one, but if I might phone first? The
babies do need to go into care as quickly as possible.'

A cheerful West Country voice answered her.
They'd be there right away, she was told, just let her
sit tight till they came. Much relieved, she drank
her tea, thanked the farmer and drove back to tell
the travellers that help was on the way.

'Likely they'll move us on,' said one woman.

'It's common land, isn't it? I dare say they'll let
you stay as long as the babies are taken care of. I expect they'll take them to hospital and transfer them to
the nursery until they are well again. You'll be able
to see them whenever you all want to. Some of you
may want to go with them.' She looked around her.
'I can give three of you lifts, if you like.'

One of the younger women offered to go.

'How ever will you get back?' asked Emma.

'Thumb a lift and walk the last bit—no problem.'

The ambulance came then, and Emma stood aside
while the paramedics took over. They lifted the
babies into the ambulance presently, offered the

young woman who was to have gone with Emma a
seat, and drove away. That left her free to go at last.
No one wanted a lift—they were content to wait and
see what the young woman would tell them when she
got back. Emma got into her car and drove home, to
be met at the door by an agitated Mrs Parfitt.

'You're fit to drop,' she scolded kindly. 'In you
come, madam, and straight into a nice, hot bath while
I get your breakfast. Like as not you've caught your
death of cold.'

Not quite death, as it turned out, but for the moment she was very tired and shivery. The bath was
bliss, and so were breakfast and the warm bed she
got into afterwards.

'I must ring the nursery,' she said worriedly, and
began to get out of bed again, to Queenie's annoyance.

'I'll do that,' said Mrs Parfitt. 'No good going
there for a day or two, and so I'll tell that Miss Pearson.'

'I'm not ill,' said Emma peevishly, and fell asleep.

She woke hours later with a head stuffed with cotton wool and a sore thorat and crept downstairs, to
be instantly shooed back to her bed by Mrs Parfitt
bearing hot lemon and some paracetamol.

'It's more than my job's worth, Lady Wyatt, to let
you get up. Sir Paul would send me packing.'

Emma, aware that Mrs Parfitt only called her
Lady Wyatt when she was severely put out, meekly
got back into bed.

'Did you phone the nursery?' she croaked.

'I did, and there is no need for you to go in until you are free of your cold. You'd only give it to the babies.' Mrs Parfitt eyed her anxiously. 'I wonder if I should get the doctor to you, ma'am?'

'No, no—it's only a cold; I'll be fine in a day or two.'

Sir Paul, back from his travels, drove himself straight to the hospital, listened impatiently to his senior registrar's litany of things which had gone wrong during his absence and then, eager to get back home, phoned his secretary, who read out a formidable list of patients waiting for his services.

'Give me a day?' he begged her. 'I've a short list on the day after tomorrow. I'll come to my rooms in the afternoon—I leave it to you…'

He was about to ring off when she stopped him. 'Sir Paul, Miss Pearson phoned several times, and said it was most urgent that she should see you as soon as you got back.'

He frowned. 'Why didn't she speak to my registrar?'

'I don't know, sir; she sounded upset.'

'I'll call in on my way home.'

He was tired; he wanted to go home and see Emma, watch her face light up when she saw him. She might not love him but she was always happy to be with him. He smiled as he got out of the car and went along to Diana's office.

He might be tired but good manners necessitated his cheerful greeting. 'You wanted to see me; is it very urgent? I'm now on my way home.'

'I had to see you first,' said Diana. She was, for her, very quiet and serious. 'It's about Emma. Oh, don't worry, she's not ill, but I'm so upset. You see, she went dashing off; she simply wouldn't listen...'

Sir Paul sat down. 'Start at the beginning,' he said quietly.

Which was just what Diana had hoped he would say. She began to tell him her version of what had happened and, because she was a clever young woman, it all sounded true.

Sir Paul let himself into his house quietly, took off his coat and, since there were no lights on in the drawing-room, went to the little sitting-room at the back of the house. Emma was there, with Queenie on her lap and the dogs draped over her feet.

When he walked in she turned round, saw who it was, flew to her feet and ran across to him in a flurry of animals. 'Paul—you're back!' Her voice was still hoarse, and her nose pink from constant blowing, and it was a silly thing to say but she couldn't hide her delight.

He closed the door behind him and stood leaning against it, and it was only then that she realised that he was in a rage. His mouth was a thin hard line and his eyes were cold.

'What possessed you to behave in such a foolish

manner?' he wanted to know. 'Why all the melo-
drama? What are the ambulances for? Or the police,
for that matter? What in the name of heaven possessed you, Emma? To go racing off on to the moor
in bad weather, sending dramatic messages, spending the night in a God-forsaken camp. Ignoring Diana's pleading to wait and give her time to phone
for help. No, you must race away like a heroine in a
novel, bent on self-glory.'

Emma said in a shaky voice, 'But Diana—'

'Diana is worth a dozen of you.'

It was a remark which stopped her from uttering
another word.

'We'll talk later,' said Sir Paul, and went away to
his study and sat down behind his desk, his dogs at
his feet. He'd been too hard on her; he tried not to
think of her white, puzzled face with its pink nose,
but he had been full of rage, thinking of all those
things which could have happened to her. 'The little idiot,' he told the dogs. 'I could wring her darling neck.'

Emma gave herself ten minutes to stop shaking,
then went in search of Mrs Parfitt. 'Sir Paul's home,'
she told her. 'Can we stretch dinner for three?'

Mrs Parfitt gave her a thoughtful look, but all
she said was, 'I'll grill some more cutlets and shall
I serve a soup first? No doubt he's hungry after that
journey.'

'That would be fine, Mrs Parfitt. I dare say he's
famished. Could we have dinner quite soon?'

'Half an hour, ma'am—gives him time to have a drink and stretch out in his study.'

Emma went to her room, re-did her face and pinned her hair back rather more severely than usual, and then practised a few expressions in the looking-glass—a look of interest, a cool aloofness—she liked that one best...

Downstairs again, in the drawing-room, she picked up her tapestry work and began poking the needle in and out in a careless fashion, practising cool aloofness. She succeeded so well that when Paul came into the room intent on making his peace with her he changed his mind at once—the look she cast him was as effective as a barbed wire fence.

All the same, after a moment or two he essayed some kind of a conversation while he wondered how best to get back on a friendly footing once more.

Emma, her hurt and anger almost a physical pain, had no intention of allowing him to do that. She sat, mangling her needlework most dreadfully, silent except when it was asolutely necessary to say yes or no.

They had their dinner in silence, and as they got up from the table Paul said, 'I think we should have a talk, Emma.'

She paused on her way to the door. 'No, I have understood you very well, Paul; there is no need to say it all over again.'

'Do I take it that you don't wish to work at the nursery any more?'

Her eyes were very large in her pale face. 'I shall go tomorrow morning as usual. Why not?'

His cold, 'Just as you wish,' was as icy as her own manner.

At breakfast she treated him with a frigid politeness which infuriated him—asking him if he would be late home, reminding him that they were due to attend a dinner party on the following evening and wishing him a cool goodbye as he got up to go.

When he had gone she allowed her rigid mouth to droop. She supposed that in a while they would return to their easy-going relationship, but it wouldn't be the same—he had believed Diana, he had mocked her attempts at helping the travellers and, worst of all, he hadn't asked her if any of the things Diana had told him were true. So, if his opinion of her was so low why had he married her? To provide a screen of respectability so that he and Diana could continue as they were? So why hadn't he married her?

Emma's thoughts swirled around in her tired head and didn't make sense. All she did know was that Diana had lied about her and Paul had listened willingly. She didn't think that Diana would expect her back but she was going. Moreover, she would behave as though nothing unusual had occurred, only now she would be on her guard. It was a pity that she had fallen in love with Paul but, since she had, there was nothing more she could do about it—only make sure that Diana didn't get him.

Her imagination working overtime, Emma took herself off to the clinic.

It was a source of satisfaction actually to see that Diana was actually surprised and a little uncomfortable when she walked in.

'Emma—I didn't expect you. You're sure you feel up to it? I heard that you had a heavy cold.'

'Not as heavy as all that. I'll wear a mask, shall I? Are there any new babies?'

Diana's eyes slid away from hers. 'Three from that camp. They're in isolation—whooping cough. They were in a pretty poor way, you know.' She added casually, 'I hear that Paul is back?'

'Yes, didn't he come to see you? I thought he might have popped in on his way home. He's got a busy day—I dare say he'll do his best to call in this evening. I'd better get on with the bathings or I'll have Maisie on my tail.'

Maisie was already busy with the first of her three babies. She looked up as Emma wrapped her pinny round her and got everything ready before picking up Charlie, who was bawling as he always did.

'I heard a lot,' said Maisie. 'Most of which I don't believe. You look like something the cat's dragged in.'

'As bad as that? And I don't think you need to believe any of it, Maisie.'

'You're a right plucky un coming back 'ere. I couldn't 'elp but 'ear wot madam was saying—being busy outside the office door as it were. And that 'usband of yours coming out like a bullet from a gun, ready to do murder. If 'e'd been a bit calmer I'd 'ave spoke up. But 'e almost knocks me over, sets me back on me feet and all without a word. 'E's got a nasty temper and no mistake.'

They sat in silence for a few minutes, then Maisie asked, 'Going to tell 'er awf, are yer?' She scowled. 'I could tell a few tales about 'er if you don't.'

'No—please, Maisie, don't do that. There's a reason...'

'Oh, yeah? Well, yer knows best, but if yer want any 'elp you just ask old Maisie.'

'I certainly will, and thank you, Maisie. I can't explain but I have to wait and see...'

'You're worth a dozen of 'er,' said Maisie, which brought a great knot of tears into Emma's throat, so that she had to bury her face in the back of Charlie's small neck until she had swallowed them back where they belonged.

Sir Paul came home late that evening and Emma, beyond asking politely if he had had a busy day, forbore from wanting to know where he had been. Anyway, Maisie, who was at the nursery for most of the day, would tell her soon enough if he had been to see Diana.

They exchanged polite remarks during dinner and then he went to his study, only coming to the drawing-room as she was folding away her tapestry. Sir Paul, a man of moral and physical courage, quailed under her stony glance and frosty goodnight.

Where, he asked himself, was his enchanting little Emma, so anxious to please, always so friendly and so unaware of his love? He had behaved badly towards her, but couldn't she understand that it was because he had been so appalled at the idea of her going off on her own like that? Perhaps Diana had exaggerated a little; he would go and see her again.

Emma wasn't going to the nursery the following morning. She took the dogs for a long walk and spent an agreeable half-hour deciding which dress she would wear to the dinner party. It was to be rather a grand affair, at one of the lovely old manor-houses on the outskirts of the village, and she wanted to make a good impression.

She had decided to wear the silver-grey dress with the long sleeves and modest neckline, deceptively simple but making the most of her charming shape. She would wear the pearls too, and do her hair in the coil the hairdresser had shown her how to manage on her own.

She had changed and was waiting rather anxiously for Paul to come home by the time he opened the door. She bade him good evening, warned him that he had less than half an hour in which to shower and change, and offered him tea.

He had taken off his coat and was standing in the doorway. 'Emma—I went to the camp this afternoon—'

She cut him short gently. 'You must tell me about it—but not now, you haven't time…'

He didn't move. 'I went to see Diana too.'

'Well, yes, I quite understand about that, but I don't want to talk about it, if you don't mind.' She added in a wifely voice, 'We're going to be late.'

He turned away and went upstairs and presently came down again, immaculate in his dinner-jacket, his face impassive, and courteously attentive to her needs. They left the cottage, got into the car and drove the few miles to the party.

It was a pleasant evening; Emma knew several of the people there and, seated between two elderly gentlemen bent on flattering her, she began to enjoy herself. Paul, watching her from the other end of the table, thought how pretty she had grown in the last few weeks. When they got home he would ask her about her night in the camp.

The men and women he had talked to there had been loud in her praise.

'Saved the kids lives,' one young man had said. 'Acted prompt, she did—and gave an 'and with cleaning 'em up too. Didn't turn a hair—took our little un and 'er mum back with 'er and then came back in that perishing fog—couldn't see yer 'and in front of yer face. Proper little lady, she were.'

He bent his handsome head to listen to what his dinner partner was talking about—something to do with her sciatica. He assumed his listening face; being a bone man, his knowledge of that illness was rudimentary, but he nodded and looked sympathetic while he wondered once again if Diana had exaggerated and why Emma hadn't told him her side of the story.

He glanced down the table once more and squashed a desire to get out of his chair, pick her up out of hers and carry her off home. The trouble was that they didn't see enough of each other.

CHAPTER EIGHT

'A VERY PLEASANT EVENING,' observed Sir Paul as they drove home.

'Delightful,' agreed Emma. It was fortunate that it was a short journey for there didn't seem to be anything else to say, and once they were at home she bade him a quiet goodnight and took herself off to bed. As she went up the stairs she hoped against hope that he would leap after her, beg her forgiveness... Of course he did no such thing!

In the morning when she went downstairs she found him on the point of leaving. 'I'll have to re-arrange my day,' he told her. 'There's a patient—an emergency—for Theatre, so the list will run late. I'll probably be home around six o'clock, perhaps later. Don't forget that we are going to Mother's for the weekend.'

'Shall I take the dogs out?'

He was already through the door. 'I walked them earlier.' He nodded a goodbye and drove away as Mrs Parfitt came out of the kitchen.

'Sir Paul will knock himself out,' she observed, 'tearing off without a proper breakfast, up half the night working, and down here this morning before six o'clock, walking his legs off with those dogs.' She shook her head. 'I never did.'

Emma said, 'It's an emergency...'

'Maybe it is, but he didn't ought to go gallivanting around before dawn after being up half the night— he's only flesh and blood like the rest of us.' She bent her gaze on Emma. 'Now you come and have your breakfast, ma'am; you look as though you could do with a bit of feeding up.'

When Emma got to the nursery she found Diana waiting for her.

'Emma, did Paul remember to tell you that I am giving a little party next week? Tuesday, I thought— it's one of his less busy days.'

She smiled, and Emma said, 'No, but we were out to dinner until late and he left early for the hospital.'

'Yes, I know,' said Diana, who didn't but somehow she made it sound like the truth. 'He works too hard; he'll overdo things if he's not careful. I'll try and persuade him to ease off a bit.'

'I think you can leave that to me, Diana. You know, you're so—so motherly you should find a husband.' Emma's smile was sweet. 'Well, I'll get started.'

She wished Maisie good morning and Maisie said, 'You're smouldering again. Been 'aving words?'

'I'm afraid so. I'm turning into a very unpleasant person, Maisie.'

'Not you—proper little lady, you are. Don't meet many of 'em these days. Now, that young woman downstairs…' She branched off into an account of the goings-on of the young couple on the landing below her flat and Emma forgot her seething rage and laughed a little.

'Doing anything nice this weekend?' asked Maisie as they sat feeding the babies.

'We're going to spend it with my husband's parents.'

'Like that, will you?'

'Oh, yes, they're such dears, and it's a nice old house with a large garden. What are you going to do, Maisie? It's your weekend off, isn't it?'

'S'right.' Maisie looked coy. 'I got a bloke—'e's the milkman; we get on proper nice. Been courting me for a bit, 'e 'as, and we're thinking of having a go…'

'Oh, Maisie, how lovely. You're going to marry him?'

'I ain't said yes, mind you, but it'll be nice not ter 'ave ter come 'ere day in day out, with Madam looking down her nose at me.'

'You'll be able to stay home—oh, Maisie, I am glad; you must say yes. Does he got on well with your family?'

'They get on a treat. Yer don't think I'm silly?'

'Silly? To marry a man who wants you, who'll

give you a home and learn to be a father to the children. Of course it's not silly. It's the nicest thing I've heard for days.'

'Oh, well, p'raps I will. Yer're 'appy, ain't yer?'

Emma was bending over Charlie's cot, tucking him in. 'Yes, Maisie.'

'Me, I'd be scared to be married to Sir Paul, that I would—never know what 'e's thinking. 'E don't show 'is feelings, do 'e?'

'Perhaps not, but they are there all the same.'

'Well, you should know,' said Maisie, and chuckled.

The weather was still bad later on, so Emma walked the dogs briefly and went home to sit by the fire. She had a lot to think about; Diana seemed very confident that Paul was in love with her and he had said nothing to give the lie to that, and there was that one remark that she would never forget—that she was worth twelve of Emma. 'Oh, well,' she told the dogs, 'we'll go to this party and see what happens.'

She was glad that they were going away for the weekend, for two days spent alone with Paul, keeping up a façade of friendliness, was rather more than she felt she could cope with. She packed a pretty dress, got into her skirt and one of her cashmere jumpers, made up her face carefully and declared herself ready to go directly after breakfast on Saturday.

It was easier in the car, for she could admire the scenery and there was no need to talk even though she longed to. She sat watching his hands on the wheel—large, capable hands, well-kept. She loved them; she loved the rest of him too and she wasn't going to sit back tamely and let Diana dazzle him…

His parents welcomed them warmly, sweeping them indoors while the dogs went racing off into the garden. 'And where is Queenie?' asked Mrs Wyatt.

'She's happy with Mrs Parfitt and they're company for each other.'

'Of course. You're quite well again after that cold? We missed seeing you while Paul was away. Such a shame. Never mind, we'll make the most of you while you are here. Let Paul take your coat, my dear, and come and sit down and have some coffee.'

It was Mrs Wyatt who asked her how she had come to catch cold. 'Paul tells me that you work twice a week in a nursery in Moretonhampstead; I dare say you caught it there.'

Emma didn't look at Paul. She murmured something and waited to see if he would tell them how she had caught a cold. He remained silent. As well he might, she reflected crossly as he stood there looking faintly amused. Really, he was a most tiresome man; if she hadn't loved him so much she would have disliked him intensely.

There might have been an awkward pause if he hadn't, with the ease of good manners, made some trifling remark about the weather. Smooth, thought Emma, and went pink when her mother-in-law said,

'Well, cold or no cold, I must say that marriage suits you, my dear.'

Emma put her coffee-cup down with care and wished that she didn't blush so easily. Blushing, she felt sure, had gone out with the coming of women's lib and feminism, whatever that was exactly. Mrs Wyatt, being of an older generation, wasn't concerned with either and found the blush entirely suitable.

Paul found it enchanting.

The weekend passed too quickly.

No one would ever replace her mother, but Mrs Wyatt helped to fill the emptiness her mother had left, and if she noticed the careful way Emma and Paul avoided any of the usual ways of the newly wed she said nothing.

Paul had never worn his heart on his sleeve but his feelings ran deep and, unless her maternal instinct was at fault, he was deeply in love with Emma. And Emma with him, she was sure of that. They had probably had one of the many little tiffs they would have before they settled down, she decided.

'You must come again soon,' she begged them as they took their leave on Sunday evening.

It was late by the time they reached the cottage, which gave Emma the excuse to go to bed at once. Paul's 'Goodnight, my dear,' was uttered in a placid voice, and he added that there was no need for her to get up for breakfast if she didn't feel like it. 'I shall be away all day,' he said. 'I've several private patients to see after I've finished at the hospital.'

In bed, sitting against the pillows with her knees under her chin, Emma told Queenie, 'This can't go on, you know; something must be done.'

The Fates had come to the same conclusion, it seemed, for as Paul opened the front door the next evening, Emma, coming down the stairs, tripped and fell. He picked her up within seconds, scooping her into his arms, holding her close.

'Emma—are you hurt? Stay still a moment while I look.'

She would have stayed still forever with his arms around her, but she managed a rather shaky, 'I'm fine, really...'

He spoke to the top of her head, which was buried in his waistcoat. 'Emma—you must tell me—this ridiculous business of spending the night at that camp. Why did you refuse to listen to Diana? She is still upset and I cannot understand...'

Emma wrenched herself free. 'You listened to her and you believed her without even asking me. Well, go on believing her; you've known her for years, haven't you? And you've only known me for months, you don't know much about me, do you? But I expect you know Diana very well indeed.'

Paul put his hands in his pockets. 'Yes. Go on, Emma.'

'Well, if I were you, I'd believe her and not me,'

she added bitterly. 'After all, she's worth a dozen of me.'

She flew back upstairs and shut her bedroom door with a snap and when Mrs Parfitt came presently to see if she should serve dinner she found Emma lying on her bed.

'I have such a shocking headache,' sighed Emma. 'Would you give Sir Paul his dinner? I couldn't eat anything.'

Indeed she did look poorly. Mrs Parfitt tut-tutted and offered one of her herbal teas. 'You just get into bed, ma'am. I'll tell Sir Paul and I dare say he'll be up to see you.'

'No, no, there's no need. Let him have his dinner first; he's had a busy day and he needs a meal and time to rest. I dare say it will get better in an hour or two.'

The headache had been an excuse, but soon it was real. Emma got herself into bed and eventually fell asleep.

That was how Paul found her when he came to see her. She was curled up, her tear-stained face cushioned on a hand, the other arm round Queenie. He stood studying her for some minutes. Her hair was loose, spread over the pillows, and her mouth was slightly open. Her cheeks were rather blotchy because of the tears but the long, curling brown lashes swept them gently. When he had fallen in love with her he hadn't considered her to be beautiful but now he could see that her ordinary little face held a beauty which had nothing to do with good looks.

He went away presently, reassured Mrs Parfitt and went to his study. There was always work.

Emma went down to breakfast in the morning, exchanged good mornings with Paul, assured him that her headache had quite gone and volunteered the information that she was going to the nursery that morning. 'And I said I would go tomorrow morning as well—they're short-handed for a few days. Will you be home late?'

'No, in time for tea I hope. There's the parish council meeting at eight o'clock this evening.'

'Oh, yes. I am helping with the coffee and biscuits.'

He left then, and very soon after she got into the Mini and drove herself to the nursery.

''Ere,' said Maisie as she sat down and picked up the first baby, 'wot yer been up ter? 'Ad a tiff?'

'No, no, Maisie. I'm fine, really. How's your intended?'

It was a red herring which took them through most of the morning.

It was just as Emma was leaving and passing the office that Diana called to her. 'Emma, don't worry if Paul is late this evening—he's coming to check one of the babies from the camp—a fractured arm as well as whooping cough.'

Emma asked, 'Did he say he'd come? He's got a parish meeting this evening; he won't want to miss it.'

Diana smiled slowly. 'Oh, I'm sure it won't matter if he's not there.' She stared at Emma. 'As a matter of fact, he said he was coming to see me anyway.'

'That's all right, then,' said Emma. She didn't believe Diana.

She had lunch, then took the dogs for a long walk and helped Mrs Parfitt get the tea. Buttered muffins and cucumber sandwiches, she decided, and one of Mrs Parfitt's rich fruit cakes.

Teatime came and went, and there was no Paul. At last she had a cup of tea anyway, and a slice of cake, helped Mrs Parfitt clear away and went upstairs to get ready. She put on a plain jersey dress suitable for a parish council meeting.

When seven o'clock came and went she told Mrs Parfitt to delay her cooking. 'Sir Paul won't have time to eat in comfort before eight o'clock. Perhaps we could have a meal when we get home?'

'No problem,' said Mrs Parfitt. 'The ragout'll only need warming up and the rest will be ready by the time you've had a drink.'

'You have your supper when you like, Mrs Parfitt.' Emma glanced at the clock; she would have to go to the meeting and make Paul's excuses.

The councillors were friendly and very nice about it. Doctors were never free to choose their comings and goings, observed old Major Pike, but he for one was delighted to see his little wife.

Emma smiled shyly at him—he was a dear old man, very knowledgeable about the moor, born and bred in Lustleigh even though he had spent years away from it. He thoroughly approved of her, for she was a local girl and looked sensible.

The meeting was drawing to a close when the door opened and Paul came in. Emma, sitting quietly at the back of the village hall, watched him as he made his excuses, exchanged a few laughing remarks with the rest of the council and sat down at the table. He hadn't looked at her, but presently he turned his head and gave her a look which shook her.

He was pale and without expression, and she knew that he was very angry. With her? she wondered. Had Diana been making more mischief between them? She hoped he would smile but he turned away and soon it was time for her to go and help the vicar's wife in the kitchen.

They made the coffee and arranged Petit Beurre biscuits on a plate and carried them through just as the chairman closed the meeting. Eventually goodnights were exchanged and everyone started to go home.

Emma, collecting cups and saucers, saw that Paul had stayed. Waiting for her, she supposed, and when she came from the kitchen presently he was still there.

He got up when he saw her, passed a pleasant time of day with the vicar's wife, helped them on with their coats, turned out the lights, locked the door and gave the key to the vicar, who had walked back for his wife. That done, he turned for home, his hand under Emma's elbow.

She sensed that it was an angry hand and, anxious not to make things worse than they apparently were, she trotted briskly beside him, keeping up with his strides.

In the drawing-room she sat down in her usual chair, but Paul stood by the door, the dogs beside him. Perhaps it would be best to carry the war into the enemy camp, Emma decided.

'You were very late; did you have an emergency?'

'No.'

'You went to see Diana…?'

'Indeed I did.'

Emma nodded. 'She told me that you would go and see her, and that you were going to see her anyway.'

'And you believed her?'

'Well, no, I didn't—but I do now.'

He said softly, 'And why do you suppose that I went to see her?'

Emma said carefully, 'Shall we not talk about that? Something has made you angry and you must be tired. I'll tell Mrs Parfitt that we are ready for dinner, shall I? While you have a drink.'

She was surprised when he laughed.

It was while they were eating that Paul said quietly, 'I do not wish you to go to the clinic any more, Emma.'

She had a forkful of ragout halfway to her mouth. 'Not go? Why ever not?'

'Would it do if I just asked you to do as I wish? There are good reasons.'

Emma allowed her imagination to run riot. Diana would have convinced him in her charming way that she was no good at the nursery, that she was too slow, too independent too. She said slowly, 'Very well, Paul, but I should like to go tomorrow morning to say goodbye to Maisie. I have been working with her and she is getting married—I've a present for her. And I'd like to see Charlie—he's so cross and unloved...'

'Of course you must go. Diana won't be there, but you could leave a note.'

'Very well. I'll think up a good excuse.'

She wrote it later when Paul was in his study. Obviously Paul didn't want her to meet Diana again. Why? she wondered. Perhaps she would never know. It had been silly of her to refuse to talk about it; she hadn't given him a chance to explain why he was angry. She thought that he still was but he had got his rage under control; his manner was imperturbable.

He had looked, she reflected, as though he could have swept the extremely valuable decanter and glasses off the side-table. She sighed—everything had gone wrong. Their marriage had seemed such a splendid idea and she had been sure that it would be a success.

* * *

The mousy little woman who deputised for Diana was at the nursery the next day.

'Is Diana ill?' asked Emma, agog for information.

'No, Lady Wyatt. She felt she should have a few days off; she's been working hard just lately. You'll be sorry to have missed her. I hear you're leaving us.'

'Yes, I'm afraid so. I shall miss the babies. May I go and say goodbye to them and Maisie?'

'Of course. I'm sure Diana is grateful for your help while you were with us.'

'I enjoyed it,' said Emma.

Maisie was on her own, and Emma resisted the urge to put on her pinny and give her a hand. 'I'm leaving, Maisie. I didn't want to but Sir Paul asked me to.'

'Did 'e now?' Maisie looked smug. She had been there yesterday evening when Sir Paul had come to see Diana and, although she hadn't been able to hear what was said, she had heard Diana's voice, shrill and then tearful, and Sir Paul's measured rumble. He had come out of the office eventually, and this time Maisie had been brave and stopped him before he got into his car.

'I don't know the ins and outs,' she had told him briskly, 'but it's time you caught on ter that Diana telling great whoppers about that little wife of yours. Little angel, she is, and never said a word, I'll bet. 'Oo pretended there weren't no doctors nor ambulances to go ter the camp? Moonshine. I 'eard 'er

with me own ears telling 'em there weren't no need
to send anyone. Sent little Emma back into all that
mist and dark, she did, and tells everyone she'd done
it awf her own bat and against 'er wishes.' Maisie had
stuck her chin out. 'Sack me if yer want to. I likes
ter see justice done, mister!'

Sir Paul had put out a hand and engulfed hers.
'Maisie—so do I. Thank you for telling me; Emma
has a loyal friend in you.'

'Don't you go telling her, now.'

He had kept his word. Emma obviously knew
nothing about his visit. Now everything would be
all right. 'I'll miss yer, but I dare say you'll 'ave a
few of yer own soon enough.'

Emma had picked up Charlie. 'I do hope Charlie
will be wanted by someone.'

'Now, as ter that, I've a bit of good news. 'E's ter
be adopted by such a nice woman and 'er 'usband—
no kids of their own and they want a boy. 'E'll 'ave
a good 'ome.'

'Oh, lovely. Maisie, will you write and tell me
when you're to be married? And here's a wedding-
present.'

Emma dived into her shoulder-bag and handed
over a beribboned box.

'Cor, love, yer didn't orter...'

Maisie was already untying the ribbons. Inside
was a brown leather handbag and, under that, a pair
of matching gloves.

'I'll wear 'em on me wedding-day,' said Maisie, and got up and offered a hand.

Emma took it and then kissed Maisie's cheek. 'I hope you'll be very happy, and please write to me sometimes.'

'I ain't much 'and with a pen, but I'll do me best,' said Maisie.

Back home again, Emma took the dogs for a walk, had her lunch and then went into the garden. She pottered about, weeding here and there, tying things up, examining the rose bushes, anxious to keep busy so that she didn't need to think too much. She supposed that sooner or later she and Paul would have to talk—perhaps it would be best to get it over with. He had said that he would be home for tea. She began to rehearse a casual conversation—anything to prevent them talking about Diana.

The rehearsal wasn't necessary; when Paul got home he treated her with a casual friendliness which quite disarmed her. It was only later that she remembered she had told him that she had no wish to discuss the unfortunate episode at the camp and Diana's accusations. Which, of course, made it impossible for her to mention it now. They spent the evening together, making trivial talk, so that by the time she went to bed she was feeling peevish from her efforts to think up something harmless to say.

Paul got up to open the door for her, and as she went past him with a quick goodnight he observed, 'Difficult, isn't it, Emma?'

She paused to look up at him in surprise.

'Making polite small talk when you're bursting to utter quite different thoughts out loud.' He smiled down at her—a small, mocking smile with a tender edge to it, but she didn't see the tenderness, only the mockery.

For want of anything better, she said, 'I've no idea what you mean.'

Over the next few days they settled down to an uneasy truce—at least, it was uneasy on Emma's part, although Paul behaved as though nothing had occurred to disturb the easy-going relationship between them.

He was due up in Edinburgh at the beginning of the following week, but he didn't suggest that she should go with him. Not that I would have gone, reflected Emma, all the same annoyed that he hadn't asked her.

He would be back in three days he told her. 'Why not call Father to take you up to the Cotswolds, and spend a couple of days with them?'

'Well, Mrs Parfitt did say that she would like a few days to visit her sister at Brixham. I thought I might drive her there and fetch her back Willy and Kate can sit in the back and I can leave Queenie for most of the day.'

'You would like to do that? Then by all means go. I don't really like your being alone in the house, though, Emma.'

'It won't be the first time, and I have the dogs. I'm not nervous.'

'I'll leave my phone number, of course. Perhaps it would be better if Mrs Parfitt waited until I am back home.'

'No, it wouldn't. There's lots more to do around the house and more cooking when you're home.'

'A nuisance in my own house, Emma?' He sounded amused.

'No—oh, no, of course not. But I know she'd prefer to go away when you're not here.'

'As you wish. In any case, I shall phone each evening.'

Paul left soon after breakfast, so Emma was able to drive Mrs Parfitt to her sister's very shortly after that.

It was a pleasant drive and the morning was fine, and when she reached Brixham she delivered Mrs Parfitt and then drove down to the harbour, where she parked the car and took the dogs for a run. She had coffee in a small café near by and then drove back to Lustleigh. When she reached the cottage and let herself in she realised that she felt lonely, despite the animals' company.

She wandered through the house, picking things up and putting them down again and, since Mrs Parfitt had left everything in apple-pie order, there was nothing for her to do except get the lunch.

A long walk did much to dispel her gloom and took up the time nicely until she could get her tea, and then it was the evening and Paul had said that he would phone…

She wondered how long it would take him to get there; it was a long way and he might be too tired to ring up.

Of course he did, though; she was watching the six o'clock news when the phone rang and she rushed to it, fearful that he might ring off before she reached it.

Yes, his cool voice assured her, he had had a very pleasant drive, not all that tiring, and he had already seen two patients who needed his particular skills. 'I have a clinic tomorrow morning,' he told her, 'and then a lecture before dining with friends. I may phone rather later. You enjoyed your drive to Brixham?'

'Yes. We went for a long walk this afternoon; Willy got a thorn in his paw but I got it out. I'm getting their suppers…'

'In that case, don't let me keep you. Sleep well, Emma.'

He didn't wait for her answer but hung up.

An unsatisfactory conversation, thought Emma, snivelling into the dog food. He hadn't asked her if she was lonely or cautioned her kindly about locking up securely; indeed, he had asked hardly any questions about her at all.

She poked around in the fridge and ate two cold sausages and a carton of yoghurt, then took herself off to bed after letting the dogs out and then bolting and barring all the doors and the windows. She had no reason to feel nervous—it was a pity that she didn't know that the village constable, alerted by Sir Paul, had made it his business to keep an eye on her.

She lay awake for a long time, thinking about Paul. She missed him dreadfully; it was as though only half of her were alive—to have him home was all she wanted, and never mind if they no longer enjoyed their pleasant comradeship. She would have to learn to take second place to Diana and be thankful for that.

'But why he couldn't have married her and been done with it, I don't know,' Emma observed to the sleeping Queenie and, naturally enough, got no answer.

She walked to the village stores after breakfast, took her purchases home and went off for another walk with the dogs. The fine weather held and the sun shone, and out on the moors her worries seemed of no account. They went back home with splendid appetites and, having filled the dogs' bowls and attended to Queenie's more modest needs, Emma had her own lunch. The day was half done, and in the evening Paul would phone again.

She was putting away the last spoons and forks when there was a thump on the door-knocker. She wiped her hands on her apron and went to open it.

Diana stood there, beautifully dressed, exquisitely made-up, and smiling.

'Emma—I've been lunching at Bovey Tracey and I just had to come and see you. I know Paul's in Edinburgh and I thought you might like a visit. I'm surprised he didn't take you with him. It's great for a professor's image to have a wife, you know.'

She had walked past Emma as she held the door open and now stood in the hall, looking round. 'Nothing's changed,' she observed and heaved a sigh. 'I never liked that portrait over the table, but Paul said he was a famous surgeon in his day and he wouldn't move him.'

She smiled at Emma, and Emma smiled back. 'Well, it is Paul's house,' she said pleasantly. 'Would you like a cup of coffee?'

'I'd love one.' Diana had taken off her jacket and thrown it over a chair. 'I had the most ghastly lunch at the Prostle-Hammetts and the coffee was undrink-able.'

It was the kind of remark Diana would make, thought Emma as she led the way into the draw-ing-room.

'Oh, the dogs,' cried Diana. 'We always had such fun together…'

Neither dog took any notice of her, which cheered Emma enormously—they were on her side.

'Do sit down,' she said. 'I'll fetch the coffee.'

'Can I help? I know my way around, you know.'

'No, no. Sit down here—you look a bit pinched. I expect you're tired.' She saw Diana's frown and the quick peek in the great Chippendale mirror over the fireplace.

In the kitchen she poured the coffee and wondered why Diana had come. To see how she had settled in as Paul's wife? Or just to needle her? Emma told herself stoutly that she wasn't going to believe anything Diana said. After all, so far she had done nothing but hint at her close friendship with Paul; all that nonsense about her love distracting him from his work had been nothing but moonshine. All the same, Diana had played a dirty trick on her when she had been at the nursery and she wasn't to be trusted.

She took the coffee-tray in, offered sugar and cream and sat down opposite her unwelcome guest. She didn't believe that Diana had called out of friendliness—it was probably just out of curiosity.

'Paul has a busy few days in Edinburgh,' said Diana. 'Patients yesterday and today after that long drive, and a clinic tomorrow. What a blessing it is that he has good friends—we always dined there...' She cast a sidelong look at Emma and gave a little laugh. 'Of course, everyone expected us to marry.'

'Then why didn't you?' Emma lifted the coffee-pot. 'More coffee?'

'No, thanks—I have to think of my figure.'

Emma said pertly, 'Well, yes, I suppose you do; we none of us grow any younger do we?'

Diana put her cup and saucer down. 'Look, Emma, you don't like me and I don't like you, but that doesn't alter the fact that Paul still loves me. He married you for all kinds of worthy reasons: you're an ideal wife for a busy man who is seldom at home; you don't complain; you're not pretty enough to attract other men. I dare say you're a good housewife and you won't pester him to take you out to enjoy the bright lights. As I said, you're an ideal wife for him. He's fond of you, I suppose—but loving you? I don't suppose you know what that means; you're content with a mild affection, aren't you? Whereas he…'

She had contrived to get tears in her eyes and Emma, seeing them, had sudden doubts.

'We love each other,' said Diana quietly. 'He has married you and he'll be a kind and good husband to you but you must understand that that is all he will ever be. I know you think I'm not worthy of him, and I know I'm not.' She blinked away another tear. 'He's not happy, you know, Emma.'

Emma said, 'You could go away—right away.'

Diana said simply, 'He would come after me—don't you know that? There's nothing I can do—I've talked and talked and he won't listen.' She looked at Emma. 'It is you who must go, Emma.'

Emma, looking at her and not trusting her an inch, found herself half believing her. She detested Diana, but if Paul loved her that didn't matter, did it? However, she didn't quite believe Diana; she would need proof.

Where would she get proof? It would have to be something that would hold water, not vague hints. She said, 'I don't intend to go, Diana.'

She got up to answer the phone and it was Paul. His quiet voice sounded reassuring to her ear. 'It will be late before I can phone you this evening so it seemed sensible to do so now. Is everything all right at home?'

'Yes, thank you—have you been busy?'

'Yes. I'll be here for another two days. Do you fetch Mrs Parfitt back tomorrow?'

'No, the day after.'

'You're not lonely?'

'No. Diana is here, paying a flying visit.'

She heard the change in his voice. 'I'll speak to her, Emma.'

'It's Paul; he'd like a word with you.' Emma handed the phone to Diana. 'I'll take the coffee out to the kitchen.'

Which she did, but not before she heard Diana's rather loud, 'Darling...'

CHAPTER NINE

EMMA hesitated for a moment; to nip back and listen at the door was tempting, but not very practical with the coffee-tray in her hands. She went to the kitchen, letting the door bang behind her, put the tray on the table and then returned noiselessly to the hall. The drawing-room door was ajar; she could hear Diana very clearly.

'I'll be at home until Friday. Goodbye, Paul.'

Emma retreated smartly to the kitchen and rattled a few cups and saucers and then went back to the drawing-room, shutting the baize door to the kitchen with a thump. Diana was putting on her coat.

'My dear, I must go. Thanks for the coffee, and I'm so glad to see that you've altered nothing in the cottage.' She paused, pulling on her gloves. 'Emma, you will think over what I have said, won't you? It sounds cruel but we are all unhappy now, aren't we? If you let Paul go then there would be only one of us unhappy, and since you don't love him you'll get over it quickly enough. He'll treat you well—financially, I mean.'

'I think you'd better go,' said Emma, 'before I throw something at you.' She went ahead of Diana and opened the cottage door. 'You're very vulgar, aren't you?'

She shut the door before Diana could reply.

She went back to the drawing-room and sat down; Queenie got on to her lap while Willy and Kate settled beside her. She didn't want to believe Diana but she had sounded sincere and she had cried. Moreover, she had told Paul that she would be at home until Friday. Why would she do that unless she expected him to go and see her? There was no way of finding out—at least, until Paul came home again.

He phoned the following evening. 'You're all right?' he wanted to know. 'Not lonely?'

'Not in the least,' said Emma airily. 'I had tea with the Postle-Hammets. I like Mrs Postle-Hammet and the children are sweet; I enjoyed myself.'

Largely because Mrs Postle-Hammet had been remarkably frank about her opinion of Diana, she thought. 'Cold as a fish and selfish to the bone and clever enough to hide it,' she had said—hardly information she could pass on to Paul.

'I should be home tomorrow evening, but if I should be delayed will you leave the side-door locked but not bolted? You'll fetch Mrs Parfitt tomorrow?'

'Yes, after lunch.'

'Good. I'll say goodnight, Emma. I've several more phone calls to make.' One of them to Diana? she wondered, and tried not to think about that.

* * *

She had an early lunch the next day and drove to Brixham through driving rain to fetch Mrs Parfitt, and then drove home again, listening to that lady's account of her few days' holiday. 'Very nice it was too, ma'am, but my sister isn't a good cook and I missed my kitchen. Still, the sea air was nice and there are some good shops. You've not been too alone, I hope?'

'No, no, Mrs Parfitt. I've been out to tea and Miss Pearson came to see me and Sir Paul has phoned each evening, and of course there were the dogs to take out. I had no time to be lonely—' Emma turned to smile at her companion '—but it's very nice to have you back, Mrs Parfitt. The cottage doesn't seem the same without you. Sir Paul is coming back this evening.'

'He'll need his dinner if he's driving all that way. Did you have anything in mind, ma'am?'

They spent the rest of the journey deciding on a menu to tempt him when he got home. 'Something that won't spoil,' cautioned Emma, 'for I've no idea exactly when he'll be back.'

Mrs Parfitt took off her best hat and her sensible coat and went straight to the kitchen. 'A nice cup of tea,' she observed, 'and while the kettle's boiling I'll pop a few scones in the oven.'

Emma went from room to room, making sure that everything was just so, shaking up cushions, rearranging the flowers, laying the pile of letters on the table by Paul's chair and, since it was going to be a gloomy evening, switching on lamps here and there so that there was a cheerful glow from the windows.

Satisfied that everything was as welcoming as she could make it, she went upstairs and changed into a patterned silk jersey dress, did her face with care and brushed her hair into a knot at the back of her head; it took a long time to get it just so but she was pleased with the result. Then she went downstairs to wait.

At ten o'clock she sent Mrs Parfitt to bed and ate a sketchy meal off a tray in the kitchen. When the long case clock in the hall chimed one o'clock she went to bed herself.

She was still awake when it chimed again, followed by the silvery tinkle of the carriage clock in the drawing-room. She slept after that but woke when it was barely light to creep downstairs to see if Paul was home. If he was, the back door would be bolted. It wasn't!

Emma stared at it for a long moment and then went to the phone and picked it up. The night porter answered it. Yes, Sir Paul had been in the hospital during the late evening and had left again shortly after—he had seen him leave in his car.

He sounded a little surprised at her query and she hastened to say that it was perfectly all right. 'Sir Paul said that he might do that. I'll ring him now. Thank you.'

She went to the kitchen then, and put on the kettle. She spooned tea into the pot, trying not to think about the previous evening, trying not to believe Diana's remarks but quite unable to forget them.

She was making tea when the kitchen door opened and Paul walked in. Emma caught her breath and choked on a surge of strong feelings.

'A fine time to come home,' she snapped, rage for the moment overcoming the delight of seeing him again, and she made unnecessary work of refilling the kettle and putting it back on the Aga.

Sir Paul didn't speak, but stood in the doorway looking at her indignant back, and since the silence was rather long she asked stiffly, 'Would you like a cup of tea?'

'Er—no, thank you, Emma. I'm sorry if you were worried.'

'Worried? Why should I be worried?' said Emma at her haughtiest. 'I phoned the hospital early this morning and I was told that you had been in and gone again late last night.' She drew a long breath. 'So I had no need to worry, had I?'

When he most annoyingly didn't answer, she said, 'I knew where you were…'

'Indeed.'

She had her back to him, busy with mug and sugar and milk and pouring tea. 'Well, Diana came to see me—I told you that—you spoke to her…'

'Ah, Diana—of course. *Latet anguis in herba*!' murmured Sir Paul.

Emma's knowledge of Latin was sketchy and,

anyway, what had grass got to do with it? For she
had recognised the word *herba*, and if he was trailing
a red herring she meant to ignore it. In any case her
tongue was running on now, regardless of prudence.

'So of course I knew you'd go to her when you got
back. She was very—very frank.' She gave an angry
snuffle. 'She was glad I hadn't altered the pictures
or anything.' She wouldn't look at him. 'Would you
like breakfast?'

'No, Emma, I'll shower and change and go to the
hospital.'

'You'll be back later? Teatime?'

'Don't count on that.' He spoke quietly, and something in his voice made her turn to look at him. He
looked very tired but he gave her a bland stare from
cold eyes. She had no doubt that he was angry. She
was angry too, and miserable, and she loved him so
much that she felt the ache of it. The urge to tell him
so was so great that she started to speak, but she had
barely uttered his name when he went away.

He had left the house by the time she had dressed
and gone back downstairs to find Mrs Parfitt in the
kitchen.

'Gone again,' cried Mrs Parfitt. 'I saw him drive
off not ten minutes ago. By the time I'd got downstairs he'd gone. He'll wear himself out, that he will.
How about a nice leg of lamb for dinner this evening?
He'll need his strength kept up.'

When Emma said that he had come home very
early in the morning Mrs. Parfitt commented, 'Must

have been an accident. Now you go and eat your breakfast, ma'am, for no doubt you've been worrying half the night. Who'd be a doctor's wife, eh?' She laughed, and Emma echoed it in a hollow way.

She took the dogs for their walk after breakfast while Mrs Parfitt took herself off to the village shop and paid a visit to the butcher. It was while she was drying the dogs in the outhouse by the kitchen that Mrs Parfitt joined her.

'Postie was in the stores—there's been a nasty accident on the M5 where it turns into the A38.' Mrs Parfitt paused for breath, bursting with her news. 'Nine cars, he said, all squashed together, and Sir Paul right behind them on his way back here. Goes back to the hospital and spends the night in the operating theatre, he does. He's back there now, no doubt, working himself to death. He didn't ought to do it. He didn't say nothing to you, ma'am? No— well, of course, he wouldn't; he'd have known how upset you'd have been.'

Emma had gone very pale. 'Not a word. He didn't want tea or his breakfast but he said he had to go back.' The full horror of what she had said to him dawned on her—she had accused him of being with Diana while all the time he had been saving lives. She hadn't even given him the chance to tell her anything. She felt sick at the thought, and Mrs Parfitt took her arm and sat her down by the table.

'There, I shouldn't have come out with it so quick;

you're that pale—like a little ghost. You stay there while I fetch you a drop of brandy.'

Emma was only too willing to sit. It was chilly in the little room, and the dogs, released from the tiresome business of being cleaned up before going into the house, had slipped away to lie by the Aga.

Mrs Parfitt came back with the brandy. 'It don't do to give way, ma'am,' she urged Emma. 'He's safe and sound even if he's tired to his bones, but you must show a bright face when he gets home, for that'll be what he needs.'

Emma drank the brandy, although she thought he wouldn't care if her face was bright or not. He would be polite, because he had beautiful manners and they wouldn't allow him to be otherwise, but he would have gone behind the barrier she had always sensed was between them—only now that barrier was twice as high and she doubted if she would ever climb it.

She spent a restless day, dreading his return and yet longing for it, going over and over in her aching head the awful things she had said and rehearsing the humble speech she would offer him when he came home. Which he did just as Mrs Parfitt brought in the tea-tray, following her into the drawing-room.

'There,' said Mrs Parfitt. 'Didn't I bake that fruit cake knowing you'd be here for your tea? I'll fetch another cup and a sandwich or two.'

She trotted off; she firmly believed that the way to a man's heart was through his stomach, and his doubtless needed filling.

He thanked her quickly and stooped to fondle the dogs weaving around his feet. 'Hello, Emma,' he said quietly.

'Paul.' The strength of her feelings was choking her as she got out of her chair, spilling an indignant Queenie on to the carpet. She said stupidly, 'I didn't know…' Her tongue shrivelled under his cold stare; underneath his quietness he was furiously angry, and suddenly she was angry again. 'Why didn't you tell me?'

He sat down in his chair and the dogs curled up beside him. 'I don't believe that I had the opportunity,' he observed mildly.

'You could have—' Emma burst out, only to be interrupted by Mrs Parfitt with fresh tea, cup and saucer and a plate of sandwiches.

'Gentleman's Relish,' she pointed out in a pleased voice. 'Just what you fancy, sir, and cucumber and cress. I shall be serving dinner a bit earlier, ma'am? I dare say the master's peckish.'

Emma glanced at Paul, who said, 'That would be very nice, Mrs Parfitt.' He sounded like any man just home and sitting by his own fireside but Emma, unwittingly catching his eye, blinked at its icy hardness.

After Mrs Parfitt had gone Emma poured the tea, offered sandwiches and strove to think of something to say; she would have to apologise, and she wanted to, but for the moment the right words eluded her. All the same she made a halting start, only to have it swept aside as Paul began a conversation which gave her no chance to utter a word.

It was an undemanding and impersonal stream of small talk, quiet and unhurried. He could have been soothing a scared patient before telling her his diagnosis. Well, she wasn't a patient but she was scared, and the diagnosis, when it came, left her without words.

She was pouring his second cup of tea when he said casually, 'I've been offered a lecture tour in the States…'

He watched her pale face go even paler and saw the shock in it.

'The States? America? For how long?'

'Four months.'

She gulped back a protesting scream. 'That's a long time.'

'Yes. Time enough for us to consider our future, don't you agree?'

If only he wasn't so pleasant about it, Emma thought unhappily, and if only I could think of the right thing to say. After a minute she said, 'I expect you'd like to go?'

He didn't answer that so she tried again, asking a question her tongue uttered before she could stop it. 'Will you go alone?'

'Oh, yes.'

He didn't add to that, and she seized the opportunity and plunged into a muddled apology. None of the things she had meant to say came out properly.

'I'm sorry, Paul, I'm so very sorry; it was terribly stupid of me and unkind...'

He stopped her quite gently. 'Don't say any more, Emma. I thought that when we married...' He paused. 'You must see that if you don't trust me our marriage is going to be unhappy. That is why I shall go on this tour; you will have time to decide what you want to do with your future.'

She gave him a bewildered look. 'You mean, you don't want me to be your wife?'

'I didn't say that...'

'Well, no—but I think you meant that, only you are too polite to say so. I expect it's a good idea.'

At the end of four months, she thought sadly, he would come back, and they would separate without fuss and he would go his way and she would go hers. What about Diana? He hadn't mentioned her, had he? And she didn't dare to ask.

'I've made you very angry.'

'Indeed you have,' he agreed politely.

'I think it would have been better if you had shouted at me...'

'I could never shout at you, Emma.'

He smiled a little, thinking that he wanted to pick her up and shake her and carry her off somewhere and never let her go—his darling Emma.

Perhaps he was too old for her; perhaps she regretted marrying him. Certainly she had been a constantly good companion, and at times he had thought that she might become more than that, but once she had got over the shock she had given no sign that she didn't want him to go away. Indeed, she had taken it for granted that she would stay here.

He got up. 'I've one or two letters to write,' he told her. 'I'll go and do them before dinner—I can take the dogs out later.'

Emma nodded, and when he had gone carried the tray out to the kitchen. She stayed there for ten minutes, getting in Mrs Parfitt's way, and presently went back to the drawing-room and got out her embroidery. She wasn't being very successful with it and spent the next half-hour unpicking the work she had done the previous evening. It left her thoughts free and she allowed them full rein.

Somehow she must find a way to convince Paul that she was truly sorry. If he wanted to be free—perhaps to marry Diana—then the least she could do was to make it easy for him. She owed him so much that she could never repay him. She must find out when this lecture tour was to start; if she were to go away first, then he wouldn't need to go.

Her head seethed with plans; she could tell everyone that an aunt or uncle needed her urgently. That she had no relations of any kind made no difference—no one was to know that. She would do it in a way that would arouse no suspicions. Diana would guess, of course—she had suggested it in the first place—but she wasn't likely to tell anyone.

She would write a letter to Paul, saying all the things she wanted to say—that she loved him and

wanted him to be happy and thanked him for his
kindness and generosity. Her mind made up, she at-
tacked her embroidery with vigour and a complete
disregard for accuracy.

Out-patients' sister watched Sir Paul's vast back dis-
appear down the corridor. 'Well, what's the matter with him?' she asked her staff nurse. 'I've never
known him dash off without his cup of tea, and him
so quiet too. Something on his mind, do you suppose? He's got that nice little wife to go home to and
you're not telling me that they're not happy together.
Mention her and his face lights up—looks ten years
younger. Ah, well, he'll go home and spend a lovely
evening with her, I dare say.'

Sir Paul drove himself to the nursery, got out of
his car and walked into Diana's office. She was getting ready to go home but put her jacket down as
he went in. 'Paul, how lovely to see you—it's ages.'

He closed the door behind him—a disappointment
to Maisie, who was getting ready to go home too,
standing in the cloakroom near enough to the office
to hear anything interesting which might be said.

'Perhaps you will spare me ten minutes, Diana?'

He hadn't moved from the door and she sat down
slowly. 'All the time in the world for you, Paul.'

'You went to see Emma—why?'

She shrugged her shoulders. 'I thought she might
be lonely.'

'The truth, Diana...'

Now Maisie edged nearer the door. She couldn't hear what was being said but she could hear Diana's voice getting more and more agitated, and Sir Paul's voice sounding severe and, presently, angry.

Sir Paul wasn't mincing his words. 'I have never at any time given you reason to believe that I was in love with you.' He added, with brutal frankness, 'Indeed, you are the last woman I would wish to have for a wife.'

Maisie, her ear pressed to the keyhole, just had time to nip back into the cloakroom as he opened the door.

He saw at once on his return home that this was not the right time to talk to Emma. She was being carefully polite and the expression on her face warned him not to be other than that; so the evening was spent in a guarded manner, neither of them saying any of the things they wanted to say, both waiting for some sign…

Emma went to bed rather early, relieved that she was alone and could grizzle and mope and presently go over her plans to leave. Just for a little while that evening, despite their coolness towards each other, she had wondered if she could stay, if they could patch things up between them. But trying to read Paul's thoughts was an impossible task; they were far too well hidden behind his bland face. He wasn't going to reproach her; he wasn't going to say another word about the whole sorry business. Presumably it was to be forgotten and they would go on as before, just good friends and then, when the right moment came, parting.

'I hate Diana,' said Emma, and kicked a cushion across the floor. 'I hope she makes him very unhappy.' It was a palpable lie which did nothing to restore her spirits.

She didn't sleep much—she was too busy making plans. Many were wildly unsuitable to begin with, but by the early morning she had discarded most of them in favour of one which seemed to her to be simple and foolproof.

She would give Mrs Parfitt a day off—it would have to be in two days' time, when Paul had his theatre list and a ward round, which meant he wouldn't be home before about six o'clock. Once Mrs Parfitt was out of the house she would pack a few things in a suitable bag, write a letter to Paul and one to Mrs Parfitt—the illness of a fictitious aunt would do very well—walk to Bovey Tracey, get a bus down to the main road and another bus to Plymouth.

She could lose herself there and get a job in a restaurant or a hotel—surely there would be temporary jobs in the tourist trade. She would have to buy some kind of a bag—a knapsack would do. In the morning she would take her car into Exeter and get one. It was morning already, she reminded herself, and got up and dressed and did the best she could to disguise her sleepless night.

Sir Paul bade her good morning in his usual manner, remarked on the fine day and studied her tired face. She looked excited, too, in a secret kind of way, as though she were hatching some plot or other. He decided to come home early but told her smoothly when she asked if he would be home for tea that he thought it unlikely, watching the relief on her face.

It was easy to get Mrs Parfitt to take a day off; Emma knew that she wanted to go to Exeter and buy a new hat. 'Take the whole day,' she suggested. 'I might go over to Mrs Postle-Hammett's—it's a good walk for the dogs and she's very fond of them. I'm sure Sir Paul will give you a lift tomorrow morning.'

'Well, if you don't mind, ma'am. I must say I'd like a day to shop around.'

'I'm going to Exeter this morning,' said Emma. 'One or two things I want. Do we need anything for the house while I'm there?'

There was nothing needed. She went to her room and got into her jacket, found her car keys and drove herself to Exeter. She soon found exactly what she wanted in a funny little shop at the bottom of the high street, walked back to the car park in Queen Street and on the way came face to face with Maisie.

'Come and have a cup of coffee?' said Emma. She was glad to see her and steered her into a café. 'Aren't you at the nursery any more?'

'Leaving on Saturday,' said Maisie and looked coy. 'Getting married, yer see.'

'On Saturday? Oh, Maisie, I am glad; I hope you'll both be very happy. In church?'

'Baptist. Just the kids and 'is mum and dad.'

Maisie sugared her coffee lavishly. 'Saw yer old man at the nursery—leastways, 'eard 'im. In a bit of a rage, it sounded like, and that Diana going 'ammer and tongs. Sounded all tearful she did—kept saying, "Oh, Paul, oh, Paul." Didn't come to work today nei- ther. Nasty piece of work she is; turns on the charm like I switches on the electric.'

'She's very attractive,' said Emma, and felt sick. So, he was still seeing Diana; it was a good thing she had decided to go…

'Suppose so,' said Maisie. 'Leastways, to men. Good thing you're married to yer old man!'

She chuckled and Emma managed a laugh. 'Yes, isn't it? Tell me what you're going to wear…'

Which filled the next ten minutes very nicely be- fore Maisie declared that she still had some shop- ping to do.

'We'll 'ave some photos,' she promised. 'I'll send you one.'

'Please do, Maisie, and it was lovely meeting you like that.'

They said goodbye and Emma went back to the car and drove home. The small hopeful doubt she had had about leaving had been doused by Maisie's news. Tomorrow she would go.

She was surprised when Paul came home at tea- time, but she greeted him in what she hoped was a normal voice, and, when he asked her, told him that she had been to Exeter—'One or two things I wanted'—and had met Maisie. Maisie's approaching wedding made a good topic of conversation; Emma wore it threadbare and Paul, listening to her repeating herself, decided that whatever it was she was planning it wouldn't be that evening.

He went to his study presently and spent some time on the phone rearranging the next day's work. When his receptionist complained that he had several patients to see on the following afternoon he told her ruthlessly to change their appointments. 'I must have the whole of tomorrow afternoon and evening free,' he told her, and then spent ten minutes charming Theatre Sister into altering his list.

'I'll start at eight o'clock instead of nine,' he told her, and, since she liked him and admired him, she agreed, aware that it would mean a good deal of rearranging for her to do.

As for his registrar, who admired him too, he agreed cheerfully to take over out-patients once the ward-round was done.

Sir Paul ate his supper, well aware that he had done all he could to avert whatever disaster his Emma was plotting.

The cottage seemed very empty once Paul and Mrs Parfitt had gone the next morning. It was still early; she had all day before her. Emma took the dogs for a long walk, went from room to room tidying up, clearing the breakfast things Mrs Parfitt hadn't had the time to do, and then she sat down to write her letters.

This took her a long time, for it was difficult to

write exactly what she wanted to say to Paul. She
finished at last, wrote a letter to Mrs Parfitt about
the sick aunt and went to pack her knapsack. Only
the necessities went into it—her lavish wardrobe she
left. She left her lovely sapphire and diamond ring
too, putting it in its little velvet box on the tallboy
in his dressing-room.

She wasn't hungry but she forced herself to eat
some lunch, for she wasn't sure where she would
get her supper. She had some money too—not very
much but enough to keep her for a week, and as soon
as she had a job she would pay it back; she had been
careful to put that in her letter.

It was going on for three o'clock by then. She
got her jacket, changed into sensible shoes, took the
dogs for a quick run and then carefully locked up the
house. It only remained for her to take her letter and
leave it in Paul's study.

She left the knapsack in the hall with Mrs Parfitt's
letter and went to the study. The letter in her hand,
she sat for a moment in his chair, imagining him sitting in it presently, reading her letter, and two tears
trickled down her cheeks. She wiped them away, got
out of the chair and went round the desk and leaned
over to prop the letter against the inkstand.

Sir Paul's hand took it gently from her just as she
set it down, and for a moment she didn't move. The
sight of the sober grey sleeve, immaculate linen and
gold cufflinks, and his large, well-kept hand appear-
ing from nowhere, had taken her breath, but after a

moment she turned round to face him. 'Give it to me, please, Paul.' Her voice was a whisper.

'But it is addressed to me, Emma.'

'Yes, yes, I know it is. But you weren't to read it until after…'

'You had gone?' he added gently. 'But I am here, Emma, and I am going to read it.'

The door wasn't very far; she took a step towards it but he put out an arm and swept her close. 'Stay here where you belong,' he said gently and, with one arm holding her tight, he opened the letter.

He read it and then read it again, and Emma tried to wriggle free.

'Well, now you know,' she said in a watery voice. 'What are you going to do about it? I didn't mean to fall in love with you—it—it was an accident; I didn't know it would be so—so… What are you going to do, Paul?'

His other arm was round her now. 'Do? Something I wanted to do when I first saw you.' He bent and kissed her, taking his time about it.

Emma said shakily, 'You mustn't—we mustn't—what about Diana?'

'I can see that we shall have to have a cosy little talk, my darling, but not yet.' He kissed her again. 'I've always loved you. You didn't know that, did you? I didn't tell you, for I hurried you into marriage and you weren't ready for me, were you? So I waited, like a fool, and somehow I didn't know what to do.'

'It was me,' said Emma fiercely into his shoulder.

'I listened to Diana and I don't know why I did. I suppose it was because I love you and I want you to be happy, and I thought it was her and not me.' She gave a great sniff. 'She's so beautiful and clever and the babies were darlings and she told me to go to the travellers' camp...'

Sir Paul, used to the occasional incoherence of his patients, sorted this out. 'Darling heart, you are beautiful and honest and brave, and the only woman I have ever loved or could love.' He gave a rumble of laughter. 'And you shall have a darling baby of your own...'

'Oh, I shall love that—we'll share him. Supposing he's a girl?'

'In that case we must hope that we will be given a second chance.'

His arms tightened round her and she looked up at him, smiling. 'We'll start all over again—being married, I mean.'

He kissed her once more. 'That idea had occurred to me too.'

* * * * *

NANNY BY CHANCE

CHAPTER ONE

ARAMINTA POMFREY, a basket of groceries over one arm, walked unhurriedly along the brick path to the back door, humming as she went. She was, after all, on holiday, and the morning was fine, the autumn haze slowly lifting to promise a pleasant September day—the first of the days ahead of doing nothing much until she took up her new job.

She paused at the door to scratch the head of the elderly, rather battered cat sitting there. An old warrior if ever there was one, with the inappropriate name of Cherub. He went in with her, following her down the short passage and into the kitchen, where she put her basket on the table, offered him milk and then, still humming, went across the narrow hall to the sitting room.

Her mother and father would be there, waiting for her to return from the village shop so that they might have coffee together. The only child of elderly parents, she had known from an early age that although they loved her dearly, her unexpected late arrival had upset their established way of life. They were clever, both authorities on ancient Celtic history, and had published books on the subject—triumphs of knowledge even if they didn't do much to boost their finances.

Not that either of them cared about that. Her father had a small private income, which allowed them to live precariously in the small house his father had left him, and they had sent Araminta to a good school, confident that she would follow in their footsteps and become a literary genius of some sort. She had done her best, but the handful of qualifications she had managed to get had been a disappointment to them, so that when she had told them that she would like to take up some form of nursing, they had agreed with relief.

There had been no question of her leaving home and training at some big hospital; her parents, their heads in Celtic clouds, had no time for household chores or cooking. The elderly woman who had coped while Araminta was at school had been given her notice and Araminta took over the housekeeping while going each day to a children's convalescent home at the other end of the village. It hadn't been quite what she had hoped for, but it had been a start.

And now, five years later, fate had smiled kindly upon her. An elderly cousin, recently widowed, was coming to run the house for her mother and father and Araminta was free to start a proper training. And about time too, she had reflected, though probably she would be considered too old to start training at twenty-three. But her luck had held; in two weeks' time she was to start as a student nurse at a London teaching hospital.

Someone was with her parents. She opened the door and took a look. Dr Jenkell, a family friend as well as their doctor for many years.

She bade him good morning and added, 'I'll fetch the coffee.' She smiled at her mother and went back to the kitchen, to return presently with a tray laden with cups and saucers, the coffeepot and a plate of biscuits.

'Dr Jenkell has some splendid news for you, Araminta,' said her mother. 'Not too much milk, dear.' She took the cup Araminta offered her and sat back, looking pleased about something.

Araminta handed out coffee and biscuits. She said, 'Oh?' in a polite voice, drank some coffee and then, since the doctor was looking at her, added, 'Is it something very exciting?'

Dr Jenkell wiped some coffee from his drooping moustache. 'I have a job for you, my dear. A splendid opportunity. Two small boys who are to go and live for a short time with their uncle in Holland while their parents are abroad. You have had a good deal of experience dealing with the young and I hear glowing accounts of you at the children's home. I was able to recommend you with complete sincerity.'

Araminta drew a steadying breath. 'I've been taken as a student nurse at St Jules'. I start in two

weeks' time.' She added, 'I told you and you gave
me a reference.'

Dr Jenkell waved a dismissive hand. 'That's easily
arranged. All you need to do is to write and say that
you are unable to start training for the time being.
A month or so makes no difference.'

'It does to me,' said Araminta. 'I'm twenty-three,
and if I don't start my training now I'll be too old.'
She refilled his coffee cup with a steady hand. 'It's
very kind of you, and I do appreciate it, but it means
a lot to me—training for something I really want
to do.'

She glanced at her mother and father and the eu-
phoria of the morning ebbed way; they so obviously
sided with Dr Jenkell.

'Of course you must take this post Dr Jenkell has
so kindly arranged for you,' said her mother. 'Indeed, you cannot refuse, for I understand that he has
already promised that you will do so. As for your
training, a few months here or there will make no
difference at all. You have all your life before you.'

'You accepted this job for me without telling me?'
asked Araminta of the doctor.

Her father spoke then. 'You were not here when
the offer was made. Your mother and I agreed that it
was a splendid opportunity for you to see something
of the world and agreed on your behalf. We acted in
your best interests, my dear.'

I'm a grown woman, thought Araminta wildly,
and I'm being treated like a child, a mid-Victorian

child at that, meekly accepting what her elders and betters have decided was best for her. Well, I won't, she reflected, looking at the three elderly faces in turn.

'I think that, if you don't mind, Dr Jenkell, I'll go and see this uncle.'

Dr Jenkell beamed at her. 'That's right, my dear—get some idea of what is expected of you. You'll find him very sympathetic to any adjustments you may have in mind.'

Araminta thought this unlikely, but she wasn't going to say so. She loved her parents and they loved her, although she suspected that they had never quite got over the surprise of her arrival in their early middle age. She wasn't going to upset them now; she would see this man, explain why she couldn't accept the job and then think of some way of telling her parents which wouldn't worry them. Dr Jenkell might be annoyed; she would think about that later.

Presently the doctor left and she collected the coffee cups and went along to the kitchen to unpack her shopping and prepare the lunch, leaving her mother and father deep in a discussion of the book of Celtic history they were writing together. They hadn't exactly forgotten her. The small matter of her future having been comfortably settled, they felt free to return to their abiding interest...

As she prepared the lunch, Araminta laid her plans. Dr Jenkell had given her the uncle's address, and unless he'd seen fit to tell the man that she in-

tended visiting him she would take him by surprise,
explain that she wasn't free to take the job and that
would be that. There was nothing like striking while
the iron was hot. It would be an easy enough journey;
Hambledon was barely three miles from Henley-on-
Thames and she could be in London in no time at
all. She would go the very next day...

Her mother, apprised of her intention, made no
objection. Indeed, she was approving. 'As long as
you leave something ready for our lunch, Araminta.
You know how impatient your father is if he has to
wait for a meal, and if I'm occupied...'

Araminta promised cold meat and a salad and
went to her room to brood over her wardrobe. It was
early autumn. Too late in the year for a summer outfit and too warm still for her good jacket and skirt.
It would have to be the jersey two-piece with the
corn silk tee shirt.

Her mother, an old-fashioned woman in many
respects, considered it ladylike, which it was. It
also did nothing for Araminta, who was a girl with
no looks worth glancing at twice. She had mousy
hair, long and fine, worn in an untidy pile on top of
her head, an unremarkable face—except for large,
thickly fringed hazel eyes—and a nicely rounded
person, largely unnoticed since her clothes had always been chosen with an eye to their suitability.

They were always in sensible colours, in fabrics
not easily spoilt by small sticky fingers which would
go to the cleaners or the washing machine time and

time again. She studied her reflection in the looking glass and sighed over her small sharp nose and
wide mouth. She had a lovely smile, but since she
had no reason to smile at her own face she was unaware of that.

Not that that mattered; this uncle would probably
be a prosey old bachelor, and, since he was a friend
of Dr Jenkell, of a similar age.

She was up early the following morning to take
tea to her parents, give Cherub his breakfast and
tidy the house, put lunch ready and then catch the
bus to Henley.

A little over two hours later she was walking
along a narrow street close to Cavendish Square. It
was very quiet, with tall Regency houses on either
side of it, their paintwork pristine, brass doorknock-
ers gleaming. Whoever uncle was, reflected Araminta, he had done well for himself.

The house she was looking for was at the end of
the terrace, with an alley beside it leading to mews
behind the houses. Delightful, reflected Araminta,
and she banged the knocker.

The man who answered the door was short and
thin with sandy hair, small dark eyes and a very
sharp nose. Just like a rat, thought Araminta, and
added, a nice rat, for he had a friendly smile and the
little eyes twinkled.

It was only then that she perceived that she should
have made an appointment; uncle was probably out
on his rounds—did doctors who lived in grand

houses have rounds? She didn't allow herself to be discouraged by the thought.

'I would like to see Dr van der Breugh. I should have made an appointment but it's really rather urgent. It concerns his two nephews...'

'Ah, yes, miss. If you would wait while I see if the doctor is free.'

He led the way down a narrow hall and opened a door. His smile was friendly. 'I won't be two ticks,' he assured her. 'Make yourself comfortable.'

The moment he had closed the door behind him, she got up from her chair and began a tour of the room. It was at the back of the house and the windows, tall and narrow, overlooked a small walled garden with the mews beyond. It was furnished with a pleasant mixture of antique cabinets, tables and two magnificent sofas on either side of an Adam fireplace. There were easy chairs, too, and a vast mirror over the fireplace. A comfortable room, even if rather grand, and obviously used, for there was a dog basket by one of the windows and a newspaper thrown down on one of the tables.

She studied her person in the mirror, something which brought her no satisfaction. The jersey two-piece, in a sensible brown, did nothing for her, and her hair had become a little ruffled. She poked at it impatiently and then looked round guiltily as the door opened.

'If you will come this way, miss,' said the rat-faced man. 'The boss has got ten minutes to spare.'

Was he the butler? she wondered, following him out of the room. If so, he wasn't very respectful. Perhaps modern butlers had freedom of speech…

They went back down the hall and he opened a door on the other side of it.

'Miss Pomfrey,' he announced, and gave her a friendly shove before shutting the door on her.

It was a fair-sized room, lined with bookshelves, one corner of it taken up by a large desk. The man sitting at it got to his feet as Araminta hesitated, staring at him. This surely couldn't be uncle. He was a giant of a man with fair hair touched with silver, a handsome man with a high-bridged nose, a thin, firm mouth and a determined chin. He took off the glasses he was wearing and smiled as he came to her and shook hands.

'Miss Pomfrey? Dr Jenkell told me that you might come and see me. No doubt you would like some details—'

'Look,' said Araminta urgently, 'before you say any more, I've come to tell you that I can't look after your nephews. I'm starting as a student nurse in two weeks' time. I didn't know about this job until Dr Jenkell told me. I'm sure he meant it kindly, and my parents thought it was a splendid idea, but they arranged it all while I wasn't there.'

The doctor pulled up a chair. 'Do sit down and tell me about it,' he invited. He had a quiet, rather slow way of speaking, and she felt soothed by it, as was intended.

'Briskett is bringing us coffee...'

Araminta forgot for the moment why she was there. She felt surprisingly comfortable with the doctor, as though she had known him for years. She said now, 'Briskett? The little man who answered the door? Is he your butler? He called you "the boss"—I mean, he doesn't talk like a butler...'

'He runs the house for me, most efficiently. His rather unusual way of talking is, I fancy, due to his addiction to American films; they represent democracy to him. Every man is an equal. Nevertheless, he is a most trustworthy and hard-working man; I've had him for years. He didn't upset you?'

'Heavens, no. I liked him. He looks like a friendly rat,' she explained. 'Beady eyes, you know, and a sharp nose. He has a lovely smile.'

Briskett came in then, with the coffee tray, which he set down on a small table near Araminta's chair. 'You be mother,' he said, and added, 'Don't you forget you've to be at the hospital, sir.'

'Thank you, Briskett, I'll be leaving very shortly.'

Asked to do so, Araminta poured their coffee. 'I'm sorry if I'm being inconvenient,' she said. 'You see, I thought if you didn't expect me it would be easier for me to explain and you wouldn't have time to argue.'

The doctor managed not to smile. He agreed gravely. 'I quite see that the whole thing is a misunderstanding and I'm sorry you have been vexed.' He added smoothly, with just a touch of regret allowed to

show, 'You would have done splendidly, I feel sure.
They are six years old, the boys, twins and a handful. I must find someone young and patient to cope
with them. Their parents—their mother is my sister—are archaeologists and are going to the Middle
East for a month or so. It seemed a good idea if the
children were to make their home with me while
they are away. I leave for Holland in a week's time,
and if I can't find someone suitable, I'm afraid their
mother will have to stay here in England. A pity, but
it can't be helped.'

'If they went to Holland with you, would they live
with you? I mean, don't you have a wife?'

'My dear Miss Pomfrey, I am a very busy man.
I've no time to look for a wife and certainly no time
to marry. I have a housekeeper and her husband, both
too elderly to cope with small boys. I intend sending them to morning school and shall spend as much
time with them as I can, but they will need someone
to look after them.'

He put down his coffee cup. 'I'm sorry you had
to come and see me, but I quite understand that you
are committed. Though I feel that we should all have
got on splendidly together.'

She was being dismissed very nicely. She got up.
'Yes, I think we would too. I'm sorry. I'll go—or
you'll be late at the hospital.'

She held out a hand and had it taken in his large,
firm clasp. To her utter surprise she heard herself

234   NANNY BY CHANCE

say, 'If I cancelled my place at the hospital, do you
suppose they'd let me apply again? It's St Jules'...'

'I have a clinic there. I have no doubt that they
would allow that. There is always a shortage of student nurses.'

'And how long would I be in Holland?'

'Oh, a month, six weeks—perhaps a little longer.
But you mustn't think of altering your plans just to
oblige me, Miss Pomfrey.'

'I'm not obliging you,' said Araminta, not beating
about the bush. 'I would like to look after the boys,
if you think I'd do.' She studied his face; he looked
grave but friendly. 'I've no idea why I've changed
my mind,' she told him, 'but I've waited so long to
start my training as a nurse, another month or two
really won't matter.' She added anxiously, 'I won't
be too old, will I? To start training...?'

'I should imagine not. How old are you?'

'Twenty-three.'

'You aren't too old,' he assured her in a kind voice,
'and if it will help you at all, I'll see if I can get you
on to the next take-in once you are back in England.'

'Now that would be kind of you. Will you let me
know when you want me and how I'm to get to Holland? I'm going now; you'll be late and Briskett will
hate me.'

He laughed then. 'Somehow I think not. I'll be
in touch.'

He went into the hall with her and Briskett was
there, too.

'Cutting it fine,' he observed severely. He opened the door for Araminta. 'Go carefully,' he begged her.

Araminta got on a bus for Oxford Street, found a café and over a cup of coffee sorted out her thoughts. That she was doing something exactly opposite to her intentions was a fact which she bypassed for the moment. She had, with a few impulsive words, re-arranged her future. A future about which she knew almost nothing, too.

Where exactly was she to go? How much would she be paid? What about free time? The language question? The doctor had mentioned none of these. Moreover, he had accepted her decision without surprise and in a casual manner which, when she thought about it, annoyed her. He should be suitably grateful that she had delayed her plans to accommodate his. She had another cup of coffee and a bun and thought about clothes.

She had a little money of her own. In theory she kept the small salary she had been getting at the convalescent home to spend as she wished, but in practice she used it to bolster up the housekeeping money her father gave her each month.

Neither he nor her mother were interested in how it was spent. The mundane things of life—gas bills, the plumber, the most economical cuts of meat— meant nothing to them; they lived in their own world of the Celts, who, to them at least, were far more important and interesting.

Now she must spend some of her savings on clothes. She wouldn't need much: a jacket, which would stand up to rain, a skirt and one or two woollies, and shoes—the sensible pair she wore to the convalescent home were shabby. No need for a new dress; she wasn't likely to go anywhere.

And her parents; someone would have to keep an eye on them if she were to go to Holland in a week's time and if Aunt Millicent, the elderly cousin, was unable to come earlier than they had arranged. Mrs Snow in the village might oblige for a few days, with basic cooking and cleaning. Really, she thought vexedly, she could make no plans until she heard from Dr van der Breugh.

Her parents received her news with mild interest. Her mother nodded her head in a knowledgeable way and observed that both she and Araminta's father knew what was best for her and she was bound to enjoy herself, as well as learn something of a foreign land, even if it was only a very small one like Holland. She added that she was sure that Araminta would arrange everything satisfactorily before she went. 'You'll like looking after the dear little boys.'

Araminta said that, yes, she expected she would. Probably they were as tiresome and grubby as all small boys, but she was fond of children and had no qualms about the job. She would have even less when she knew more about it.

A state of affairs which was put right the next morning, when she received a letter from Dr van der Breugh. It was a long letter, typed, and couched in businesslike language. She would be called for at her home on the following Sunday at eleven o'clock and would spend a few hours with her charges before travelling to Holland on the night ferry from Harwich. She would be good enough to carry a valid passport and anything she might require overnight. It was hoped that her luggage might be confined to no more than two suitcases.

She would have a day off each week, and every evening after eight o'clock, and such free time during the day as could be arranged. Her salary would be paid to her weekly in Dutch guldens… She paused here to do some arithmetic—she considered it a princely sum, which certainly sweetened the somewhat arbitrary tone of the letter. Although there was no reason why it should have been couched in friendlier terms; she scarcely knew the doctor and didn't expect to see much of him while she was in Holland.

She told her mother that the arrangements for her new job seemed quite satisfactory, persuaded Mrs Snow to undertake the housekeeping until Aunt Millicent could come, and then sifted through her wardrobe. The jersey two-piece and the corn silk blouse, an equally sober skirt and an assortment of tops and a warmer woolly or two, a short wool jacket to go over everything and a perfectly plain dress in a soft blue crêpe; an adequate choice of clothes, she considered, adding a raincoat, plain slippers and undies.

She had good shoes and a leather handbag; gloves

and stockings and a headscarf or two would fill the
odd corners in the one case she intended taking. Her
overnight bag would take the rest. She liked clothes,
but working in the children's convalescent home had
called for sensible skirts and tops in sensible colours,
and she had seldom had much of a social life. She
was uneasily aware that her clothes were dull, but
there was no time to change that, and anyway, she
hadn't much money. Perhaps she would get a new
outfit in Holland…

The week went quickly. She cleaned and polished,
washed and ironed, laid in a stock of food and got a
room ready for Aunt Millicent. And she went into
Henley and bought new shoes, low-heeled brown
leather and expensive, and when she saw a pink an-
gora sweater in a shop window she bought that too.
She was in two minds about buying a new jacket,
but caution took over then. She had already spent
more money than she'd intended. Though caution
wasn't quite strong enough to prevent her buying
a pretty silk blouse which would render the sober
skirt less sober.

On Sunday morning she was ready and waiting
by eleven o'clock—waiting with her parents who, despite their wish to get back to researching the Ancient
Celts, had come into the hall to see her off. Cherub
was there too, looking morose, and she stooped to
give him a final hug; they would miss each other.

Exactly on the hour a car drew up outside and
Briskett got out, wished them all good morning,

stowed her case in the boot and held the rear car door open for her.

'Oh, I'd rather sit in front with you,' said Araminta, and she gave her parents a final kiss before getting into the car, waved them a cheerful goodbye and sat back beside Briskett. It was a comfortable car, a Jaguar, and she could see from the moment Briskett took the wheel that despite his unlikely looks they hid the soul of a born driver.

There wasn't much traffic until they reached Henley and here Briskett took the road to Oxford.

'Aren't I to go to the London address?' asked Araminta.

'No, miss. The doctor thought it wise if you were to make the acquaintance of the boys at their home. They live with their parents at Oxford. The doctor will come for you and them later today and drive to Harwich for the night ferry.'

'Oh, well, I expect that's a good idea. Are you coming to Holland too?'

'No, miss. I'll stay to keep an eye on things here; the boss has adequate help in Holland. He's for ever to-ing and fro-ing—having two homes, as it were.'

'Then why can't the two boys stay here in England?'

'He'll be in Holland for a few weeks, popping over here when he is needed. Much in demand, he is.'

'We won't be expected to pop over, too? Very unsettling for the little boys…'

'Oh, no, miss. That's why you've been engaged;

he can come and go without being hampered, as you might say.'

The house he stopped before in Oxford was in a terrace of similar comfortably large houses, standing well back from the road. Araminta got out and stood beside Briskett in the massive porch waiting for someone to answer the bell. She was a self-contained girl, not given to sudden bursts of excitement, but she was feeling nervous now.

Supposing the boys disliked her on sight? It was possible. Or their parents might not like the look of her. After all, they knew nothing about her, and now that she came to think about it, nor did Dr van der Breugh. But she didn't allow these uncertain feelings to show; the door was opened by a girl in a pinafore, looking harassed, and she and Briskett went into the hall.

'Miss Pomfrey,' said Briskett. 'She's expected.'

The girl nodded and led them across the hall and into a large room overlooking a garden at the back of the house. It was comfortably furnished, extremely untidy, and there were four people in it. The man and woman sitting in easy chairs with the Sunday papers strewn around them got up.

The woman was young and pretty, tall and slim, and well dressed in casual clothes. She came to meet Araminta as she hesitated by the door.

'Miss Pomfrey, how nice of you to come all this way. We're so grateful. I'm Lucy Ingram, Marcus's sister—but of course you know that—and this is my husband, Jack.'

Araminta shook hands with her and then with Mr Ingram, a rather short stout man with a pleasant rugged face, while his wife spoke to Briskett, who left the room with a cheerful, 'So long, miss, I'll see you later.'

'Such a reliable man, and so devoted to Marcus,' said his sister. 'Come and meet the boys.'

They were at the other end of the room, sitting at a small table doing a jigsaw puzzle, unnaturally and suspiciously quiet. They were identical twins which, reflected Araminta, wasn't going to make things any easier, and they looked too good to be true.

'Peter and Paul,' said their mother. 'If you look carefully you'll see that Peter has a small scar over his right eye. He fell out of a tree years ago—it makes it easy to tell them apart.'

She beckoned them over and they came at once, two seemingly angelic children. Araminta wondered what kind of a bribe they had been offered to behave so beautifully. She shook their small hands in turn and smiled.

'Hello,' she said. 'You'll have to help me to tell you apart, and you mustn't mind if I muddle you up at first.'

'I'm Peter. What's your name—not Miss Pomfrey, your real name?'

'Araminta.'

The boys looked at each other. 'That's a long name.'

They cast their mother a quick look. 'We'll call you Mintie.'

'That's not very polite,' began Mrs Ingram.

'If you've no objection, I think it's a nice idea. I don't feel a bit like Miss Pomfrey…'

'Well, if you don't mind—go and have your milk, boys, while we have our coffee and then you can show Miss…Mintie your room and get to know each other a bit.'

They went away obediently, eyeing her as they went, and Araminta was led to a sofa and given coffee while she listened to Mrs Ingram's friendly chatter. From time to time her husband spoke, asking her quietly about her work at the children's home and if she had ever been to Holland before.

'The boys,' he told her forthrightly, 'can be little demons, but I dare say you are quite used to that. On the whole they're decent kids, and they dote on their uncle.'

Araminta, considering this remark, thought that probably it would be quite easy to dote on him, although, considering the terseness of his letter to her, not very rewarding. She would have liked to get to know him, but common sense told her that that was unlikely. Besides, once she was back in England again, he would be consigned to an easily forgotten past and she would have embarked on her nursing career…

She dismissed her thoughts and listened carefully to Mrs Ingram's instructions about the boys' clothing and meals.

'I'm telling you all these silly little details,' explained Mrs Ingram, 'because Marcus won't want to be bothered with them.' She looked anxious. 'I hope you won't find it too much…'

Araminta made haste to assure her that that was unlikely. 'At the children's home we had about forty children, and I'm used to them—two little boys will be delightful. They don't mind going to Holland?'

'No. I expect they'll miss us for a few days, but they've been to their uncle's home before, so they won't feel strange.'

Mrs Ingram began to ask carefully polite questions about Araminta and she answered them readily. If she had been Mrs Ingram she would have done the same, however well recommended she might be. Dr van der Breugh had engaged her on Dr Jenkell's advice, which was very trusting of him. Certainly he hadn't bothered with delving into her personal background.

They had lunch presently and she was pleased to see that the boys behaved nicely at the table and weren't finicky about their food. All the same, she wondered if these angelic manners would last. If they were normal little boys they wouldn't…

The rest of the day she spent with them, being shown their toys and taken into the garden to look at the goldfish in the small pond there, and their behaviour was almost too good to be true. There would be a reason for it, she felt sure; time enough to discover that during the new few weeks.

They answered her questions politely but she took care not to ask too many. To them she was a stranger, and she would have to earn their trust and friendship.

They went indoors presently and found Dr van der Breugh in the drawing room with their father and mother. There was no doubt that they were fond of him and that he returned the affection. Emerging from their boisterous greeting, he looked across at Araminta and bade her good afternoon.

'We shall be leaving directly after tea, Miss Pomfrey. My sister won't mind if you wish to phone your mother.'

'Thank you, I should like to do that...'

'She's not Miss Pomfrey,' said Peter. 'She's Mintie.'

'Indeed?' He looked amused. 'You have rechristened her?'

'Well, of course we have, Uncle. Miss Pomfrey isn't *her*, is it? Miss Pomfrey would be tall and thin, with a sharp nose and a wart and tell us not to get dirty. Mintie's nice; she's not pretty, but she smiles...'

Araminta had gone a bright pink and his mother said hastily, 'Hush, dear. Miss Pomfrey, come with me and I'll show you where you can phone.'

Leading Araminta across the hall, she said apologetically, 'I do apologise. Peter didn't mean to be rude—indeed, I believe he was paying you a compliment.'

Araminta laughed. 'Well, I'm glad they think of
me as Mintie, and not some tiresome woman with a
wart. I hope we're going to like each other.'

The boys had been taken upstairs to have their
hands washed and the two men were alone.

'Good of you to have the boys,' said Mr Ingram.
'Lucy was getting in a bit of a fret. And this treasure
you've found for them seems just like an answer to
a prayer. Quiet little thing and, as Peter observed,
not pretty, but a nice calm voice. I fancy she'll do.
Know much about her?'

'Almost nothing. Old Jenkell told me of her; he's
known her almost all her life. He told me that she was
entirely trustworthy, patient and kind. They loved her
at the children's home. She didn't want to come—
she was to start her training as a nurse in a week or
so—but she changed her mind after refusing the job.
I don't know why. I've said I'll help her to get into
the next batch of students when we get back.'

The doctor wandered over to the windows. 'You'll
miss your garden.' He glanced over his shoulder. 'I'll
keep an eye on the boys, Jack. As you say, I think
we have found a treasure in Miss Pomfrey. A nice,
unassuming girl who won't intrude. Which suits me
very well.'

Tea was a proper meal, taken at the table since
the boys ate with them, but no time was wasted on
it. Farewells were said, the boys were settled by their
uncle in the back seat of his Bentley, and Araminta
got into the front of the car, composed and very neat.

The doctor, turning to ask her if she was comfortable, allowed himself a feeling of satisfaction. She was indeed unassuming, both in manner and appearance.

CHAPTER TWO

ARAMINTA, HAPPILY UNAWARE of the doctor's opinion of her, settled back in the comfort of the big car, but she was aware of his voice keeping up a steady flow of talk with his little nephews. He sounded cheerful, and from the occasional words she could hear he was talking about sailing. Would she be expected to take part in this sport? she wondered. She hoped not, but, being a sensible girl, she didn't allow the prospect to worry her. Whatever hazards lay ahead they would be for a mere six weeks or so. The salary was generous and she was enjoying her freedom. She felt guilty about that, although she knew that her parents would be perfectly happy with Aunt Millicent.

The doctor drove through Maidenhead and on to Slough and then, to her surprise, instead of taking the ring road to the north of London, he drove to his house.

Araminta, who hadn't seen Briskett leave the Ingrams', was surprised to see him open the door to them.

'Right on time,' he observed. 'Not been travelling

over the limit, I hope, sir. You lads wait there while I see to Miss Pomfrey. There's a couple of phone calls for you, Doc.'

He led Araminta to the cloakroom at the back of the hall. 'You tidy yourself, miss; I'll see to the boys. There's coffee ready in the drawing room.'

Araminta, not in the least untidy, nonetheless did as she was bid. Briskett, for all his free and easy ways, was a gem. He would be a handy man in a crisis.

When she went back into the hall he was there, waiting to usher her into the drawing room. The doctor was already there, leaning over a sofa table with the boys, studying a map. He straightened up as she went in and offered her a chair and asked her to pour their coffee. There was milk for the boys as well as a plate of biscuits and a dish of sausage rolls, which Peter and Paul demolished.

They were excited now, their sadness at leaving their mother and father already fading before the prospect of going to bed on board the ferry. Presently the doctor excused himself with the plea that there were phone calls he must make and Araminta set to work to calm them down, something at which she was adept. By the time their uncle came back they were sitting quietly beside her, listening to her telling them a story.

He paused in the doorway. 'I think it might be a good idea if you sat in the back with the boys in the car, Miss Pomfrey...'

'Mintie,' said Peter. 'Uncle Marcus, she's Mintie.'

'Mintie,' said the doctor gravely. 'If Miss Pomfrey does not object?'

'Not a bit,' said Araminta cheerfully.

They left shortly after that, crossing London in the comparative calm of a Sunday evening, onto the A12, through Brentford, Chelmsford, Colchester and finally to Harwich. Long before they had reached the port the two boys were asleep, curled up against Araminta. She sat, rather warm and cramped, with an arm around each of them, watching the doctor driving. He was a good driver.

She reflected that he would be an interesting man to know. It was a pity that the opportunity to do that was improbable. She wondered why he wasn't married and allowed her imagination to roam. A widower? A love affair which had gone wrong and left him with a broken heart and dedicated to his work? Engaged? The last was the most likely. She had a sudden urge to find out.

They were amongst the last to go on board, and the doctor with one small sleeping boy and a porter with the other led the way to their cabins.

Araminta was to share a cabin with the boys; it was roomy and comfortable and well furnished, with a shower room, and once her overnight bag and the boys' luggage had been brought to her she lost no time in undressing them and popping them into their narrow beds. They roused a little, but once tucked up slept again. She unpacked her night things and won-

dered what she should do. Would the doctor mind if
she rang for a pot of tea and a sandwich? It was almost midnight and she was hungry.

A tap on the door sent her to open it and find
him outside.

'A stewardess will keep an eye on the boys. Come
and have a meal; it will give me the opportunity to
outline your day's work.'

She was only too glad to agree to that; she went
with him to the restaurant and made a splendid supper while she listened to him quietly describing the
days ahead.

'I live in Utrecht. The house is in the centre of the
city, but there are several parks close by and I have
arranged for the boys to attend school in the mornings. You will be free then, but I must ask you to be
with them during the rest of the day. You will know
best how to keep them happy and entertained.

'I have a housekeeper and a houseman who will
do all they can to make life easy for you and them.
When I am free I will have the boys with me. I am
sure that you will want to do some sightseeing. I expect my sister has told you her wishes concerning
their clothes and daily routine. I must warn you that
they are as naughty as the average small boy...they
are also devoted to each other.'

Araminta speared a morsel of grilled sole. 'I'll do
the best I can to keep them happy and content, Dr
van der Breugh. And I shall come to you if I have any

problems. You will be away during the day? Working? Will I know where you are?'

'Yes, I will always leave a phone number for you or a message with Bas. He speaks English of a sort, and is very efficient.' He smiled at her kindly. 'I'm sure everything will be most satisfactory, Miss Pomfrey. And now I expect you would like to go to your bed. You will be called in good time in the morning. We will see how the boys are then. If they're too excited to eat breakfast we will stop on the way and have something, but there should be time for a meal before we go ashore. You can manage them and have them up and ready?'

Araminta assured him that she could. Several years in the convalescent home had made her quite sure about that. She thanked him for her dinner, wished him goodnight, and was surprised when he went back to her cabin with her and saw her into it.

Nice manners, thought Araminta, getting undressed as fast as she could, having a quick shower and jumping into her bed after a last look at the boys—deeply asleep.

The boys woke when the stewardess brought morning tea. They drank the milk in the milk jug and ate all the biscuits. Talking non-stop, they washed and cleaned their teeth and dressed after a fashion. Araminta was tying shoelaces and inspecting fingernails when there was a knock on the door and the doctor came in.

'If anyone is hungry there's plenty of time for

breakfast,' he observed. He looked at Araminta. 'You all slept well?'

'Like logs,' she told him, 'and we're quite ready, with everything packed.'

'Splendid. Come along, then.' He sounded briskly cheerful and she wondered if he found this disruption in his ordered life irksome. If he did, he didn't allow it to show. Breakfast was a cheerful meal, eaten without waste of time since they were nearing the Hoek of Holland and the boys wanted to see the ferry dock.

Disembarking took time, but finally they were away from the customs shed, threading their way through the town.

'We'll go straight home,' said the doctor. He had the two boys with him again and spoke to Araminta over his shoulder. 'Less than an hour's drive.' He picked up the car phone and spoke into it. 'I've told them we are on our way.'

There was a great deal of traffic as they neared Rotterdam, where they drove through the long tunnel under the Maas. Once through it, the traffic was even heavier. But presently, as they reached the outskirts of the city and were once more on the motorway, it thinned, and Araminta was able to look about her.

The country was flat, and she had expected that, but it was charming all the same, with farms well away from the highway, small copses of trees already turning to autumn tints, green meadows separated by narrow canals, and cows and horses roaming freely. The motorway bypassed the villages and towns, but she caught tantalising glimpses of them from time to time and promised herself that if she should get any free time, she would explore away from the main roads.

As though he had read her thoughts, the doctor said over his shoulder, 'This is dull, isn't it? But it's the quickest way home. Before you go back we must try and show you some of rural Holland. I think you might like it.'

She murmured her thanks. 'It's a very good road,' she said politely, anxious not to sound disparaging.

'All the motorways are good. Away from them it's a different matter. But you will see for yourself.'

Presently he turned off into a narrow country road between water meadows. 'We're going to drive along the River Vecht. It is the long way round to Utrecht, but well worth it. It will give you a taste of rural Holland.'

He drove north, away from Utrecht, and then turned into another country road running beside a river lined with lovely old houses set in well-kept grounds.

'The East Indies merchants built their houses here—there's rather a splendid castle you'll see presently on your right. There are a number in Utrecht province—most of them privately owned. You must find time to visit one of those open to the public before you go back to England.'

Apparently satisfied that he had given her enough to go on with, he began a lively conversation with the boys, leaving her to study her surroundings. They were certainly charming, but she had the feeling that he had offered the information in much the same manner as a dutiful and well mannered host would offer a drink to an unexpected and tiresome guest.

They were on the outskirts of Utrecht by now, and soon at its heart. Some magnificent buildings, she conceded, and a bewildering number of canals. She glimpsed several streets of shops, squares lined by tall, narrow houses with gabled roofs and brief views of what she supposed were parks.

The boys were talking now, nineteen to the dozen, and in Dutch. Well, of course, they would, reflected Araminta. They had a Dutch mother and uncle. They were both talking at once, interrupted from time to time by the doctor's measured tones, but presently Paul shouted over his shoulder, 'We're here, Mintie. Do look, isn't it splendid?'

She looked. They were in a narrow *gracht*, tree-lined, with houses on either side of the canal in all shapes and sizes: some of them crooked with age, all with a variety of gabled roofs. The car had stopped at the end of the *gracht* before a narrow red-brick house with double steps leading up to its solid door. She craned her neck to see its height—four storeys, each with three windows. The ground floor ones were large, but they got progressively smaller at each storey so that the top ones of all were tucked in between the curve of the gable.

The doctor got out, went around to allow the boys

to join him and then opened her door. He said kindly,
'I hope you haven't found the journey too tiring?'

Araminta said, 'Not in the least,' and felt as elderly as his glance indicated. Probably she looked
twice her age; her toilet on board had been sketchy...

The boys had run up the steps, talking excitedly
to the man who had opened the door, and the doctor,
gently urging her up the steps said, 'This is Bas, who
runs my home with his wife. As I said, he speaks
English, and will do all he can to help you.'

She offered a hand and smiled at the elderly lined
face with its thatch of grey hair. Bas shook hands and
said gravely, 'We welcome you, miss, and shall do
our best to make you happy.'

Which was nice, she thought, and wished that the
doctor had said something like that.

What he did say was rather absent-minded. 'Yes,
yes, Miss Pomfrey. Make yourself at home and ask
Bas for anything you may need.'

Which she supposed was the next best thing to
a welcome.

The hall they entered was long and narrow, with
a great many doors on either side of it, and halfway
along it there was a staircase, curving upwards between the panelled walls. As they reached a pair
of magnificent mahogany doors someone came to
meet them from the back of the house. It was a short,
stout woman in a black dress and wearing a printed
pinny over it. She had a round rosy face and grey hair

screwed into a bun. Her eyes were very dark and as she reached them she gave Araminta a quick look.

'Jet…' Dr van der Breugh sounded pleased to see her and indeed kissed her cheek and spoke at some length in his own language. His housekeeper smiled then, shook Araminta's hand and bent to hug the boys, talking all the time.

The doctor said in English, 'Go with Jet to the kitchen, both of you, and have milk and biscuits. Miss Pomfrey shall fetch you as soon as she has had a cup of coffee.'

Bas opened the doors and Araminta, invited to enter the room, did so. It was large and lofty, with two windows overlooking the *gracht*, a massive fireplace along one wall and glass doors opening into a room beyond. It was furnished with two vast sofas on either side of the fireplace and a number of comfortable chairs. There was a Pembroke table between the windows and a rosewood sofa table on which a china bowl of late roses glowed.

A walnut and marquetry display cabinet took up most of the wall beside the fireplace on one side, and on the other there was a black and gold laquer cabinet on a gilt stand. Above it was a great *stoel* clock, its quiet tick-tock somehow enhancing the peace of the room. And the furnishings were restful: dull mulberry-red and dark green, the heavy curtains at the windows matching the upholstery of the sofas and chairs. The floor was highly polished oak with Kasham silk rugs, faded with age, scattered on it.

A magnificent room, reflected Araminta, and if it had been anyone other than the doctor she would have said so. She held her tongue, however, sensing that he would give her a polite and chilly stare at her unasked-for praise.

He said, 'Do sit down, Miss Pomfrey. Jet shall take you to your room when you have had coffee and then perhaps you would see to the boys' things and arrange some kind of schedule for their day? We could discuss that later today.'

Bas brought the coffee then, and she poured it for them both and sat drinking it silently as the doctor excused himself while he glanced through the piles of letters laid beside his chair, his spectacles on his handsome nose, oblivious of her presence.

He had indeed forgotten her for the moment, but presently he looked up and said briskly, 'I expect you would like to go to your room. Take the boys with you, will you? I shall be out to lunch and I suggest that you take the boys for a walk this afternoon. They know where the park is and Bas will tell you anything you may wish to know.'

He went to open the door for her and she went past him into the hall. She would have liked a second cup of coffee...

Bas was waiting for her and took her to the kitchen, a semi-basement room at the back of the house. It was nice to be greeted by cheerful shouts from the boys and Jet's kind smile and the offer of another cup of coffee. She sat down at the old-fash-

ioned scrubbed table while Bas told her that he would
serve their lunch at midday and that when they came
back from their walk he would have an English afternoon tea waiting for her.

His kind old face crinkled into a smile as he told
her, 'And if you should wish to telephone your family, you are to do so—*mijnheer's* orders.'

'Oh, may I? I'll do that now, before I go to my
room...'

Her mother answered the phone, expressed relief that Araminta had arrived safely and observed
that there were some interesting burial mounds in
the north of Holland if she should have the opportunity to see them. 'And enjoy yourself, dear,' said
her parent.

Araminta, not sure whether it was the burial
mounds or her job which was to give her enjoyment,
assured her mother that she would do so and went in
search of the boys.

Led upstairs by Jet, with the boys running ahead,
she found herself in a charming room on the second floor. It overlooked the street below and was
charmingly furnished, with a narrow canopied bed,
a dressing table under its window and two small
easy chairs flanking a small round table. The colour
scheme was a mixture of pastel colours and the furniture was of some pale wood she didn't recognise.
There was a large cupboard and a little door led to a
bathroom. The house might be old, she thought, but

the plumbing was ultra-modern. It had everything one could wish for...

The boys' room was across the narrow passage, with another bathroom, and at the end of the passage was a room which she supposed had been a nursery, for it had a low table and small chairs round it and shelves full of toys.

She was right. The boys, both talking at once, eager to show her everything, told her that some of the toys had belonged to their uncle and his father; even his grandfather.

'We have to be careful of them,' said Paul, 'but Uncle Marcus lets us play with them when we're here.'

'Do you come here often?' asked Araminta.

'Every year with Mummy and Daddy.'

Bas came to tell them that lunch was ready, so they all trooped downstairs and, since breakfast seemed a long time ago, made an excellent meal.

The boys were still excited, and Araminta judged it a good idea to take them for the walk. She could unpack later, when they had tired themselves out.

Advised by Bas and urged on by them, she got her own jacket, buttoned them into light jackets and went out into the street. The park was five minutes' walk away, small and beautifully kept, a green haven in the centre of the city. There was a small pond, with goldfish and seats under the trees, but the boys had no intention of sitting down. When they had tired of the goldfish they insisted on showing her some of the surrounding streets.

'And we'll go to the Dom Tower,' they assured her. 'It's ever so high, and the Domkerk—that's a cathedral—and perhaps Uncle will take us to the university.'

They were all quite tired by the time they got back to the house, and Araminta was glad of the tea Bas brought to them in a small room behind the drawing room.

'*Mijnheer* will be home very shortly,' he told her, 'and will be free to have the boys with him for a while whilst you unpack. They are to have their supper at half past six.'

Which reminded her that she should have some kind of plan ready for him to approve that evening.

'It's all go,' said Araminta crossly, alone for a few moments while the boys were in the kitchen, admiring Miep—the kitchen cat—and her kittens.

She had gone to the window to look out onto the narrow garden behind the house. It was a pretty place, with narrow brick paths and small flower-beds and a high brick wall surrounding it.

'I trust you do not find the job too tiresome for you?' asked the doctor gently.

She spun round. He was standing quite close to her, looking amused.

She said tartly, 'I was talking to myself, doctor, unaware that anyone was listening. And I do not find the boys tiresome but it has been a long day.'

'Indeed it has.' He didn't offer sympathy, merely

agreed with her in a civil voice which still held the thread of amusement.

He glanced at his watch. 'I dare say you wish to unpack for the boys and yourself. I'll have them with me until half past six.'

He gave her a little nod and held the door open for her.

In her room, she put away her clothes, reflecting that she must remember not to voice her thoughts out loud. He could have been nasty about it—he could also have offered a modicum of sympathy...

She still wasn't sure why she had accepted this job. True, she was to be paid a generous salary, and she supposed that she had felt sorry for him.

Upon reflection she thought that being sorry for him was a waste of time; it was apparent that he lived in some comfort, surrounded by people devoted to him. She supposed, too, that he was a busy man, although she had no idea what he did. A GP, perhaps? But his lifestyle was a bit grand for that. A consultant in one of the hospitals? Or one of those unseen men who specialised in obscure illnesses? She would find out.

She went to the boys' room and unpacked, put everything ready for bedtime and then got out pen and paper and wrote out the rough outline of a routine for the boys' day. Probably the doctor wouldn't approve of it, in which case he could make his own suggestions.

At half past six she went downstairs and found

the boys in the small room where they had their tea earlier. The doctor was there, too, and they were all on the floor playing a noisy game of cards. There was a dog there too, a black Labrador, sitting beside his master, watching the cards being flung down and picked up.

They all looked up as she went in and the doctor said, 'Five minutes, Miss Pomfrey.' When the dog got to its feet and came towards her, he added, 'This is Humphrey. You like dogs?'

'Yes.' She offered a fist and then stroked the great head. 'He's lovely.'

She sat down until the game came to an end, with Peter declared the winner.

'Supper?' asked Araminta mildly.

The doctor got on to his feet, towering over them. 'Come and say goodnight when you're ready for bed. Off you go, there's good fellows.'

Bas was waiting in the hall. 'Supper is to be in the day nursery on the first floor,' he explained. 'You know the way, miss.' And they all went upstairs and into the large room, so comfortably furnished with an eye to a child's comfort.

'Uncle Marcus used to have his supper here,' Paul told her, 'and he says one day, when he's got some boys of his own, they'll have their supper here, too.'

Was the doctor about to marry? Araminta wondered. He wasn't all that young—well into his thirties, she supposed. It was high time he settled down.

It would be a pity to waste this lovely old house and this cosy nursery...

Bas came in with a tray followed by a strapping girl with a round face and fair hair who grinned at them and set the table. Supper was quickly eaten, milk was drunk and Araminta whisked the boys upstairs, for they were tired now and suddenly a little unhappy.

'Are Mummy and Daddy going a long way away?' asked Peter as she bathed them.

'Well, it would be a long way if you had to walk there,' said Araminta, 'but in an aeroplane it takes no time at all to get there and get back again. Shall we buy postcards tomorrow and write to them?'

She talked cheerfully as she popped them into their pyjamas and dressing gowns and they all went back downstairs, this time to the drawing room, where their uncle was sitting with a pile of papers on the table beside him.

He hugged them, teased them gently, told them he would see them at breakfast in the morning and bade them goodnight. As they went, he reminded Araminta that dinner would be in half an hour.

The boys were asleep within minutes. Araminta had a quick shower and got into another skirt and a pretty blouse, spent the shortest possible time over her face and hair and nipped downstairs again with a few minutes to spare. She suspected that the doctor was a man who invited punctuality.

He was in the drawing room still, but he got up as

she went in, offered her a glass of sherry, enquired if
the boys were asleep and made small talk until Bas
came to tell them that dinner was ready.

Araminta was hungry and Jet was a splendid
cook. She made her way through mushrooms in a
garlic and cream sauce, roast guinea fowl, and apple
tart with whipped cream. Mindful of good manners,
she sustained a polite conversation the while.

The doctor, making suitable replies to her pains-
taking efforts allowed his thoughts to wander.

After this evening he would feel free to spend
his evenings with friends or at the hospital; breakfast wasn't a problem, for the boys would be there,
and he was almost always out for lunch. Miss Pomfrey was a nice enough girl, but there was nothing
about her to arouse his interest. He had no doubt that
she would be excellent with the boys, and she was a
sensible girl who would know how to amuse herself
on her days off.

Dinner over, he suggested that they had their coffee in the drawing room.

'If you don't mind,' said Araminta, 'I'd like to
go to bed. I've written down the outlines of a day's
schedule, if you would look at it and let me know
in the morning if it suits you. Do we have breakfast
with you or on our own?'

'With me. At half past seven, since I leave for the
hospital soon after eight o'clock.'

Araminta nodded. 'Oh, I wondered where you
worked,' she observed, and wished him goodnight.

   The doctor, politely opening the door for her, had
the distinct feeling that he had been dismissed.

   He could find no fault with her schedule for the
boys. He could see that if she intended to carry it out
to the letter she would be tired by the end of the day,
but that, he felt, was no concern of his. She would
have an hour or so each morning while the boys were
at school and he would tell her that she could have
her day off during the week as long as it didn't interfere with his work.

   He went back to his chair and began to read the
patients' notes that he had brought with him from
the hospital. There was a good deal of work waiting
for him both at Utrecht and Leiden. He was an ac-
knowledged authority on endocrinology, and there
were a number of patients about which he was to be
consulted. He didn't give Araminta another thought.

   Araminta took her time getting ready for bed.
She took a leisurely bath, and spent time search-
ing for lines and wrinkles in her face; someone had
told her that once one had turned twenty, one's skin
would start to age. But since she had a clear skin,
as soft as a peach, she found nothing to worry her.
She got into bed, glanced at the book and magazines someone had thoughtfully put on her bedside
table and decided that instead of reading she would
lie quietly and sort out her thoughts. She was asleep
within minutes.

   A small, tearful voice woke her an hour later. Paul

was standing by her bed, in tears, and a moment later Peter joined him.

Araminta jumped out of bed. 'My dears, have you had a nasty dream? Look, I'll come to your room and sit with you and you can tell me all about it. Bad dreams go away if you talk about them, you know.'

It wasn't bad dreams; they wanted their mother and father, their own home, the cat and her kittens, the goldfish… She sat down on one of the beds and settled the pair of them, one on each side of her, cuddling them close.

'Well, of course you miss them, my dears, but you'll be home again in a few weeks. Think of seeing them all again and telling them about Holland. And you've got your uncle…'

'And you, Mintie, you won't go away?'

'Gracious me, no. I'm in a foreign country, aren't I? Where would I go? I'm depending on both of you to take me round Utrecht so that I can tell everyone at home all about it.'

'Have you got little boys?' asked Peter.

'No, love, just a mother and father and a few aunts and uncles. I haven't any brothers and sisters, you see.'

Paul said in a watery voice, 'Shall we be your brothers? Just while you're living with us?'

'Oh, yes, please. What a lovely idea…'

'I heard voices,' said the doctor from the doorway. 'Bad dreams?'

Peter piped up, 'We woke up and we wanted to

go home, but Mintie has explained so it's all right, Uncle, because she'll be here with you, and she says we can be her little brothers. She hasn't got a brother or a sister.'

The doctor came into the room and sat down on the other bed. 'What a splendid idea. We must think of so many things to do that we shan't have enough days in which to do them.'

He began a soothing monologue, encompassing a visit to some old friends in Friesland, another to the lakes north of Utrecht, where he had a yacht, and a shopping expedition so that they might buy presents to take home...

The boys listened, happy once more and getting sleepy. Araminta listened too, quite forgetting that she was barefoot, somewhere scantily clad in her nightie and that her hair hung round her shoulders and tumbled untidily down her back.

The doctor had given her an all-seeing look and hadn't looked again. He was a kind man, and he knew that the prim Miss Pomfrey, caught unawares in her nightie, would be upset and probably hate him just because he was there to see her looking like a normal girl. She had pretty hair, he reflected.

'Now, how about bed?' he wanted to know. 'I'm going downstairs again but I'll come up in ten minutes, so mind you're asleep by then.'

He ruffled their hair and took himself off without a word or a look for Araminta. It was only as she was tucking the boys up once more that she realised that she hadn't stopped to put on her dressing gown. She kissed the boys goodnight and went away to swathe herself in that garment now, and tie her hair back with a ribbon. She would have to see that man again, she thought vexedly, because the boys had said they wouldn't go to sleep unless she was there, but this time she would be decently covered.

He came presently, to find the boys asleep already and Araminta sitting very upright in a chair by the window.

'They wanted me to stay,' she told him, and he nodded carelessly, barely glancing at her. Perhaps he hadn't noticed, she thought, for he looked at her as though he hadn't really seen her. She gave a relieved sigh. Her, 'Goodnight, doctor,' was uttered in Miss Pomfrey's voice, and he wished her a quiet goodnight in return, amused at the sight of her swathed in her sensible, shapeless dressing gown. Old Jenkell had told him that she was the child of elderly and self-absorbed parents, who hadn't moved with the times. It seemed likely that they had not allowed her to move with them either.

Nonetheless, she was good with the boys, and so far had made no demands concerning herself. Give her a day or two, he reflected, and she would have settled down and become nothing but a vague figure in the background of his busy life.

His hopes were borne out in the morning; at breakfast she sat between the boys, and after the exchange of good mornings, neither she nor they tried to distract him from the perusal of his post.

Presently he said, 'Your schedule seems very satisfactory, Miss Pomfrey. I shall be home around teatime. I'll take the boys with me when I take Humphrey for his evening walk. The boys start school today. You will take them, please, and fetch them at noon each day. I dare say you will enjoy an hour or so to go shopping or sightseeing.'

'Yes, thank you,' said Araminta.

Peter said, 'Uncle, why do you call Mintie Miss Pomfrey? She's Mintie.'

'My apologies. It shall be Mintie from now on.' He smiled, and she thought how it changed his whole handsome face. 'That is, if Mintie has no objection?'

She answered the smile. 'Not in the least.'

That was the second time he had asked her that. She had the lowering feeling that she had made so little impression upon him that nothing which they had said to each other had been interesting enough to be remembered.

CHAPTER THREE

THE BOYS HAD no objection to going to school. It was five minutes' walk from the doctor's house and in a small quiet street which they reached by crossing a bridge over the canal. Araminta handed them over to one of the teachers. Submitting to their hugs, she promised that she would be there at the end of the morning, and walked back to the house, where she told Bas that she would go for a walk and look around.

She found the Domkerk easily enough, but she didn't go inside; the boys had told her that they would take her there. Instead she went into a church close by, St Pieterskerk, which was Gothic with a crypt and frescoes. By the time she had wandered around, looking her fill, it was time to fetch the boys. Tomorrow she promised herself that she would go into one of the museums and remember to have coffee somewhere...

The boys had enjoyed their morning. They told her all about it as they walked back, and then de-

manded to know what they were going to do that
afternoon.

'Well, what about buying postcards and stamps
and writing to your mother and father? If you know
the way, you can show me where the post office is.
If you show me a different bit of Utrecht each day
I'll know my way around, so that if ever I should
come again...'

'Oh, I 'spect you will, Mintie,' said Paul. 'Uncle
Marcus will invite you.'

Araminta thought this highly unlikely, but she
didn't say so. 'That would be nice,' she said cheerfully. 'Let's have lunch while you tell me some more
about school.'

The afternoon was nicely filled in by their walk
to the post office and a further exploration of the
neighbouring streets while the boys, puffed up with
self-importance, explained about the *grachten* and
the variety of gables, only too pleased to air their
knowledge. They were back in good time for tea,
and when Bas opened the door to them they were
making a considerable noise, since Araminta had at-
tempted to imitate the Dutch words they were intent
on teaching her.

A door in the hall opened and the doctor came
out. He had his spectacles on and a book in his hand
and he looked coldly annoyed.

Araminta hushed the boys. 'Oh, dear, we didn't
know you were home. If we had we would have been
as quiet as mice.'

'I am relieved to hear that, Miss Pomfrey. I hesitate to curtail your enjoyment, but I must ask you to be as quiet as possible in the house. You can, of course, let yourself go once you are in the nursery.'

She gave him a pitying look. He should marry and have a houseful of children and become human again. He was fast becoming a dry-as-dust old bachelor. She said kindly, 'We are really sorry, aren't we, boys? We'll creep around the house and be ourselves in the nursery.' She added, 'Little boys will be little boys, you know, but I dare say you've forgotten over the years.'

She gave him a sweet smile and shooed the boys ahead of her up the stairs.

'Is Uncle Marcus cross?' asked Paul.

'No, no, of course not. You heard what he said— we may make as much noise as we like in the nursery. There's a piano there, isn't there? We'll have a concert after tea…'

The boys liked the sound of that, only Peter said slowly, 'He must have been a bit cross because he called you Miss Pomfrey.'

'Oh, he just forgot, I expect. Now, let's wash hands for tea and go down to the nursery. I dare say we shall have it there if your uncle is working.'

The doctor had indeed gone back to his study, but he didn't immediately return to his reading. He was remembering Araminta's words with a feeing of annoyance. She had implied that he was elderly, or at least middle-aged. Thirty-six wasn't old, not even middle-aged, and her remark had rankled. True, he was fair enough to concede, he hadn't the lifestyle of other men of his age, and since he wasn't married he was free to spend as much time doing his work as he wished.

As a professor of endocrinology he had an enviable reputation in his profession already, and he was perfectly content with his life. He had friends and acquaintances, his sister, of whom he was fond, and his nephews; his social life was pleasant, and from time to time he thought of marriage, but he had never met a woman with whom he wanted to share the rest of his life.

Sooner or later, he supposed, he would have to settle for second best and marry; he had choice enough. A man of no conceit, he was still aware that there were several women of his acquaintance who would be only too delighted to marry him.

He read for a time and then got up and walked through the house to the kitchen, where he told Bas to put the tea things in the small sitting room. 'And please tell Miss Pomfrey and the boys that I expect them there for tea in ten minutes.'

After tea, he reflected, they would play the noisiest game he could think of!

He smiled then, amused that the tiresome girl should have annoyed him. She hadn't meant to annoy him; he was aware of that. He had seen enough of her to know that she was a kind girl, though perhaps given to uttering thoughts best kept to herself.

Araminta, rather surprised at his message, went downstairs with the boys to find him already sitting in the chair by the open window, Humphrey at his feet. He got up as they went in and said easily, 'I thought we might as well have tea together round the table. I believe Jet has been making cakes and some of those *pofferjes* which really have to be eaten from a plate, don't they?'

He drew out a chair and said pleasantly. 'Do sit down, Miss Pomfrey.'

'Mintie,' Peter reminded him.

'Mintie,' said his uncle meekly, and Araminta gave him a wide smile, relieved that he wasn't annoyed.

Tea poured and Jet's *botorkeok* cut and served, he asked, 'Well, what have you done all day? Was school all right?'

The boys were never at a loss for words, so there was little need for Araminta to say anything, merely to agree to something when appealed to. Doubtless over dinner he would question her more closely. She would be careful to be extra polite, she thought; he was a good-natured man, and his manners were beautiful, but she suspected that he expected life to be as he arranged it and wouldn't tolerate interference. She really must remember that she was merely the governess in his employ—and in a temporary capacity. She would have to remember that, too.

They played Monopoly after tea, sitting at the table after Bas had taken the tea things away. The boys were surprisingly good at it, and with a little help and a lot of hints Peter won with Paul a close second. The doctor had taken care to make mistakes and had even cheated, although Araminta had been the only one to see that. As for her, she would never, as he had mildly pointed out, be a financial wizard.

She began to tidy up while the boys said a protracted goodnight to their uncle. 'You'll come up and say goodnight again?' they begged.

When he agreed they went willingly enough to their baths, their warm milk drinks with the little sugar biscuits, and bed. Araminta, rather flushed and untidy, was tucking them in when the doctor came upstairs. He had changed for the evening and she silently admired him. Black tie suited him and his clothes had been cut by a masterly hand. The blue crêpe would be quite inadequate…

He bade the boys goodnight and then turned to her. 'I shall be out for dinner, Miss Pomfrey,' he told her with a formal politeness which she found chilling. 'Bas will look after you. Dinner will be at the usual time, otherwise do feel free to do whatever you wish.'

She suppressed an instant wish to go with him. To some grand house where there would be guests? More likely he was taking some exquisitely gowned girl to one of those restaurants where there were little pink-shaded table lamps and the menus were the size of a ground map…

And she was right, for Paul asked sleepily, 'Are you going out with a pretty lady, Uncle Marcus?'

The doctor smiled. 'Indeed I am, Paul. Tomorrow I'll tell you what we had for dinner.'

He nodded to Araminta and went away, and she waited, sitting quietly by the window, until she judged that he had left the house. Of course, there was no reason for him to stay at home to dine with her; she had been a fool to imagine that he would do so. Good manners had obliged him to do so yesterday, since it had been her first evening there, but it wasn't as if she was an interesting person to be with. Her mother had pointed out kindly and rather too frequently that she lacked wit and sparkle, and that since she wasn't a clever girl, able to converse upon interesting subjects, then she must be content to be a good listener.

Araminta had taken this advice in good part, knowing that her mother was unaware that she was trampling on her daughter's feelings. Araminta made allowances for her, though; people with brilliant brains were quite often careless of other people's feelings. And it was all quite true. She knew herself to be just what her mother had so succinctly described. And she had taught herself to be a good listener...

She might have had to dine alone, but Bas treated her as though she was an honoured guest and the food was delicious.

'I will put coffee in the drawing room, miss,' said

Bas, so she went and sat there, with Humphrey for comfort and companionship, and presently wandered about the room, looking at the portraits on its walls and the silver and china displayed in the cabinet. It was still early—too early to go to bed. She slipped upstairs to make sure that the boys were sleeping and then went back to the drawing room and leafed through the magazines on the sofa table. But she put those down after a few minutes and curled up on one of the sofas and allowed her thoughts to wander.

The day had, on the whole, gone well. The boys liked her and she liked them, the house was beautiful and her room lacked nothing in the way of comfort. Bas and Jet were kindness itself, and Utrecht was undoubtedly a most interesting city. There was one niggling doubt: despite his concern for her comfort and civil manner towards her, she had the uneasy feeling that the doctor didn't like her. And, of course, she had made it worse, answering him back. She must keep a civil tongue in her head and remember that she was there to look after the boys. He was paying her for that, wasn't he?

'And don't forget that, my girl,' said Araminta in a voice loud enough to rouse Humphrey from his snooze.

She went off to bed then, after going to the kitchen to wish Bas and Jet goodnight, suddenly anxious not to be downstairs when the doctor came home.

He wasn't at breakfast the next morning; Bas told them that he had gone early to Amsterdam but hoped to be back in the late afternoon. The boys were disappointed and so, to her surprise, was Araminta.

He was home when they got back from their afternoon walk. The day had gone well and the boys were bursting to tell him about it, so Araminta took their caps and coats from them in the hall, made sure that they had wiped their shoes, washed their hands and combed their hair, and told them to go and find their uncle.

'You'll come, too? It's almost time for tea, Mintie.' Paul sounded anxious.

'I'll come presently, love. I'll take everything upstairs first.'

She didn't hurry downstairs. There was still ten minutes or so before Bas would take in the tea tray. She would go then, stay while the boys had their tea and then leave them with their uncle if he wished. In that way she would need only to hold the briefest of conversations with him. The thought of dining with him later bothered her, so she began to list some suitable subjects about which she could talk…

She arrived in the drawing room as Bas came with the tea things, and the doctor's casual, 'Good afternoon, Miss Pomfrey. You have had a most interesting walk, so the boys tell me,' was the cue for her to enlarge upon that. But after a moment or so she realised that she was boring him.

'The boys will have told you all this already,' she observed in her matter-of-fact way. She gave the boys their milk and handed him a cup of tea. 'I hope you had a good day yourself, doctor?'

He looked surprised. 'Yes—yes, I did. I'll keep the boys with me until their bedtime, if you would fetch them at half past six?'

There was really no need to worry about conversation; the boys had a great deal to say to their uncle, often lapsing into Dutch, and once tea was finished, she slipped away with a quiet, 'I'll be back presently.'

She put everything ready for the boys' bedtime and then went quietly downstairs and out of the kitchen door into the garden. Jet, busy preparing dinner, smiled and nodded as she crossed the kitchen, and Araminta smiled and nodded back. There was really no need to talk, she reflected, they understood each other very well—moreover, they liked each other.

The garden was beautifully kept, full of sweet-smelling shrubs and flowers, and at its end there was a wooden seat against a brick wall, almost hidden by climbing plants. The leaves were already turning and the last of the evening sun was turning them to bronze. It was very quiet, and she sat idly, a small, lonely figure.

The doctor, looking up from the jigsaw puzzle he was working on with the boys, glanced idly out of the window and saw her sitting there. At that distance she appeared forlorn, and he wondered if she

was unhappy and then dismissed the idea. Miss Pomfrey was a sensible, matter-of-fact girl with rather too
sharp a tongue at times; she had her future nicely
mapped out, and no doubt, in due course, she would
make a success of her profession.

He doubted if she would marry, for she made no
attempt to make herself attractive; her clothes were
good, but dowdy, and her hairstyle by no means flattering. She had pretty hair too, he remembered, and
there was a great deal of it. Sitting there last night
in her cotton nightie she had been Mintie, and not
Miss Pomfrey, but she wouldn't thank him for reminding her of that.

The boys took his attention again and he forget
her.

The boys in bed, Araminta went to her room and
got into the blue crêpe. A nicely judged ten minutes
before dinner would be served, she went downstairs.
She could see Bas putting the finishing touches to
the table through the half-open dining room door
as she opened the door into the drawing room. The
few minutes before he announced dinner could be
nicely filled with a few remarks about the boys and
their day…

The doctor wasn't alone. The woman sitting opposite him was beautiful—quite the most beautiful Araminta had ever seen; she had golden hair, a
straight nose, a curving mouth and large eyes. Araminta had no doubt that they were blue. She was
wearing a silk trouser suit—black—and gold jew-

ellery, and she was laughing at something the doctor had said.

Araminta took a step backwards. 'So sorry, I
didn't know that you had a guest...'

The doctor got to his feet. 'Ah, Miss Pomfrey,
don't go. Come and meet Mevrouw Lutyns.' And, as
she crossed the room, 'Christina, this is Miss Pomfrey, who is in charge of the boys while Lucy and
Jack are away.'

Mevrouw Lutyns smiled charmingly, shook
hands and Araminta felt her regarding her with cold
blue eyes. 'Ah, yes, the nanny. I hope you will find
Utrecht interesting during your short stay here.'

Her English was almost perfect, but then she herself was almost perfect, reflected Araminta, at least
to look at.

'I'm sure I shall, *Mevrouw*.' She looked at the doctor, gave a little nod and the smallest of smiles and
went to the door.

'Don't go, Miss Pomfrey, you must have a drink...
I shall be out this evening, by the way, but I'll leave
you in Bas's good hands.'

'I came down to tell you that the boys were in
bed, Doctor. I'll not stay for a drink, thank you.'
She wished them good evening and a pleasant time,
seething quietly.

She closed the door equally quietly, but not before she heard Mevrouw Lutyns' voice, pitched in
a penetrating whisper. 'What a little dowd, Marcus.
Wherever did you find her?'

She stood in the hall, trembling with rage. It was
a pity she didn't understand the doctor's reply.

'That is an unkind remark, Christina. Miss Pomfrey is a charming girl and the boys are devoted to
her already. Her appearance is of no consequence; I
find her invaluable.'

They were speaking Dutch now, and Mevrouw
Lutyns said prettily, 'Oh, my dear, I had no intention
of being unkind. I'm sure she's a treasure.'

They left the house presently and dined at one of
Utrecht's fine restaurants, and from time to time,
much against his intention, the doctor found himself
thinking about Araminta, eating her solitary dinner
in the blue dress which he realised she had put on
expecting to dine with him.

He drove his companion back later that evening,
to her flat in one of the modern blocks away from
the centre of the city. He refused her offer of a drink
with the excuse that he had to go to the hospital to
check on a patient, and, when she suggested that they
might spend another evening together, told her that
he had a number of other consultations, not only in
Utrecht, and he didn't expect to be free.

An answer which didn't please her at all.

It was almost midnight as he let himself into his
house. It was very quiet in the dimly lit hall but
Humphrey was there, patiently waiting for his evening walk, and the doctor went out again, to walk
briskly through the quiet streets with his dog. It was
a fine night, but chilly, and when they got back home

he took Humphrey to the kitchen, settled him in his basket and poured himself a mug of coffee from the pot keeping hot on the Aga. Presently he took himself off to bed.

The evening, he reflected, had been a waste of time. He had known Christina for some years but had thought of her as an amusing and intelligent friend; to fall in love with her had never entered his head. He supposed, as he had done from time to time, that he *would* marry, but neither she nor the other women of his acquaintance succeeded in capturing his affection. His work meant a great deal to him, and he was wealthy, and served by people he trusted and regarded as friends. He sometimes wondered if he would ever meet a woman he would love to the exclusion of everything else.

He was already at breakfast when Araminta and the two boys joined him the next day. Peter and Paul rushed to him, both talking at once, intent on reminding him that he had promised to take them out for the day at the weekend. He assured them that he hadn't forgotten and wished Araminta good morning in a friendly voice, hoping that she had forgotten the awkwardness of the previous evening.

She replied with her usual composure, settled the boys to their breakfast and poured herself a cup of coffee. She had spent a good deal of the night reminding herself that she was the boys' nanny, just as the hateful Mevrouw Lutyns had said. It had been silly to suppose that he would wish to spend what little spare time he had with her when he had friends of his own.

Probably he was in love with the woman, and Araminta couldn't blame him for that for she was so exactly right for him—all that golden hair and a lovely face, not to mention the clothes. If Mevrouw Lutyns had considered her a dowd in the blue crêpe, what on earth would she think of her in her sensible blouse and skirt? But the doctor wouldn't think of Araminta; he barely glanced at her and she didn't blame him for that.

She replied now to his civil remark about the weather and buttered a roll. She really must remember her place; she wasn't in Hambledon now, the daughter of highly respected parents, famous for their obscure Celtic learning...

The doctor took off his spectacles and looked at her. There was no sign of pique or hurt feelings, he was relieved to observe. He said pleasantly, 'I shall be taking the boys to Leiden for the day tomorrow. I'm sure you will be glad to have a day to yourself in which to explore. I have a ground map of Utrecht somewhere; I'll let you have it. There is a great deal to see and there are some good shops.'

When she thanked him, he added, 'If you should wish to stay out in the evening, Bas will let you have a key.'

She thanked him again and wondered if that was a polite hint not to return to the house until bedtime.

'What about the boys? Putting them to bed...?'

He said casually, 'Oh, Jet will see to that,' then added, 'I shall be away for most of Sunday, but I'm sure you can cope.'

'Yes, of course. I'm sure the boys will think up something exciting to do.'

The days were falling into a pattern, she reflected: school in the morning, long walks in the afternoon, shopping expeditions for postcards, books or another puzzle, and an hour to herself in the evening when the boys were with their uncle.

She no longer expected the doctor to dine with her in the evening.

All the same, for pride's sake, she got into the blue crêpe and ate her dinner that evening with every appearance of enjoyment. She was living in the lap of comfort, she reminded herself, going back to the drawing room to sit and read the English papers Bas had thoughtfully provided for her until she could go to bed once the long case clock in the hall chimed ten o'clock.

She took a long time getting ready for bed, refusing to admit how lonely she was. Later she heard quiet footsteps in the hall and a door close. The doctor was home.

The doctor and the boys left soon after breakfast on Saturday. Araminta, standing in the hall to bid them goodbye, was hugged fiercely by Peter and Paul.

'You will be here when we get back?' asked Peter.

'Couldn't you come with us now?' Paul added

urgently, and turned to his uncle, waiting patiently to usher them into the car. 'You'd like her to come, wouldn't you, Uncle?'

'Miss Pomfrey—' at a look from Peter he changed it. 'Mintie is only here for a few weeks and she wants to see as much of Utrecht as possible. This is the first chance she's had to go exploring and shopping. Women like to look at shops, you know.'

'I'll have a good look round,' promised Araminta, 'and when we go out tomorrow perhaps you can show me some of the places I won't have seen.'

She bent to kiss them and waited at the door as they got into the car, with Humphrey stretched out between them. She didn't look at the doctor.

Bas shut the door as soon as the car had gone. 'You will be in to lunch, miss?' he wanted to know. 'At any time to suit you.'

'Thank you, Bas, but I think I'll get something while I'm out; there's such a lot to see. Are you sure Jet can manage with the boys at bedtime?'

'Oh, yes, miss. The doctor has arranged that he will be out this evening...' He paused and looked awkward.

'So she won't need to cook dinner—just something for the boys.'

He looked relieved. 'I was given to understand that you would be out this evening, miss. I am to give you a key, although I will, of course, remain up until you are back.'

'How kind of you, Bas. I'll take a key, of course,

but I expect I shall be back by ten o'clock. When I come in I'll leave the key on the hall table, shall I? Then you'll know that I'm in the house.'

'Thank you, miss. You will have coffee before you go out?'

'Please, Bas, if it's not too much trouble.'

She left the house a little later and began a conscientious exploration of the city. The boys would want to know what she had seen and where she had been... She had been to the Domkerk with them, now she went to the Dom Tower and then through the cloister passage to the University Chapter Hall. The Central Museum was next on her list—costumes, jewellery, some paintings and beautiful furniture. By now it was well after noon, so she looked for a small café and lingered over a *kaas broodje*. She would have liked more but she had no idea when she would be paid and she hadn't a great deal of money.

The day, which had begun with sunshine and gentle wind, had become overcast, and the wind was no longer gentle. She was glad of her jacket over the jersey two-piece as she made her way to the shopping centre. The shops were fine, filled with beautiful things: clothes, of course, and shoes, but as well as these splendid furniture, porcelain, silver and glass... There were bookshops, too, and she spent a long time wandering round them, wishing she could buy some of their contents. It surprised her to find so many English books on sale, and to find a shop selling

Burberrys and Harris Tweed. It would be no hard-
ship to live here, she reflected, and took herself off
to find the *hofjes* and patrician houses, to stand and
admire their age-old beauty.

She found another small coffee shop where she
had tea and a cake while she pondered what to do
with her evening. She thought she might go back
around nine o'clock. By then the boys would be in
bed and asleep, and if the doctor was out, Bas and Jet
would be in kitchen. A cinema seemed the answer.
It would mean that she couldn't afford a meal, but
she could buy a sandwich and a cup of coffee before
she went back to the house.

There were several cinemas; she chose one in a
square in the centre of the city, paid out most of
her remaining guldens and sat through an American
film. Since she was a little tired by now, she dozed
off and woke to see that it was over and that the advertisements were on. After that the lights went up
and everyone went out into the street.

It was almost dark now, but it was still barely eight
o'clock. She went into a crowded café and had a cup
of coffee, then decided that she had better save what
guldens she had left. There was a small tin of biscuits by her bed; she could eat those. She couldn't sit
for ever over one cup of coffee, though, so she went
into the street and started her walk back to the house.

She was crossing the square when she saw the

little stall at one corner. *Pommes Frites* was painted across its wooden front.

'Chips,' said Araminta, her mouth watering. 'But why do they have to say so in French when we're in Holland?' She went over to the corner and in exchange for two gulden was handed a little paper cornet filled with crisp golden chips. She bit into one; it was warm and crunchy and delicious...

Dr van der Breugh, on his way to dine with old friends, halting at traffic lights, glanced around him. Being a Saturday evening there were plenty of people about; the cafés and restaurants were doing a good trade and the various stalls had plenty of customers.

He saw Araminta as the light changed, and he had to drive on, but instead of going straight ahead, as he should have done, he turned back towards the square and stopped the car a few feet from her.

She hadn't seen him; he watched her bite into a chip with the eager delight of a child and then choke on it when she looked up and saw him. He was astonished at his feelings of outrage at the sight of her. Outrage at his own behaviour. He should have taken her with them, or at least made some arrangement for her day. He got out of his car, his calm face showing nothing of his feelings.

As for Araminta, if the ground had obligingly opened and allowed her to fall into it, she would have been happy; as it was, she would have to do the best she could. She swallowed the last fragment of chip and said politely, 'Good evening, doctor. What delicious chips you have in Holland...'

He had no intention of wasting time talking about chips. 'Why are you here, Miss Pomfrey? Why are you not at the house, eating your dinner....' He paused, frowning. He hadn't given her a thought when he returned with the boys, hadn't asked Bas if she was back, had forgotten her.

Araminta saw the frown and made haste to explain. 'Well, you see, it's like this. Bas thought that I would be out until late; he gave me a key, too, so I expect there was a misunderstanding. I thought—' she caught his eye '—well, I thought that perhaps you expected me to stay out. I mean, you did say that Jet would put the boys to bed, so you didn't expect me back, did you?' She hesitated. 'Am I making myself clear?'

When he didn't speak, she added, 'I've had a most interesting day, and I went to the cinema this evening. I'm on my way back to the house now, so I'll say good evening, doctor.'

'No, Miss Pomfrey, you will not say good evening. You will come with me and we will have dinner together. I have no doubt that you have eaten nothing much all day and I cannot forgive myself for not seeing that you had adequate money with you and arrangements made for your free day. Please forgive me?'

She stared up at him, towering over her. 'Of course I forgive you. I'm not your guest, you know,

and I'm quite used to being by myself. And please
don't feel that you have to give me a meal; I've just
eaten all those chips.'

'All the same, we will dine together.' He swept her
into the car and picked up the car phone. He spoke
in Dutch so that she wasn't to know that he was ex-
cusing himself from a dinner party.

'Oh, that hospital again,' said his hostess. 'Do you
never get a free moment, Marcus?'

He made a laughing rejoinder, promised to dine
at some future date, and started the car.

Araminta, still clutching her chips, said in a tight
little voice, 'Will you take me back to the house,
doctor? It's kind of you to offer me a meal, but I'm
not hungry.'

A waste of breath, for all she got in reply was
a grunt as he swept the car back into the lighted
streets, past shop windows still blazing with light,
cafés spilling out onto the pavements, grand hotels…
She tried again. 'I'm not suitably dressed…'

He took no notice of that either, but turned into a
narrow side street lined with elegant little shops. At
its far end there was a small restaurant.

There was a canal on the opposite side of the
street, and the doctor parked beside it—dangerously near the edge, from her point of view—and
got out. There was no help for it but to get out when
he opened her door, to be marched across the street
and into the restaurant.

It was a small place: a long, narrow room with

tables well apart, most of them occupied. Araminta was relieved to see that although the women there were well dressed, several of them were in suits and dark dresses so that her jacket and skirt weren't too conspicuous.

It seemed the doctor was known there; they were led to a table in one corner, her jacket was taken from her and a smiling waiter drew out her chair.

The doctor sat down opposite to her. 'What will you drink?' he asked. 'Dry sherry?'

When she agreed, he spoke to the waiter, who offered menus. There was choice enough, and she saw at a glance that everything was wildly expensive. She stared down at it; she hadn't wanted to come, and it would be entirely his fault if she chose caviar, plover's eggs and truffles, all of which were on the menu, their cost equivalent to a week's housekeeping money. On the other hand, she had no wish to sample any of these delicacies and, since she must have spoilt his evening, it seemed only fair to choose as economically as possible.

The doctor put down his menu. 'Unless you would like anything special, will you leave it to me to order?'

'Oh, please.' She added, 'There's such a lot to choose from, isn't there?'

'Indeed. How about marinated aubergine to start with? And would you like sea bass to follow?'

She agreed; she wasn't shy, and she was too much her parents' daughter to feel awkward. She had never been in a restaurant such as this one, but she wasn't going to let it intimidate her. When the food came she ate with pleasure and, mindful of manners, made polite conversation. The doctor was at first secretly amused and then found himself interested. Miss Pomfrey might be nothing out of the ordinary, but she had self-assurance and a way of looking him in the eye which he found disquieting. Not a conceited man, but aware of his worth, he wasn't used to being studied in such a manner.

For a moment he regretted his spoilt evening, but told himself that he was being unjust and then suggested that she might like a pudding from the trolley.

She chose sticky toffee pudding and ate it with enjoyment, and he, watching her over his biscuits and cheese, found himself reluctantly liking her.

They had talked in a guarded fashion over their meal—the weather, the boys, her opinion of Utrecht, all safe subjects. It was when they got back to the house and she had thanked him and started for the stairs that he stopped her.

'Miss Pomfrey, we do not need to refer again to the regrettable waste of your free day. Rest assured that I shall see to it that any other free time you have will be well spent.'

'Thank you, but I am quite capable of looking after myself.'

He smiled thinly. 'Allow me to be the best judge of that, Miss Pomfrey.' He turned away. 'Goodnight.'

She paused on the stairs. 'Goodnight, doctor.' And

then she added, 'I bought the chips because I was hungry. I dare say you would have done the same,' she told him in a matter-of-fact voice.

The doctor watched her small retreating back and went into his study. Presently he began to laugh.

CHAPTER FOUR

ARAMINTA WOKE EARLY on Sunday morning and re-membered that the doctor had said that he would be away all day—moreover, he had remarked that he had no doubt that she and the boys would enjoy their day. Doing what? she wondered, and sat up and wor-ried about it until Jet came in with her morning tea, a concession to her English habit.

They smiled and nodded at each other and ex-changed a *'Goeden Morgen'*, and the boys, hearing Jet's voice, came into the room and got onto Ara-minta's bed to eat the little biscuits which had come with the tea.

'We have to get up and dress,' they told her. 'We go to church with Uncle Marcus at half past nine.'

'Oh, do you? Then back to your room, boys, I'll be along in ten minutes or so.'

Church would last about an hour, she supposed, which meant that a good deal of the morning would be gone; they could go to one of the parks and feed the ducks, then come back for lunch, and by then

surely she would have thought of something to fill
the afternoon hours. A pity it wasn't raining, then
they could have stayed indoors.

Jet had told her that breakfast would be at half past
eight—at least, Araminta was almost sure that was
what she had said; she knew the word for breakfast
by now, and the time of day wasn't too hard to guess
at. She dressed and went to help the boys. Not that
they needed much help, for they dressed themselves,
even if a bit haphazardly. But she brushed hair, tied
miniature ties and made sure that their teeth were
brushed and their hands clean. She did it without
fuss; at the children's convalescent home there had
been no time to linger over such tasks.

The doctor wasn't at breakfast, and they had almost finished when he came in with Humphrey. He
had been for a walk, he told them. Humphrey had
needed to stretch his legs. He sat down and had a cup
of coffee, explaining that he had already breakfasted.
'Church at half past nine,' he reminded them, and
asked Araminta if she would care to go with them.
'The church is close by—a short walk—you might
find it interesting.'

She sensed that he expected her to accept. 'Thank
you, I would like to come,' she told him. 'At what
time are we to be ready?'

'Ten past nine. The service lasts about an hour.'

They each had a child's hand as they walked to the
church, which was small and old, smelling of damp,
flowers and age and, to Araminta's mind, rather

bleak. They sat right at the front in a high-backed pew with narrow seats and hassocks. The boys sat between them, standing on the hassocks to sing the hymns and then sitting through a lengthy sermon.

Of course, Araminta understood very little of the service, although some of the hymn tunes were the same, but the sermon, preached by an elderly dominee with a flowing beard, sounded as though it was threatening them with severe punishments in the hereafter; she was relieved when it ended with a splendid rolling period of unintelligible words and they all sang a hymn.

It was a tune she knew, but the words in the hymn-book the doctor had thoughtfully provided her with were beyond her understanding. The boys sang lust-ily, as did the doctor, in a deep rumbling voice, and since they were singing so loudly, she hummed the tune to herself. It was the next best thing.

Back at the house, the doctor asked Bas to bring coffee into the drawing room.

'I shall be leaving in a few minutes,' he told Ara-minta. 'I expect you intend to take a walk before lunch, but in the afternoon Bas will drive you to Steijner's toy shop. They have an exhibition of toys there today and I have tickets. And next door there is a café where you may have your tea. Bas will come for you at about five o'clock. If you want him earlier, telephone the house.'

The boys were delighted, and so was Araminta, although she didn't allow it to show. The day had been nicely taken care of and the boys were going to enjoy themselves. She had no doubt that she would too.

The doctor stooped to kiss the boys. 'Have fun,' he told them, and to Araminta, 'Enjoy your afternoon, Miss Pomfrey. I leave the boys in your safe hands.'

It was only after he had gone that she realised that she hadn't much money—perhaps not enough to pay for their tea. She need not have worried. The boys showed her the notes their uncle had given to them to spend and a moment later, Bas, coming to collect the coffee cups, told her quietly that there was an envelope for her in the doctor's study if she would be good enough to fetch it.

There was, in her opinion, enough money in it to float a ship. She counted it carefully, determined to account for every cent of it, and went back to collect the boys ready for their walk.

They decided against going to one of the parks but instead they walked to one of the squares, the 'neude', and so into the Oudegracht, where there was the fourteenth-century house in which the Treaty of Utrecht had been signed. They admired the patrician house at some length, until Araminta said, 'Are we very far from your uncle's house? We should be getting back.'

They chorused reassurance. 'Look, Mintie, we just go back to the *neude* and Vredeburg Square, and it's only a little way then.'

She had been there the day before, spending hours looking at the windows of the shopping centre. The doctor's house was only a short distance from the Singel, the moat which surrounded the old city— much of its length was lined with attractive promenades backed by impressive houses.

'By the time we go home I shall know quite a lot about Utrecht,' she told the boys. 'Now, let's go back to the house and have lunch; we don't want to miss one moment of the exhibition…'

Steijner's toy shop was vast, housed in a narrow building, several storeys high, each floor reached by a narrow, steep staircase. The front shop was large and opened out into another smaller room which extended, long and narrow, as far as a blank wall. Both rooms were lined with shelves packed with toys of every description, and arranged down their centres were the larger exhibits: miniature motor cars, dolls' houses, minute bicycles, magnificent model boats.

The place was crowded with children, tugging the grown-ups to and fro, and it was some time before Araminta and the boys managed to climb the first flight of stairs to the floor above. The rooms here were mostly given over to dolls, more dolls' houses and miniature kitchens and furniture, so they stayed only for a few minutes and then, together with a great many other people, made their way to the next floor.

This was very much more to the boys' liking— more cars and bikes, kites of every kind, skates, trumpets and drums, puppets and toy animals. Araminta, with the beginnings of a headache, suggested hopefully that they might go and have their tea and wait for Bas in the café. More and more people were filling the shop, the narrow stairs were packed, but the children were reluctant to move from the displays they fancied.

'There's camping stuff on the next floor,' said Peter, and he tugged at her hand. 'Could we just have a look—a quick peep?' He looked so appealing and since Paul had joined him, raising an excited face to her, she gave in. 'All right. But we won't stay too long, mind.'

The last flight of stairs was very narrow and steep, and the room it led to was low-ceilinged and narrow, with a slit window set in the gable. But it was well lit and the array of camping equipment was impressive. There were only a handful of people there and before long they had gone back down the staircase, leaving the boys alone to examine the tents and camping equipment to their hearts' content.

They must have a tent, they told Araminta excitedly, they would ask Uncle Marcus to buy them one. 'We could live in it in the garden, Mintie. You'd come too, of course.'

They went round and round, trying to decide which tent was the one they liked best. They were still longing to have one and arguing about it when Araminta looked at her watch.

'Time for tea, my dears,' she told them. 'We mustn't keep Bas waiting.'

It was another five minutes before she could prise them away and start down the stairs in single file. Peter was in front and he stopped on the last stair.

'The door's shut,' he said.

Araminta reached over. 'Well, we'll just turn the handle.'

Only there wasn't a handle, only an old-fashioned lock with no key. She changed places with Peter and gave the door a good push. Nothing happened; the door could have been rock. She told the boys to sit on the stairs and knocked hard. There was no reply, nor did anyone answer her 'hello'. The place was quiet, though when she looked at her watch she wondered why. The exhibition was due to close at five o'clock and it was fifteen minutes to that hour. All the same, surely someone would tour the building and make sure that everyone had left. She shouted, uneasily aware of the thickness of the door.

'What an adventure!' she said bracingly. 'Let's all shout…'

Which brought no result whatever.

'Well, we'd better go back to the room. Someone will come presently; it's not quite time for people to have to leave yet.' She spoke in a matter-of-fact voice and hoped that the boys would believe her.

Back upstairs again, she went to the narrow window. The glass was thick and, although it had once opened, it had been long since sealed up. She looked around for something suitable to break it, picked up

a tent peg and, urged on by the boys, who were rev-
elling in the whole thing, began to bash the glass.

It didn't break easily, and only some of it fell into
the street below, but anyone passing or standing
nearby could have seen it. She shouted hopefully, unaware that there was no one there. The doctor's second car, another Jaguar, was standing close by, but
Bas had gone into the café to see if they were there.

Of course, they weren't; he went to the toy shop,
where the doors were being locked.

'Everyone has left,' he was told, and when he
asked why they had closed a quarter of an hour
sooner than expected, he was told that an electrical
fault had been found and it was necessary to turn
off the current.

'But no one's inside,' he was assured by the owner,
who was unaware that the assistant who had checked
the place hadn't bothered to go to the top room but
had locked the door and gone home.

They could have gone back to the house, thought
Bas. Miss Pomfrey was a sensible young woman, and
instead of lingering about waiting for him she would
have taken the boys home to let him know that they
had left earlier than they had planned.

He got into the car and drove back, to find the
Bentley parked by the canal and the doctor in his
study. He looked up as Bas went in, but before he
could speak Bas said urgently, 'You're just this minute back, *mijnheer*? You do not know about the ex-

hibition closing early? I thought Miss Pomfrey and the boys would be here.'

The doctor was out of his chair. 'At the toy shop? It is closed? Why? You're sure? They were not in the café?'

'No one had seen them. I spoke to the man closing the place—there's been an electrical fault, that's why they shut early. He was sure that there was no one left inside.'

The doctor was already at the door. 'They can't be far, and Miss Pomfrey isn't a girl to lose her head. Come along. We'll find them. You stay in the car, Bas, in case they turn up.'

With Bas beside him he drove to Steijner's shop. There were few people about—the proprietor and his assistants had gone home—but there was a van parked outside and men unloading equipment.

The doctor parked the car and walked over to them. 'You have keys? I believe there are two boys and a young woman still inside. I'm not sure of it, but I must check.'

He looked up as a small splattering of glass fell between them. He looked up again and saw what appeared to be a stocking waving from the gabled window.

The man looked up, too. 'Best get them down, *mijnheer.* I'll open up—you won't need help? I've quite a bit of work here…'

He opened the door, taking his time over its bolts and chains, giving the doctor time to allow for his relief, mingled, for some reason which he didn't understand, with rising rage. The silly girl. Why didn't she leave the place with everyone else? There must have been some other people there, and the boys would have understood what was said—everyone would have been warned in good time.

He raced up the stairs, turned the key in the lock of the last door and went up the staircase two at a time. The boys rushed to meet him, bubbling about their adventure, delighted to see him, and he put his great arms around their small shoulders.

He said, very softly, 'I hope you have a good explanation for this, Miss Pomfrey.' The look he gave her shrivelled her bones.

Araminta, ready and eager to explain, bit back the words. He was furiously angry with her. No doubt any other man would have sworn at her and called her names, but he had spoken with an icy civility which sent shivers down her spine. A pity he hadn't shouted, she reflected, then she could have shouted back. Instead she said nothing at all, and after a moment he turned to the boys.

'Bas is below with the car. If you haven't had tea we will have it together.'

'Shall we tell you about it, Uncle Marcus?' began Peter.

'Later, Peter, after tea.' He crossed the room and took Araminta's stocking off the glass window. It was hopelessly torn and laddered, but he handed it to her very politely. Her 'thank you' was equally po-

lite, but she didn't look at him. She felt a fool with
only one stocking, and he had contrived to make her
feel guilty about something which hadn't been her
fault. Nor had he asked what had happened, but had
condemned her unheard.

At the bottom of the staircase she paused; she
would show him that there was no handle on the
door. But he was already going down the next stairs
with the boys.

She was going to call him back, but his impatient,
'Come along, Miss Pomfrey,' gave her no chance.
She followed the three of them out to the car and got
in wordlessly. Once back at the house, she tidied up
the boys ready for tea, excused herself on account
of a headache and went to her room.

The doctor's curled lip at her excuse boded ill for
any further conversation he might wish to have with
her. And she had no doubt that he would have more
to say about feather-brained women who got left behind and locked up while in charge of small boys….

Bas brought in the tea. 'Miss Pomfrey will be with
you presently?' he wanted to know. He had seen her
pale face and his master's inscrutable features in the
car. 'You could have cut the air between them with
a pair of scissors,' he had told Jet.

'Miss Pomfrey has a headache. Perhaps you would
take her a tray of tea,' suggested the doctor.

'Mintie never has a headache,' declared Peter.
'She said so; she said she's never ill…'

'In that case, I dare say she will be with us again

in a short time,' observed his uncle. 'I see that Jet has baked a *boterkeok*, and there are *krentenbollejes*...'

'Currant buns,' said Paul. 'Shall we save one for Mintie?'

'Why not? Now, tell me, did you enjoy the exhibition? Was there anything that you both liked?'

'A tent—that's why we were in the room at the very top. It was full of tents and things for camping. We though we'd like a tent. Mintie said she'd come and live in it with us in the garden. She made us laugh, 'specially when we tried to open the door...'

The doctor put down his teacup. 'And it wouldn't open?'

'It was a real adventure. Mintie supposed that the people who went downstairs before us forgot and shut the door, and of course there wasn't a handle. You would have enjoyed it, too, Uncle. We banged on the door and shouted, and then Mintie broke the glass in the window and took off a stocking and hung it through the hole she'd made. She said it was what those five children in the Enid Blyton books would have done and we were having an adventure. It was real fun, wasn't it, Peter?'

His uncle said, 'It sounds a splendid adventure.'

'I 'spect that's why Mintie's got a headache,' said Peter.

'I believe you may be right, Peter. Have we finished tea? Would you both like to take Humphrey into the garden? He likes company. I have something to do, so if I'm not here presently, go to Jet in the kitchen, will you?'

The boys ran off, shouting and laughing, throwing a ball for the good-natured Humphrey, and when Bas came to clear away the tea things, the doctor said, 'Bas, would you be good enough to ask Miss Pomfrey to come to my study as soon as she feels better?'

He crossed the hall and shut the study door behind him, and Bas went back to the kitchen. Jet, told of this, pooh-poohed the idea that the doctor was about to send Miss Pomfrey packing. 'More like he's got the wrong end of the stick about what happened this afternoon and wants to know what did happen. You don't know?'

Bas shook his head. 'No idea. But it wasn't anything to upset the boys; they were full of their adventure.'

Araminta had drunk her tea, had a good cry, washed her face and applied powder and lipstick once more, tidied her hair and sat down to think. She had no intention of telling the doctor anything; he was arrogant, ill-tempered and she couldn't bear the sight of him. Anyone else would have asked her what had happened, given her a chance to explain. He had taken it for granted that she had been careless and unreliable. 'I hate him,' said Araminta, not meaning it, but it relieved her feelings.

When Bas came for the tea tray and gave her the message from the doctor she thanked him and said that she would be down presently. When he had gone she went to the gilt edged triple mirror on the dressing table and took a good look. Viewed from all sides, her face looked much as usual. Slightly puffy eyelids could be due to the headache. Perhaps another light dusting of powder on her nose, which was still pink at its tip… She practised one or two calm and dignified expressions and rehearsed several likely answers to the cross questioning she expected, and, thus fortified, went down to the study.

The doctor was sitting at his desk, but he got up as she went in.

He said at once, 'Please sit down, Miss Pomfrey, I owe you an apology. It was unpardonable of me to speak to you in such a fashion, to give you no chance to explain—'

Araminta chipped in, 'It's quite all right, doctor, I quite understand. You must have been very worried.'

'Were you not worried, Mintie?'

He so seldom called her that that she stared at him. His face was as impassive as it always was; he was looking at her over his spectacles, his brows lifted in enquiry.

'Me? Yes, of course I was. I was scared out of my wits, if you must know—so afraid that the boys would suddenly realise that we might be shut up for hours and it wasn't an adventure, after all.' She added matter-of-factly, 'Of course, I knew you'd come sooner or later.'

'Oh, and why should you be so sure of that?'

She frowned. 'I don't know—at least, I suppose…
I don't know.'

'I hope you accept my apology, and if there is
anything—'

'Of course I accept it,' she interrupted him again.
'And there isn't anything. Thank you.'

'You are happy here? You do not find it too dull?'

'I don't see how anyone could feel dull with Peter
and Paul as companions.'

She looked at him and smiled.

'You have been crying, Miss Pomfrey?'

So she was Miss Pomfrey again. 'Certainly not.
What have I got to cry about?'

'I can think of several things, and you may be
a splendid governess, Miss Pomfrey, but you are a
poor liar.'

She went rather red in the face. 'What a nasty
thing to say about me,' she snapped, quite forgetting
that he was her employer, who expected politeness
at all times, no doubt, 'I never tell lies, not the kind
which harm people. Besides, my father has always
told me that a weeping woman is a thorn in the flesh
of any man.'

The doctor kept a straight face. 'A very sensible
opinion,' he murmured. 'All the same, if it was I who
caused your tears, I'm sorry. I have no wish to upset
you or make you unhappy.'

She sought for an answer, but since she couldn't
think of one, she stayed silent.

'You behaved with commendable good sense.' He

smiled then. 'Dr Jenkell assured me that you were the most level-headed young woman he had ever known. I must be sure and tell him how right he was.'

If that's a compliment, thought Araminta, I'd as soon do without it. She wondered what would have happened if she had been pretty and empty-headed and screamed her head off. Men being men, they would have rushed to her rescue, poured brandy down her throat and offered a shoulder for her to cry into. They would probably have called her poor little girl and made sure that she went to her bed for the rest of the day. And the doctor was very much a man, wasn't he? Being plain had its drawbacks, thought Araminta.

The doctor, watching her expressive face, wondered what she was thinking. How fortunate it was that she was such a sensible girl. The whole episode would be forgotten, but he must remember to make sure that her next free day was a success.

He said now, 'I expect you want to go to the boys. I told them that they might have supper with us this evening, but that they must have their baths and be ready for bed first.'

Dismissed, but with her evening's work already planned, Araminta went in search of the boys and spent the next hour supervising the cleaning of teeth, the brushing of hair and the riotous bath. With the boys looking like two small angels, she led them downstairs presently. There had been little time to do anything to her own person; she had dabbed her nose with powder, brushed her own hair, and sighed into the mirror, aware that the doctor wouldn't notice if she wore a blonde wig and false eyelashes.

'Not that I mind in the least,' she had told her reflection.

Her supposition was regrettably true, he barely glanced at her throughout the meal, and when he did he didn't see anyone other than the dependable Miss Pomfrey, suitably merging into the background of his life.

The next days were uneventful, a pleasant pattern of mornings at school, afternoons spent exploring and evenings playing some game or other. When their uncle was at home, the boys spent their short evenings with him, leaving her free to do whatever she wanted.

She supposed that she could have gone and sat in the little room behind the drawing room and watched the TV, but no one had suggested it and she didn't like to go there uninvited. So she stayed in her room, doing her nails, sewing on buttons and mending holes in small garments. It was a pleasant room, warm and nicely furnished, but it didn't stop her feeling lonely.

It was towards the end of the week that Paul got up one morning and didn't want his breakfast. Probably a cold, thought Araminta, and kept an eye on him.

He seemed quite his usual self when she fetched them both from school, but by the evening he was feverish, peevish and thoroughly out of sorts. It was a pity that the doctor had gone to the Hague and wouldn't be back until late that evening. Araminta put him to bed and, since the twins didn't like to be separated, Peter had his bath and got ready for bed, too. With Bas's help she carried up their light supper.

But Paul didn't want his; his throat was sore and his head ached and when she took his temperature it was alarmingly high. She sat him on her lap, persuaded him to drink the cold drinks Bas brought and, while Peter finished his supper, embarked on a story. She made it up as she went along, and it was about nothing in particular, but the boys listened and presently Paul went to sleep, his hot little head pressed against her shoulder.

Peter had come to sit beside her, and she put an arm around him, carrying on a cheerful whispered conversation until he, reassured about his brother, slept too.

It was some time later when Bas came in quietly to remind her that dinner was waiting for her.

'I'm sorry, Bas, but I can't come. They're both sound asleep and Paul isn't well. They're bound to wake presently, then I can put them in their beds... Will you apologize to Jet for me? I'm not hungry; I can have some soup later.'

Bas went reluctantly and she was left, her insides rumbling, while she tried not to think of food. Just like the doctor, she thought testily, to be away just when he was wanted. She wouldn't allow herself to panic. She had coped with childish ailments at the children's convalescent home and knew how resilient they were and how quickly they got well once whatever it was which had afflicted them had been diagnosed and dealt with. All the same, she wished that the doctor would come home soon.

Minutes ticked themselves slowly into an hour, but she managed a cheerful smile when Bas put a concerned head round the door.

'They'll wake soon,' she assured him in a whisper. But they slept on: Peter sleeping the deep sleep of a healthy child, Paul deeply asleep too but with a mounting fever, his tousled head still against her shoulder. She longed to changed her position; she longed even more for a cup of tea. It did no good to dwell on that, so she allowed her thoughts free rein and wondered what the doctor was doing and who he was with. She hoped that whoever it was wasn't distracting him from returning home at a reasonable hour.

It was a good thing that she didn't know that on the point of his leaving the hospital in the Hague he had been urgently recalled…

When he did get home it was ten o'clock. Bas came hurrying into the hall to meet him, his nice elderly face worried.

'What's wrong?' asked the doctor.

'Little Paul. He's not well, *mijnheer*. He's asleep, but Miss Pomfrey has him on her lap; he's been there for hours. Peter's there too. Miss Pomfrey asked me to phone the hospital, but you were not available…'

The doctor put a hand on Bas's shoulder. 'I'll go up. Don't worry, Bas.'

Araminta had heard him come home, and the voices in the hall, and relief flooded through her. She peered down into Paul's sleeping face and then looked up as the doctor came quietly into the room.

'Have you had the mumps?' she asked him.

He stopped short. 'Good Lord, yes, decades ago.'

He looked at his nephew's face, showing distinct signs of puffiness, then stopped and lifted him gently off her lap.

'How long have you been sitting there?'

'Since six o'clock. He's got a temperature and a headache and his throat's sore. Peter's all right so far.'

The doctor laid the still sleeping boy in his bed and bent to examine him gently. 'We will let him sleep, poor scrap.' He came and took Peter in his arms and tucked him up in his bed, talking softly to the half-awake child. Only then did he turn to Araminta, sitting, perforce, exactly as she had been doing for the past few hours, so stiff that she didn't dare to move.

The doctor hauled her gently to her feet, put an arm around her and walked her up and down.

'Now, go downstairs, tell Bas to ask Jet to get us something to eat and send Nel up here to sit with the boys for a while.'

And when she hesitated, he added, 'Go along, Miss Pomfrey. I want my supper.'

She gave him a speaking look; she wanted her supper, too, and the unfeeling man hadn't even bothered to ask her if she needed hers.

'So do I,' she snapped, and then added, 'Is Paul all right? It is only mumps?'

He said coolly, 'Yes, Miss Pomfrey. Hopefully only mumps.'

She went downstairs and gave Bas his messages, then went and sat in the small sitting room. She was tired and rather untidy and she could see ahead of her several trying days while the mumps kept their hold on Paul—and possibly Peter.

'Twelve days incubation,' she said, talking to herself, 'and we could wait longer than that until we're sure Peter doesn't get them, too.'

'Inevitable, Miss Pomfrey. Do you often talk to yourself?'

The doctor had come silently into the room. He poured a glass of sherry and gave it to her and didn't wait for her answer. 'It will mean bed for a few days for Paul, and of course Peter can't go to school. Will you be able to manage? Nel can take over in the afternoons while you take Peter for a walk?'

He watched her toss back the sherry and refilled her glass. Perhaps he was expecting too much of her. 'See how you go on,' he told her kindly. 'If necessary, I'll get some more help.'

'If Peter were to get the mumps within the next few days I shall be able to manage very nicely,' she said matter-of-factly.

'It is to be hoped that he will. Let us get them over with, by all means.'

Bas came then, so she finished her second sherry far too quickly and went to the dining room with the doctor.

Jet had conjured up an excellent meal: mushroom soup, a cheese soufflé, salad and a lemon mousse. Araminta, slightly light-headed from the sherry, ate everything put before her, making somewhat muddled conversation as she did so. The doctor watched with faint amusement as she polished off the last of the mousse.

'Now go to bed, Miss Pomfrey. You will be called as usual in the morning.'

'Oh, that won't do at all,' she told him, emboldened by the sherry. 'I'll have a bath and get ready for bed, then I'll go and sit with the boys for a bit. Once I'm sure they are all right, I'll go to bed. I shall hear them if they wake.'

'You will do as I say. I have a good deal of reading to do; I will do it in their room.'

'Aren't you going to the hospital in the morning?'

'Certainly I am.'

'Then you can't do that; you'll be like a wet rag in the morning. You need your sleep.'

'I'm quite capable of knowing how much sleep I need, Miss Pomfrey. Kindly do as I ask. Goodnight.'

She wanted to cry, although she didn't know why, but she held back the tears, wished him a bleak goodnight and went upstairs. She felt better after a hot bath, and, wrapped in her dressing gown, she crept into the boys' room to make sure they were asleep. Nel, the housemaid, had gone downstairs again and they slept peacefully. Promising herself that she would get up during the night to make sure that they were all right, Araminta took herself off to bed.

She was asleep at once, but woke instantly at a peevish wail from Paul. She tumbled out of bed and crept to the half-open door. Paul was awake and the doctor was sitting on his bed, giving him a drink. There were papers scattered all over the floor and the chair was drawn up to the table by the window. She crept back to bed. It was two o'clock in the morning. She lay and worried about the doctor's lack of sleep until she slept once more.

She was up very early, to find the boys sleeping and the doctor gone. She dressed, crept down to the kitchen and made herself tea, filled a jug with cold lemonade and went back to the boys' room. They were still asleep. Paul's face was very swollen but Peter looked normal. She had no idea how she would manage for the next few days; it depended on whether Peter got mumps, too.

She was going silently around the room, getting clean clothes for the boys, when the doctor came in.

She wished him a quiet good morning and saw how tired he was, despite his immaculate appearance. Despite his annoyance the previous evening, she said in her sensible way, 'I hope you'll have the good sense to have a good night's sleep tonight. What would we do if you were to be ill?'

'My dear Miss Pomfrey, stop fussing. I am never ill. If you're worried during the day, tell Bas; he knows where to find me.'

And he had gone again, with a casual nod, hardly looking at her.

CHAPTER FIVE

THE DAY WAS every bit as bad as Araminta had expected it to be. Paul woke up peevish, hot and sorry for himself, and it took a good deal of coaxing to get him washed and into clean pyjamas, his temperature taken and a cold drink swallowed. Bas had produced some coloured straws, which eased the drinking problem, but the mumps had taken hold for the moment and her heart ached for the small swollen face.

Nevertheless, she got through the day, reading to the invalid until she was hoarse, playing games with Peter and then taking him for a walk with Humphrey while Nel sat with Paul. They returned, much refreshed, armed with drawing books, crayons, a jigsaw puzzle and a couple of comics, had their tea with Humphrey in the sitting room and then went to spend the rest of the afternoon with Paul. He still felt ill, but his headache was better, he said, although it still hurt him to swallow.

'You'll feel better tomorrow,' Araminta assured

him. 'Not quite well, but better, and when your uncle comes home I expect he'll know what to do to take away the pain in your throat.'

The doctor came home just after six o'clock, coming into the boys' room quietly, his civil good evening to Araminta drowned in the boisterous greeting from Peter and the hoarse voice of Paul. Humphrey, who had been lying on his bed, lumbered up to add his welcome and the doctor stooped to pat him.

Before the doctor could voice any disapproval of dogs on beds, Araminta said firmly, 'I said that Humphrey could get on the bed. He's company for Paul and comforting, too, so if you want to scold anyone, please scold me.'

He looked at her with raised eyebrows and a little smile which held no warmth. 'I was not aware that I had given my opinion on the matter, Miss Pomfrey. I see no reason to scold anyone, either you or Humphrey.'

And, having disposed of the matter, he proceeded to ask her how the day had gone. He sat on the bed while she told him, examining Paul's face and neck, taking his temperature, listening to his small bony chest, looking down his throat.

'You're better,' he declared cheerfully. 'You're going to feel horrible for a few days, and you'll have to stay in bed for a while, but I've no doubt that Miss Pomfrey will keep you amused.'

'Does Miss Pomfrey—well, you mean Mintie, of course—amuse you too, Uncle?' This from Peter.

The doctor glanced across at Araminta. 'Oh, decidedly,' he said, and smiled at her, a warm smile this time, inviting her to share the joke.

It was impossible to resist that smile. She agreed cheerfully and listened to Peter, like all small boys, enlarging upon the idea with gruff chuckles from his twin.

The doctor got up presently. 'Ice cream and yoghurt for supper,' he suggested. 'Miss Pomfrey, if you would come down to my study, I will give you something to ease that sore throat. Peter, I leave you in charge for a few minutes.'

In the study, with Humphrey standing between them, he said, 'You have had a long day. I'm afraid the next few days will be equally long. Paul is picking up nicely, and the swelling should go down in another five or six days. He must stay in bed for another day or so, then he could be allowed to get up, wrapped up warmly and kept in the room. Peter seems all right...'

'Yes, and so good with his brother.'

'I shall be at home this evening. I'll keep an eye on the boys while you have dinner, and then if you would be with them for half an hour or so, I'll take over. You could do with an early night...'

She said, before she could stop her tongue, 'Do I look so awful?'

He surveyed her coolly. 'Let us say you do not look at your best, Miss Pomfrey.'

He took no notice of her glare but went to his case.

'Crush one of these and stir it into Paul's ice cream. Get him to drink as much as possible.' He added, 'You will, of course, be experienced in the treatment of childish ailments?'

'Yes,' said Araminta. The horrible man. What did he expect when she'd been kept busy the whole day with the boys? Not look her best, indeed!

She went to the door and he opened it for her and then made matters worse by observing, 'Never mind, Miss Pomfrey, as soon as the mumps have been routed, you shall have all the time you want for beauty treatment and shopping.'

She spun round to face him, looking up into his bland face. 'Why bother? And how dare you mock me? You are an exceedingly tiresome man, but I don't suppose anyone has dared to tell you so!'

He stared down at her, not speaking.

'Oh, dear, I shouldn't have said that,' said Araminta. 'I'm sorry if I've hurt your feelings, although I don't see why I should be, for you have no regard for mine. Anyway,' she added defiantly, 'it's a free world and I can say what I like.'

'Indeed you can, Miss Pomfrey. Feel free to express your feelings whenever you have the need.'

He held the door wide and she flounced through. Back with the boys once more, she wondered if he would give her the sack. He was entitled to do so; she had been more than a little outspoken. On the other hand, he would have to get someone to replace her pretty smartly, someone willing to cope with two small boys and the mumps…

Apparently he had no such intention. Paul was soon readied for the night and Peter was prancing round in his pyjamas, demanding that he should have his supper with his brother.

'Well, I don't see why not,' said Araminta. 'Put on your dressing gown, there's a good boy, and I'll see what Bas says…'

'And what should Bas say?' asked the doctor, coming in in his usual quiet fashion.

'That he won't mind helping me bring supper up here for Peter as well as Paul.'

'By all means. Ask him to do so, Miss Pomfrey, and then have your dinner—a little early, but I dare say you will enjoy a long evening to yourself.'

There was nothing to say to that, so she went in search of Bas.

Peter said. 'You must say Mintie, Uncle. Why do you always call her Miss Pomfrey?'

'I have a shocking memory. How about a game of Spillikins after supper?'

Araminta still felt annoyed, and apprehensive as well, but that didn't prevent her from enjoying her meal. Jet sent in garlic mushrooms, chicken à la king with braised celery, and then a chocolate mousse. It would be a pity to miss these delights, reflected Araminta, relishing the last of the mousse. She must keep a curb on her tongue in future.

She went back to sit with the boys and the doctor

went away to eat his dinner, urged to be quick so that there would be time for one more game of Spillikins before their bedtime.

'It's already past your bedtime,' said Araminta.

'Just for once shall we bend the rules?' said the doctor as he went out of the room.

He was back within half an hour, and another half an hour saw the end of their game. He got up from Paul's bed.

'I'll be back in five minutes,' he told them, 'and you'll both be asleep.'

When he came back he said, 'Thank you, Miss Pomfrey, goodnight.'

She had already tucked the boys in, so she wished him a quiet goodnight and left him there.

A faint grizzling sound wakened her around midnight. Peter had woken up with a headache and a sore throat...

She went down to breakfast in the morning feeling rather the worse for wear. The doctor glanced up briefly from his post, wished her good morning and resumed his reading. Araminta sat down, poured her coffee, and, since he had nothing further to say, observed, 'Peter has the mumps.'

The doctor took off his spectacles, the better to look at her.

'To be expected. I'll go and have a look at him. He had a bad night?'

'Yes,' said Araminta, and stopped herself just in time from adding, And so did I.

'And so did you,' said the doctor, reading her peevish face like an open book. He passed her the basket
of rolls and offered butter. 'You'll feel better when
you've had your breakfast.'

Araminta buttered a roll savagely. She might have
known better than to have expected any sympathy.
She thought of several nasty remarks to make, but
he was watching her from his end of the table and
for once she decided that prudence might be the best
thing.

She bit into her roll with her splendid teeth,
choked on a crumb and had to be thumped on the
back while she whooped and spluttered. Rather red
in the face, she resumed her breakfast and the doctor his seat.

He said mildly, 'You don't appear to be your usual
calm self, Miss Pomfrey. Perhaps I should get extra
help while the boys are sick.'

'Quite unnecessary,' said Araminta. 'With both
of them in bed there will be very little to do.'

She was aware that she was being optimistic; there
would be a great deal to do. By the end of the day she
would probably be at her wits' end, cross-eyed and
sore-throated from reading aloud, headachey from
jigsaw puzzles and worn out by coaxing two small
fractious boys to swallow food and drink which they
didn't want...

'Just as you wish,' observed the doctor, and gathered up his letters. 'I'll go and have a look at Peter.
Did Paul sleep?'

'For most of the night.'

He nodded and left her to finish her breakfast, and presently, when he had seen Paul, he returned to tell her that Peter was likely to be peevish and out of sorts. 'I'll give you something before I leave to relieve his sore throat. Paul is getting on nicely. Bas will know how to get hold of me if you are worried. Don't hesitate if you are. I'll be home around six.'

The day seemed endless, but away from the doctor's inimical eye Araminta was her practical, unflappable self, full of sympathy for the two small boys. Naturally they were cross, given to bursts of crying, and unwilling to swallow drinks and the ice cream she offered. Still, towards teatime she could see that Paul was feeling better, and although Peter's temperature was still too high, he was less peevish.

She hardly left them; Nel relieved her when she had a meal, and offered to sit with them while she went out for a while, but Araminta, with Bas translating, assured her that she was fine and that when the doctor came home she would have an hour or two off.

She was reading *The Lion, the Witch and the Wardrobe* when he walked into the room. He sat down on Paul's bed and didn't speak for a moment.

'I see Paul's feeling better; what about Peter?'

He could at least have wished her good evening or even said hello.

'He's feeling off colour, and he's been very good—they both have—and they've taken their drinks like Trojans. Jet is making them jelly for supper.'

'Splendid. Go and have a stroll round the garden, Miss Pomfrey, and then have dinner.'

'I'm perfectly…' she began.

'Yes, I know you are, but kindly do as I say.' He said something in Dutch to the boys, and they managed to giggle despite the mumps.

Araminta went. First to her room to get a cardigan, and to take a dispirited look at her reflection. There seemed no point in doing more than brushing her hair into tidiness and powdering her nose; she went downstairs and passed Humphrey on his way up to join his master. She would have liked his company as she wandered to and fro in the garden.

It was growing chilly and she was glad of the cardigan and even more glad when Bas came to tell her that dinner would be ready in five minutes.

It was a delicious meal, but she didn't linger over it. The doctor would need his dinner, too, and probably he had plans for his evening. It was Bas who insisted that she went to the drawing room to have her coffee.

Sitting by the cheerful fire presently, with the tray on a table beside her, she felt at peace with everyone…

She was pouring her second cup when she heard Bas admit someone. A minute later the door was thrust open and Christina Lutyns pushed past him and came into the room.

Araminta put the coffeepot down carefully. Her

polite 'Good evening, *Mevrouw*,' went unanswered, though.

'Why are you sitting here in the drawing room? Where is Dr van der Breugh? Why aren't you looking after the children?'

Araminta didn't need to answer, for the doctor had come into the room. His '*Dag*, Christina,' was uttered quietly, and he smiled a little. 'Miss Pomfrey is taking a well-earned hour or so from her duties. The reason she is not with the children is because she has been with them almost constantly since the early hours of today. They both have the mumps.'

Christina gave a small shriek. She lapsed into Dutch. 'Don't come near me; I might get them too. And that girl sitting there, she shouldn't be here; she should stay with the boys. I shall go away at once.' She contrived to look tearful. 'And I was looking forward to our evening together. How long will they be ill?'

'Oh, quite a while yet,' said the doctor cheerfully. 'But both Miss Pomfrey and I have had mumps as children, so we aren't likely to get them again.'

'I shall go,' said Christina. 'When there is no more infection you will tell me and we will enjoy ourselves together.'

She went then, ignoring Araminta, escorted to the door by the doctor who showed her out, taking care, at her urgent request, not to get too near to her.

When he went back into the drawing room Araminta had drunk her coffee and was on her feet. She said politely, 'I enjoyed my dinner, thank you. I'll see to the boys now.'

He nodded in an absent-minded manner. 'Yes, yes, by all means. I'll be back later on.'

'There is no need—' began Araminta, then she caught his eye and ended lamely, 'Very well, doctor,' and went meekly upstairs.

She had the boys ready for bed when he came back upstairs, bade her a civil goodnight, waited while she tucked the boys up and hugged them and then held the door open for her. As she went past him, he told her that he would be away from home for the next two days.

'Unavoidable, I'm afraid, but I have asked a colleague of mine to call in each day. The boys have met him on previous visits and they like him. Don't hesitate to call upon him if you need advice.'

Getting ready for bed, Araminta supposed that she should be glad that the doctor would be away from home. They didn't get on and he was indifferent to her, although she had to admit that he was thoughtful for her comfort, while at the same time indifferent to her as a person.

'Not that I mind,' said Araminta, talking to herself, lying half-sleep in the bath. She said it again to convince herself.

Paul was much better in the morning and Peter, although still sorry for himself, was amenable to swallowing his breakfast. The doctor had left very early, Bas told her, but Dr van Vleet would be calling at about ten o'clock to see the boys.

They were sitting up in their beds, well enough now to talk while Araminta tidied the room, when the doctor came.

He was young, thickset and of middle height with a rugged face which just missed being handsome, but he had bright blue eyes and a wide smile. He shook hands with her, said something to the boys which made them laugh and added in English, 'Van Vleet— I expect Marcus told you that I would look in.'

'Yes, he did. They're both much better. Peter's still got a slight temperature, but the swellings have gone down since yesterday.'

'I'll take a look...'

Which he did, sitting on their beds while he examined them in turn, talking all the time, making them laugh.

'They're fine. I should think they might get up tomorrow. Though they must stay in a warm room...'

'There's a nursery close by. They could spend the day there.'

'Don't let them get tired.' He smiled nicely at her. 'Marcus told me that you were very experienced with small children, so I don't have to bother you with a great many instructions.'

He closed his bag just as Bas came in. 'Coffee is in the drawing room, Miss Pomfrey, Doctor...Nel will come and stay with the boys while you drink it.'

And when Araminta hesitated, he added, 'Dr van der Breugh instructed me.'

So they went downstairs together and spent a short time over their coffee. Too short, thought Araminta, bidding him goodbye. She liked Dr van Vleet and he seemed to like her. It had been delightful to talk to someone who didn't treat her with indifference, who actually appeared to like talking to her. She was glad that he would be coming again in the morning.

The boys were so much better the next day that there was really no need for Dr van Vleet to call, but he came, looked down their throats, peered into their ears, examined the receding mumps and pronounced himself satisfied.

'Marcus will be back tonight,' he told her. 'I'll phone him in the morning, but will you tell him that the boys are both fine.'

They had coffee together again, and when he got up he asked, 'Do you get time off? I'd like to show you something of Utrecht while you're here.'

Araminta beamed at him. 'I'd like that. I get time off, of course, but it has to fit in with Dr van der Breugh.'

He took out his pocketbook and wrote in it. 'Here's my phone number. When you are free, will you phone me? Perhaps we could arrange something.'

'Thank you, I'll let you know.'

She smiled at him, her eyes sparkling at the prospect of a day out with someone with whom she felt so completely at ease.

The pleasant feeling that she had met someone who liked her—enough to ask her out for a whole day—made the day suddenly become perfect, her chores no trouble at all, the boys little angels…

The glow of her pleasure was still in her face when the doctor came home. He had come silently into the house as he so often did, to be welcomed by Humphrey. Bas hurried to greet him, offered tea or coffee, and took his overnight bag. The doctor went into his study, put away his bag, tossed his jacket on a chair and went upstairs two at a time, to pause in the open doorway of the nursery where the two boys and Araminta were crouched on the floor before a cheerful fire playing Happy Families.

They looked round as he went in and the boys rushed to greet him. Araminta got to her feet and he stared at her for a long moment. He had thought about her while he had been away, unwillingly, aware that she disturbed him in some way, and he had returned home determined to relegate her to where she belonged—the vague background, which he didn't allow to interfere with his work.

But the face she turned to him wasn't easily dismissed; she looked happy. He was so accustomed to her quiet face and self-effacing manner that he was taken aback. Surely that look wasn't for him? He dismissed the idea as absurd and knew it to be so as he watched the glow fade and her features assume their usual calm.

He wished her good evening, listened while she gave him a report on the boys' progress, expressed himself satisfied and, when Bas came to tell him that he had taken his coffee to the drawing room, bore the two boys downstairs with him.

'Fetch them in an hour, if you will, Miss Pomfrey. When they are in bed we can discuss their progress.'

Left alone, she tidied up the room, got everything ready for bedtime and sat down by the fire. Why was a fire so comforting? she wondered. The house was already warm but there were handsome fireplaces in the rooms in which fires were lighted if a room was in use. She had got used to living in comfort and she wondered now how she would like hospital life.

In a few weeks now they would be returning to England. She thought of that with regret now that she had met Dr van Vleet. She wondered if she should ask for a day off—she was certainly entitled to one—but Dr van der Breugh hadn't looked very friendly—indeed, the look he had given her had made her vaguely uncomfortable…

She fetched the boys presently, and once they were finally in their beds went to her room to change for the evening. The skirt and one of the blouses, she decided. There seemed little point in dressing up each evening, for the doctor was almost never home. But she felt that if Bas took the trouble to set the table with such care, and Jet cooked such delicious din-

ners for her, the least she could do was to live up to
that. She heard the doctor come upstairs and go into
the boys' room, and presently, making sure that they
were on the verge of sleep, and with a few minutes so
spare before Bas came to tell her dinner was ready,
she went downstairs.

There was no sign of the doctor, but she hadn't
expected to see him. He would probably tell her at
breakfast of any plans for the boys. Bas, crossing
the hall, opened the drawing room door for her and
she went in.

The doctor was sitting in his chair, with Humphrey at his feet. He got up as she went in, offered her
a chair, offered sherry and when he sat down again,
observed, 'I think we may regard Peter and Paul as
being almost back to normal. I think we should keep
them from school for another few days, but I see no
reason why they shouldn't have a short brisk walk
tomorrow if the weather is fine. Children have astonishing powers of recovery.'

Araminta agreed pleasantly and sipped her sherry.
She hoped he wasn't going to keep her for too long;
she was hungry and it was already past the dinner
hour.

'You must have a day to yourself,' said the doctor.
'I'm booked up for the next two days, but after that I
will be at home, if you care to avail yourself of a day.
And this time I promise to make sure that you enjoy
yourself. You may have the Jaguar and a driver, and

if you will let me know where you would like to go, I will arrange a suitable tour for you.'

Araminta took another sip of sherry. So she was to be given a treat, was she? Parcelled up and put in a car and driven around like a poor old relative who deserved a nice day out.

She tossed back the rest of the sherry and sat up straight. 'How kind,' she said in a voice brittle with indignation, 'but there is no need of your thoughtful offer. I have other plans.'

The doctor asked carelessly, 'Such as?' and when she gave him a chilly look he said, 'I do stand, as it were, *in loco parentis*.'

'I am twenty-three years old, doctor,' said Araminta in a voice which should have chilled him to the bone.

He appeared untouched. 'You don't look it. Had I not known, I would have guessed nineteen, twenty at the most.' He smiled, and she knew that she would have to tell him.

'Dr van Vleet has asked me to spend the day with him.'

She had gone rather red, so that she frowned as she spoke.

'Ah, a most satisfactory arrangement. And it absolves me from the need to concern myself over you. Telephone him and make any arrangements you like; I am sure you will enjoy yourself with him.' He put down his glass. 'Shall we go in to dinner?'

'Oh, are you going to be here?' Araminta paused;

she had put that rather badly. 'What I meant was, you're dining at home this evening?'

The doctor said gravely, 'That is my intention, Miss Pomfrey.' She didn't see his smile, for she was looking at her feet and wondering if she should apologise.

He, aware of that, maintained a steady flow of small talk throughout the meal so that by the time they had finished she felt quite her normal calm self again.

Getting ready for bed later, she even decided that the doctor could, if he chose, be a pleasant companion.

The next few days went well. The boys, making the most of their last free days before going back to school, took her about the city, spending their pocket money, feeding the ducks in the park, taking her to the Oudegracht to look at the ancient stone—a legendary edifice which, they told her, with suitable embellishments, had to do with the devil.

She saw little of the doctor, just briefly at breakfast, with occasional glimpses as he came and went during the day, but never in the evenings. Somehow he made time to be with his nephews before their bedtime, when she was politely told that she might do whatever she wished for a couple of hours, but they didn't dine together again.

Not that Araminta minded. She had phoned Dr van Vleet and, after gaining the doctor's indifferent consent, had agreed to spend the day with him on the following Saturday.

She worried as to what she should wear. It was too chilly for the two-piece; it would have to be a blouse and skirt and the jacket. A pity, she reflected crossly, that she never had the time to go shopping. In the meantime she would have to make do with whatever her meagre wardrobe could produce. She had money, the doctor was punctilious about that, so the very first morning she had an hour or two to herself she would go shopping.

The sun was shining when Dr van Vleet came for her; the doctor had already breakfasted, spent a brief time in his study and was in the garden with the boys, but they all came to see her off, the boys noisily begging her to come back soon. 'As long as you're here in the morning when we wake up,' said Peter.

Dr van Vleet drove a Fiat and she quickly discovered that he liked driving fast. 'Where are we going?' she wanted to know.

'To Arnhem first. We go through the Veluwe—that's pretty wooded country—and at Arnhem there's an open-air village museum you might like to see. You've seen nothing of Holland yet?'

'Well, no, though I've explored Utrecht pretty thoroughly. With the boys.'

'Nice little chaps, aren't they?' He gave her a smiling glance. 'My name's Piet, by the way. And what is it the boys call you?'

'Mintie. Short for Araminta.'

'Then I shall call you Mintie.'

He was right, the Veluwe was beautiful: its trees glowing with autumn colours, the secluded villas half hidden from the road. They stopped for coffee and, after touring the village at Arnhem, had lunch there.

After lunch he drove to Nijmegen and on to Culemborg, and then north to Amersfoort and on to Soestdijk so that she could see the royal palace.

They had tea in Soest and then drove back to Appeldoorn to look at the palace there. Piet finally took the Utrecht road, and she said, 'You've given me a lovely day. I can't begin to thank you; I've loved every minute of it…'

'It's not over yet. I hope you'll have dinner with me. There's rather a nice hotel near Utrecht—Auberge de Hoefslag. Very pretty surroundings, woods all round and excellent food.'

'It sounds lovely, but I'm not dressed…' began Araminta.

'You look all right to me.'

And she need not have worried; the restaurant was spread over two rooms, one modern, the other delightfully old-fashioned, and in both there was a fair sprinkling of obvious tourists.

The food was delicious and they didn't hurry over it. By the time they had driven the ten kilometres to Utrecht it was almost eleven o'clock.

Piet got out of the car with her and went with her to the door, waiting while she rang the bell, rather

worried as it was later than she had intended. Bas
opened the door, beamed a greeting at her and ushered her inside. He wished Dr van Vleet a civil
goodnight and shut the door, and just for a moment
Araminta stood in the hall, remembering her happy
day and smiling because before they had said goodnight he had asked her to go out with him again.

'A happy day, miss?' asked Bas. 'You would like
coffee or tea?'

'A lovely day, Bas.' Her eyes shone just thinking
about it. 'I don't want anything, thank you. I do hope
I haven't kept you up?'

'No, miss. Goodnight.'

She crossed the hall to the staircase. The doctor's
study door was half open and she could see him at
his desk. He didn't look up, and after a moment's
pause she went on up the stairs. He must have heard
her come in but he had given no sign. She wouldn't
admit it, but her lovely day was a little spoilt by that.

At breakfast he asked her if she had enjoyed her
day out, and, quite carried away by the pleasure, she
assured him that she had and embarked on a brief
description of where they had been, only to realise
very quickly that he wasn't in the least interested.
So she stopped in mid-sentence, applied herself to
attending to the boys' wants and her own breakfast,
and when he got up from the table with a muttered
excuse took no notice.

He turned back at the door to say, 'I see no reason
why the boys shouldn't attend church this morning.

Kindly have them ready in good time, Miss Pomfrey. And, of course, yourself.'

So they went to church, the boys delighted to be with their uncle, she at her most staid. The sermon seemed longer than ever, but she didn't mind, she was planning her new clothes. Piet had said he would take her to Amsterdam, a city worthy of a new outfit.

The doctor, sitting so that he could watch her face, wondered why he had considered her so plain—something, someone had brought her to life. He frowned; he must remember to warn her...

There was a general upsurge of the congregation and presently they were walking home again.

They had just finished lunch and were full of ideas as to how they might spend their afternoon when Christina Lutyns was ushered in.

She kissed the doctor on both cheeks, nodded to the boys and ignored Araminta, breaking into a torrent of Dutch.

The doctor had got up as she entered, and stood smiling as she talked. When she paused he said something to make her smile, and then said in English, 'I shall be out for the rest of the day, Miss Pomfrey.' When the boys protested, he promised that when he came home he would be sure to wish them goodnight. 'Although you may be asleep,' he warned them.

They had been asleep for hours when he came home. He went to their room and bent to kiss them and tuck the bedclothes in, and Araminta, who had

had a difficult time getting them to go to sleep, hoped that he would have a good excuse in the morning.

Whatever it was, it satisfied the boys, but not her, for he spoke Dutch.

That evening he asked her when she would like her free day. Piet had suggested Thursday, but she felt uncertain of having it. If the doctor had work to do he wouldn't change that to accommodate her. But it seemed that Thursday was possible. 'Going out with van Vleet again?' asked the doctor casually.

'Yes, to Amsterdam.' She added, in a voice which dared him to disagree with her, 'I hear it is a delightful city. I am looking forward to seeing it.'

'Miss Pomfrey, there is something I should warn you about…'

'Is there? Could it wait, Doctor? The boys will be late for school if I don't take them now.'

'Just as you like, Miss Pomfrey.' And somehow she contrived not to be alone with him for the rest of the day; she felt sure he was going to tell her that they would be returning to England sooner than he had expected, and she didn't want to hear that. Not now that she had met Piet.

Rather recklessly she went shopping during the morning hours while the boys were in school. Clothes, good clothes, she discovered, were expensive, but she couldn't resist buying a dress and loose jacket in a fine wool. It was in pale amber, an impractical colour and probably she wouldn't have much chance to wear it, but it gave her mousy hair an added glint and it was a perfect fit. She bought shoes, too, and a handbag and a pretty scarf.

Thursday came and, much admired by the boys, she went downstairs to meet Piet. He was in the hall talking to the doctor and turned to watch her as she came towards them. His hello was friendly. 'How smart you look—I like the colour; it suits you.'

'We told her that she looks beautiful,' said Peter.

'She does, doesn't she, Uncle?' Paul added.

The doctor, appealed to, observed that indeed Miss Pomfrey looked charming. But his eyes when he glanced at her were cold.

Amsterdam was everything that she had hoped for, and Piet took her from one museum to the other, for a trip on the canals, a visit to the Rijksmusee and there they had a quick look at the shops. They had coffee and had a snack lunch and, later, tea. And in the evening, as the lights came on, they strolled along the *grachten*, looking at the old houses and the half-hidden antique shops.

He took her to the Hotel de L'Europe for dinner, and it was while they drank their coffee that he told her that he was to marry in the New Year.

'Anna is in Canada, visiting her grandparents,' he told her. 'I miss her very much, but soon she will be home again. You would like each other. She is like you, I think, rather quiet—I think you say in English, a home bird? She is a splendid cook and she is fond of children. We shall be very happy.'

He beamed at her across the table and she smiled back while the half-formed daydreams tumbled down into her new shoes. She had been a fool, but, thank heaven, he had no idea…

'Tell me about her,' said Araminta. Which he did at some length, so that it was late by the time they reached the doctor's house.

'We must go out together again,' said Piet eagerly.

'Well, I'm not sure about that. I believe we're going back to England very shortly. Shall I let you know?' She offered a hand. 'It's been a lovely day, and thank you so very much for giving me dinner. If we don't see each other again, I hope that you and your Anna will be very happy.'

'Oh, we shall,' he assured her.

'Don't get out of the car,' said Araminta. 'There's Bas at the door.'

It was quiet in the hall, and dimly lit. Bas wished her goodnight and went away, and she stood there feeling very alone. She had only herself to thank, of course. Had she really imagined that someone as uninteresting as herself could attract a man? He had asked her out of kindness—she hoped he hadn't pitied her…

She was aware that the study door was open and the doctor was standing there watching her. She made for the stairs, muttering goodnight, but he put out an arm and stopped her.

'You look as though you are about to burst into tears. You'll feel better if you talk about it.'

'I haven't anything to talk about…'

He put a vast arm round her shoulders. 'Oh, yes, you have. I did try to warn you, but you wouldn't allow me to.'

He sounded quite different: kind, gentle and understanding.

'I've been such a fool,' began Araminta as she laid her head against his shoulder and allowed herself the luxury of a good cry.

CHAPTER SIX

THE DOCTOR, WAITING PATIENTLY while Araminta sniv-
elled and snorted into his shoulder, became aware
of several things: the faint scent of clean mousy hair
under his chin, the slender softness of her person and
a wholly unexpected concern for her. Presently he
gave her a large white handkerchief.

'Better?' he asked. 'Mop up and give a good blow
and tell me about it.'

She did as she was told, but said in a watery voice,
'I don't want to talk about it, thank you.' And then
she added, 'So sorry...' She had slipped from his
arm. 'You've been very kind. I'll wash your hanky...'

He sat her down in a small chair away from the
brightness of his desk lamp.

'You don't need to tell me if you don't wish to.'
He had gone to a small table under the window and
come back with a glass. 'Drink that; it will make
you feel better.'

She sniffed it. 'Brandy? I've never had any...'

'There's always a first time. Of course, van Vleet

told you that he was going to be married shortly.' He watched her sip the brandy and draw a sharp breath at its strength. 'And you had thought that he was interested in you. He should have told you when you first met him, but I imagine that it hadn't entered his head.' He sighed. 'He's a very decent young man.'

Araminta took another sip, a big one, for the brandy was warming her insides. She felt a little sick and at the same time reckless.

She said, in a voice still a little thick from her tears, 'I have been very silly. I should know by now that there is nothing about me to—to make a man interested. I'm plain and I have no conversation, and I wear sensible clothes.'

The doctor hid a smile. 'I can assure you that when you meet a man who will love you, none of these things will matter.'

She said in her matter-of-fact way, 'But I don't meet men—young men. Father and Mother have friends I've known for years. They're all old and mostly married.' She tossed back the rest of the brandy, feeling light-headed. Vaguely she realised that in the morning she was going to feel awful about having had this conversation. 'I shall, of course, make nursing my career and be very successful.' She got to her feet. 'I'll go to bed now.' She made for the door. 'I feel a little sick.'

He crossed the hall with her and stood watching while she made her way upstairs. She looked forlorn and he ignored a wish to help her. Her pride had been shattered; he wouldn't make it worse.

Thanks to the brandy, Araminta slept all night, but everything came rushing back into her head when she woke up. She remembered only too clearly the talk she had had with the doctor. To weep all over him had been bad enough, but she had said a great deal too much. She got up, went to call the boys and prayed that he would have left the house before they went down to breakfast.

Her prayers weren't answered; he was sitting at the table just as usual, reading his letters, his spectacles perched on his splendid nose.

He got up as they went in, received the boys' hugs and wished her good morning with his usual cool politeness. She gave him a quick look as she sat down; there was no sign of the gentle man who had comforted her last night. He was as he always was: indifferent, polite and totally uninterested in her. Her rather high colour subsided; it was clear their conversation was to be a closed book. Well, she had learned her lesson; if ever a man fell in love with her—and she doubted that—he would have to prove it to her in no uncertain fashion. And she would take care to stay heartwhole.

The day passed in its well-ordered fashion; there was plenty to keep her occupied. The boys, fit again, were full of energy, noisy, demanding her attention and time. She welcomed that, just as she welcomed the routine, with their uncle's return in the evening and the hour of leisure while they were with him. He went out again as soon as they were in bed, wishing her a cool goodnight as he went.

Araminta, eating her dinner under Bas's kindly eye, wondered where he was. Probably with Christina Lutyns, she supposed. Much as she disliked the woman there was no doubt that she would make a suitable wife for the doctor. Suitable, but not the right one. There was a side to him which she had only glimpsed from time to time—not the cool, bland man with his beautiful manners and ease; there was a different man behind that impassive face and she wished she could know that man. A wish not likely to be granted.

The following week wore on, and there had been no mention of her free day. Perhaps he thought she wouldn't want one. It was on Friday evening, when she went to collect the boys at bedtime that he asked her to stay for a moment.

'I don't know if you had any plans of your own, Miss Pomfrey, but on Sunday I'm taking the boys up to Friesland to visit their aunt and uncle. I should say their great-aunt and great-uncle. They live near Leeuwarden, in the lake district, and I think we might make time to take you on a quick tour of the capital. The boys and I would be delighted to have you with us, and my aunt and uncle will welcome you.' His smile was kind. 'You may, of course, wish to be well rid of us!'

It was a thoughtful kindness she hadn't expected. 'I wouldn't be in the way?'

'No. No, on the contrary. I promise you the boys won't bother you, and if you feel like exploring on your own you have only to say so. It would give you the opportunity of seeing a little more of Holland before we go back to England.'

'Then I'd like to come. Thank you for asking me. Is it a long drive?'

'Just over a hundred miles. We shall need to leave soon after eight o'clock; that will give us an hour or so at Huis Breugh and then after lunch we can spend an hour in Leeuwarden before going back for tea. The boys can have their supper when we get back and go straight to bed.'

Even if she hadn't wanted to go, she would never have been able to resist the boys' eager little faces. She agreed that it all sounded great fun and presently urged them upstairs to baths and bed. When she went down later it was to find the doctor had gone out. She hadn't expected anything else, but all the same she was disappointed.

Which is silly of me, said Araminta to herself, for he must be scared that I'll weep all over him again. He must have hated it, and want to forget it as quickly as possible.

In this she was mistaken. The doctor had admitted to himself that he had found nothing disagreeable in Araminta's outburst of crying. True, she had made his jacket damp, and she had cried like a child, uncaring of sniffs and snivels, but he hadn't forgotten any moment of it. Indeed, he had a vivid memory of the entire episode.

He reminded himself that she would leave his household in a short while now, and doubtless in a short time he would have forgotten all about her. In the meantime, however, there was no reason why he shouldn't try and make up for her unhappy little episode with van Vleet.

He reminded himself that he had always kept her at arm's length and would continue to do so. On no account must she be allowed to disrupt his life. His work was his life; he had a wide circle of friends and some day he would marry. The thought of Christina flashed through his mind and he frowned—she would be ideal, of course, for she would allow him to work without trying to alter his life.

He picked up his pen and began making notes for the lecture he was to give that evening.

Araminta, getting up early on Sunday morning, was relieved to see that it was a clear day with a pale blue sky and mild sunshine. She would wear the new dress and jacket and take her short coat with her. That important problem solved, she got the boys dressed and, on going down to breakfast, found the doctor already there.

'It's a splendid day,' he assured them. 'I've been out with Humphrey. The wind is chilly.' He glanced at Araminta. 'Bring a coat with you, Miss Pomfrey.'

'Yes, I will. The boys have their thick jerseys on, but I'll put their jackets in the car. Is Humphrey coming with us?'

'Yes, he'll sit at the back with the boys.'

The boys needed no urging to eat their breakfast, and a few minutes after eight o'clock they were all in the car, with Bas at the door waving them away.

The doctor took the motorway to Amsterdam and then north to Purmerend and Hoorn and so on to the Afsluitdijk.

'A pity we have no time to stop and look at some of the towns we are passing,' he observed to Araminta. 'Perhaps some other time...'

There wasn't likely to be another time, she reflected, and thrust the thought aside; she was going to enjoy the day and forget everything else. She had told herself sensibly that she must forget about Piet van Vleet. She hadn't been in love with him, but she had been hurt, and was taken by surprise and she was still getting over that. But today's outing was an unexpected treat and she was going to enjoy every minute of it.

Once off the *dijk* the doctor took the road to Leeuwarden and, just past Franeker, took a narrow country road leading south of the city. It ran through farm land: wide fields intersected by narrow canals, grazed by cows and horses. There were prosperous-looking farmhouses and an occasional village.

'It's not at all like the country round Utrecht.'

'No. One has the feeling of wide open spaces here,

which in a country as small as Holland seems a so-
lecism. You like it?'

'Yes, very much.'

He drove on without speaking, and when the road
curved through a small copse and emerged on the
further side, she could see a lake.

It stretched into the distance, bordered by trees
and shrubs. There was a canal running beside it and
a narrow waterway leading to a smaller lake. There
were sailing boats of every description on it and,
here and there, men fishing from its banks, sitting
like statues.

The boys were excited now, begging her to look
at first one thing, then another. 'Isn't it great?' they
wanted to know. 'And it gets better and better. Aren't
you glad you came, Mintie?'

She assured them that she was, quite truthfully.

There were houses here and there on the lake's
bank, each with its own small jetty, most of them
with boats moored there. She didn't like to ask if
they were almost there, but she did hope that it might
be one of these houses, sitting four-square and solid
among the sheltering trees around it.

The doctor turned the car into a narrow brick lane
beside a narrow inlet, slowed to go through an open
gateway and stopped before a white-walled house
with a gabled roof. It had a small square tower to
one side and tall chimneys, and it was surrounded
by a formal garden. The windows were small, with
painted shutters. It was an old house, lovingly main-

tained, and she could hardly wait to see what it was like inside.

The entrance was at the foot of the tower and led into a small lobby which, in turn, opened into a long wide hall. As they went in two people came to meet them. They were elderly, the man tall and spare, with white hair and still handsome, and the woman with him short and rather stout, with hair which had once been fair and was now silver. In her youth she might have been pretty, and she had beautiful eyes, large and blue with finely marked eyebrows. She was dressed in a tweed skirt and a cashmere twinset in a blue to match her eyes. When she spoke her voice was rather high and very clear.

'Marcus—you're here. I told Bep we would answer the door; she's getting deaf, poor dear.' She stood on tiptoe to receive Marcus's kiss on her cheek and then bent to hug the boys.

'And this is Miss Pomfrey,' said the doctor, and the little lady beamed and clasped Araminta's hand.

'You see I speak English, because I am sure you have no time to speak our language, and it is good practice for me.' Her eyes twinkled. 'We are so glad to meet you, Miss Pomfrey, now you must meet my husband...'

The two men had been greeting each other while the boys stood one each side of them, but now her host came to her and shook her hand.

'You are most welcome, Miss Pomfrey. I hear

from Marcus that you are a valued member of his household.'

'Thank you. Well, yes, just for a few weeks.' She smiled up into his elderly face and liked him.

He stared back at her and then nodded his head. She wondered what he was thinking, and then forgot about it as his wife reminded them that coffee was waiting for them in the drawing room. Araminta, offered a seat by her hostess, saw that the doctor had the two boys with him and his uncle and relaxed.

'Of course, Marcus did not tell you our name? He is such a clever man, with that nose of his always in his books, and yet he forgets the simplest things. I am his mother's sister—of course, you know that his parents are dead, some years ago now—our name is Nos-Wieringa. My husband was born and brought up in this house and we seldom leave it. But we love to see the family when they come to Holland. You have met the boys' mother?'

Araminta said that, yes, she had.

'And you, my dear? Do you have any brothers and sisters and parents?'

'Parents. No brothers or sisters. I wish I had.'

'A family is important. Marcus is the eldest, of course, and he has two younger brothers and Lucy. Of course you know she lives in England now that she is married, and the two boys are both doctors; one is in Canada and the other in New Zealand. They should be back shortly—some kind of exchange posts.'

Mevrouw Nos-Wieringa paused for breath and Araminta reflected that she had learned more about the doctor in five minutes than in the weeks she had been working for him.

Coffee drunk, the men took the boys down to the home farm, a little distance from the house. There were some very young calves there, explained the doctor, and one of the big shire horses had had a foal.

'And I will show you the house,' said Mevrouw Nos-Wieringa. 'It is very old but we do not wish to alter it. We have central heating and plumbing and electricity, of course, but they are all concealed as far as possible. You like old houses?'

'Yes, I do. My parents live in quite a small house,' said Araminta, anxious not to sail under false pretences. 'It is quite old, early nineteenth-century, but this house is far older than that, isn't it?'

'Part of it is thirteenth-century, the rest seventeenth-century. An ancestor made a great deal of money in the Dutch East Indies and rebuilt the older part.'

The rooms were large and lofty, with vast oak beams and white walls upon which hung a great many paintings.

'Ancestors?' asked Araminta.

'Yes, mine as well as my husband's. All very alike, aren't they? You must have noticed that Marcus has the family nose. Strangely enough, few of the women had it. His mother was rather a plain little thing—the van der Breughs tend to marry plain women. They're a very old family, of course, and his grandfather still lives in the family home. You haven't been there?'

Araminta said that, no, she hadn't, and almost added that it was most unlikely that she ever would. Seeking a change of subject, she admired a large oak pillow cupboard. She mustn't allow her interest in the doctor to swamp common sense.

They lunched presently, sitting at a large oak table on rather uncomfortable chairs; it was a cheerful meal, since the children were allowed to join in the conversation. As they rose from the table Mevrouw Nos-Wieringa said, 'Now, off you go, Marcus, and take Mintie—I may call you Mintie?—with you. We will enjoy having the boys to ourselves for a while, but be back by six o'clock for the evening meal.'

Araminta, taken by surprise, looked at the doctor. He was smiling.

'Ah, yes, it slipped my memory. The boys and I decided that I should take you to Leeuwarden and give you a glimpse of it...'

When she opened her mouth to argue, he said, 'No, don't say you don't want to come; the boys will be disappointed. It was their idea that you should have a treat on your free day.'

The boys chorused agreement. 'We knew you'd like to go with Uncle Marcus. He'll show you the weigh house and the town hall, and there's a little café by the park where you could have tea.'

In the face of their eager pleasure there was nothing she could say.

'It sounds marvellous,' she told them. 'And what dears you are to have thought of giving me a treat.'

In the car presently, driving along the narrow fields towards Leeuwarden, she said stiffly, 'This is kind of you, but it's disrupting your day. You must wish to spend time with your aunt and uncle.'

He glanced at her rather cross face. 'No, no, Miss Pomfrey, I shall enjoy showing you round. Besides, I can come here as often as I wish, but you are not likely to come to Friesland—Holland—again, are you? What free time you get from hospital you will want to spend at your own home.'

She agreed, at the same time surprised to discover that the prospect of hospital was no longer filling her with happy anticipation. She should never have taken this job, she reflected. It had unsettled her—a foreign country, living in comfort, having to see the doctor each day. She rethought that—he might unsettle her, but she had to admit that he had made life interesting...

She asked suddenly, and then could have bitten out her tongue, 'Do you mean to marry Mevrouw Lutyns?' Before he could reply she added, 'I'm sorry, I can't think why I asked that. It was just—just an idle thought.'

He appeared unsurprised. 'Do you think that I should?' He added pleasantly, 'Feel free to speak your mind, Miss Pomfrey. I value your opinion.'

This astonished her. 'Do you? Do you really? Is it because I'm a stranger—a kind of outside observer? Though I don't suppose you would take any notice of what I say.'

'Very likely not.'

'Well, since you ask… Mevrouw Lutyns is very beautiful, and she wears lovely clothes—you know, they don't look expensive but they are, and they fit. Clothes off the peg have to be taken up or let out or hitched up, and that isn't the same…'

They were on the outskirts of Leeuwarden, and she watched the prosperous houses on either side of the street. 'This looks a nice place.'

'It is. Answer my question, Miss Pomfrey.'

'Well…' Why must she always begin with 'well'? she wondered. Her mother would say it was because she was a poor conversationalist. 'I think that perhaps you wouldn't be happy together. I imagine that she has lots of friends and likes going out and dancing and meeting people, and you always have your nose in a book or are going off to some hospital or other.' She added suddenly, 'I'm sure I don't know why you asked me this; it's none of my business.' She thought for a moment. 'You would make a handsome pair.'

The doctor turned a laugh into a cough. 'I must say that your opinion is refreshing.'

'Yes, but it isn't going to make any difference.'

He didn't answer but drove on into the inner city and parked the car by the weigh house. 'I should have liked to take you to the Friesian Museum, but if I do there will be no time to see anything of the city. We will go to the Grote Kerk first, and then the Olde-hove Tower, and then walk around so that you may see some of the townhouses. They are rather fine…'

He took her from here to there, stopping to point out an interesting house, the canals and bridges, interesting gables, and the town hall. Araminta gazed around, trying to see everything at once, determined to remember it all.

'Now we will do as the boys suggested and have tea—there is the café. They remember it because it has such a variety of cakes. We had better sample some or they will be disappointed.'

It was a charming place, surrounded by a small lawn and flowerbeds which even in autumn were full of colour. The tea was delicious, pale and weak, with no milk, but she was thirsty and the dish of cakes put before them were rich with cream and chocolate and crystallised fruit. Araminta ate one with a simple pleasure and, pressed to do so, ate another.

The doctor, watching her enjoyment, thought briefly of Christina, who would have refused for fear of adding a few ounces to her slimness. Araminta appeared to have no such fear. She was, he conceded silently, a very nice shape.

'That was a lovely tea,' said Araminta, walking back to the car. 'I've had a marvellous afternoon. Thank you very much. And your aunt and uncle have been very kind.'

He made a vague, casual answer, opened the car door for her and got in beside her. When she made some remark about the street they were driving along, he gave a non-commital reply so that she concluded that he didn't want to talk. Perhaps he felt that he had done his duty and could now revert to his usual manner. So she sat silently until they had reached the house, and then there was no need to be silent, for the boys wanted to know if she had enjoyed herself, what she had thought of Leeuwarden and, above all, what kind of cakes she had had for tea.

She was glad of their chatter, for it filled the hour or so before they sat down to their meal. They had had a wonderful afternoon, she was told. They had fished in the lake with their great-uncle, and gone with their great-aunt to see the kitchen cat with her kittens—and did she know that there were swans on the lake and that they had seen a heron?

She made suitable replies to all this and then sat with Mevrouw Nos-Wieringa and listened to that lady's gentle flow of talk. There was no need to say anything to the doctor, and really there was no need even to think of that, for he went away with his uncle for a time to look at something in the study, and when they came back they were bidden to the table.

As a concession to the boys, the meal was very similar to an English high tea, and the food had been chosen to please them, finishing with a plate of *poffertjes*—small balls of choux pastry smoth-

ered in fine sugar. Araminta enjoyed them as much
as the boys.

They left soon afterwards. The boys eager to
come again with their mother and father, the doctor
saying that he would spend a weekend with his aunt
and uncle when next he came to Holland. Araminta,
saying all the right things, wished very much that
she would be coming again, too.

The boys were tired by now, and after a few minutes of rather peevish wrangling they dozed off, leaning against Humphrey's bulk. The doctor drove in
silence, this time travelling back via Meppel and
Zwolle, Hardewijk and Hilversum, so that Araminta
might see as much of Holland as possible.

He told her this in a disinterested manner, so that
she felt she shouldn't bother him with questions. She
sat quietly, watching his large capable hands on the
wheel, vaguely aware that she was unhappy.

It was dark by the time they reached Utrecht, and
she urged the sleepy boys straight up to bed with the
promise of hot milk and a biscuit once they were
there. They were still peevish, and it took time and
patience to settle them. She was offering the milk
when the doctor came to say goodnight, and when he
added a goodnight to her, she realised that he didn't
expect her to go downstairs again.

She thanked him for her pleasant day in a damp-
ened down voice, since he was obviously impatient
to be gone, and when he had, she tucked up the boys
and went to her room.

It wasn't late, and she would have liked a cup of tea or a drink of some sort. There was no reason why she shouldn't go down to the kitchen and ask for it, but the thought of encountering him while doing so prevented her. She undressed slowly, had a leisurely bath and got into bed. It had been a lovely day—at least, it would have been lovely if the doctor had been friendly.

She fell asleep presently, still feeling unhappy.

The boys woke early in splendid spirits so that breakfast was a lively meal. The doctor joined in their chatter, but beyond an austere good morning he had nothing to say to Araminta.

It's just as though I'm not here, she reflected, listening to plans being made by the boys to go shopping for presents to take back with them.

'You must buy presents, too,' they told Araminta. 'To take home, you know. We always do. Uncle comes with us so's he can pay when we've chosen.'

'I expect Miss Pomfrey will prefer to do her shopping without us. Let me see, I believe I can spare an afternoon this week.'

'Mintie?' Paul looked anxious.

'Your uncle is quite right; I'd rather shop by myself. But I promise you I'll show you what I've bought and you can help me wrap everything up.'

Suddenly indignant, she suggested that the boys should go and fetch their schoolbooks, and when they had gone she turned her eyes, sparkling with ill temper, on the doctor.

'Presumably we are to return to England shortly?' she enquired in a voice to pulverise a stone. 'It would be convenient for me if you were to be civil enough to tell me when.'

The doctor put down the letter he was reading. 'My dear Miss Pomfrey, you must know by now that I'm often uncivil. If I have ruffled your feelings, I am sorry.' He didn't look in the least sorry, though, merely amused.

'We shall return in five days' time. I have various appointments which I must fulfil but the boys will remain with me until their parents return within the next week or so. I hope that you are agreeable to remain with them until they do? You will, of course, be free to go as soon as their parents are back.'

'You said that you would arrange for me to start my training...'

'Indeed I did, and I will do so. You are prepared to start immediately? Frequently a student nurse drops out within a very short time. If that were the case, you would be able to take her place. I will do what I can for you. You are still determined to take up nursing?'

'Yes. Why do you ask?'

'I'm not sure if the life will suit you.'

'I'm used to hard work,' she told him. 'This kind of life—' she waved a hand around her '—is something I've never experienced before.'

'You don't care for it?'

She gave him an astonished look. 'Of course I

like it. I had better go and see if the boys are ready
for school.'

That morning she went shopping, buying a scarf
for her mother, a book on the history of the Nether-
lands for her father and a pretty blouse for her cousin,
who would probably never wear it. She bought cigars
for Bas, too, and another scarf for Jet, and a box of
sweets for Nel and the elderly woman who came each
day to polish and clean. Mindful of her promise to
the boys, she found pretty paper and ribbons. Wrapping everything up would keep them occupied for
half an hour at least, after their tea, while they were
waiting impatiently for their uncle to come home.

They were still engrossed in this, sitting on the
floor in the nursery with Araminta, when the door
opened and the doctor and Mevrouw Lutyns came in.

The boys ran to him at once and Araminta got to
her feet, feeling at a disadvantage. Mevrouw Lutyns
was, as always, beautifully dressed, her face and
hair utter perfection. Araminta remembered only too
clearly the conversation she had had with the doctor in Leeuwarden and felt the colour creep into her
cheeks. How he must have laughed at her. Probably
he had shared the joke with the woman.

Mevrouw Lutyns ignored her, greeted the boys in
a perfunctory manner and spoke sharply to the doctor. He had hunkered down to tie a particularly awkward piece of ribbon and answered her in a casual
way, which Araminta saw annoyed her. He spoke
in English, too, which, for the moment at any rate,

made her rather like him. A tiresome man, she had to admit, but his manners were beautiful. Unlike Mevrouw Lutyns'.

He glanced at Araminta and said smoothly. 'Mevrouw Lutyns is thinking of coming to England for a visit.'

'I expect you know England well?' said Araminta politely.

'London, of course. I don't care for the country. Besides, I must remain in London. I need to shop.' Her lip curled. 'I don't expect you need to bother with clothes.'

Araminta thought of several answers, all of them rude, so she held her tongue.

The doctor got to his feet. 'Come downstairs to the drawing room, Christina, and have a drink.' And to the boys he added, 'I'll be back again presently— we'll have a card game before bed.'

They went away and Peter whispered. 'We don't like her; she never talks to us. Why does Uncle like her, Mintie?'

'Well, she's very pretty, you know, and I expect she's amusing and makes him laugh, and she wears pretty dresses.'

Paul flung an arm round her. 'We think you're pretty, Mintie, and you make us laugh and wear pretty clothes.'

She gave him a hug. 'Do I really? How nice of you to say so. Ladies like compliments, you know.'

She found a pack of cards. 'How about a game of Happy Families before your uncle comes?'

They were in the middle of a noisy game when he returned. When she would have stopped playing he squatted down beside her.

'One of my favourite games,' he declared, 'and much more fun with four.'

'Has Mevrouw Lutyns gone home?' asked Paul.

'Yes, to dress up for the evening. We are going out to dinner.'

He looked at Araminta as he spoke, but she was shuffling her cards and didn't look up.

Two days later the boys went with their uncle to do their shopping, leaving Araminta to start packing. She had been happy in Holland and she would miss the pleasant life, but now she must concentrate on her future. Her mother, in one of her rare letters, had supposed that she would go straight to the hospital when she left the doctor's house. Certainly she wasn't expected to stay home for any length of time. All the same, she would have to go home for a day or so to repack her things.

'We may be away,' her mother had written. 'There is an important lecture tour in Wales. Your cousin will be here, of course.' She had added, as though she had remembered that Araminta was her daughter, whom she loved, 'I am glad you have enjoyed your stay in Holland.'

Neither her mother or her father would be interested in her life there, nor would her cousin, and there would scarcely be time for her to look up her friends. There would be no one to whom she could describe the days she had spent in the doctor's house. Just for a moment she gave way to self-pity, and then reminded herself that she had a worthwhile future before her despite the doctor's doubts.

For the last few days before they left she saw almost nothing of the doctor. The boys, excited at the prospect of going back to England, kept her busy, and they spent the last one or two afternoons walking the, by now, well known streets, pausing at the bridges to stare down into the canals, admiring the boatloads of flowers and, as a treat, eating mountainous ices in one of the cafés.

They were to leave early in the morning, and amidst the bustle of departure Araminta had little time to feel sad at leaving. She bade Jet and Bas goodbye, shook hands with Nel and the daily cleaner, bent to hug Humphrey, saw the boys settled on the back seat and got in beside the doctor.

It was only as he drove away that she allowed herself to remember that she wouldn't be coming again. In just a few weeks she had come to love the doctor's house, and Utrecht, its pleasant streets and small hidden corners where time since the Middle Ages had stood still. I shall miss it, she thought and then, I shall miss the doctor, too. Once she had left his house she wasn't likely to see him again. There was no chance of their lives converging; he would become part of this whole interlude. An important part.

I do wonder, thought Araminta, how one can fall in love with someone who doesn't care a row of pins for one, for that's what I have done. And what a good thing that I shall be leaving soon and never have to see him again.

The thought brought tears to her eyes and the doctor, glancing sideways at her downcast profile, said kindly, 'You are sorry to be leaving Holland, Miss Pomfrey? Fortunately it is not far from England and you will be able to pay it another visit at some time.'

Oh, no, I won't, thought Araminta, but murmured in agreement.

Their journey was uneventful. They arrived back at his London home to be welcomed by Briskett, with tea waiting. It was as though they had never been away.

CHAPTER SEVEN

BRISKETT HANDED THE DOCTOR his post, informed him that there were a number of phone calls which needed to be dealt with at once, took the boys' jackets and invited Araminta to go with him so that he might show her to her room.

'The boys are in their usual room. They'd better come with you, miss; the doctor won't want to be bothered for a bit. Had a good time, have you? Hope the boss took time off to show you round a bit.'

'Well, yes, we went to Friesland.'

He turned to smile at her, his cheerful rat face split in a wide smile. 'Nice to have him back again, miss. Here's your room. Make yourself at home.'

It would be difficult not to feel at home in such a delightful room, thought Araminta, with its satinwood bed, tall chest and dressing table. The curtains and bedspread were white and pale yellow chintz, and someone had put a vase of freesias by the bed. The window overlooked the long narrow garden, with a high brick wall and trees screening it from its neighbours.

She would have liked to linger there, but the boys would need to be seen to. They had been good on the journey, but now they were tired and excited. Tea and an early bedtime were indicated, unless the doctor had other plans. She went to their room, tidied them up and took them downstairs.

The study, where she had first been interviewed by the doctor, had its door open. The doctor was at his desk, sitting back in his chair, on the phone, and speaking in Dutch. Araminta's sharp ears heard that. He looked up as they went past.

'Go into the sitting room. Briskett will have tea waiting. I'll join you presently.'

So the boys led her across the hall into quite a small room, very cosy, where Briskett was putting the finishing touches to the tea table.

'I've laid a table,' he told her. 'I don't hold with little nippers balancing plates on their knees. Just you sit down, miss, and I'll give the boss a call.'

The doctor joined them presently, ate a splendid tea and then excused himself with the plea of work. 'I have to go out,' he told the boys, 'and I don't think I'll be back before you go to bed, but I'm not doing anything tomorrow morning; we will go to the park and feed the ducks.' He glanced at Araminta. 'I'm sure Miss Pomfrey will be glad of an hour or two to get your clothes unpacked.' He added casually, 'I expect you would like to let your parents know you are back in England; do ring them if you wish.'

She thanked him. 'And, if you don't mind, I'll

go and unpack the boys' night things. I thought an early bedtime…'

'Very wise. I'm sure Briskett will have something extra special for their supper.'

'Perhaps I could have my supper at the same time with them?'

'You would prefer that? Then by all means do so. I'll let Briskett know. You'll bathe them and have them ready for bed first? Shall I tell him seven o'clock?'

'That would do very well, thank you.' She hesitated. 'Are you going out immediately? If you are, then I'll wait and unpack later.'

He glanced at his watch. 'Half an hour or so, but I need to change first.'

'If I can have ten minutes?'

'Of course.'

She unpacked the overnight bag, put everything ready in the boys' bathroom and whisked herself back downstairs with a minute to spare. The doctor bade the boys goodnight, nodded to her and went away. She was in the boys' room, which overlooked the street, when she heard him in the hall and went to look out of the window. He was getting into his car, wearing black tie, looking remarkably handsome.

'I wonder when he gets any work done,' reflected Araminta. 'Talk about a social whirl.' She knew that wasn't fair, he worked long hours and he was good at it, but it relieved her feelings. She hoped lovingly that he wouldn't stay out too late; he needed his sleep like anyone else…

She sighed; she had managed all day not to think too much about him and it had been made easier by his distant manner towards her, but loving him was something she couldn't alter, even though it was hopeless. No one died of a broken heart; they went on living like everyone else and made a success of their lives. Something which she was going to do. But first she must learn to forget him, once she had left his house. Until then, surely it wouldn't do any harm if she thought about him occasionally?

The boys came tumbling in then, and she allowed stern common sense to take over.

Life in London would be very different from that of Utrecht. For one thing there would be no school in the mornings.

Their parents would be returning in a few days now, and the boys were excited and full of high spirits; she filled the mornings with simple lessons and the afternoons with brisk walks, returning in time for tea and games before bedtime. The doctor was seldom at home; as Briskett put it, 'Up early and home late. No time for anything but his work. Good thing he's got a bit of social life of an evening. You know what they say, miss, "All work and no play"…'

But the doctor still found time to spend an hour with the boys each evening, although it was very evident that he had no time for Araminta. His brief good mornings and good evenings were the extent of his conversations with her. And what else did she expect? she asked herself.

They had been back in England for three days before he told her that the boys' parents would be arriving in two days time.

'Perhaps you would be good enough to remain for a day or so after their return; my sister is bound to wish to talk to you, and their clothes and so on will need to be packed up. She will be glad of your help.'

Three days, thought Araminta, four at the outside, and after that I shan't see him again. 'Of course I'll stay on, if Mrs Ingram wishes me to,' she told him.

She was surprised when he asked, 'You will go home? Your people expect you?'

'Yes.' She didn't add that they would probably still be away. Her cousin would be there, of course, and she supposed she would stay there until she heard from the hospital. Which reminded her to add, 'You told me that there was a chance that I might be accepted at the hospital...'

'Ah, yes. It slipped my memory. There is indeed a vacancy; one of the students has left owing to illness. If you can start within a few days and are prepared to work hard in order to catch up with the other students you will be accepted.'

She should have been elated. He had made everything easy for her; she could embark on her plans for a nursing career. And it had been so unimportant to him that he had forgotten to tell her.

'That is what you wanted?' He had spoken so

sharply that she hurried to say that, yes, there was nothing she wished for more.

'I'm very grateful,' she added. 'Is there anything that I should do about it?'

'No, no. You will receive a letter within the next day or two. And you have no need to be grateful. You have been of great help while the boys have been with me. They will miss you.'

The doctor spoke with an austere civility which chilled her, but he was aware as he said it that *he* would miss her too: her small cheerful person around the house, her quiet voice which could on occasion become quite sharp with annoyance. He had a sudden memory of her weeping into his shoulder and found himself thinking of it with tenderness...

He chided himself silently for being a sentimental fool. Miss Pomfrey had fulfilled a much needed want for a few weeks, and he was grateful for that, but once she had gone he would forget her.

Mr and Mrs Ingram duly arrived, late in the afternoon. It was a chilly October day, with a drizzling rain, and Araminta had been hard pushed to keep the boys happy indoors. But at last they shouted to Araminta from their perch by the front windows that their uncle's car had just arrived with their mother and father.

'Then off you go downstairs, my dears. Go carefully.'

She went to the window when they had gone, in

time to see Mr and Mrs Ingram enter the house, followed at a more leisurely pace by the doctor. They
would all have tea, she supposed, and sat down quietly to wait until Briskett brought her own tea tray.
She had sought him out that morning and he had
agreed with her that it might be a good idea if she
were to have her tea in her room.

'The boys will be so excited, and they will all
have so much to talk about that I won't be needed,'
she had pointed out.

He came presently with the news that there was
a fine lot of talk going on downstairs and she hadn't
been missed.

'They'll send for you presently, miss, when they're
over the first excitement,' he assured her. 'The boss'll
want you there to give a report, as it were.' He gave
her a friendly nod. 'Sets great store on you, he does.'

She drank her tea and nibbled at a cake, her usually splendid appetite quite gone. She would start
packing this evening, once the boys were in bed, so
that when she had done all she could do to help Mrs
Ingram, she would be able to leave at once.

She was pouring another cup of tea when the door
opened and the doctor came in.

'I didn't hear you knock,' said Araminta in her
best Miss Pomfrey voice.

'My apologies. Why did you not come downstairs
to tea?'

'It's a family occasion.'

He leaned forward and took a cake and ate it—

one of Briskett's light-as-air fairy cakes—and the simple act turned him from a large, self-assured man into a small boy.

Araminta swallowed the surge of love which engulfed her. However would she be able to live without him?

The doctor finished his cake without haste. 'You have finished your tea? Then shall we go downstairs?'

She shot him a look and encountered a bland stare. There was nothing for it but to do as he asked. How is it possible, she thought, to love someone who is so bent on having his own way? She accompanied him downstairs to the drawing room, to be warmly greeted by the boys' parents. Presently Mrs Ingram drew her on one side.

'They were good?' she wanted to know anxiously. 'Peter and Paul can be perfect little horrors...' She said it with love.

'Well, they weren't; they have been really splendid—very obedient and helpful and never bored.'

'Oh, good. I expect you're longing to go home. Could you stay over tomorrow and help me pack their things?'

'Yes, of course. You must be glad to be going home again. I know the boys will be, although they enjoyed living in Utrecht. It seemed like a second home to them.'

'Well, they love Marcus, of course, and since they've both spoken Dutch and English ever since they could utter words they don't feel strange. I'm sure they will have a lot to tell us. You were happy in Holland?'

'Oh, yes. I enjoyed it very much…'

'Marcus tells me that you're to start nursing training very shortly. That's something you want to do?' Mrs Ingram smiled. 'No boyfriend?'

'No, I expect I'm meant to be a career girl!'

If Mrs Ingram had any opinion about that she remained silent, and presently Araminta took the boys off to bed and supper, before slipping away to her room while their parents came to say goodnight. This was a lengthy business, with a great deal of giggling and talk until they consented to lie down and go to sleep. Excitement had tired them out; they slept in the instant manner of children and she was free to go to her room and change her dress.

She excused herself as soon as she decently could after dinner; it had been a pleasant meal, and she had borne her part in the conversation when called upon to do so, but although the talk had been general, she had no doubt that her company hindered the other three from any intimate talk.

She was bidden a friendly goodnight and the doctor got up to open the door for her. She went past him without a look and went off to her room and started to pack her things. Tomorrow she knew that she would be kept busy getting the boys' clothes packed. She felt lonely; Humphrey's company would have been welcome, but of course he was miles away in Utrecht. So she was forced to talk to herself.

'I'm perfectly happy,' she assured herself. 'My future is settled, I have money, I shall make friends with the other nurses, and in a year or two I shall be able to pick and choose where I mean to work.' Not London. The chance of meeting the doctor was remote but, all the same, not to be risked.

There was no one at breakfast when she went down with the boys: the doctor had already left and Mr and Mrs Ingram weren't yet down. They had almost finished when they joined them. Araminta left the boys with them and at Mrs Ingram's suggestion began the task of packing up for the boys. They were to leave that evening but first they were to go shopping with their father and mother. So Araminta had a solitary lunch and spent the afternoon collecting up the boys' toys and tidying them away into various boxes. They were to be driven home by the doctor directly after tea, and she had been asked to have everything ready by then.

Briskett, going round the house retrieving odds and ends for her to pack, was of the opinion that the house would be very dull once they had gone. 'And you'll be leaving, miss—we shall miss you, too. Very quiet, it'll be.'

'I expect the doctor will be quite glad to have the house to himself,' said Araminta.

'Well, now, as to that, I'd venture to disagree,

miss. The boss is fond of children and you've fitted in like a glove on a hand.'

She thanked him gravely. He was a kind little man, despite his ratty looks, and he was devoted to the doctor. 'Maybe you'll be back, miss,' said Briskett, to her surprise.

'Me? Oh, I don't think so, Briskett. You mean as a governess when the doctor marries and has children? By then I'll be a trained nurse and probably miles away.'

It took some time for the doctor to get his party settled with their possessions in the car and still longer for them to make their goodbyes. The boys hugged and kissed Araminta and rather silently handed her a parcel, painstakingly wrapped in fancy paper. Seeing the look on their small faces, she begged to be allowed to open it there and then.

'They chose it themselves,' said their mother rather apologetically.

It was a coffret of face cream, powder and lipstick, and a little bottle of scent. When Araminta exclaimed over it, Peter said, 'We know you're not pretty, but these things will make you beautiful. The lady behind the counter said so.'

'It's just exactly what I've always wanted,' declared Araminta, 'and thank you both very much for thinking of such a lovely present. I'll use it every day and I'm sure I'll be beautiful in no time at all.'

She hugged them both, told them to be good boys and then watched with Briskett as they all got into the car, parcels and packages squashed into the back seat with the boys and their mother. They all waved and smiled, but not the doctor, of course; he raised a casual hand as he drove away but he didn't turn his head.

Araminta finished her packing, ate a solitary dinner and decided to go to bed. There was no sign of the doctor; probably he would stay the night at his sister's house. She was halfway up the stairs when he came in and Briskett appeared in the hall to offer supper.

'No, no, I've had a meal, thanks, Briskett, but will you see to the car? I'll be in my study.'

He glanced at Araminta, poised on the stairs. 'Miss Pomfrey, if you would spare me a few minutes…?'

She went with him to his study and sat down in the chair he offered her.

'You've had the letter from the hospital?' And when she said yes, he went on, 'Briskett will drive you to your home in the morning. I expect you are anxious to get back. Is there anything you want to know about your appointment as a student nurse? I presume you have been given instructions?'

'Yes, thank you. There is no need for Briskett to drive me…'

He said in a level voice, 'If you will just tell him when you are ready to leave, Miss Pomfrey. I shall see you in the morning before you go. I won't keep you now; you must be tired.'

She got up quickly. 'Yes, yes, I am. Goodnight, Doctor.'

His goodnight was very quiet.

She went down to breakfast after a wakeful night to find that the doctor had been called away very early in the morning. 'Not knowing when he'll be back, he said not to wait for him, miss. I'll have the car round as soon as you've had breakfast.'

Araminta crumbled toast onto her plate and drank several cups of coffee. Now she would never say goodbye to the doctor. Possibly he had left the house early, so that he might avoid a last meeting. She had no idea what she had expected from it, but at least she had hoped that they would part in a friendly fashion. She went suddenly hot and cold at the idea that he might have guessed that she had fallen in love with him. Now her one thought was to leave his house as quickly as possible…her one regret that Hambledon wasn't thousands of miles away.

It was almost noon when Briskett drew up before her home, took her case from the boot and followed her up the path to the front door.

'Looks empty,' he observed. 'Expecting you, are they?'

'My mother and father are in Wales on a lecture tour. A cousin is staying here, though—housekeeping now that I'm not at home.'

Briskett took the key from her and opened the door. There were letters on the doormat and an open note on the hall table. His sharp eyes had read it

before Araminta had seen it. 'Gone with Maud—'
Maud was a friend of Millicent, the cousin '—for a
couple of days. Good luck with your new job.'

He was bending over her case as she saw it and
read it.

'Where will I put this, miss? I'll take it upstairs
for you.'

'Thank you, Briskett. It's the room on the left on
the landing. Will you stay while I make a cup of tea?
I'd offer you lunch, but I'm not quite sure…'

'A cuppa would be fine, miss.'

Briskett hefted the case and went upstairs. Nice
little house, he decided, and some nice furniture—
good old-fashioned stuff, no modern rubbish. But
the whole place looked unlived-in, as though no one
much bothered about it. He didn't like leaving Miss
Pomfrey alone, but she hadn't said anything about
the note so he couldn't do much about that.

He went down to the kitchen, again old-fashioned
but well equipped, and found her making the tea.

'I've found some biscuits,' she told him cheerfully. 'Will you get back in time to make lunch for
yourself?'

'Easy, miss, there won't be all that much traffic.' He eyed Cherub, who had come in though the
kitchen window she had opened and was making
much of Araminta.

'Nice cat. Yours, is he?'

'Yes, I found him. Have another biscuit. I shall
miss Humphrey in Utrecht…'

Briskett's long thin nose quivered. 'I'm sure he'll
miss you. Pity the boss wasn't home. Beats me, it
does, him at the top of the tree, so to speak, and still
working all the hours God made.'

When he had gone Araminta unpacked. Presently
she would sort out her clothes and repack, ready to
leave the next day, but for now she went to inspect the
fridge. Even those with broken hearts needed to be fed.

As the doctor let himself into his house that evening
Briskett came into the hall.

'A bit on the late side, aren't you?' he observed.
'Had a busy day, I'll be bound. I've a nice little dinner ready for you.'

'Thanks, Briskett. You took Miss Pomfrey back
to her home?'

Briskett nodded. 'There's a nice young lady for
you. I didn't fancy leaving her in that empty house.'
He met the doctor's sudden blue stare and went on,
'Her ma and pa are in Wales. There's a cousin or
some such looking after the house, but she'd gone
off for a few days. Only living thing to greet us was
a tatty old cat.'

He watched the doctor's face; he really looked
quite ferocious but he didn't speak. Briskett reck-
oned he was pretty angry...

'Nice house,' he went on. 'Small, some nice stuff
though, good and solid, a bit old-fashioned. Nice bits
of silver and china too.' He paused to think. 'But it
weren't a home.'

And, when the doctor still remained silent, 'We had a cuppa together—very concerned, she was, about me not having my dinner.'

'Did Miss Pomfrey tell you that this cousin was away?'

'Not a word. I happened to see the note on the table.'

'She seemed quite happy?'

'Now, as to that, Boss, I wouldn't like to venture an opinion.'

He hesitated, cautious of the doctor's set face. 'I'd have brought her back, but that wouldn't have done, would it?'

'No, Briskett, it wouldn't have done at all. You did right. Miss Pomfrey will be going to St Jules' tomorrow, and I dare say this cousin will have returned by then.'

The doctor went into his study and sat down at his desk, staring at the papers on it, not seeing them. I miss her, he thought. I can't think why. She has no looks, she wears drab clothes, she has at times a sharp tongue and yet her voice is delightful and she is kind and patient and sensible. And she has beautiful eyes.

He drew the papers towards him and picked up his pen. This feeling of loss is only temporary, he mused. She has been a member of the household for some weeks; one gets used to a person. I shall forget her completely in a few weeks.

He went to his solitary dinner then, agreeing with

Briskett that it was pleasant to have a quiet house once more. Now he would be able to prepare the notes on the learned treatise he was writing without the constant interference of small boys' voices—and Mintie's voice telling them to hush.

He went to his desk after dinner but he didn't write a word, his mind occupied with thoughts of Araminta, alone at her home with only a cat for company. There was no use trying to work, so he took himself for a brisk walk and went to bed—but he didn't sleep.

Araminta had had a boiled egg and some rather stale bread for a late lunch, fed Cherub, put on the washing machine and started packing again. She was to report to the hospital at two o'clock the next day and, since there was no indication as to when her cousin would return, she went down the lane to Mrs Thomas's little cottage and asked her to feed Cherub.

'I'll leave the food out for you in the shed. If you wouldn't mind feeding him twice a day? I've no idea when my cousin will be back…'

Mrs Thomas listened sympathetically. 'Don't you worry, dear, I'll look after him. He's got the cat flap so's he can get into the house, hasn't he?'

'Yes. I hate leaving him, but there's nothing I can do about it.'

'Well, she only went yesterday morning, I saw the car…and your mother and father will be back soon, I dare say?'

'I'm not sure when.'

It wasn't very satisfactory, as she explained to Cherub later, but surely someone would come home soon. Besides, she would have days off. She cheered up at the thought.

Her mother phoned in the evening. 'I thought you might be home,' she said vaguely. 'I expect you're happy to be starting at St Jules'. You see that we were right, my dear. This little job you have had hasn't made any difference at all, just a few weeks' delay. I'm sure you'll have no difficulty in catching up with the other students. Your father and I will be coming home very shortly. I can't say exactly when. The tour is such a success we may extend it. Is your cousin there?'

Araminta started to say that she wasn't, but her mother had already begun to tell her about some remarkable Celtic documents they had been examining. It took a long time to explain them and when she had finished Mrs Pomfrey said a hurried goodbye. 'I have so much to think of,' she explained. 'I'll send a card when we are coming home.'

St Jules' Hospital was old, although it had been added to, patched up and refurbished from time to time. It was a gloomy place, looming over the narrow streets surrounding it, but the entrance hall was handsome enough, with portraits of dead and gone medical men on its panelled walls and the handsome staircase sweeping up one side of it. A staircase which no one except the most senior staff were allowed to tread.

Araminta was bidden to take herself and her case
to the nurses' home, reached by a rather dark tunnel
at the back of the hall. There was a door at the other
end and when she opened it cautiously she found
herself in a small hallway with stairs ahead of her
and a door marked 'Office' at one side.

It seemed sense to knock, and, bidden to go in,
she opened the door.

The woman behind the small desk was middle-
aged with a pale face and colourless hair, wearing a
dark maroon uniform.

'Araminta Pomfrey? Come in and shut the door.
I'll take you to your room presently. You can leave
your outdoor things there before you go to see the
Principal Nursing Officer.' She shuffled through a
pile of papers.

'Here is a list of rules. You are expected to keep
them while you live here. When you have completed
your first year you will be allowed to live out if you
wish. No smoking or drinking, no men visitors unless they visit for some good reason.'

She drew a form from a pile on the desk. 'I'll
check your particulars. You are twenty-three? A good
deal older than the other students. Unmarried? Parents living? British by birth?' She was ticking off the
items as she read them. 'Is that your case? We will
go to your room.'

They climbed the stairs, and then another flight
to the floor above, and the woman opened a door
halfway down a long corridor. 'You'll have your own

key, of course. You will make your bed and keep
your room tidy.'

The room was small and rather dark, since its
window overlooked a wing of the hospital, but it was
furnished nicely and the curtains and bedcover were
pretty. There was a washbasin in one corner and a
built-in wardrobe.

Araminta was handed a key. She asked, 'What
should I call you? You are a sister?'

'I am the warden—Miss Jeff.' She looked at her
watch. 'Come back to my office in ten minutes and
I'll take you for your interview.'

Left alone, Araminta turned her back on the view
from the window, took off her jacket and tidied her
hair. She hoped she looked suitably dressed; her skirt
was too long for fashion, but her blouse was crisply
ironed and her shoes were well polished. She went
out of the room, locked the door, put the key in her
shoulder bag and found her way to Miss Jeff.

The Principal Nursing Officer's office was large,
with big windows draped with velvet curtains, a carpet underfoot and a rather splendid desk. She herself was just as elegant. She was a tall woman, still
good-looking, dressed in a beautifully tailored suit.
She shook Araminta's hand, and told her crisply that
she was fortunate that there had been an unexpected
vacancy.

'Which I could have filled a dozen times, but
Dr van der Breugh is an old friend and very highly
thought of here in the hospital. He assured me that

you had given up your place in order to cope with an emergency in his family.' She smiled. 'You are a lucky young woman to have such an important sponsor.' She studied Araminta's face. 'I hope that you will be happy here. I see no reason why you shouldn't be. You will work hard, of course, but you will make friends. You are older than the other student nurses, but I don't suppose that will make any difference.'

She nodded a friendly dismissal and Araminta went back to her room, where she unpacked and took a look at the uniform laid out on the bed. It was cotton, in blue and white stripes with a stiff belt, and there was a little badge she was to wear pinned on her chest with her name on it.

The warden had told her to go down to the canteen for her tea at four o'clock. She made her way back down the stairs and into the hospital, down more stairs into the basement. The canteen was large, with a long counter and a great many tables—most of them occupied. Araminta went to the counter, took a tray, loaded it with a plate of bread and butter and a little pot of jam, collected her tea and then stood uncertainly for a moment, not sure where she should sit. There was a variety of uniforms, so she looked for someone wearing blue and white stripes.

Someone gave her a little shove from behind. 'New, are you?'

The speaker was a big girl, wearing, to Araminta's relief, blue and white stripes, and when she nodded, she said, 'Come with me, we have to sit with our own set—the dark blue are sisters, the light blue are staff nurses. Don't go sitting with them.'

She led the way to the far end of the room to where several girls were sitting round a table. 'Here's our new girl,' she told them. 'What's your name?'

'Araminta Pomfrey.'

Several of the girls smiled, and one of them said, 'What a mouthful. Sister Tutor isn't going to like that.'

'Everyone calls me Mintie.'

'That's more like it. Sit down and have your tea. Any idea which ward you are to go to in the morning?'

'No. Whom do I ask?'

'No one. It'll be on the board outside this place; you can look presently. Have you unpacked? Supper's at eight o'clock if you're off duty. What room number are you? I'll fetch you.'

'Thank you.'

The big girl grinned. 'My name's Molly Beckett.' She waved a hand. 'And this is Jean, and that's Sue in the corner…' She named the girls one by one.

'We're all on different wards, but not all day, we have lectures and demonstrations. You'll be run off your feet on the ward, and heaven help you if Sister doesn't like you.' She got up. 'We're all on duty now, but I'm off at six o'clock; I'll see you then. Come with us and we'll look at the board.'

There was a dismayed murmur as they crowded round to look for Araminta's name.

'Baxter's,' said Molly. 'That's Sister Spicer. I don't want to frighten you, but look out for her, Mintie.

She's got a tongue like a razor and if she takes a dislike to you you might as well leave.'

Araminta went back to her room, put her family
photos on the dressing table, arranged her few books
on the little shelf by the bed and sat down to think.
She had very little idea of what hospital life would
be like and she had to admit that Sister Spicer didn't
sound very promising. But she was a sensible girl
and it was no use thinking about it too much until
she had found her feet.

The other girls seemed very friendly, and she
would be free for a few hours each day, and she could
go home each week. She allowed her thoughts to
wander. What was the doctor doing? she wondered.
Had he missed her at all? She thought it unlikely. I
must forget him, she told herself firmly. Something
which should be easy, for she would have more than
enough to think about.

Molly came presently and, since it wasn't time for
supper, took her on a tour of the home, explaining
where the different wards were and explaining the
off duty. 'You'll get a couple of evenings off each
week. Trouble is, you're too tired to do much. Otherwise it's a couple of hours in the morning or in the
afternoon. Days off are a question of luck. We come
bottom of the list, though if you've got a decent sister she'll listen if you want special days.'

The canteen was full and very noisy at suppertime. Araminta ate her corned beef and salad and the
stewed apple and custard which followed it, drank

a cup of strong tea and presently went to the sitting room for the more junior nursing staff. Molly had gone out for the rest of her free evening and she couldn't see any of the other girls she had met at tea. She slipped away and went to her room, had a bath and got into bed.

She told herself that it would be all right in the morning, that it was just the sudden drastic change in her lifestyle which was making her feel unhappy. She lay thinking about the doctor, telling herself that once she started her training she wouldn't let herself think of him again.

Marcus van der Breugh, dining with friends, bent an apparently attentive ear to his dinner companion while he wondered what Mintie was doing. He had told her that he didn't think she would make a good nurse and he very much feared that he was right. Possibly it was this opinion which caused his thoughts to return to her far too frequently.

CHAPTER EIGHT

LYING IN BED at the end of her first day at St Jules',
Araminta tried not to remember all the things which
had gone wrong and reminded herself that this was
the career she had wished for. Now that she had
started upon it, nothing was going to deter her from
completing it.

Of course, she had started off on the wrong foot.
The hospital was large, and had been built in the days
when long corridors and unexpected staircases were
the norm. Presumably the nurses then had found
nothing unusual in traipsing their length, but to Araminta, who had never encountered anything like
them before, they'd spelt disaster. She had gone the
wrong way, up the wrong staircase and presented
herself at Sister's office only to be told that she had
come to Stewart's ward, Baxter's was at the other
end of the hospital and up another flight of stairs.

So she had arrived late, to encounter Sister Spicer's basilisk stare.

'You're late,' she was told. 'Why?'

'I got lost,' said Araminta.

'A ridiculous excuse. Punctuality is something I insist upon on my ward. Have you done any nursing before coming here?'

Araminta explained about the children's convalescent home, but decided against mentioning her work for the doctor.

Sister Spicer sighed. 'You will have to catch up with the other students as best you can. I suppose Sister Tutor will do what she can with you. I have no time to mollycoddle you, so you had better learn pretty fast.'

Araminta nodded her head.

'If you don't you might as well leave.'

Once upon a time Sister Spicer had probably been a nice person, reflected Araminta. Perhaps she had been crossed in love. Although she could see little to love in the cold handsome face. Poor soul, thought Araminta, and then jumped at Sister Spicer's voice. 'Well, go and find staff nurse.'

The ward was in the oldest part of the hospital, long, and lighted by a row of windows along one side, with the beds facing each other down its length occupied by women of all ages. There were two nurses making beds, who took no notice of her. At the far end Staff Nurse, identified by her light blue uniform, was bending over a trolley with another nurse beside her.

She was greeted briefly, told to go and make beds with the nurse, and thrown, as it were, to the lions.

Araminta didn't like remembering that rest of the morning. She had made beds, carried bedpans, handed round dinners and helped any number of patients in and out of bed, but never, it seemed, quite quickly enough.

'New, are yer, ducks?' one old lady had asked, with an alarming wheeze and a tendency to go purple in the face when she coughed. 'Don't you mind no one. Always in an 'urry and never no time ter tell yer anything.'

Her dinner hour had been a respite. She had sat at the table with Molly and the other students and they had been sympathetic.

'It's because you're new and no one has had the time to tell you anything. You're off at six o'clock, aren't you? And you'll come to the lectures this afternoon. Two o'clock, mind. Even Sister Spicer can't stop you.'

She had enjoyed the lectures, although she'd discovered that there was a good deal of catching up to do.

'You must borrow one of the other students' books and copy out the lectures I've already given,' Sister Tutor had said. This was an exercise which would take up several days off duty.

'But it's what I wanted,' said Araminta to herself now.

She had to admit by the end of the week that things weren't quite as she had expected them to be. According to Sister Spicer, she was lazy, slow and wasted far too much time with the patients. There was plenty of work, she had been told, without stopping to find their curlers and carry magazines to and fro, fill water jugs and pause to admire the photos sent from home of children and grandchildren. It was all rather unsatisfactory, and it seemed that she would be on Baxter's ward for three months...

She longed for her days off, and when they came she was up early and out of the hospital, on her way home as quickly as she could manage. She scooted across the forecourt as fast as her legs could carry her, watched, if she had but known, by Dr van der Breugh, who had been called in early and was now enjoying a cup of coffee before he went back home.

The sight of her small scurrying figure sent the thought of her tumbling back into his head and he frowned. He had managed for almost a whole week to think of her only occasionally. Well, perhaps rather more than occasionally! She would be going home for her days off and he toyed with the idea of driving to Hambledon to find out if she had settled in. He squashed the idea and instead, when he encountered one of the medical consultants on his way out of the hospital, asked casually how the new student nurses were shaping.

'I borrowed one of them for a few weeks and she's been accepted late.'

'Oh, yes, I remember hearing about that. They're quite a good bunch, but of course she has to catch up. She's on Baxter's and Sister Spicer is a bit of a martinet. Don't see much of the nurses, though, do we? If I remember she was being told off for getting the wrong patient out of bed when I saw her, something like that. Rather quiet, I thought, but Sister Spicer can take the stuffing out of anyone. Terrifies me occasionally.'

They both laughed and went on their way.

Araminta, home by mid-morning, found her cousin and Cherub to welcome her. Over coffee she made light of her first week at St Jules'.

'Have you heard from your mother?' asked Millicent. 'She phoned, but they were still busy with some new Celtic finds. She said they might not be home yet...'

'They'll be back before Christmas, though?'

'Oh, I'm sure they will! It's still October. Will you get off for the holiday?'

Araminta shook her head. 'I don't think so, I'm very junior, but of course I'll get my days off as near to Christmas Day as possible.'

'You like it? You're happy?'

Araminta assured her that she was.

The two days were soon over, but they had given her a respite, and she went back on the ward determined to make the week a better one than her first had been. It was a pity that Sister Spicer was bent on making that as difficult as possible.

Molly had told her that Sister Spicer, if she took a dislike to anyone, would go to great lengths to make life as unpleasant as possible for her. Araminta hadn't quite believed that, but now she saw that it was true. Nothing she did was quite right; she was too slow, too clumsy, too careless. She tried not to let it worry her and took comfort from the patients, who liked her. Staff Nurse was kind, too, and the two senior student nurses, although the other student nurse who was in the same set as she now was, did nothing to make life easier for her.

Melanie was a small, pretty girl, always ready with the right answers during the lectures they both attended, and, since Sister Spicer liked her, the fact that she sometimes skimped her work and was careless of the patients' comfort, went unnoticed. She was young, barely nineteen, and made it obvious that Araminta need not expect either her friendship or her help on the ward.

When once she came upon Araminta speaking to one of the house doctors she said spitefully, 'Don't you know better than to talk to the housemen? Is that why you're here? To catch yourself a husband? Just you wait and see what happens to you if Sister Spicer catches you.'

Araminta looked at her in blank astonishment. 'He was asking me the way to Outpatients; he's new.'

Melanie giggled. 'That's as good an excuse as any, I suppose, but watch out.'

Thank heavens I've got days off tomorrow, Araminta thought. Since she was off duty at six o'clock that evening, she would be able to catch a train home.

She hadn't told her cousin, but she would be home by nine o'clock at the latest…

The afternoon was endless, but she went about getting patients in and out of bed, helping them, getting teas, bedpans, filling water jugs, but it was six o'clock at last and she went to the office, thankful that she could at last ask to go off duty.

Sister Spicer barley glanced up from the report she was writing.

'Have you cleaned and made up the bed in the side ward? And the locker? It may be needed. You should have done it earlier. I told Nurse Jones to tell you. Well, it's your own fault for not listening, Nurse. Go and do it now and then you may go off duty.'

'I wasn't told to do it, Sister,' Araminta said politely, 'and I am off duty at six o'clock.'

Sister Spicer did look up then. 'You'll do as you are told, Nurse—and how dare you answer back in that fashion? I shall see the Principal Nursing Sister in the morning and I shall recommend that you are entirely unsuitable for training. If I can't train you, no one else could.'

She bent her head over her desk and Araminta went back into the ward where there was a third-year nurse and Melanie, who had taken such a dislike to her. Neither of them took any notice of her as she went to the side ward and started on the bed. She very much wanted to speak her mind, but that might upset the patients and, worse, she might burst into tears. She would have her days off and when she came back *she* would go and see the Principal Nursing Officer and ask to be moved to another ward. Unheard of, but worth a try!

It was almost seven o'clock by the time she had finished readying the room and making up the bed. She went down the ward, wishing the patients a cheerful goodnight as she went, ignoring the nurses and ignoring, too, Sister's office, walking past it, out of the ward and along the corridor, then going down the wide stone staircase to the floor below and then another staircase to the ground floor.

She was trying to make up her mind as to whether it was too late to go home, or should she wait for the morning, but she was boiling with rage and misery. Nothing was turning out as she had hoped, not that that mattered now that she would never see Marcus van der Breugh again. The pain of loving him was almost physical. She swallowed the tears she must hold back until she was in her room.

'I shall probably be given the sack,' she said out loud, and jumped the last two steps, straight into the doctor's waistcoat.

'Oh,' said Araminta, as she flung her arms around as much of him as she could reach and burst into tears.

He stood patiently, holding her lightly, and not until her sobs had dwindled into hiccoughs and sniffs did he ask, 'In trouble?'

'Yes, oh, yes. You have no idea.' It seemed the most natural thing in the world to tell him, and, for the moment, the delight of finding him there just when she wanted him so badly had overridden all her good resolutions not to see him again, to forget him…

He said calmly in a voice she wouldn't have dreamt of disobeying, 'Come with me,' and he urged her across the corridor and into a room at its end.

'I can't come in here,' said Araminta. 'It's the consultants' room. I'm not allowed…'

'I'm a consultant and I'm allowing you. Sit down, Mintie, and tell me why you are so upset.'

He handed her a very white handkerchief. 'Mop up your face, stop crying and begin at the beginning.'

She stopped crying and mopped her face, but to begin at the beginning was impossible. She told him everything, muddling its sequence, making no excuses. 'And, of course, I'll be given the sack,' she finished. 'I was so rude to Sister Spicer, and anyway, she said I was no good, that I'd never make a nurse.'

She gave a sniff and blew her nose vigorously. 'It's kind of you to listen; I don't know why I had to behave like that. At least, I do, I had been looking forward to my days off, and I would have been home by now. But it's all my own fault; I'm just not cut out to be a nurse. But that doesn't matter,' she added defiantly. 'There are any number of careers these days.'

The doctor made no comment. All he said was, 'Go and wait in the nurses' sitting room until I send you a message. No, don't start asking questions. I'll explain later.'

He led her back, saw her on her way and went without haste to the Principal Nursing Officer's office. He was there for some time, using his powers of persuasion, cutting ruthlessly through rules and regulations with patience and determination which couldn't be gainsaid.

Araminta found several of her new friends in the sitting room, and it was Molly who asked, 'Not gone yet?' and then, when she saw Araminta's face, added, 'Come and sit down. We were just wondering if we'd go down to the corner and get some chips.'

Araminta said carefully, 'I meant to go home this evening, but I got held up. I—I was rude to Sister Spicer. I expect I'll be dismissed.'

She didn't feel like a grown woman, more like a disobedient schoolgirl and she despised herself for it.

Molly said bracingly, 'It can't be as bad as all that, Mintie. You'll see, when you come back from your days off you'll find it will all have blown over.'

Araminta shook her head. 'I don't think so. You see, Molly, I think Sister Spicer is probably right; I'm not very efficient, and I'm slow. I like looking after people and somehow there's never enough time. Oh, you know what I mean—someone wants a bedpan but I'm not allowed to give it because the consultant is due in five minutes—that sort of thing.'

'You've not been happy here, have you, Mintie?'

'No, to be honest I haven't. I think it will be best if I go and see the Principal Nursing Officer and tell her I'd like to leave.'

'You don't want to give it another try?' someone asked, but Araminta didn't answer because the warden had put her head round the corner.

'Nurse Pomfrey, you're to go to the consultants' room immediately.'

She went out, banging the door after her.

'Mintie, whatever is happening? Why do you have to go there?'

Araminta was at the door. 'I'll come back and tell you,' she promised.

Dr van der Breugh was standing with his vast back to the room, looking out of the window, when she knocked and went in. He turned round and gave her a thoughtful look before he spoke.

'Have you decided what you want to do?'

'Yes, I'll go and ask if I may leave. At once, if that's allowed. But I don't suppose it is.'

'And what do you intend to do?'

'It's kind of you to ask, doctor,' said Araminta, hoping that her voice wouldn't wobble. 'I shall go home and then look for the kind of job I can do. Probably they will take me back at the convalescent home.'

They wouldn't; someone had taken her place and there was no need of her services there now. But he wasn't to know that.

'I feel responsible for this unfortunate state of affairs,' said the doctor slowly, 'for it was I who persuaded you to look after the twins and then arranged for you to come here. I should have known that it would be difficult for you, having to catch up with the other students. And Sister Spicer...'

He came away from the window. 'Sit down, Mintie, I have a suggestion to make to you. I do so reluctantly, for you must have little faith in my powers to help you. I have a patient whose son is the owner and headmaster of a boys' prep school at Eastbourne. I saw her today and she told me that he is looking urgently for a temporary assistant matron. The previous one left unexpectedly to nurse her mother and doesn't know when she intends to return. I gave no thought to it until I saw you this evening. Would you consider going there? You would need to be interviewed, of course, but it is a job with which you are already familiar.'

'Little boys? But how can I take the job? I am not sure, but I expect I'd have to give some sort of notice.' She added sharply, 'Of course I have faith in you, I'm very grateful that you should have thought of me.'

'But if it could be arranged, you would like the job, provided the interview was satisfactory?'

'Yes. You see, that's something I can do—little boys and babies and girls.' She paused, then explained, 'It's not like nursing.'

'No, I realise that. So you are prepared to give it a try? I have seen the Principal Nursing Officer. If you go to her office now you may make a request to leave. It is already granted, but you need to go through the motions. I will contact my patient and ask her to arrange things with her son. You should hear shortly.'

He went to the door and opened it for her. 'I will drive you home tomorrow morning. Ten o'clock in the forecourt.'

'There is really no need…' began Araminta. 'I'm perfectly able…'

'Yes, yes, I know, but I have no time in which to argue about it. Kindly do as I ask, Mintie.'

If he had called her Miss Pomfrey in his usually coolly civil way, she would have persisted in arguing, but he had called her Mintie, in a voice kind enough to dispel any wish to argue with him. Besides, she loved him, and when you love someone, she had discovered, you wish to do everything to please them.

She said, 'Very well, doctor,' and added politely, 'Good evening.'

She went off to the office, buoyed up by the knowledge that if Marcus had said that everything was arranged, then that would be so and she had no need to worry. She knocked and, bidden to enter, received a bracing but kind lecture, a recommendation to find work more suited to her capabilities and permission to leave.

'Be sure and hand in your uniform and notify the warden. There is no need for you to see Sister Spicer.' She was offered a hand. 'I have no doubt that you will find exactly what you want, Nurse.'

So Araminta shook hands and got herself out of the office, leaving her superior thoughtful. Really,

Dr van der Breugh had gone to great lengths to arrange the girl's departure. After all, he wasn't responsible for her, whatever he said. The Principal Nursing Officer wouldn't have allowed her arm to be twisted by anyone else but him; she liked him and respected him and so did everyone else at the hospital. All the same, he must be interested—such a plain little thing, too.

Araminta went back to the sitting room and half a dozen pairs of eyes fastened on her as she went in.

'Well?' asked Molly. 'Who was it? What's happened? Was Sister Spicer there?'

Araminta shook her head. 'No, just me. I'm leaving in the morning...'

'But you can't. I mean, you have to give notice that you want to, and reasons.'

Araminta decided to explain. 'Well, I didn't come with the rest of you because I was asked to take on a job in an emergency. I did tell you that. But the thing is the person I worked for was Dr van der Breugh—with his nephews—and I went to look after them provided he would do his best to get me a place here as soon as possible. Well, he did, but it hasn't worked out, so now he has arranged for me to leave. The Principal Nursing Officer was very nice about it.'

There was a chorus of voices. 'What will you do? Try another hospital? Find another job?'

'Go home.'

Molly said, 'It's good of Dr van der Breugh to

help you. I can quite see that he feels responsible—I mean, you obliged him in the first place, didn't you?'

'Yes. And he did warn me that he didn't think I'd be any good at nursing. Only I'd set my heart on it. I'll start again, but not just yet.'

'If you're going in the morning you'll have to pack and sort out your uniform. We'll give you a hand.'

So several of them went to Araminta's room and helped her to pack. She went in search of the warden and handed in her uniform, taking no heed of the lecture she was given by that lady, and presently they all went down to supper and then to make tea and talk about it, so that Araminta had no time at all to think or make plans. Which was a good thing, for her head was in a fine muddle. Tomorrow, she told herself, she would sit down quietly and think things out. Quite what she meant by that she didn't know.

She woke very early, her head full of her meeting with the doctor. It was wonderful that he had come into her life once more—surely for the last time. And since he had gone to so much trouble she would take this job at Eastbourne and stay there for as long as they would have her. It was work she could do, she would have some money, she could go home in the holidays and she would take care never to see Marcus again. That shouldn't be difficult, for he had never shown a wish to see more of her. She got up, and dressed, then said goodbye to her friends, and promptly at ten o'clock went down to the entrance with her case. She hadn't been particularly happy at the hospital but all the same she felt regret at leaving it.

The doctor came to meet her, took her case and put it in the boot, and settled her beside him in the car. He had wished her good morning, taken a look at her face and then decided to say nothing more for the moment. Mintie wasn't a girl to cry easily, he was sure, but he suspected that there were plenty more tears from where the last outburst had come, and it would only need a wrong word to start them off.

He drove out of the forecourt into the morning traffic.

'We will go home and have coffee, for Briskett wants to bid you goodbye. You have an appointment to see Mr Gardiner at three o'clock this afternoon. He will be at the Red Lion in Henley. Ask for him at Reception.'

He didn't ask her if she had changed her mind, and he had nothing further to say until he stopped in front of his house.

Briskett had the door open before they reached it, delighted to see her again.

'There's coffee in the small sitting room,' said Briskett, 'and I'll have your coat, Miss Pomfrey.'

They sat opposite each other by the fire, drinking Briskett's delicious coffee and eating his little vanilla biscuits, and the doctor kept up an undemanding conversation: the boys were fine, he had seen them on the previous weekend, they were all going over

to Friesland for Christmas. 'They sent their love—
they miss you, Mintie.'

He didn't add that he missed her, too. He must go
slowly, allow her to find her feet, prove to herself that
she could make a success of a job. He had admitted to
himself that she had become the one thing that really
mattered to him, that he loved her. He had waited a
long time to find a woman to love, and now that he
had he was willing to wait for her to feel the same
way, something which might take time...

He drove her to Hambledon later, and once more
found the house empty save for a delighted Cherub.
There was another note, too, and, unlike Briskett,
the doctor coolly took it from Araminta's hand when
she had read it.

The cousin had gone to Kingston to shop and
would be back after tea. He put the note back, ignoring her indignant look, and glanced around him.
Briskett had given a faithful description of the house:
pleasant, old-fashioned solid furniture and lacking
a welcome.

'It's a good thing, really,' said Araminta. 'I've an
awful lot to do, especially if I get this job and they
want me as soon as possible.'

He rightly took this as a strong hint that he should
go. He would have liked to have taken her somewhere for a meal but she would have refused. When
she thanked him for the lift and his help in getting
her another job, he made a noncommittal reply,
evincing no wish to see her again, but wishing her a

happy future. And in a month or two he would contrive to see her again…

Araminta, wishing him goodbye and not knowing that, felt as though her heart would break—hearts never did, of course, but it was no longer a meaningless nonsense.

But there was little time to indulge in unhappiness. In three hours' time she would have to be at the Red Lion in Henley, and in the meantime there was a lot to do.

There had been no time to have second thoughts; that evening, washing and ironing, sorting out what clothes she would take with her while she listened to her cousin's chatter, Araminta wondered if she had been too hasty.

Mr Gardiner had been no time-waster. He was a man of early middle age, quiet and taciturn, asking her sensible questions and expecting sensible answers. His need for an assistant matron was urgent, with upwards of fifty little boys and Matron run off her feet. He'd read her credentials, then voiced the opinion that they seemed satisfactory.

'In any case,' he told her, 'my mother tells me that Dr van der Breugh is a man of integrity and highly respected. He gave you a most satisfactory reference. Now, as to conditions and salary…'

He dealt with these quite swiftly and asked, 'Are you prepared to come? As soon as possible?' He smiled suddenly. 'Could you manage tomorrow?'

The sooner she had something to occupy her thoughts the better, reflected Araminta. She agreed to start on the following day. 'In the late afternoon? Would that do? There are several things I must see to...'

'Of course, we'll expect you around teatime. Take a taxi from the station and put it down to expenses. I don't suppose you have a uniform? I'll get Matron to find something.'

He had given her tea and she had come back home to find her cousin returned. A good thing, for she'd offered to cook them a meal while Araminta began on her packing. She'd phoned her mother later to tell her that she had left the hospital and was taking up a job as an assistant school matron.

'What a good idea,' observed her parent comfortably. 'You liked the convalescent home, didn't you? A pity you couldn't have stayed with Dr van der Breugh's nephews, for it seems to me, my love, that you are cut out to be a homebody. I'm sure you will be very happy at Eastbourne.

'We shall be home very shortly and we must make plans for Christmas. We still have a good deal of research to do and the publishers are anxious for us to have our book ready by the spring, but we shall be home soon, although we may need to make a trip to Cornwall—there have been some interesting discoveries made near Bodmin.'

Araminta was sorry to leave Cherub once again. It was fortunate that he was a self-sufficient cat, content as long as he was fed and could get in and out of the house. Araminta, on her way to Eastbourne the next day, wondered if it would be possible for her to have him with her at the school. There was a flatlet, Mr Gardiner had told her, and Cherub would be happy in her company. She would wait until she had been there for a time and then see what could be done. It depended very much on the matron she would be working with. Araminta, speculating about her, decided that no one could be worse than Sister Spicer...

The school was close to the sea front, a large rambling place surrounded by a high brick wall, but the grounds around it were ample; there were tennis courts and a covered swimming pool and a cricket pitch. And the house looked welcoming.

She was admitted by a friendly girl who took her straight to Mr Gardiner's office. He got up to shake hands, expressed pleasure at her arrival and suggested that she might like to go straight to Matron.

'I'll take you up and leave you to get acquainted. The boys will be at supper very shortly, and then they have half an hour's recreation before bed. Perhaps you could work alongside Matron for a while this evening and get some idea of the work?'

Matron had a sitting room and a bedroom on the first floor next to the sick bay. She was a youngish woman with a round, cheerful face and welcomed Araminta warmly. Over a pot of tea she expressed her relief at getting help.

'It's a good job here,' she observed. 'The Gardiners are very kind and considerate, but it does need two of us. You like small boys? Mr Gardiner told me that you had worked with them.'

She took Araminta along to her room presently, at the other end of the house but on the same floor. It was quite large, with a shower room leading from it, an electric fire, a gas ring and a kettle. It was comfortably furnished and on the bed there was an assortment of blue and white striped dresses.

'I've done the best I could,' said Matron. 'See if any of them fit—the best of them can be altered.' She hesitated. 'Mr Gardiner always calls me Matron— but the name's Pagett, Norma. I should call you Matron as well, when the boys are around, but...' She paused enquiringly.

'Would you call me Mintie? It's Araminta, really, but almost no one calls me that. Do I call you Miss Pagett?'

'Heavens no, call me Norma. I'm sure we shall get on well together.'

Norma went back to her room and left Araminta to try on the dresses. One or two were a tolerable fit, so she changed, unpacked her few things and went back to Norma's room.

There was just time to be given a brief resumé of her work before the boys' suppertime, and presently, presiding over a table of small boys gobbling their suppers, Araminta felt a surge of content. She wasn't happy, but it seemed that she had found the right job at last—and who could be miserable with all these little boys talking and shouting, pushing and shoving and then turning into pious little angels when Mr Gardiner said grace at the end of the meal?

Later that evening, sitting in her dressing gown, drinking cocoa in Norma's room, Araminta reminded herself that this was exactly what she had wanted. She would never be a career girl, but she hoped there would be a secure and pleasant future ahead for her.

Hard on this uplifting thought came another one. She didn't want security and life could be as unpleasant as it liked, if only she could see Marcus again.

The next few days gave her no chance to indulge in self-pity. Accustomed as she was to the care of small children, she still found the day's workload heavy. Norma was well organised, being a trained children's nurse, and efficient. She was kind and patient, too, and the boys liked her. They liked Araminta, too, and once she had learned her day's routine, and her way round the school, she found that life could be pleasant enough even if busy— provided, of course, that she didn't allow herself to think about Marcus.

The following weekend was an exeat, and the boys would have Saturday, Sunday and Monday to go home, save for a handful whose parents were abroad.

'We will split the weekend between us,' Norma told her, 'I'll have Friday evening—you can manage, can't you?—and come back on Sunday at midday.

You can have the rest of Sunday and Monday, only
be back in the evening, won't you? The boys will
come back after tea. Mr Gardiner doesn't mind how
we arrange things as long as one of us is here to keep
an eye on the boys who are staying—there aren't
many; all but half a dozen have family or friends to
whom they go.'

'I don't mind if I don't go home,' said Araminta.
'I've only just got here...'

'Nice of you, but fair's fair, and you'll be glad of
a couple of days away. This is always a busy term—
Christmas and the school play and parents coming
and the boys getting excited.'

Marcus van der Breugh, busy man though he was,
still found time to phone Mrs Gardiner senior. 'A
happy coincidence,' he told her, 'that you should have
mentioned your son's urgent need for help. I am sure
that Miss Pomfrey will be suitable for the work.'

Mrs Gardiner, with time on her hands, was only
too glad to chat.

'I heard from him yesterday evening. He is very
satisfied. She seems a nice girl—the boys like her
and the matron likes her. So important that these
people should get on well together, don't you agree?
And, of course, she is fortunate in that it is an exeat
at the weekend and she will be free for part of the
time to go home. She and Matron will share the days
between them, of course; someone has to be there
for the boys who stay at the school.' She gave a sat-

isfied laugh. 'I feel we must congratulate ourselves on arranging things so successfully.'

The doctor, making suitable replies when it seemed necessary, was already making plans.

Araminta was surprised to get a letter the next morning; her parents were still away and the writing on the envelope wasn't her cousin's. She opened it slowly; her first delighted thought that it was from the doctor was instantly squashed. The writing was a woman's; his writing was almost unreadable.

It was from Lucy Ingram. She had asked her brother where Araminta was, she wrote, and he had given her the school's address. Could Araminta come and stay for a day or two when she was next free? The boys were so anxious to see her again. 'It's an exeat next weekend and I dare say all the schools are the same. So if you are free, do let us know. I'll drive over and fetch you. Do come if you can; it will be just us. Will you give me a ring?'

Araminta phoned that evening. It would be nice to see Peter and Paul again, and perhaps hear something of Marcus from his sister. She accepted with pleasure but wondered if it was worth Mrs Ingram's drive. 'It's only a day and a half,' she pointed out, 'and it's quite a long way.'

'The M4, M25, and a straight run down to Eastbourne. I'll be there on Sunday at noon. And we shall love to see you again.'

The school seemed very empty once most of the

boys had gone and Norma had got into her elderly car and driven away. There were eight boys left, and with Mr Gardiner's permission Araminta had planned one or two treats for the next day. The pier was still open and some of the amusements—the slot machines, the games which never yielded up a prize, the fortune-teller—were still there.

After their midday dinner she marshalled her little flock and, armed with a pocket full of tenpenny pieces which she handed out amongst them, she let them try everything and then trotted them along the esplanade and into the town, where they had tea at one of the smartest cafés.

Mr Gardiner had told her to give them a good time, that she would be reimbursed, so they ate an enormous tea and, content with their outing, walked back through the dusk to the school. Since it was a holiday they were allowed to stay up for an hour and watch television after their supper. Araminta, going from bed to bed wishing them goodnight, was almost as tired as they were.

She put everything ready for the morning before she went to bed, praying that Norma would be as good as her word and return punctually.

She did. Araminta, back from church with the boys and Mr Gardiner and his wife, wished everyone a hurried goodbye and went out of the school gate to find Mrs Ingram waiting there.

'You've not been waiting long?' she asked breathlessly. 'It's been a bit of a scramble.'

'Five minutes. How nice to see you again, Mintie. I thought we'd stop for lunch on the way; we'll be home before three o'clock and then we'll have an early tea with the boys. They can't wait to see you again.'

'It's very kind of you to invite me. I—I didn't expect to see you or the boys again.'

'You like this new job?' Mrs Ingram was driving fast along the almost empty road.

'Yes, very much. I've only been here for a week. I started nursing, but I wasn't any good at it. Dr van der Breugh happened to see me at the hospital and arranged for me to give up training, and he happened to know of this school. He's been very kind.'

Mrs Ingram shot her a quick look. 'Yes, he is. Far too busy, too. We don't see enough of him, so thank heaven for the phone. Now, tell me, what exactly do you do?'

The drive seemed shorter than it was; they found plenty to talk about, and stopped for a snack meal at a service station. The time passed pleasantly and, true to her word, Mrs Ingram stopped the car at her home just before three o'clock.

CHAPTER NINE

PETER AND PAUL fell upon her with a rapturous welcome. They had missed her, they chorused, and did she still remember the Dutch they had taught her when they were in Holland? And did she remember that lovely toy shop? And why did she have to live so far away? And was she to stay for a long, long time? For they had, assured Peter, an awful lot to tell her. But first she must go into the garden and see the goldfish...

They had a splendid tea presently, and then everyone sat around the table and played Snakes and Ladders, Ludo and the Racing Game, relics from Mr Ingram's childhood. Then it was time for supper, and nothing would do but that Araminta should go upstairs when they were in bed and tell them a story.

'You always did in Uncle Marcus's house,' they reminded her.

The day was nicely rounded off by dinner with the Ingrams and an hour or so round the drawing room fire talking about everything under the sun, except Marcus.

It was still dark when she awoke in the pretty bedroom.

'It's a bit early,' said Peter as the pair of them got onto her bed and pulled the eiderdown around them, 'but you've got to go again at tea time, haven't you? So we thought you might like to wake up so's we can talk.'

The day went too quickly. They didn't go out, for the weather had turned nasty—a damp, misty, chilly November day—but there had been plenty to do indoors. It was mid-afternoon when Mr Ingram took the boys into the garden to make sure that the goldfish were alive and waiting for their food, leaving Mrs Ingram and Araminta sitting in the drawing room, talking idly.

They were discussing clothes. 'It must be delightful—' began Araminta, and stopped speaking as the door opened and the doctor came in.

He nodded, smiling, at his sister, and said, 'Hello, Mintie.'

Nothing could have prevented her glorious smile at the sight of him. He noted it with deep satisfaction and watched her pale cheeks suddenly pinken.

'Good afternoon, Doctor,' said Araminta, replacing the smile with what she hoped was mild interest, bending to examine one of her shoes.

Mrs Ingram got up to kiss him. 'Marcus, how very punctual you are. We're about to have tea. Such a pity that Araminta has to go back this evening.'

The doctor glanced at his watch. 'You have to be

back to get the boys settled in again?' he asked Araminta. 'If we leave around four o'clock that should get you there in good time.'

Araminta looked at Mrs Ingram, who said airily, 'Oh, you won't mind if Marcus drives you back, will you, Araminta? After all, you do know each other, and you'll have plenty to talk about.'

'But it's miles out of your way...?'

Araminta, filled with delight at the thought of several hours in Marcus's company, nonetheless felt it her duty to protest.

'I am interested to hear how you are getting on at the school,' he observed blandly. 'I feel sure that there will be no chance to discuss that once the boys have come indoors.'

Which was true enough. They swarmed over their uncle and grown-up conversation of any kind was at a minimum. Tea was eaten at the table: plates of thinly cut bread and butter, crumpets, toasted teacakes, a sponge cake and a chocolate cake.

'The boys chose what we should have for tea—all the things you like most, Araminta,' said Mrs Ingram. 'And, I suspect, all the things they like most, too! We always have an old-fashioned tea with them. I can't say I enjoy milkless tea and one biscuit at four o'clock.'

She glanced at her brother. 'Did you have time for lunch, Marcus?'

'Oh, yes. It's Briskett's day off, but he leaves me something.' He sounded vague. But there was nothing vague about his manner when presently he said that they must leave if Araminta needed to be back at the school by six o'clock. She fetched her overnight bag and got into her coat, then made her farewells—lengthy ones when it came to the boys, who didn't want her to go.

'Araminta must come and see us all again soon,' said Mr Ingram. 'She gets holidays just like you do.'

A remark which served to cheer up the boys so that she and Marcus left followed by a cheerful chorus of goodbyes.

Beyond asking her if she were comfortable, the doctor had nothing to say. It wasn't until they were on the M4, travelling fast through the early dusk, that he began a desultory conversation about nothing in particular. He was intent on putting Araminta at her ease, for she was sitting stiff as a poker beside him, giving him the strong impression that given the opportunity she would jump out of the car.

She had said very little to him at his sister's house, something which no one but himself had noticed, and now she was behaving as though he were a stranger. Driving to Oxford that afternoon, he had decided to ask her to marry him, but now he could see that that was something he must not do. For some reason she was keeping him at arm's length, and yet at St Jules' she had flung those arms around him with every appearance of relief and delight at seeing him. She seemed happy enough at the school. Perhaps she was trying to make it plain that she resented his reappearance now that she had settled into a job that she liked.

They reached the M25 and he was relieved to see that her small stern profile had resolved itself into her usual habitual expression of serenity. He waited until they had left the motorway, going south now towards Eastbourne.

'You are happy at the school?' he asked casually. 'You feel that you can settle there, if permanent job should be offered, or would you prefer to use it as a stop-gap? You can always enrol at another hospital, you know.'

'No. That was a mistake. I hope that I can stay at the school. Matron is thinking of leaving next year; there's always the chance that I might get her job. I would be very happy there for the rest of my life.'

She spoke defiantly, expecting him to disagree about that, but all he did was grunt in what she supposed was agreement, which should have pleased her but left her illogically disappointed.

Presently he said, 'You feel that you have found your niche in life?' He shot past a slow-moving car. 'Have you no wish to marry? Have a home of your own, a husband and children?'

It was on the tip of her tongue to tell him that was exactly what she wished, but what would be the point of wishing? Where was she to find a home and a husband and children? And anyway, the only husband she wanted was beside her, although he might just as well have been on the moon.

She wasn't going to answer that; instead she asked, 'And you, doctor, don't you wish for a wife and children?'

'Indeed I do. What is more, I hope to have both in due course.'

Not Christina, hoped Araminta, he would be unhappy. She said, at her most Miss Pomfrey-ish, 'That will be nice.'

A silly answer, but what else was there to say? She tried to think of a suitable remark which might encourage him to tell her more, but her mind was blank. Only her treacherous tongue took matters into its own hands.

'Is she pretty?' asked Araminta, and went scarlet with shame, thankful that it was too dark for him to see her face.

The doctor managed not to smile. He said in a matter-of-fact way, as though there was nothing unusual in her question, 'I think she is the loveliest girl in the world.'

To make amends, Araminta said, 'I hope you will be very happy.'

'Oh, I am quite certain of that. Paul and Peter are looking very fit, don't you agree?'

Such a pointed change in the conversation couldn't be ignored. She was aware of being snubbed and her reply was uttered in extreme politeness with waspish undertones. It seemed the right moment to introduce that safest of topics, the weather.

She spun it out, making suitable comments at intervals, and the doctor, making equally suitable answers in a casual fashion, was well content. True, his Araminta had shown no sign of love, even liking for him, but she was very much on her guard and anxious to impress him with her plans for her solitary future.

But he had seen her gloved hands clenched together on her lap and the droop of her shoulders. She wasn't happy, despite her assurances. He wished very much to tell her that he loved her, but it was only too obvious that she was holding him at arm's length. Well, he could wait. In a week or so he would find a reason to meet her again…

They were in the outskirts of Eastbourne and he glanced at the clock on the dashboard. 'Ten minutes to six. Do you go on duty straight away?'

'I expect so. There'll be the unpacking to do, and the boys will want their supper.'

He stopped the car by the school entrance and she undid her seat belt. 'Thank you for bringing me back; I have so enjoyed my weekend. Don't get out—you must be anxious to get home.'

He took no notice of that but got out, opened her door, got her case from the boot and walked her to the door.

She held out a hand. 'Goodbye, Dr van der Breugh. I hope you have a lovely time at Christmas.'

He didn't speak. He put her case down in the vestibule and bent and kissed her, slowly and gently. And only by a great effort was she able to keep her arms from flinging themselves round him. He got back into his car then, and drove away, and she stood, a prey to a great many thoughts and feelings, oblivious of the small boys trooping to and fro in the hall behind her.

Their small voices, piping greetings, brought her to her senses and back into the busy world of the school. It was only that night in bed that she had the time to go over those last few moments.

Had he meant to kiss her like that? she wondered. Or was it a kind of goodbye kiss? After all, if he intended to marry, he would have no further interest in her, and any interest he might have had had been more or less thrust upon him.

She was glad that she had been so positive about the future she had planned for herself. She must have convinced him that she had no interest in getting married. There were hundreds of girls who had made independent lives for themselves and there was no reason why she shouldn't be one of them.

No one would mind. Her mother and father would want her to be happy, but it wouldn't worry them if she didn't marry.

She was too tired to cry and tomorrow morning was only a few hours away. She went into an uneasy sleep and dreamed of Marcus.

With Christmas only weeks away there was a good deal of extra activity at the school: the play, the school concert, the older boys carol-singing in the town, and all of the boys making Christmas presents. Model aeroplanes, boats, spacecraft were all in the process of being glued, nailed and painted, destined for brothers and sisters at home. Cards were designed and painted, drawings framed for admiring mothers and fathers, calendars cut out and suitably ornamented for devoted grannies, and, as well as all this, there were lessons as usual.

Araminta, racing round making beds, looking for small lost garments, helping to write letters home, helping with the presents and making suitable costumes for the play, and that on top of her usual chores, had no time to think about her own life. Only at last when she had her free day did she take time to think about the future.

She didn't go home; her parents would be coming back during the following week and she would go then. She wrapped up warmly and walked briskly along the promenade, oblivious of the wind and the rain.

It seemed obvious to her that she wouldn't see Marcus again. It must have been pure chance which led him to visit his sister while she was staying there. Indeed, it was always pure chance when they met. He had had no choice but to offer to drive her back to Eastbourne.

'I must forget him,' said Araminta, shouting it into the wind.

She turned her back on that same wind presently and got blown back the way she had come. In the town she found a small, cosy restaurant and had a meal, then spent the afternoon shopping. Dull items like toothpaste, hand cream and a new comb, some of the ginger nuts Norma liked with her evening cocoa and coloured wrapping paper for some of the boys whose gifts were finished and ready to pack up.

She had an extravagant tea presently, prolonging it as long as possible by making a list of the Christmas presents she must buy. Then, since the shops were still open, she spent a long time choosing cards, but finally that was done and there was nothing for her to do but go back to the school.

The cinema was showing a horror film, which didn't appeal, and besides, she didn't like the idea of going alone. The theatre was shut prior to opening with the yearly pantomime.

She bought a packet of sandwiches and went back to her room; she would make tea on her gas ring and eat her sandwiches and read the paperbacks she had chosen. She had enjoyed her day, she assured herself. All the same she was glad when it was morning and she could plunge headfirst into the ordered chaos of little boys.

At the end of another week she went home for the day. It was a tedious journey, travelling to London by train and then on to Henley where her father met her with the car. He was glad to see her, observed that she looked very well and plunged into an account of his and her mother's tour. It had been an undoubted success, he told her, and they would be returning at a future date. The details of their trip lasted until they reached the house, where her mother was waiting for them.

'You look very well, my dear,' she told Araminta. 'This little job is obviously exactly right for you. Did your father tell you about our success? I'm sure he must have left out a good deal…'

Even if Araminta had wanted to talk to her mother there was no chance; they loved her, but she couldn't compete against the Celts. After all, they had been involved with them long before she was born. Her unexpected late arrival must have interfered with their deep interest in Celtic lore, but only for a short time. Nannies, governesses and school had made her independent at an early age and she had accepted that.

She listened now, made suitable comments and, since her cousin had gone to Henley to the dentist, cooked lunch. It was only later, while they were having tea, that her mother asked, 'You enjoyed your stay with those little boys? Dr Jenkell has told us what a charming man their uncle is. You were well treated?'

'Oh, yes, Mother, and the boys were delightful children. We got on well together and I liked Holland. Utrecht is a lovely old city…'

'I dare say it is. A pity you had no time to explore the *hunebedden* in Drenthe and the *terps* in Friesland; so clever of those primitive people to build their villages on mounds of earth. Your father and

I must find the time to visit them. I'm sure something can be arranged; he knows several people at Groningen University.'

Araminta poured second cups and passed the cake. 'You will be home for Christmas?'

'Yes, yes, of course we shall. We are going to Southern Ireland next week, for your father has been invited to give a short lecture tour and there are several places I wish to see—verifying facts before we revise the book. It will be published next year, I hope…'

'I get almost three weeks' holiday,' said Araminta.

Her mother said vaguely, 'Oh, that's nice, dear. You'll come home, of course?'

'Yes.' Araminta looked at her cousin. 'I could take over for a week or so if you wanted to go away.'

An offer which was accepted without hesitation.

Back at school, activities became feverish; the play was to be presented to an audience of parents who could get there, friends who lived locally and the school staff. So costumes had to have last-minute fittings, boys who suddenly lost their nerve had to be encouraged, the school hall had to be suitably decorated, and refreshments dealt with. Everyone was busy and Araminta told herself each night when she went to bed that with no leisure to brood she would soon forget Marcus; he would become a dim figure in her past.

She shut her eyes, willed herself to sleep and

there he was, his face behind her lids, every well-remembered line of it; the tiny crow's feet round his eyes when he smiled, the little frown mark where he perched his spectacles, the haughty nose, the thin, firm mouth, the lines when he was tired…

It will take time, thought Araminta, shaking up her pillows, and she tried to ignore the thought that it would take the rest of her life and beyond.

It wasn't only the school play. The carol-singers had to be rounded up and rehearsed, and someone had discovered that she could play the piano, so that each evening for half an hour she played carols, not always correctly but with feeling, sometimes joining in the singing.

The school concert would be held on the very last day, so that parents coming to collect their small sons could applaud their skills. There were to be recitations, duets on the piano, and a shaky rendering of 'Silent Night' by a boy who was learning the violin and a promising pianist. It was a pity that the two boys didn't get on well and rehearsals were often brought to a sudden end while they squabbled.

But it was a happy time for them all and Araminta, sitting up in bed long after she should have been asleep, fashioning suitable costumes for the Three Kings, to be sung by three of the older boys, although she was unhappy, was learning to live with her unhappiness. The answer was work; to be occupied for as many hours as there was daylight and longer than that so that she was too tired to think when she went to bed.

She didn't go home on her next day off, but spent the day buying Christmas presents and writing cards. Her parents had never celebrated Christmas in the traditional way; they exchanged presents and Araminta made Christmas puddings and mince pies, but there was never a tree or decorations in the house. This year, now that she had money to spend, she determined to make it a festive occasion. So she shopped for baubles for the tree, and tinsel, candles in pretty holders, crackers in pretty wrappings.

There was a tree set up in the Assembly Hall at school, too, and the boys were allowed to help decorate it. The nearer the end of term came the more feverish became the activity. End of term examinations were taken, reports made out and the boys' clothes inspected ready for packing. After the concert there would be a prize giving, and then the boys would go home. Araminta was to stay for another day, helping Norma leave the dormitories and recreation rooms tidy, before they, too, would go home.

Before the end of term the Gardiners gave a small party for the staff. Araminta had met them all, of course, but saw very little of them socially. She changed into a pretty dress and went with Norma to drink sherry and nibble savoury biscuits and exchange small talk with the form masters, the little lady who taught music and the French girl who taught French. Mr Gardiner was kind, asking her if she enjoyed her work, wanting to know what she was doing for Christmas, and Mrs Gardiner admired her dress.

The last day came, a round of concert, prize-giving and seeing the boys all safely away. Even those few whose parents were abroad were going to stay with friends or relatives, so that by suppertime the school was empty of boys and several of the staff.

Araminta and Norma began on the task of stripping beds, making sure that the cupboards and lockers were empty, checking the medicine chest and the linen cupboard, and then they spent the next morning sorting bed linen, counting blankets and making sure that everything was just so. They would return two days before the boys to make up beds and get things shipshape.

Norma was ready to leave after lunch. 'I'll go and see Mr Gardiner,' she told Araminta, 'and then go straight out to the car. So I'll say goodbye and a Happy Christmas now. You'll catch the train later? Have a lovely Christmas.'

Araminta finished her own packing, took her case and the bag packed with presents down to the hall and went in search of Mr Gardiner.

He was in his study, sitting at his desk, and looked up as she went in.

'Ah, Miss Pomfrey, you have come to say goodbye. You have done very well and I am more than pleased with you; you certainly helped us through a dodgy period.' He leaned back in his chair and gave her a kind smile.

'I am only sorry that we cannot offer you a permanent position here; I have heard from our assistant matron, who tells me that her mother has died and she has begged for her job back again. She has been with us for a number of years and, given that your position was temporary, I feel it only fair to offer her the post again. I am sure you will have no difficulty in finding another post; I shall be only too glad to recommend you. There is always a shortage of school matrons, you know.'

Araminta didn't say anything; she was dumb with disappointment and surprise, her future crumbling before her eyes just as she had felt sure that she had found security at last. She had really convinced herself that the previous Matron would not return. Mr Gardiner coughed. 'We are really sorry,' he added, 'but I'm sure you will understand.'

She nodded. 'Yes, of course, Mr Gardiner...'

He looked relieved. 'The post was brought to me a short while ago; there is a letter for you.' He handed her an envelope and stood up, offering a hand. 'Your train goes shortly? Stay here as long as you wish. I'm sure they will give you a cup of tea if you would like that before you go.'

'Thank you, there is a taxi coming for me.'

She shook hands and smiled, although smiling was very difficult, and went quickly out of the room.

In the hall she sat down and opened her letter. It was from her mother.

Araminta would understand, she felt sure, that she and her father had been offered a marvellous opportunity to go to Italy, where there had been the most interesting finds. Splendid material for the book, wrote her mother, and an honour for her father. They would return as soon as they could—some time in the New Year. 'You will have your cousin for company,' finished her mother, 'and I'm sure you will be glad of a quiet period.'

Araminta read the letter twice, because she simply hadn't believed it the first time, but it was true, written clearly in ink in her mother's flowing hand. She folded the letter carefully, then crossed the hall to the telephone and dialled her home number.

Her cousin answered. 'I've had a letter from mother,' began Araminta. 'It was a bit of a surprise. I'm catching the five o'clock train from here, so I'll be home for supper...'

There was silence for a few minutes. 'Araminta, I won't be here. Didn't your mother tell you? No, of course, she would have forgotten. I'm on the point of leaving—Great Aunt Kate is ill and I'm going to Bristol to nurse her. I've left food in the fridge and Cherub is being looked after until you come. I'm sorry, dear. Your mother and father left in a hurry and I don't suppose they thought... Could you not stay with friends? I'll come back just as soon as I can.'

Araminta found her voice; it didn't sound quite

like hers, but she forced it to sound cheerful. 'Don't worry, I'll be quite glad of a quiet time after rushing round here. I'll look up some friends in the village. I'm sorry you won't be at home, and I hope Christmas won't be too busy for you.'

She must end on a bright note. 'My taxi's just arrived and I mustn't keep it waiting. Let me know how you get on. I'll be at home for a couple of weeks, and you may be back by then.' She added, 'Happy Christmas,' with false brightness.

The taxi had arrived. It was too early for the train but she had planned to leave her luggage at the station and have tea in the town. Now all she wanted was to go somewhere and sit as far away from people as possible. She didn't want to think, not yet. First she must come to terms with disappointment.

She got into the taxi. 'Will you drive me along the promenade? I'll tell you where I want to be put down.'

It was dusk already, and cold. The promenade was bare of people and only a handful of cars were on it. Away from the main street it was quiet, only the sound of the sea and the wind whistling down a side street. She asked the driver to stop and got out, took her case and bag, then paid him, assuring him that this was where she wished to be, and watched him drive away.

She crossed the road to a shelter facing the sea. It was an old-fashioned edifice, with its benches sheltered from the wind and the rain by a roof and glassed-in walls. She put her luggage down and sat down in one corner facing the sea. It was cold, but she hadn't noticed that; she was arranging her thoughts in some kind of order. Just for a short time she allowed disappointment to engulf her, a disappointment all the more bitter because she hadn't really expected it—nor would it have been as bad if she had gone home to a loving family, waiting to welcome her.

'Wallowing in self-pity will do you no good, my girl,' said Araminta loudly. 'I must weigh the pros and cons.'

She ticked them off on her gloved fingers. 'I have some money, I have a home to go to, I can get another job after Christmas, Mother and Father...' She faltered. 'And there is Cherub waiting for me.'

Those were the pros, and for the moment she refused to think of anything else. But presently she had to, for she couldn't sit there for the rest of the evening and all night. The idea of going home to an empty house was something she couldn't face for the moment, although she could see that there was nothing else that she could do. She had friends in the village, but she had lost contact with them; her parents were liked and respected, but hardly neighbourly. There was no one to whom she could go and beg to stay with, especially at Christmas, when everyone had family and friends staying.

The tears she had been swallowing back crawled slowly down her cheeks.

* * *

The doctor was well aware that school had broken
up, and upon which day Araminta would be going
home for the holidays; old Mrs Gardiner had been
delighted to have another little gossip when she had
visited him at his consulting rooms. She had even
volunteered the information that the teaching staff
and the matrons stayed at the school for an extra day
in order to leave everything tidy. And she had added,
'Miriam—my daughter-in-law—told me that the matrons stay until the late afternoon. They have a good
deal to see to, but she is always glad when they have
gone and the school is empty. I shall be going there
for Christmas, of course.'

It took a good deal of planning, but by dint of
working early and late the doctor achieved his object. By two o'clock he was driving away from St
Jules', on his way to Eastbourne.

Araminta had left the school ten minutes before
he stopped before its gates.

'Gone to catch the five o'clock train,' the maid
who answered his ring told him. 'I said she was too
early, but she was going to have tea somewhere first.'

The doctor thanked her with a civility which quite
belied his feelings, then drove into the town, parked
the car and began his search. The station first, and
then every tea room, café, restaurant and snack bar.
Araminta had disappeared into thin air in the space
of half an hour or so.

The doctor went back to the station. He was

tired, worried and angry, but nothing of his feelings showed on his face. He searched the station again, enquired at the ticket office, questioned the porters and went back to the entrance. There was a row of taxis lined up, waiting for the next train from London, and he went from one to the other, making his enquiries in a calm unhurried manner.

The third cabby, lolling beside his cab, took a cigarette out of his mouth to answer him.

'Young lady? With a case? Booked to go to the station, but changed her mind. Looking for her, are you?'

'Yes, will you tell me where you took her?'

'Well, now, I could do that, but I don't know who you are, do I?'

'You're quite right to ask. My name is van der Breugh. I'm a doctor. The young lady's name is Miss Araminta Pomfrey. She is my future wife. If you will take me to her, you could perhaps wait while we talk and then bring us back here. My car is in the car park.' He smiled. 'If you wish you may accompany me when I meet her.'

The man stared at him. 'I'll take you and I'll wait.'

Araminta, lost in sad thoughts, didn't hear the taxi, and didn't hear the doctor's footsteps. Only when he said quietly, 'Hello, Mintie,' did she look up, her mouth open and her eyes wide. All she said was, 'Oh.'

It was apparently enough for the doctor. He picked

up her case and the plastic bag and said in a brisk voice, 'It's rather chilly here. We'll go somewhere and have a cup of tea.'

'No,' said Araminta, then added, 'I'm going home.'

'Well, of course you are. Come along, the taxi's waiting.'

The utter surprise of seeing him had addled her wits. She crossed the road and got into the taxi, and when the cabby asked, 'OK, miss?' she managed to give him a shaky smile. She was cold, her head felt empty, and it was too much trouble to think for the moment. She sat quietly beside Marcus until the taxi stopped before a tea room, its lighted windows welcoming in the dark evening. She stood quietly while the doctor paid the cabby, picked up her luggage, opened the tea room door and sat her down at a table.

The place was half full, for it was barely five o'clock, and it was warm and cosy with elderly waitresses carrying loaded trays. The doctor gave his order, took off his overcoat, then leaned across and unbuttoned her jacket, and in those few minutes Araminta had pulled herself together.

'I do not know why you have brought me here,' she said frostily.

'I was hoping that you would tell me,' said Marcus mildly. 'The school has broken up for the holidays, everyone has gone home but you are still here, sitting in a shelter on the promenade with your luggage. Why are you not at home, Mintie?'

His voice would have melted the Elgin Marbles, and Araminta was flesh and blood.

She said gruffly, 'I've been made redundant—the other girl is coming back. I thought I'd just stay here for a day or two.'

'And why would you wish to do that?' His voice was very quiet—a voice to calm a frightened child…

'Well,' began Araminta, 'there's really no need for me to go home. Mother and father have gone to Italy—the Celts, you know—and my cousin has had to go to an aunt who is ill. There's only Cherub…'

He perceived that Cherub was the only close tie she had with her home. He said nothing, but his silence was comforting, so that she went on, pot-valiant, 'I shall have no trouble in getting another job. I'm well qualified…'

A gross exaggeration, this, in a world of diploma holders and possessors of degrees, but she wouldn't admit that, not even to herself, and certainly not to him.

The doctor remained silent, watching her from under his lids while she drank her tea.

'Well, I must be going.' She had never been so unhappy in her life, but she must get away before she burst into tears. 'I cannot think why I have wasted my time here. I suppose you were just curious?'

'Yes.' He had spent a good deal of time and trouble looking for her, but he found himself smiling. He said in his quiet voice, 'Will you marry me, Mintie?' and watched the colour creep into her pale face as she stared at him across the table. 'I fell in love with you the moment I set eyes on you, although I wasn't aware of that at the time. Now I love you so deeply I find that I cannot live without you, my darling.'

Araminta took a minute to understand this. 'Me? You love me? But I thought you didn't like me—only you always seemed to be there when I had got into a mess. You—you ignored me.'

'I did not know what else to do. I am years older than you; you might have met a younger man.' He smiled suddenly and she felt a warm tide of love sweep over her. 'Besides, you were always Miss Pomfrey, holding me at arm's length, so I have waited patiently, hoping that you might learn to love me. But now I can wait no longer.' He added, 'If you want me to go away, I will, Mintie.'

Her voice came out in a terrified squeak. 'Go away? Don't go—oh, please, don't go. I couldn't bear it, and I want to marry you more than anything else in the world.'

The doctor glanced around him, for those sitting near their table were showing signs of interest. He laid money on the table, got into his overcoat, buttoned her jacket and said, 'Let us leave…'

'Why?' asked Araminta, awash with happiness.

'I want to kiss you.'

They went outside into the dark afternoon, into their own private heaven. The narrow street was almost empty—there were only two women laden with shopping bags, an old man with his dog, and a posse of carol-singers about to start up. Neither the doctor nor Araminta noticed them. He wrapped his great arms round her and held her close, and as the first rousing verse of 'Good King Wenceslas' rang out, he kissed her.

* * * * *

JUST CAN'T GET ENOUGH
ROMANCE
Looking for more?

Harlequin has everything from contemporary, passionate and heartwarming to suspenseful and inspirational stories.

Whatever your mood, we have a romance just for you!

Connect with us to find your next great read, special offers and more.

Facebook.com/HarlequinBooks
Twitter.com/HarlequinBooks
HarlequinBlog.com
Harlequin.com/Newsletters

www.Harlequin.com

Read on for an exclusive sneak preview of
INTERVIEW WITH A TYCOON by Cara Colter…

KIERNAN WAITED FOR it to happen. All his strength had not been enough to hold the lid on the place that contained the grief within him.

The touch of her hand, the look in her eyes, and his strength had abandoned him, and he had told her all of it: his failure and his powerlessness.

Now, sitting beside her, her hand in his, the wetness of her hair resting on his shoulder, he waited for everything to fade: the white-topped mountains that surrounded him, the feel of the hot water against his skin, the way her hand felt in his.

He waited for all that to fade, and for the darkness to take its place, to ooze through him like thick black sludge freed from a containment pond, blotting out all else.

Instead, astounded, Kiernan became *more* aware of everything around him, as if he were soaking up life through his pores, breathing in glory through his nose, becoming drenched in light instead of darkness.

He started to laugh.

"What?" she asked, a smile playing across the lovely fullness of her lips.

"I just feel alive. For the last few days, I have felt alive. And I don't know if that's a good thing or a bad thing."

His awareness shifted to her, and being with her seemed to fill him to overflowing.

He dropped his head over hers and took her lips. He kissed her with warmth and with welcome, a man who had thought he was dead discovering not just that he lived but, astonishingly, that he wanted to live.

Stacy returned his kiss, her lips parting under his, her hands twining around his neck, pulling him in even closer to her.

There was gentle welcome. She had seen all of him, he had bared his weakness and his darkness to her, and still he felt only acceptance from her.

But acceptance was slowly giving way to something else. There was hunger in her, and he sensed an almost savage need in her to go to the place a kiss like this took a man and a woman.

With great reluctance he broke the kiss, cupped her cheeks in his hands and looked down at her.

He felt as if he was memorizing each of her features: the green of those amazing eyes, her dark brown hair curling even more wildly from the steam of the hot spring, the swollen plumpness of her lips, the whiteness of her skin.

"It's too soon for this," he said, his voice hoarse.

"I know," she said, and her voice was raw, too.

Don't miss this heart-wrenching story, available September 2014 from Harlequin® Romance.

Resisting Mr. Off-Limits!

Owner of Obsidian Studios, Garrett Black
might be scarred both inside and out, but
with the Hollywood Hills Film Festival fast
approaching, there's no time for distractions.
Especially not those as tempting as event
coordinator Tori Randall....

Who cares if he's gorgeous? Tori's frustrated
by this brooding CEO's aloof attitude and near
impossible demands. Even if Garrett wasn't
her boss, she'd never risk her heart to another
emotionally closed man. Normally she'd run in
the opposite direction...so why does she feel
so compelled to stay?

Her Boss by Arrangement
by
Teresa Carpenter

Available September 2014 from
Harlequin Romance, wherever
books and ebooks are sold.

HARLEQUIN® *Romance*

You can't help who you fall for…

The arrival of Dominic Brabant is like something
out of a movie. Walking into Suzanna Zelensky's
shop in his buttoned-up suit, he can't help but
make an impression. She can't control the erratic
beating of her heart—but this stranger's here for
more pressing matters…her home is top of his
redevelopment list!

Zanna soon discovers you can't help falling in
love with the wrong person…but ending up in
her rival's arms might be the best decision she's
ever made!

In Her
Rival's Arms
by
Alison Roberts

*Available September 2014 from Harlequin Romance,
wherever books and ebooks are sold.*

www.Harlequin.com

HR74306